Kylie & Skip

C.R. Cummings

Also By
CHRISTOPHER CUMMINGS

*Kylie & Skip
The Boy and the Battleship
The Green Idol of Kanaka Creek
Ross River Fever
Train to Kuranda
The Mudskipper Cup
Davey Jones's Locker
Fourteen
Air Cadet
Below Bartle Frere
Bowling Green Bay
Airship Over Atherton
Cockatoo
The Cadet Corporal
Stannary Hills
Sugar & Spice
Coast of Cape York
Kylie and the Kelly Gang
Beyond the Barrier Reef
Behind Mt. Baldy
The Cadet Sergeant Major
Cooktown Christmas
Secret in the Clouds
Mischief at Mingela
The Word of God
The Cadet Under-Officer
Through the Devil's Eye
Barbara in the Bush
Barbara and the Smiley People
Barbara at her Best
Barbara's Bivouac

Kylie & Skip

C.R. Cummings

DoctorZed
Publishing
www.doctorzed.com

This 1st edition Published 2023 by DoctorZed Publishing

DoctorZed Publishing books may be ordered through booksellers or by contacting:

DoctorZed Publishing
10 Vista Ave
Skye, South Australia 5072
www.doctorzed.com

ISBN: 978-0-6457955-7-8 (hc)
ISBN: 978-0-6457955-8-5 (sc)
ISBN: 978-0-6457955-9-2 (ebk)

National Library of Australia Cataloguing-in-Publication entry

Author: Cummings, C. R., author.

Title: Below Bartle Frere / Christopher Cummings.

ISBN: 978-0-6457955-7-8 (hardcover)

Target Audience: For young adults.

Subjects: Adventure stories, Australian.

Queensland--Fiction.

Cover image Angry dog with open mouth © Annaav | Dreamstime.com
Cover design © Scott Zarcinas

DoctorZed Publishing rev. date: 25/04/2023

Dedicated to

With thanks
To
The Hiking Friend of my youth
Peter Bobroff
The responsible and sensible one
Whose
Intelligent plans and practical solutions
Restrained my more ambitious and enthusiastic ones.

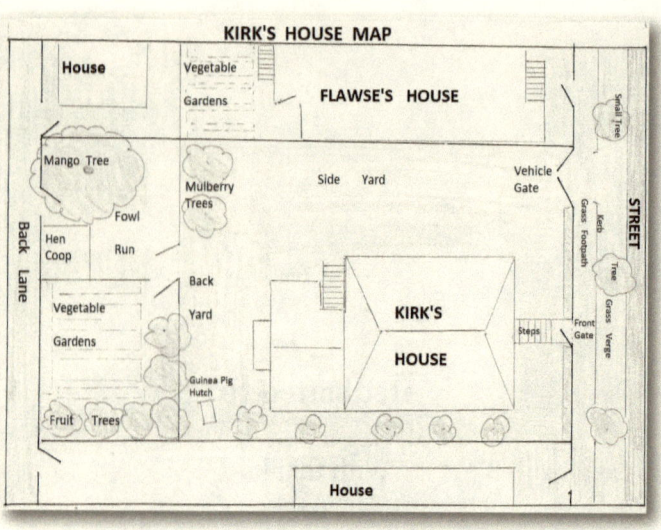

KIRK'S HOUSE MAP

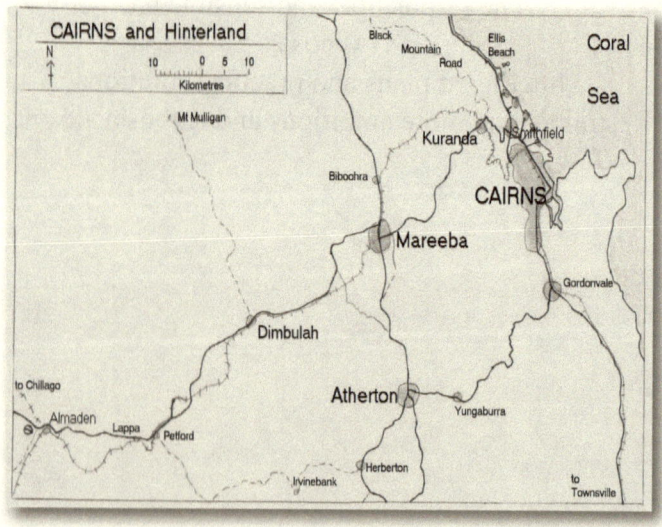

CAIRNS and Hinterland

Chapter 1

SKIP

Cairns, North Queensland, May
A suburban back yard in a wide street lined with trees and high-set old 'Queenslanders'

"Hold him, Kylie! Don't be such a sook!" called 11-year-old Margaret to her friend.

Kylie tried to but Claud the cat did not want to stay in the washbasin. He squirmed and struggled to break free.

"I can't! You hold him," Kylie replied. Then she let out a little shriek as the cat wriggled and drops of water wet her. She changed her grip and knelt on the lawn to allow Margaret to move into position beside her.

"He doesn't want a bath," Margaret commented as she took a firm grip of the old ginger cat's back and neck. "Hold still Claud!" she ordered.

"Well he needs one," Kylie replied. "He pongs. Now don't you scratch me Claud!" she cried as the cat hissed and swung his claws at her. Margaret took an even tighter grip on the sodden fur and held him firmly in the washbasin.

The two girls were on the back lawn behind Kylie's house and the minor drama had gone on for ten minutes. Just catching Claud had been an event once the cat understood what the washbasin full of water was for. Complicating matters had been the family's new dog, a Fox Terrier pup named Skip, short for 'Skipper', to indicate she was the boss. The name seemed natural as Kylie's father was also sometimes called Skipper as he was a ship's captain. More properly he was called 'Captain' as he was a Master Mariner by profession and was the ship's master. Captain Kirk, therefore, was often away from home for weeks at a time as he took vessels to places all over the north of Australia and into the Pacific Islands and even to Timor l'este and Indonesia. At this time he was away.

Skip thought that catching the cat was a great game and had rushed back and forth barking and yapping and getting under their feet as they had chased the cat. Now she came and stood up with her front paws on the rim of the washbasin and barked, provoking a furious outbreak of squirming and hissing from Claud.

Kylie used the washer with soap on it to push the puppy away. "Go away Skip! It will be your turn next," she cried. But Skip came back. In exasperation Kylie flicked water at her, using the sodden washer. Skip blinked and flinched and then withdrew.

The girls settled to washing the unhappy cat. Margaret had to use all of her strength to hold him. Kylie had to be particularly careful that the cat's sharp claws did not scratch her as he wriggled and struggled to break free.

As she worked, Kylie glanced around to check where Skip had gone. To her dismay, she saw that the puppy was at the side fence and was nosing at the bottom of a loose fence paling.

Oh no! she thought. *She mustn't go in there.*

'There' was the neighbour's back yard. Only a week before new neighbours had moved in, Mr and Mrs Flawse, and they were very unfriendly. Worse still they owned a huge black dog, a savage Doberman named 'Brute' that snarled and barked and looked very dangerous. When Kylie had first seen Brute, she had put her hand through the fence to pat him and to say hello and the dog had snarled and lunged. Just in time Kylie had pulled her hand back as Brute's jaws had snapped shut.

The incident had given her a bad fright and ever since she had been afraid of the dog and resented the fact that it barked and growled at her whenever she walked in her own garden.

Now Kylie felt her heart miss a beat as Skip ignored her and pushed through the gap where the bottom of the fence paling had swung loose. "Skip, come back! Skip!" she cried. Anxiety surged and Kylie forgot about Claud and his bath. Dropping the washer in the tub she sprang to her feet and ran across the lawn. Margaret let go of Claud and followed.

But Kylie was too late. By the time she got there, Skip had squirmed through the gap and was in the vegetable garden which took up much of the Flawse's backyard. At once the inquisitive puppy began sniffing plants and trotting around exploring the rows of vegetables.

"Skip! Come back!" Kylie cried. In the hope of not attracting the attention of the Flawses she did not raise her voice and Skip only glanced back and wagged her tail before moving in among two rows of radishes.

Oh, I hope the Flawses don't see her! Kylie thought, glancing up at the back window of the high block house as she did. Then another much more worrying thought came to her. *Where is Brute?*

But even as the idea crossed her mind Brute appeared, as though conjured up by her anxious mental waves. The huge black dog trotted into view around the far side of the Flawse's house. As yet it had not detected Skip, but it plainly knew something was up and had come to investigate.

Kylie's heart skipped several beats. *Oh my God! Brute! He will kill Skip if he catches her,* she told herself. But what to do?

In a fluster of anxiety, Kylie called again. "Skip! Here girl!"

But that didn't have the desired result. Instead it caused Brute to look at her. The dog let out a growl and began bounding across the garden beds. Kylie gasped with fear and her anxious mind rapidly calculated the distances.

Skip is just there. Brute will smell her or see her any moment, she reasoned. *I must save her.*

But how?

Only one way seemed obvious at that moment and Kylie took it. She grabbed the bottom of the paling and wrenched it aside. Then she bent and began to squirm through. As she did, realisation burst on her that she might have made a very bad mistake. Stuck in the fence as she was she was very exposed to attack by the Doberman. Fear surged, sending her heart rate pounding and causing her mouth to go dry. She looked up and saw the slavering jaws, the huge fangs and the evil yellow eyes of the big dog as it leapt towards her.

At the last moment it was Skip who saved her. Skip yapped and Brute saw her and instantly changed direction. Skip scampered away, scurrying through the vegetables while the bigger dog bounded after her. Both dogs ploughed through the radishes and the tomato plants and then in among the cabbages.

Kylie hauled herself through the gap, scraping some skin and tearing her clothes but not caring, Heart in mouth she straightened up and watched with horror as Skip dodged and scurried about in a frantic attempt to escape Brute's jaws. By this time both dogs were barking, Skip's sharp yaps almost being drowned out by the savage growls and louder barking of Brute.

Kylie put her hand to her mouth and wanted to scream. But she still had enough courage to try to save Skip. Calling out for Skip to come she moved forward several paces, uncertain where the rapidly moving chase would next take the two dogs. Then Skip heard her and turned towards her.

Brute followed, eyes blazing and foam flecking its mouth. A spasm of sheer terror ran through Kylie as she realised that the huge dog was heading straight at her.

At that moment, Margaret yelled from behind her. "Kylie, the rake! Grab the rake!"

Kylie risked a glance and saw that Margaret was holding the handle of a lawn rake out for her. In a flash she grabbed the rake and swung it in front of her. She was just in time. Skip flashed past between her legs with Brute close behind, but the flexing metal tines of the rake came down between them.

Brute ran into the rake at full speed. The shock almost wrenched the rake from Kylie's grasp but she knew that her own safety now depended on that tool so she gripped it with desperation. Brute recoiled back, snarling and yelping. The dog then scrambled back to its feet and prepared to attack again.

At that moment, a man's angry voice drew Kylie's attention to the back of the house. Standing at the door was Mr Flawse and behind him appeared the face of his horrible wife. Mr Flawse's face contorted with rage and he shook his fist.

"Don't you dare hit my dog!" he screamed.

But Kylie had no choice. To save herself she had to whack at Brute to make the animal back off. Luckily, she only caught it a glancing blow on the back, but it was enough to make the dog retreat. Gasping for breath and so frightened she could hardly think, Kylie gripped the rake and held it out to ward off another attack.

Now, where is Skip? she wondered.

To her dismay, she saw that Skip had run around behind Brute and was yapping at the bigger dog from behind. As she did, Skip dashed back and forth, shredding vegetables and causing more damage to the gardens.

Mr Flawse saw this, and his eyes bulged and anger suffused his ugly face. "Stop that you mongrel!" he screamed at Skip.

He ran forward and Kylie's heart again went into her mouth. "Skip! Run Skip, run!" she shrilled.

But Skip was only used to nice people and turned to Mr Flawse to save her. To Kylie's horror Mr Flawse stamped on Skip with his boot, pinning her against the ground and the wooden border to a patch of cabbages.

"Bloody little mongrel! Wrecking my garden!" Mr Flawse yelled. Then he kicked at Skip, sending her tumbling head over heels.

Brute turned to attack Skip. Kylie knew that the puppy would be dead if the bigger dog once latched into her, so she acted. Desperate to save her puppy she jumped forward and slammed the rake down, pinning the big dog to the ground.

Mrs Flawse screamed angrily and Mr Flawse looked up. To Kylie's horror he stamped his boot on Skip again. Then Mr Flawse looked at Kylie and snarled, "Stop hurting my dog!"

"You stop hurting mine!" Kylie retorted, her voice cracking with anxiety.

"I should kill the little mongrel. Look at the mess it's made of my garden," Mr Flawse screamed back. He glared at Kylie and for a moment she feared he would kill Skip.

Kylie trembled and had to resist the urge to step back. She feared Mr Flawse as only a little girl can fear a large and repulsive man. Mr Flawse was a big, solid brute of a man in late middle-age. He was overweight, with a protruding beer gut and a pudgy, wrinkled face. His teeth were yellowed and gapped and he always looked as though he needed a shave. He had a nervous habit of running his left hand through his thinning grey hair. To make him even less attractive, he had gross habits. To Kylie's disgust he often picked his nose, a big, reddish nose from which bristled tufts of hair. Worse still, Kylie had often seen him blow snot on the ground by covering one nostril. He also hawked and spat, a process which made her stomach turn over with nausea when she witnessed it. To cap it all off, Mr Flawse always looked as though he slept in his dirty clothes.

Of equal concern to Kylie was 'Brute'. She glanced at him now and experienced another shiver of fear. Knowing she would be horribly mauled if she let the dog go she kept the rake pressed firmly down on the scrabbling, snarling animal. Brute's yellow eyes glared at her and gave her the impression that they radiated pure evil. The huge dog clamped its jaws with audible 'chomps' and let out a series of savage barks and snarls, all the while straining to break free. Dribbles of saliva dripped from its jaws.

But Kylie knew the situation could not last. *Brute is much stronger and faster than me,* she thought. *I can't hold him much longer.*

The whole situation terrified her and made her feel sick. Mixed with dread at what might happen to her or Skip if Brute got loose was concern that she was harming the big dog by pressing down so hard. It really distressed her to hurt Brute.

I might break his neck, she worried, noting how the rake was across the big dog's throat.

There was movement beside her and Margaret appeared. She had a garden rake and now stepped forward to push down on Brute with it. Mr Flawse shouted again to stop hurting his dog, 'Or else!"

Heartened by Margaret's presence, Kylie stood her ground. Concern for Skip overrode her fear. "Please don't hurt my puppy," she cried.

"Bloody thing's bin diggin' up me radishes, the little mongrel!" Mr Flawse growled, gesturing at the newly turned earth.

"She's only a puppy. She doesn't understand," Kylie replied. "She didn't mean any harm."

Kylie could feel her heart thumping hard, choking right up into her throat. She gripped the rake tightly and pressed down as hard as she could, her emotions torn by the pain in Skip's eyes and the pitiful whimpering she was making. The pup looked so tiny under the huge boot. Even as she watched Skip struggled feebly and whimpered again, the sound tearing at Kylie's emotions.

For a moment Kylie thought Mr Flawse was going to kick Skip again, but instead he bent down to grip Skip by the scruff of the neck.

"You keep the little mongrel out of my yard, do ya hear?" Mr Flawse snarled, "Or I'll let Brute loose in your yard to have some fun."

Mr Flawse lifted the whimpering, twitching puppy up. Skip squirmed and yelped in pain. Kylie gasped and put out her left arm imploringly. But instead of handing the puppy to either girl Mr Flawse suddenly swung his arm and flung Skip high over the fence. Kylie cried out in dismay and spun round, just in time to see Skip land heavily on the lawn. The pup went tumbling and sprawling and let out sharp yelps of pain.

Mr Flawse then advanced towards the two girls, mouthing crude words as he did. Both Kylie and Margaret retreated, terrified of both the man and his dog. Brute squirmed free and sprang to his feet, snarling, barking, and biting at the rakes. In desperation Kylie fended him off.

"Get back through the fence Margaret!" she screamed.

To her relief, Margaret did. Kylie risked a glance. Through her mind flashed the hope that help might arrive, perhaps one of her brothers or her mother. But there was no sign of anyone. Margaret crawled through the broken fence and then stood up and leaned over the top, her rake swinging out to cover Kylie.

"Come on Kylie, you now," Margaret called. Then she yelled at Mr Flawse, "Grab your dog, mister! If she attacks Kylie I will really hurt him, and then we will get the police."

Mr Flawse kept advancing and he swore back, "You dare, you little bitch!"

But he did reach forward and grab at Brute's collar. The huge dog snarled and tried to break free. Failing in that Brute squirmed and tried to bite at Mr Flawse until he belted it a savage whack on the side of the head. "Calm down ya mongrel!" he snarled.

The brutality made Kylie feel sick, but she was so scared of both man and dog that she hastily backed over to the fence and then crouched to wriggle through. To her relief, she made it and she was able to drag the rake through after her to cover her retreat. As soon as she was in her own yard, she jammed the rake in the gap and then turned to look for Skip. Skip was lying ten paces away in the middle of the lawn.

"Oh Skip!" she sobbed, running to her.

As Kylie and Margaret ran towards her, Skip struggled to her feet and tried to stagger towards them, only to flop on her side.

"Oh Skip!" Kylie cried in dismay. She knelt and gently tried to take hold of the injured puppy. "Oh Skip, lie still! Don't move."

Margaret stood watching, still gripping her rake, her face a mask of conflicting emotions: horror, concern, anger. The anger won. She turned to face Mr Flawse and shouted at him, "You cruel brute! You had no call to do that."

"Don't you call me names, Missy!" Mr Flawse snarled back. "Or you'll regret it."

Margaret went very pale under her freckles as she was scared but she stood her ground and clenched her fists at her sides. "Don't be a bully! I think you are an awful man!"

"You keep outa this! It ain't none of your business," Mr Flawse growled. "And give me back my rake."

He ran his fingers through his hair, hitched up his filthy grey trousers and spat. Brute barked and snarled and tried to break free of his grip.

Margaret curled her lip in disgust and tossed the rake over the fence, noting with satisfaction that it landed among the vegetables. *Good!* she thought. Then she turned her back on the angry man and knelt beside Kylie, shaking with fear because she was afraid Mr Flawse might climb the fence or let Brute go.

"I wish Graham was here," she said.

Normally Kylie would have teased her at a comment like this because Margaret was always trying to attract the attention of her older brother, but now she was too upset over Skip. By this time Kylie had managed to take hold of Skip and was gently holding him down.

"Lie still Skip, lie still! You will hurt yourself little doggie. Lie still," she said.

As gently as she could, she ran her hands over the puppy, feeling to see if she had any broken bones. Skip whimpered and squirmed. Her black and white fur was blotched with smudges of dirt and she looked very miserable. There was blood on her fur just over the left ear and she yipped in pain when Kylie felt her left hind leg.

"Is she alright?" Margaret asked, her brown eyes soft with concern and sympathy.

"I don't know," Kylie replied with a catch in her voice. She had trouble speaking and could feel tears forming. "I'm worried that she might have internal injuries."

"We'd better take her to the vet," Margaret suggested.

Kylie nodded, wiped a tear from her cheek, then gently scooped Skip into her arms. Skip whimpered but snuggled against her. A tiny pink tongue poked out to lick at Kylie's hand, causing her to break into sobs. She hurried across the side lawn, hardly able to see for the tears which now streamed down her face. She was shaking violently with reaction.

"Mum! Mum!" she cried as she made her way up the back stairs.

Margaret followed, pausing at the bottom of the stairs to turn and curl her lip at Mr Flawse, who stood scowling across the wooden picket fence. Brute made another lunge and let loose a volley of terrifying barks. The threat so frightened Margaret that she hurried up the back stairs and closed the door behind her.

Once upstairs Kylie made her way through the house, looking into the rooms and calling. There was no response. *Mum's not home yet,* she decided.

Kylie and Margaret had come to Kylie's straight from school and begun playing with the new puppy. They had found the house open which indicated that someone was home, or had been.

When she reached the enclosed front veranda Kylie stopped and slumped onto Graham's bed, cradling Skip in her arms. Margaret sat next to her and put her arm around her, while also gently stroking Skip. "What will we do?" she asked.

Kylie shook her head in distress. "I don't know. Someone must be home."

But who? she wondered: Graham or Alex? Kylie felt very young and vulnerable and was acutely aware that she would have trouble taking Skip to the vet on her own. Both she and Margaret were only eleven. Graham was twelve, nearly thirteen, and Alex two years older again. Both boys were very independent types and Kylie knew that they would be able to cope. Her father was away at sea. Captain Kirk would not be home for weeks yet.

A fit of trembling shook Kylie and she wept with relief and anxiety. Margaret sat beside her and put her arms around her.

"You were very brave Kylie!" she said.

"So were you. You are a great friend," Kylie replied.

She hugged both Margaret and Skip and for a few minutes both girls cried and shivered as the reaction set in. Then Kylie remembered Skip. *No time for hysterics,* she told herself.

"We must take Skip to a vet," she said.

"But where? How?" Margaret asked.

"In a box, so her injuries don't get worse," Kylie said.

She was thinking hard and remembered seeing her mother do that for their previous dog 'Bounce', after she had been hit by a car. That had been in vain, and Bounce had died. The memory of that horrible outcome caused Kylie's chest to tighten up with dread.

Margaret nodded her agreement. "I'll get a box."

"There are some cardboard boxes in the storeroom. You get one while I hold her," Kylie instructed.

Margaret stood up and walked down the front stairs. She had been visiting the Kirk's house for years and knew the layout intimately, from numerous games of 'hide and seek'. It was, she thought, a lovely old house, and a very friendly and homely one. It was an 'Old Queenslander' set on high blocks (wooden posts 3 metres high). The whole downstairs area had a concrete floor. The house was set in a very large yard, taking up 2 allotments. The yard extended right through from one street to the lane at the rear. At the front was a small garden and lawn. The house was set on one side of the block so that the side lawn on the right was only 3 metres wide but the lawn on the other side (beside the Flawse's house), was about 10 metres wide. At the back was more lawn, then nearly half the block was taken up by gardens, of both flowers and vegetables, and a fowl run.

At the front of the house was the enclosed veranda (which was one of the places Margaret was most interested in since it was also Graham's bedroom). Underneath that was an open, concrete floored area the width of the house (about 4 metres wide by 12 metres across). This area was divided into two. The end nearest the wide side lawn had been converted into an aviary where Kylie kept her budgerigars. The other end was hung with pot plants and orchids and was the special preserve of Captain Kirk when he was home.

From the second row of posts to the fifth row under the house was an area which was fully enclosed on the far side but had only open slats around the other three. Two gates led into this area, one from the wide side lawn and one from the rear. This was the 'Ship Room' and was Graham's special place. In there he had a collection of model sailing ships and was his play area. The models were made only from the waterline up so they could be pushed around the floor. To add interest they were crewed by tiny people made from coloured plasticine. Graham had also manufactured whole armies of tiny plasticine soldiers and he would spend hours playing Napoleonic War games.

Behind the Ship Room was the car port and storeroom, with an opening to the narrow side lawn. The back stairs came down here to the wide side lawn, from a passageway in front of the toilet and bathroom. The kitchen was a large room at the back of the house and underneath was the laundry.

From fear of Brute, Margaret went to her right and around the far side of the house, keeping it between her and the Flawse's house, Reaching the entrance to the car port she stopped and peeked through the to check that Brute was not in the yard. To her relief, there was no sign of either the dog or either Flawse so she went quickly to the storeroom and rummaged through a stack of cardboard cartons and boxes piled in a heap in the corner. Having found one she retraced her steps, alert for any sign of danger, and hurried back upstairs.

At Kylie's instructions Margaret hurried through the 'Sitting Room' and 'Dining Room' to the 'Sewing Room'. Here she opened the linen cupboard and found an old towel. This was placed in the bottom and she then took the box back to the veranda.

Skip was gently placed in the box. She whimpered as this was done and struggled to stay in Kylie's arms. To Kylie, that was heart-rending but she managed to hold Skip down till she understood and stopped struggling. The puppy then lay and looked up at her with big brown eyes while Kylie stroked her.

"Where do we take her?" Margaret asked.

"I don't know. Where is the nearest vet?" Kylie asked.

"I don't know either," Margaret replied, shaking her head in dismay.

Kylie bit her lip and thought hard, then her face brightened. "I know! We will look in the telephone book."

Margaret ran to the table in the sewing room where the telephone book lay. She snatched it up and ran back to the front.

"In the 'Yellow Pages'," Kylie instructed.

Margaret quickly found a vet and read the address. She sighed with relief. "There is one over in Draper Street. That's only a couple of blocks, isn't it?"

"Yes, it is. I know where that is. Come on," Kylie replied. She stood up and walked quickly to the front door.

As they went down the front stairs Margaret asked if they should lock the house.

Kylie shook her head. "No. It will be alright. Besides, either Alex or Graham must have opened it."

The two girls went through the front gate, then turned left and walked along the grass footpath. This led them past the front of the Flawse's house and Kylie felt her stomach tighten with apprehension as they approached it. She had never liked Mr Flawse, or his wife ('Bloody slattern!' she had heard her father describe Mrs Flawse to her mother once), but now she positively feared them.

As she and Margaret passed the house, she cast several anxious glances at it but there was still no sign of either Flawse. She noted that the front of the Flawse's house was closer to their front fence and that it had a very small front yard.

The girls hurried on and were at the vet's within ten minutes. To Kylie's relief, the vet was willing to treat Skip, even though she had no money.

"I will send a bill," he said. "I know your dad. We went to school together."

That was a surprise to Kylie, who found it hard to imagine her dad ever having been young. The vet led the way through to his surgery and the box was placed on a side table.

"You take her out and hold her," the vet instructed. "She will wriggle less then."

Kylie had been worrying about that and was very relieved. She gently picked Skip up, wincing and biting her lip as Skip whimpered. The girls were then allowed to be present while the vet examined Skip. Several times Skip whined and struggled feebly but she had calmed down a lot by then.

After a few minutes the vet said, "Well, I can't find any broken bones. There may be internal injuries, but we won't know for a while. As for these cuts, they are superficial. I will just clean them."

That was all a relief to Kylie, although the thought of internal injuries made her feel sick with anxiety. Skip had to be held while the vet gently washed and cleaned her fur and cuts. Skip kept looking up at Kylie with her big, trusting eyes, and occasionally gave a loving little lick with her tongue. That was enough to cause tears to spring to Kylie's eyes again.

The vet then said, "Well, that's all I can do for the moment. I recommend you take her home and just keep an eye on her. If she is hurt inside, she won't want to eat and will be very tender around the tummy. If she gets sick, then bring her back again."

It was a very relieved pair of girls who walked back to Kylie's house. Once there, Skip, still in the box, was placed on the floor near the end of Graham's bed. Margaret sat with her to calm her while Kylie went through to the back of the house to check if anyone else had come home. To her disappointment, no-one had so she put some milk in a small plastic bowl and took it to Skip. To her dismay, Skip just looked at it, sniffed, then turned her head away. Kylie placed the milk to one side and went back to the kitchen where she made drinks of cordial and collected a plate of biscuits.

She and Margaret then sat and had their afternoon tea. As Kylie held a biscuit ready to bite, she noted Skip struggle up into her 'begging' position.

"She wants a biscuit!" she cried happily.

The biscuit was offered, and Skip gently took it and crunched it down, scattering crumbs all over the towel.

"That's because she thinks she is a person and knows our food is better than dog food," Margaret suggested.

Both girls laughed with relief and Kylie was enormously relieved to see Skip wag her tail and grin. Another biscuit was handed over and Skip then snuggled down again. Kylie then sat on the floor, leaning against Graham's bed while gently stroking Skip. Margaret stretched out on Graham's bed and leaned over to watch. The two girls then talked about the incident and about pets. After a time Margaret rolled over to lie full length on Graham's bed, with her head on his pillow.

That made Kylie smile. "Graham will be grumpy if he catches you.".

Margaret smiled and shook her head. "He'd better get used to me being in his bed."

At that remark, Kylie shrieked in mock scandal. "Oh Margaret, you naughty girl! You will get into trouble."

"I don't care. I'm going to marry Graham," Margaret replied.

That idea actually pleased Kylie enormously, but she shook her head and laughed. "You might not like what he will want to do to you." Having two big brothers Kylie had a fair idea of what boys were like.

"I will," Margaret replied with certainty. "I heard mum really giggling the other day when she and dad were doing it."

"Margaret!" Kylie cried. "You naughty girl! You didn't look!"

Margaret gave a guilty giggle and blushed. "They didn't know I was home," she explained. "I heard them and couldn't help myself, so I risked a peek."

"Did they see you?" Kylie asked, fascinated, having heard about 'it' but never having seen it.

Margaret shook her head. "No, and I didn't stay. I felt awfully guilty for being a Peeping Tom."

"What did they do?" Kylie asked. She was just reaching the age where she was becoming interested in boys and sex.

"I didn't really see," Margaret replied. "They were rolling on the bed and dad was tickling mum." She then went very red and Kylie knew she had seen something really rude.

"And you want Graham to do that to you?" Kylie asked.

"Yes," Margaret replied.

"You are too young. It's against the law," Kylie reminded her.

"I don't care. I won't tell," Margaret answered.

"Margaret!" Kylie gasped. "But what if he makes you pregnant?"

Margaret shook her head. "I'm too young, and I think he still is too."

Kylie dimly knew what she meant from what she had been taught at school in Human Relationships Education, and what she had learned from her mother and friends. From the way Graham was acting she was sure he was starting to go through puberty.

"You'd better be careful. I think he is reaching that age," she said. "So no more baths together."

At that Margaret blushed again and giggled. "We haven't done that for a year or so. Graham is getting too big."

Over the years, since they were babies, Kylie, Margaret, and her brothers had often had baths together after some particularly grubby play session. Kylie thought about the time when she had walked in on Graham when he was getting dressed a few days earlier.

"He certainly is," she added.

Margaret's eyes shone with interest. "Ooh! Is he!" Both girls blushed and shrieked with laughter.

At that moment, Graham came up the front steps and through the doorway. "What are you girls laughing at?" he asked. Then he spoke to Margaret, "Don't put your head on my pillow 'Maggot'. I don't want your knits!"

Margaret was hurt but also happy. Graham had arrived. She sat up and smiled, hiding her annoyance. Kylie diverted the conversation.

"Skip has been hurt."

Graham at once looked concerned and knelt down to look at Skip. "How? What happened?"

Kylie explained while Graham knelt to examine Skip. When told about Mr Flawse hurling Skip over the fence his face darkened with anger and his blue eyes glittered. "The bastard! If Skip is really hurt then he will pay!"

"Oh Graham, don't you do anything," Kylie pleaded. Sometimes her brothers could be very headstrong.

Graham tenderly stroked Skip and the puppy wagged her tail and licked his hand. "She doesn't seem too bad," he commented. He went to lift Skip out of the box, but Kylie stopped him.

"She might be hurt inside. The vet said to just watch her."

Brother and sister then discussed the treatment and how to look after Skip, with Margaret adding suggestions. During this Margaret had leaned over the side of the bed so that her head was close to Graham's. As he looked up Graham met her eyes. She smiled and he smiled back, but then said, "Come on Maggot, hop off my bed. I don't want your fleas."

"I haven't got fleas!" Margaret cried indignantly.

She rolled back onto the bed. Kylie guessed that she wanted to provoke Graham into a wrestle to get her off the bed. This is what soon happened. Margaret shrieked and giggled and clung on while Graham grabbed her legs and tried to drag her over the side.

It took Kylie a minute to realise she was being spoken to from the front door. She looked and broke into a smile. Standing there was Moira McGregor, her Guide Group Leader. Moira was quite a few years older than either her or Margaret, being already 16. She was a tall, slim girl with hazel eyes and fair hair.

"Hi! What's this? Is it a private battle or can anyone join in?" Moira asked.

"Just this pair having a 'domestic'," Kylie replied. "Come in, Moira."

Graham scowled at Kylie's implication of his relationship with Margaret but let her go and stood up. As he was introduced, Kylie noted his gaze rove quickly up and down Moira's quite nicely rounded figure. His eyes widened with evident interest, and he immediately turned on the charm and smiled.

Oh dear! Kylie thought. *I hope this isn't bad news for Margaret.*

Chapter 2

PETS AND PLANS

Moira had to be introduced to Skip as well and the story explained yet again. She crouched and patted Skip who was obviously enjoying all the attention. Another biscuit was handed over and crunched down. As the children talked, Kylie was definitely concerned about the way Graham was showing off to Moira. That Margaret was worried and hurt was obvious to Kylie, who noted the brittle smile and anxious little crinkles at the corners of her eyes.

Poor kid! Oh why can't that stupid brother of mine just accept she loves him and fall in love with her? she wondered.

More voices on the front steps led to another interruption. Kylie went to the door and met Graham's friend Peter Bronsky. Peter was a well-built lad of Graham's age. She thought he was very nice. She also knew that Graham considered Peter to be very brainy. With him was an older lad, tall and with freckles and ginger hair.

Kylie smiled a welcome. "Hello, I'm Kylie," she said, noting the newcomer's friendly smile and nice face, marred by slightly irregular teeth.

"Alistair Macalistair," replied the youth.

"Alistair is one of our Rover Leaders in Scouts," Peter explained. "He's here to help plan a hike so we can get our hiking badge."

As they talked, Kylie stepped back away from the door to allow them in. Moira and Margaret both stood up and were introduced. To Kylie it was instantly apparent that Alistair was struck by Moira. He grinned and stammered and kept glancing at her. Kylie also found it amusing to note that Graham was grumpy and displeased to have competition as Moira concentrated on talking to Alistair.

To help Moira, Kylie asked Alistair what grade he was in at school.

"Year Twelve," he replied.

Kylie thought quickly. *That makes him at least sixteen or seventeen.*

It was also obvious that Moira liked Alistair as she smiled and said that she was in Year Eleven. They then began to discuss their respective

Scout and Guide groups and people they knew in common. Graham was quite excluded from this conversation and looked miffed. He did not even notice that Margaret was sitting next to him when he plonked down on his bed.

Once again, Skip's situation had to be explained and Alistair knelt and rumpled her ears and talked to her, to the puppy's obvious delight and everyone else's amusement. "I wish I had a dog," he said. "I'd love to have a pet."

"Pets!" Peter cried. "This joint is overrun with them."

"Is it?" Alistair asked Kylie.

She blushed and smiled, then nodded. "Yes. We've got Skip, plus a cat, four budgies, fish, and six guinea pigs, and we had a tortoise, but he crawled off somewhere and we haven't seen him for a few weeks."

"That sounds great. How do you find time to look after them all?" Alistair asked.

"I look after Skip and the budgies. Graham is supposed to look after the cat and the guinea pigs, and Alex, he's my other big brother, my big-big brother, is supposed to look after the fish and the orchids," Kylie explained.

"I do look after the guinea pigs!" Graham defended indignantly.

"But not poor old Claud the Cat," Kylie replied.

"Bloody cats!" Graham muttered. "Ungrateful, lazy things."

"Claud is a good name for a cat," Alistair said. "Did he claw someone?"

"Lots of times, the grumpy old bugger," Graham replied, "But he was actually named after the ancient Roman Emperor; Gaius Germanicus Claudius Caesar."

"Good heavens! Why?" Alistair asked in astonishment.

"Seemed a good name apparently. Dad named him," Kylie said.

Alistair raised an eyebrow. "Is your dad a classical scholar or ancient history teacher?"

Kylie shook her head. "No, he's a master mariner; a ship captain."

Graham made a face and said, "He was in Captain Cook's crew and did his apprenticeship with Captain Bligh, you know; Mutiny on the *'Bounty'*."

"Graham!" Kylie cried, but she smiled because the boys had often spent weeks at sea on one of their father's ships.

Moira now asked. "Can I see the guinea pigs, please?"

"Birds first please," Alistair said.

Kylie stood up and led the way down the front steps to the aviary. That meant going left towards the wide side lawn, and as they walked that way she noted how the Flawse's house seemed to loom over her in a threatening way. She realised that she had never taken note of the fact that it was a dingy old 'two-storey' place with peeling reddish-brown paint and that it was set right against the side fence. Now she also noted that all of the downstairs windows had curtains across. That caused her to glance anxiously at the row of five upstairs windows but, to her relief, no faces were visible there.

Kylie led the way to the side of the aviary under the front veranda. As the children came into view, the budgerigars began to chirp and whistle.

"They think it is food time," Kylie explained.

Alistair murmured his approval, then complimented the birds. "They are really pretty! I love that green one. What's his name?"

"Her name," Kylie corrected. "She is called Lime. The yellow one next to her is a male, and his name is Squawker."

As Squawker was doing that very loudly, the children all laughed. Alistair then asked, "What about the blue one?"

"Her name is Misty, and she is my favourite," Kylie replied. She had a party dress of exactly the same pale blue colour and that was her favourite too.

"The one showing off at the back is a male named Chirpy," Graham added.

"Typical male," Moira commented with a laugh, "Always showing off!"

That brought indignant rebuttals from the boys. Kylie laughed and poked her finger through the wire mesh so that Misty could nibble at it. "Sorry Misty, no food yet," she said, marvelling as always at how the bird's tiny eye fixed its stare on her own.

As though she is trying to understand what I say, or read my mind, she thought.

The birds were admired and played with for a few minutes before Kylie led the way around the side of the house. As they passed the partly open side gate of the enclosed underneath area, Alistair glanced in and saw the model ships.

"Are those your model ships that I have heard about?" he asked Graham.

Graham blushed red and nodded.

"Can I see them please?" Alistair asked.

Graham blushed even redder but said yes. Kylie knew that he was very shy about his models, but could not understand why, because she thought most were very good. They went into the Ship Room and Moira gasped in amazement. The concrete floor of the large room was littered with models of sailing ships, blocks of wood, model castles and forts, and dotted with hundreds of tiny people.

"Holy Mackerel!" Alistair exclaimed. "These are great!"

He knelt and studied a model sailing ship, then stared around at the other things, obviously impressed.

Moira also knelt down and looked at the tiny people who stood around a small village which she now saw was made of cardboard houses.

"What are these little people made of?" she asked.

"Plasticine," Graham answered.

"How many ships are there?" Alistair asked.

"About seventy," Graham replied. He was obviously both pleased and embarrassed by the interest and praise.

While they were talking to Moira, Skip came to the door and sat down. She still looked stiff and sore and she let out a little whine which attracted their attention. Moira turned to where Skip sat at the door.

"Isn't the dog allowed in here?" she asked.

Graham shrugged. "She can if she likes but she knows better."

"Has she damaged some of the models?" Moira asked.

"Yeah, a couple of times," Graham said. "She chased Claud through here once, but that wasn't so bad. It was the day she cornered a rat and between them they wrecked about ten ships and scattered a dozen towns."

"Oh the poor dog! I hope you didn't hit her," Moira said.

Graham coloured and said, "I gave her a bit of a smack."

"What about the rat?" Peter asked.

"Got away," Graham admitted.

"How did all these models come about?" Alistair asked. "They aren't made from kits, are they?"

Graham shook his head. "No. They are all scratch-built," he replied.

Moira looked puzzled. "What does that mean?"

"Scratch built means I made them myself. I drew the plans and made all the pieces and stuck them together," Graham explained.

"You made them yourself!" Moira cried in wonder.

Again Graham nodded, obviously embarrassed. "Yes, from pieces of wood, dowelling, balsa and so on."

"Where did you get the plans?" Alistair asked, moving to another model, a large Spanish Galleon with brilliant colouring and silk sails.

"Most are just made from pictures," Graham admitted. "They aren't built properly to scale, but a few are." He led them across to where a whole line of ships was 'sailing' across the concrete. Along the way he cautioned them not to stand on an army of little plasticine soldiers who were 'marching' along a road chalked onto the concrete. Here he showed them several really well-made models.

"These are all Eighteenth-Century ships from the Napoleonic Wars," he explained. "This one is the HMS *Victory*, of one hundred guns, and the one behind is another Ship of the Line, that's a Battleship, HMS *Renown*. They are my best. The one that isn't finished is the HMS *Vengeance*."

"How long did it take you to make these?" Moira asked.

"I've been doing it ever since I was five or six," Graham replied. He pointed to a small, roughly built model, a small lugger. "That is my first ever model."

"Have you ever read any of the books about Captain Hornblower by C S. Forester?" Alistair asked.

Graham nodded enthusiastically. "I've got them all. That is what really inspired me a couple of years ago. And I am now collecting all the books by Patrick O'Brian about Captain Aubrey, and the 'Ramage' books by Dudley Pope."

The boys began to discuss books, which did not interest Kylie very much. She showed Moira the Austrian castle she had made out of cardboard and balsa wood. It opened up to reveal five floors and was full of tiny pieces of furniture and more small people, including a King, Queen, Princess, and servants.

"And down here is the dungeon," she said, pointing into the base "That is 'Spook' in there."

"Who?" Moira asked.

"Spook, the hairy guy in the *Wizard of Id*, the guy who is always in jail."

"I think this is fabulous," Moira said. "I love these little buildings."

Her obvious admiration filled Kylie with concern. *Oh dear. I hope she doesn't get to like Graham.* She could see that Margaret was smiling with approval at the nice things being said about Graham, but that she was also looking a bit anxious.

They moved on to admire a Spanish Fort made from balsa and cardboard. It was low and solid and had rows of small balsa cannons around the top of the crenelated battlements. Like the castle, the walls could be taken off to reveal the inside rooms. One of them held the treasure, pieces of children's jewellery and some coins.

For ten minutes they looked at the models, the tiny trees and houses being especially praised. "Kylie and Margaret helped me make them," Graham admitted.

"They are very good. You kids are very talented," Moira said.

That made Kylie blush. She shrugged and said, "Yeah, well, Graham needed some expert help."

"Oh poop!" Graham cried indignantly. "Anyway, Alex made some of them."

"Who's Alex?" Moira asked.

"My big brother," Graham answered.

"Can we see the guinea pigs now?" Moira asked.

Kylie led them out through a gate at the back and across the car port, then through the laundry and onto the back lawn. As they went through the door at the back of the laundry Kylie saw the washbasin and washer lying on the lawn. "We didn't finish washing Claud. I wonder where he is?" she said.

Graham shrugged. "Who cares? Bloody cat!" he said.

Margaret bent down and picked up the bowl and washer. "I will put these away Kylie. You show them the guinea pigs," she offered.

"Thanks," Kylie replied. "This way," she added. As they walked across the back she lawn nudged Moira and whispered, "He likes you."

"Who, Graham?" Moira whispered back.

"No, Alistair," Kylie replied.

"Oh, do you think so? Sorry, I don't want him. I don't like boys all that much," Moira replied. However she blushed and glanced at Alistair and Kylie wasn't convinced by her off-hand reply.

By then they had arrived down in the far corner of the back garden.

On the last of the lawn before the fruit trees and vegetable gardens stood a large hutch. This was made of heavy timber with fine-mesh chicken wire nailed to it. The hutch had no floor so that the guinea pigs could nibble the grass. At one end were two boxes which were the guinea pigs 'homes'. As the children and Skip approached the hutch, the guinea pigs scuttled into the boxes.

Kylie eyed the almost bare earth and profusion of food scraps and droppings. She wrinkled her nose in disgust. "You need to move the cage Graham," she said.

"I will. Help me," he said. It was obvious to Kylie that he was feeling guilty at not having remembered to do that for several days as he coloured around the neck and ears.

Once the cage was moved to a fresh area of lawn Graham knelt at the back of one of the boxes and opened a small hatch in the roof. He reached in and lifted out a guinea pig, a big old male with black and white fur.

"This is 'Guts'," he said, holding him up.

Guts looked around, quite unafraid and well used to being handled. The guinea pig sniffed and looked at them for gifts of food.

"Why do you call him Guts?" Moira asked.

"Because he is Graham's!" Peter said.

Skip came sniffing in, jealous at being neglected. Guts struggled to get clear of the dog and tried to snuggle in against Graham. Graham opened his shirt and Guts quickly scuttled in, to lie against his waistband.

"Go away Skip! Hold her, Kylie," Graham said.

Kylie did so. Graham then reached into the box and took out another. "Hold them like this," he instructed, placing the guinea pig in the palm of one hand and gently placing the other hand on top to stroke. The guinea pig was then handed to Margaret and then the others, of varying sizes and colours, were taken out and passed to the other children, who held them in their hands in the way he showed them. Kylie then released Skip who sat and looked disapproving.

"What are their names?" Moira asked.

"That one is Spike. He is a young male. The one Margaret has is Toffee and she is pregnant. She is a female."

"You don't say!" Peter added with mild sarcasm. "Be a medical marvel if she wasn't!"

They all studied the bloated Toffee. Kylie knew that Margaret was fascinated by the concept and, not for the first time, she wondered how she might cope with one day being pregnant herself.

I suppose I will manage, she thought, but the idea did not really appeal.

The other two guinea pigs, both female, were named 'Blackie' (obvious by her total black colouring, except for a tiny white area around her nose, and 'Pie'.

"Why Pie?" Moira asked.

"That's what she is going into when she is fat enough," Alistair suggested, to the outrage of the girls. "Only joking!" he cried.

"Because she is piebald," Kylie explained, indicating the brown and white colouring.

The children all held the guinea pigs and stroked them for the next few minutes. As they did, Skip whined and snuffled and showed her jealousy and displeasure. Then she expressed it even more forcibly by moving close to Alistair and doing a pee.

At that the boys burst out laughing and teased Alistair. Kylie blushed with embarrassment, then flamed even more when Skip stopped and began to grunt out a poo onto the soiled area. "Oh Skip!" she muttered.

"When ya gotta go, ya gotta go," Graham said.

He then turned to take the guinea pig Moira was holding. In her nervousness, Moira let go too soon and the guinea pig dropped to the grass.

"Oh quick! Grab him before Skip gets him!" Graham cried.

He dashed after the frightened guinea pig. There was a general rush as the others all jumped in fright or tried to join in the chase. Margaret had to step hastily aside to avoid Peter as he lunged to grab at the guinea pig. In doing so Margaret stepped back, right onto Skip.

Skip let out a yelp of pain and Margaret cried in distress, tried to lift her foot off him and then lost her balance as the puppy scuttled between her legs. With a cry of dismay she sat down heavily, then fell on her back. She looked very unhappy, and Kylie realised she had fallen right on Skip's business on the foul ground.

"Oh no!" Margaret wailed.

Chapter 3

IN THE POO

As she rolled in the mess, Margaret's emotions were in turmoil. Her main concern was whether she had hurt poor little Skip, but she could also tell by the feel, and by the looks of the others, that she had soiled her clothes. As she stood up, she bent over to anxiously reach out for Skip, who was now being delicately inspected by Kylie.

"Is she alright?" Margaret asked. "Oh I'm sorry Kylie! I didn't mean to hurt her."

"I know," Kylie replied, giving her a re-assuring smile. "I don't think anything is broken. It was only her paw."

Chuckling from Peter and Alistair now made Margaret aware of the other problem.

Peter smiled. "Margaret is the one in the poo now!" he commented.

Margaret burned with embarrassment as she twisted to try to see her back. She had worn really tight, white shorts to show off her legs to Graham and now she saw, to her horror, that the whole of her left buttock was smeared with dog poo.

"Oh no! My good shorts!" she wailed. Her eyes prickled with tears of mortification and shame.

Kylie showed her concern. Picking up Skip she moved to examine the damage. "Shut up you silly boys! Stop your laughing. Poor Margaret was only trying to avoid Skip."

"Well she met up with a good reminder of him," Alistair said. Margaret noted that his eyes looked sympathetic, but he still grinned.

What hurt Margaret more was that Graham was grinning too, although he did look sorry for her. Kylie shook her head and sucked her tongue. "You've got a big smear of... of something on your blouse too," she said.

"Doggy doo!" Peter suggested.

"Oh shut up, you horrible boys, and go away!" Kylie snapped. She thrust Skip at Graham. "Here, take Skip back to her box and look after her."

Graham took Skip. As he turned away he rumpled her ears and said,

"She might want to go to the dunny instead. Do you want to go to the potty Skip?" he asked.

At that Margaret burst into tears. Kylie snapped angrily at the boys telling them to act their age and to clear out. They retired giggling and chortling to the house.

"Oh what will I do?" Margaret wailed. "My new shorts! Mum will skin me alive."

"They are nice shorts too," Kylie complimented. "Come on, we must be able to do something." She took Margaret's hand and led her to the laundry. When she got there, she said, "I know. You go and have a shower and I will put stain remover on your shorts and top and give them a good scrubbing and then put them in the wash. They should be right in half an hour. Come one."

Margaret allowed herself to be led upstairs to the bathroom. Kylie then said, "Give me your clothes and you get in the shower."

Margaret turned her back on Kylie and undressed, then stepped into the bathtub and pulled the plastic shower curtain across. Kylie carefully picked up the clothes and made her way downstairs. To Margaret's added embarrassment a very noticeable pong was left lingering in the air.

She turned on the shower and adjusted the taps, then began to soap herself. She had often had a bath in the Kirk's bathroom so that was no novelty. As she gently rubbed the soap across her front, she had hot memories of being in the bath with Graham the previous year.

When we were little, she told herself, to excuse such wicked thoughts.

But thinking about Graham made her more upset. She studied her little girl's body and sighed. *I know he really likes girls,* she told herself. She could tell that by the way his eyes caressed them. She had also found some 'Girlie' magazines under his bed once. Thinking of them didn't help. *How can I compete with those models?* she wondered. It was no good her mother telling her that her body would just naturally develop as she got older. *I want to look sexy now,* she thought. She put her hands on her waist and shook her head.

"What waist?" she muttered bitterly. "Puppy fat, Mum calls it, but it won't get Graham excited."

She had been wondering what to wear, assuming that Kylie would bring her a dressing gown or something. Now she decided to be daring. *I will get Graham's attention,* she thought.

Even as she considered this her heart rate shot up and her mouth went dry with the anticipated thrill. She towelled herself dry and used some of the scents in the cabinet to cover up any possible remaining odour. Then she wrapped the towel around under her armpits. She then checked in the mirror and was satisfied it covered her well. It went from her armpits to her knees, so she was satisfied.

With her heart beating rapidly because of her daring dress she opened the door and walked through the house. By the time she reached the veranda her heart was hammering as though she had run a race. *Act cool,* she told herself. But by then she regretted having done it and considered turning around.

It was the sight of Graham's eyes as they skimmed down her body that gave her the courage to keep going, very aware that Peter and Alistair were also staring at her. Worse still, Moira had a little frown of disapproval on her brow. Alex was there too, having arrived home while she was in the shower.

Where shall I sit? Margaret worried, now strongly regretting her decision.

Graham and Peter sat on Graham's bed. Margaret walked past Peter and crawled onto the bed, hotly aware that she wore nothing under the towel. As quickly as she could, she curled up in a ball at the bottom of the bed, her legs tucked underneath her. Then she faced Graham and gave him a faint smile.

To her relief, he smiled back. His eyes, she noted, kept flicking down to where her legs vanished up under the towel. Alex made a few half-hearted comments about 'What is that I can smell?' but the arrival of Kylie put an end to them.

"Your clothes are in the washing machine now, Margaret," she said, her eyebrows going up fractionally when she noted what Margaret was wearing.

Fortunately the attention of the group was now diverted by the arrival of Claud the Cat. The scruffy old ginger reprobate came stalking in the front door. He sniffed suspiciously, then glared around and stalked past. Kylie scooped him up and stroked him, then passed him to Moira, who said she loved cats. Usually Claud resented strangers and did claw them but he suffered Moira's attentions without protest.

The conversation then wandered onto schools and teachers. By then

Margaret had been forgotten. She began to get sore muscles as her legs cramped under her. To ease her muscles she shifted her weight to sit on her other side. Graham noted this but to her jealous annoyance he kept his focus on Moira. That nettled her and she had to make a conscious effort to hide her feelings.

Then shame swept through her at her thoughts, and she tried to think of a dignified way of getting out of the situation without anyone noticing. The sound of a car downstairs told her that Mrs Kirk had arrived home. That introduced a whole new level of anxiety and shame.

She will think I am a little tart! Margaret thought, frantically wondering how to get to Kylie's room without anyone noting it.

She couldn't. Mrs Kirk came through from the backstairs. First, she had to be introduced to Moira and Alistair. Next, she had to be told about Mr Flawse hurting Skip and the trip to the vet. By then her eyes had noted Margaret's apparel and her raised eyebrows led to the next story, Margaret falling in the dog poo.

"Oh you poor girl!" Mrs Kirk said sympathetically.

Margaret waited for her to scold or order her to get dressed but she said nothing and went back to the kitchen. Feeling very uncomfortable Margaret sat and wished she had not been so stupid.

A few minutes later, Mrs Kirk called Kylie from the back of the house. "Yes Mum?" Kylie called, getting up and walking into the lounge next door.

Margaret took this as her cue and slid herself off the bed and followed Kylie. She had only taken two steps out of the room when she heard Mrs Kirk call, "Tell everyone to come through to the kitchen for afternoon tea."

Kylie turned and came back. Margaret said she would tell them and turned as well.

"Come and have afternoon tea," she said. As she did, the towel was jerked hard. Just in time she grabbed at it to stop it being whisked away. For a second she was too surprised to fully realise what had happened. But then the towel was tugged again, and she turned her head to see a grinning Kylie pulling at it.

Kylie is trying to take my towel away! she thought. And, to her embarrassment Kylie had partly succeeded. Margaret distinctly felt cool air on her left leg and back. Tensing up she gripped the towel to her.

"Kylie!" she cried.

Kylie grinned and let go and ran off across the lounge room, chuckling as she went. In an instant, a dozen emotions and ideas rushed through Margaret's mind. She saw a frown on Moira's face, the leering eyes of the boys, Graham staring at her wide-eyed. Their reactions left her worrying what they could now see. Blushing with shame, Margaret made sure her front was covered and began backing away. Only when she was in the next room did she step out of sight and try to adjust the towel. Burning with embarrassment, she hurried after Kylie.

Then she saw Mrs Kirk standing at the next doorway and her heart skipped with anxiety. Mrs Kirk was shaking her head and had stopped Kylie.

"Naughty little minx!" she scolded Kylie.

Kylie looked suitably abashed and fled. Margaret now flamed with shame again and hurried across the room, trying to keep herself covered as she did.

"I'm sorry Mrs Kirk," she sobbed.

Mrs Kirk gave her a faint smile. "Not your fault. Now let's put this on properly before the boys get all hot and bothered." She quickly helped Margaret wrap the towel securely around herself. "Your clothes should be dry so go and get dressed," she said.

Feeling very confused, Margaret hurried down the back stairs to the laundry. Here she found a very guilty looking Kylie putting her clothes into the tumble dryer.

"I'm sorry Margaret," Kylie said. "I don't know what came over me. I didn't mean to embarrass you."

"Well you did!" Margaret cried, her eyes watering. "I was so ashamed when your mother came into the room."

Kylie again said sorry, then grinned and added, "What about when Graham saw you?"

At that Margaret had to forgive her. "His eyes nearly popped out of his head, even though he tried to play Mr Cool," she said.

Her heart pounded so hard she felt dizzy and the sheer thrill of it made her feel light-headed. To her own wonderment she realised she was enjoying the excitement and that made her feel even more ashamed. But it also made her feel daring.

"He can look at me any time he likes," she added.

"Margaret!" Kylie cried in a scandalised tone. Margaret could tell she wasn't really shocked, only a bit surprised. "You be careful," Kylie went on Then she became serious. "Please don't get Graham into any trouble by tempting him too much."

"I won't. I love him," Margaret added.

The two girls then stood and discussed boys and what they liked to look at till Margaret's clothes were dry. Kylie then left her and went upstairs. Feeling all hot and ashamed again Margaret hurriedly dressed. Then she found it a challenge to go upstairs. Instead she contemplated leaving and going home but then shrugged.

I can't spend my life running away, she thought. *Besides, I don't think they were all that offended.*

So she meekly followed Kylie up the stairs and into the kitchen, blushing hotly as she did. To her relief, no-one mentioned the incident and she was able to find a seat and slip back out of the limelight. Mrs Kirk placed cordial and biscuits in front of her, giving her a warm smile as she did.

That left Margaret in greater turmoil. Did Mrs Kirk not care? Or was she just saving the tongue-lashing and banishment till the others had left? It was very worrying but as the minutes went by with happy chatter and more biscuits she began to relax.

I hope she doesn't tell my Mum, she thought anxiously. *Or my dad!* That would be even worse. He would give her a good spanking and a very strong talking to. *And I'll deserve it,* she told herself. But in her heart she found she didn't regret the incident.

Finally, Alistair drained his glass and put it down. "Can we get on with this planning now?" he asked. "I have to be at tennis practice by four."

"What planning is that?" Moira asked as she picked up another biscuit.

"We are going on a hike for our Hiking badge in the Scouts and I want to get my silver Duke of Edinburgh award," Alistair replied.

"Where are you going?" Kylie asked.

"We were thinking of walking from Mareeba to Kuranda," Alistair replied.

"Oh yuk! That won't be very nice, all those cars whizzing by," Margaret said.

"No, not along the main highway," Alistair replied. "We thought we would follow the railway."

"Are you allowed to walk along the railway?" Kylie asked.

"No, but there's a road beside it," Alistair replied.

"Is that the railway that goes through 'Corwa' and past the horse-riding school?" Margaret asked.

"Yes, it is," Moira answered.

"When are you going?" Kylie asked, seeing at once what Margaret wanted to know.

"Not this weekend, the weekend after," Alistair answered.

Margaret sat up. "That is when we are going horse riding for the weekend," she said. "Maybe we could see you as you go past?"

Suddenly, what had promised to be just a good weekend away promised to be a really great weekend. She gave Graham a shy smile.

Chapter 4

SILLY BOYS!

Kylie gently patted Carbine's neck before checking again that the girth strap was not too tight around the horse's middle. Then she looked around the yard and smiled with pleasure. Beside her was Moira, still nervously adjusting the bridle on Tornado, a four-year-old palomino stallion. Beyond her was Margaret, sitting confidently up on her horse, a five-year-old grey mare named Lucy. Mrs Lucas, their riding instructor, was at the door of the stables talking to her husband. In her hands she held the reins of Starblazer.

The sight of Starblazer's lovely glossy black coat shining in the sun made Kylie yearn to ride her. The two-year-old mare was the best-looking horse she had ever seen. She tried not to have negative thoughts about her own mount but knew she was jealous of Mrs Lucas. Guilt at this caused her to pat Carbine again.

"You are a lovely horse, Carbine," she said softly in the horse's ear.

Carbine, a three-year-old chestnut stallion, turned his head and looked at her, his ears waggling with interest.

Mrs Lucas, a trim, fit woman in her thirties, turned and led her horse over to them. She was very properly clad in glossy riding boots, fawn jodhpurs, white silk shirt, and white safety helmet.

"Righto girls, mount up and let's get going," she said.

Kylie at once reached up and just managed to get her riding boot into the stirrup. Carbine stood quite still, watching her as she struggled to hoist herself up onto his back. As always, Kylie felt anxious at how the saddle and animal both moved but she made it first time. Then she was struck at just how far off the ground she seemed to be. It never ceased to amaze her at how high up it was when on a horse's back. Then she felt a twinge of anxiety as Carbine moved.

It wasn't much of a movement. Carbine was just shifting his feet for comfort, but it still gave Kylie an uneasy feeling. She loved horses but she was also a bit afraid of them. That, she knew, was a bad thing.

You should feel confident, let them know you are the boss, she thought.

It was not as if she had never ridden a horse before. She had been riding for two years now and it was the third time that year she and Margaret had spent a weekend at Corwa.

Seeing Margaret grinning at her while her own mount fidgeted gave Kylie another twinge of jealousy. Margaret appeared to be completely at home on the back of a horse, even though she had no more experience. Kylie knew her jealousy was unfair, and she tried to appear calm and relaxed, even though Carbine began to move restlessly.

It was Moira who was having the problems. She had never ridden a horse in her life until that morning. Now Mrs Lucas was helping her to mount, while holding Tornado's bridle and offering quiet words of advice. Moira's anxiety was plain, but she pluckily made the attempt and swung herself into the saddle.

"Well done!" Mrs Lucas said.

Kylie gave Moira an encouraging grin and received a nervous smile in return.

Mrs Lucas then seemed to spring into Starblazer's saddle. She waved to her husband, who was holding two of the dogs at the homestead steps and turned the horse towards the front gate. "Righto girls, let's trot to the front gate, then stop. We are going across the railway to the hill paddock. Once we get there Moira can learn to canter while you two girls ride around the bush track"

The bush track was a winding dirt road that went through the open savannah woodland at the far side of the hill paddock. Kylie enjoyed riding around it because it was just different enough to be interesting. It was really only a few hundred metres long and the open paddock was always visible from it, but she liked it.

Trotting she did not like. It seemed to her to be such a peculiar way to ride a horse, uncomfortable and ridiculous looking. Despite this she managed to get Carbine to trot. She suspected he didn't like trotting either, or more likely, didn't like the way she bumped around on his back when he did. This was mainly because she had difficulty using her leg muscles to regulate the motions.

Margaret just seemed to float along, which was mildly annoying to Kylie. They crossed the railway and then the gravel road beyond. After opening the gate and passing through, Margaret leaned over and closed it. Margaret then caused Kylie even more thoughts she regretted by cantering in a wide circle. As she did, Margaret sang and laughed and appeared to be glued to the horse's back.

Moira watched this performance with obvious anxiety. Mrs Lucas stopped beside her and said to Moira, "It's easy you see, and a lot more pleasant than trotting." She then turned to Kylie and Margaret. "Righto you two girls, off you go. And remember, no galloping and no leaving the track. You are not to go out of my sight."

"Yes Mrs Lucas," Margaret replied.

She then tapped Lucy with her heels and set off. Kylie 'gee-upped' Carbine and also used her boot heels gently. To her relief, Carbine almost at once went from a walk to a canter. She loved that. It was such a smooth, rhythmic motion that she did not feel scared at all, even though it was so fast.

For the next half hour the two girls rode around the bush track while Mrs Lucas coached Moira at the basics. The bush was mostly spindly paperbarks growing in grey soil that was dry and dusty. Kylie thoroughly enjoyed the cantering and even allowed the speed to creep up to a few short gallops in an attempt to overtake Margaret. That didn't work. Margaret looked over her shoulder and urged Lucy to go faster and stayed easily ahead. Kylie slowed down because she was afraid of losing control or of falling off at the bends.

At 3pm Mrs Lucas and Moira joined them and the group happily rode around the bush track, alternately walking and cantering. By then Moira was looking a little more confident and even managed a few nervous smiles. After three laps Mrs Lucas looked at her watch and brought the horses to a stop. While patting Starblazer's neck she said, "Time these horses had a drink. It is very hot."

Kylie could only agree with that. Even though it was May and theoretically 'Autumn', the temperature was still over 27 degrees Celsius.

"Can we go down to the river to do that?" Margaret asked.

Mrs Lucas nodded. "If you like."

"Oh goodie!" Kylie cried. She loved the stretch of the Barron River near 'Corwa'.

They set off across the field towards the gate. As they trotted over the dry grass Margaret asked if they could go for a ride along the road after the horses had had a drink. Kylie knew why she was asking and smiled but Mrs Lucas wanted a reason.

"The road can be dangerous," she said.

That was true. It was only a graded gravel bush track and there wasn't all that much traffic, but the locals drove along it very fast. Margaret answered, "Some of our friends are doing a hike along the road from Mareeba today and should be passing through soon," she answered.

"My brother is one of them," Kylie added.

"Oh alright," Mrs Lucas replied. By then they were at the gate. Again Margaret opened it to let them through, then closed it behind them. Mrs Lucas led them left along the road towards Venture Creek. The creek ran in a deep little valley with steep sides and only the tops of the trees lining its banks and bed showed as they rode towards it. At the point where the road began to dip down through a cutting the railway was about fifty metres off to their right. A thin belt of dry savannah woodland grew between the road and railway.

Venture Creek was one of the few permanent creeks in the area. Most creeks were dry except for a few months during the summer rains. The valley was about two hundred metres wide and thirty metres deep. The valley sides were clothed in dry grass and scattered eucalypts. The actual creek was only five metres wide in a fifty-metre bed of dry sand. A thick belt of evergreen trees grew in the creek bed, making it a very pleasant, cool and shady place.

The road wound down a steep bench cut to the left. It then crossed over a tiny, single lane timber bridge, before climbing back up another bench cut to the dry ridge beyond. Downstream on their right the railway went straight across on a massive bridge: huge steel beams resting on four gigantic concrete pylons. The railway was laid on top of the steel beams and looked very narrow. Kylie had once walked across the railway bridge with Margaret and had found it a scary experience. Not only did it look a very long way down but there were only a few tiny safety projections for a person to get out on if a train had come along. Luckily none had and the girls had hurried off. Margaret had been so scared of falling that for her hurrying consisted of shuffling one foot ahead of the other along the two planks laid between the rails for the rail workers to walk along.

As they reached the top of the bank Kylie glanced towards the rail bridge. This was clearly visible a hundred paces to their right. Movement caught her eye and she felt her heart skip. "Oh look!" she cried. "It's the boys."

Three figures carrying packs were clearly visible walking slowly across the rail bridge. They were approaching halfway. Despite the distance Kylie could make out that Graham was leading, with Peter and Alistair behind.

Margaret gasped and shook her head. "Oh those silly boys! What if a train comes along?"

Even as she said this, they heard the distinctive blast of a diesel locomotive's air horn.

"Oh no! A train!" Kylie cried.

The train was coming from the east, from Kuranda. Kylie knew that the railway had a curve in it just before the bridge, so that a train approaching from that direction would be hidden from view until the last moment. Looking back over her right shoulder she glimpsed the top of the locomotive as it ran into the low cutting there. A string of wagons followed it.

To her consternation the three boys were still walking forwards across the bridge. "They haven't heard the train!" she cried in dismay. Hauling on the reins to stop her horse she stood up in the stirrups and screamed, "Graham! Train!"

At that moment, the boys all stopped and looked along the bridge. Their jerky body movements indicated consternation and panic.

"They've seen it!" Margaret cried, her voice choking with anxiety.

"Yes, but they'll never get off the bridge in time," added Mrs Lucas.

"They'll be killed! Oh! There is the train!" Moira screamed.

Off to the right the locomotive suddenly thundered into view onto the bridge. Its horn blared again and there was a savage hissing sound. An ear-splitting screech of metal on metal indicated that the driver had slammed on the brakes. But Kylie could see the train had no chance of stopping in the hundred metres of bridge left to it. It was simply going too fast.

Heart in mouth, all that she could do was watch. For a few moments all the boys seemed to do was stand as though mesmerised, then to jerk about in apparent panic. They were shouting but she could not understand what they were saying. Both Graham and Peter swung off their packs and threw them over the side. Alistair turned and ran back.

It appeared that Alistair was trying to reach one of the little safety projections. What Graham and Peter intended was not clear but by then the train was so close, and going so fast, that it seemed they must be run over. Even as Kylie screamed in horror, she saw Graham jump aside and Peter drop down.

"He will never make it!" wailed Moira, meaning

Alistair, who was still running back along the bridge. Heart in mouth Kylie watched as the thundering locomotive rapidly overtook him. Then it caught up and Alistair vanished from view.

"Oh no! They've been killed!" Moira screamed.

The train, a 'mixed goods', kept on going, its brakes screeching. The metallic clashing of various steel parts drowned out the girl's voices. More and more wagons roared out onto the bridge before the girl's horrified gaze.

"Graham jumped I think," Kylie yelled.

Then she kicked her heels into Carbine's flanks and set him racing down the road. There was, she knew, a vehicle track that ran along the bottom of the other side of the valley floor and underneath the rail bridge. It was the track they had been intending to take and now she headed for it as fast as she could ride. Heedless of a possible fall she urged the horse down the steep descent. A glance behind her showed the others following.

By the time Kylie reached the timber road bridge at the bottom of the slope the last wagon of the train had roared onto the bridge. Kylie had been expecting the train to stop but noted it was still rolling on across the bridge. It was definitely slowing down though, and the hissing of compressed air sounded loudly. In an agony of concern Kylie cantered across the short bridge. She then had to reef at the reins to get Carbine to slow and turn.

The horse nearly tossed her, resenting the cruel jerk. With difficulty Kylie got him around and then started him cantering along the side track. This was just two-wheel tracks through long grass and ran along the base of the steep, grassy slope. The trees of the creek bed were close on the right, some overhanging the track. Carbine did not like running in the long grass and would not be pressed. He slowed, first to a trot, then to a fast walk.

The rail bridge now loomed high above Kylie. She kept glancing up to see if there was any sign of the boys. The overhanging trees made this difficult, and the moving train also obscured much of the view. Then the last wagon rolled on across and she was granted a glimpse of someone. Because the person was on the other side of the bridge, its structure obscuring her view, she could not tell who it was. Nor could she see if they were alright.

Then the trees ended and she was able to see the creek bed under the bridge. A glance showed her that there was a person moving in the pool of water between the first and second concrete pylons. The person was swimming.

"It's Graham!" she cried. "He's alive!"

Twenty-five metres downstream of the rail bridge the creek divided. An island about fifty paces wide and a hundred long stood downstream of the second and third pylons. The island was mostly sand but had a clump of trees growing on it. Visible beyond the island was the open water of the Barron River. The pool that Graham had jumped into was only about fifty metres long and ten wide and looked to be studded with both rocks and snags. The bottom was clearly visible. The pool did not appear to Kylie to be anything like deep enough for a person to jump into from such a height.

Noting that Graham seemed to be floundering in shallow water Kylie was consumed by desperate anxiety lest he had serious injuries. She urged Carbine on under the bridge. "Graham!" she called.

She saw his head turn. Surprise gave way to a grin. "Hi Sis!"

"Are you alright?" Kylie called back, turning Carbine down into the reedy shallows.

"Yes."

"You're not hurt?"

"No."

Kylie shook her head in amazement. Her fear drained away and began to be replaced by annoyance. "So what are you doing in the water? Can't you get up?"

"Looking for Pete's pack," Graham replied, groping under the water as he did.

Kylie now spotted Graham's scout hat lying in the reeds nearby. Her emotions boiled over. "Oh you silly boy! You could have been killed! That was a really stupid thing to do!" she yelled.

Graham grinned back, raising her anger another notch. "Not as silly as being run over by a train," he retorted.

By then Carbine had halted in the shallows and put her head down to drink. Margaret arrived and reined in, then Mrs Lucas. Margaret sprang off her horse and ran down into the water.

"Oh Graham! Are you alright?" she cried.

She held her arms wide and was obviously wanting to embrace him. However he bent down and kept groping in the water. Margaret came to a stop in waist deep water next to him.

Alistair's voice came floating down from above, "Bit further to your left Graham."

Kylie looked up and saw Alistair standing on one of the tiny safety projections. Against the bright background of the sky he looked like a small, black cut-out. To Kylie it looked a long way to drop. She called up, her mind seething with concern and growing anger, "What about Peter?"

Ever since she had seen Peter drop down she had been tortured by images of him trying to lie flat between the wheels of the train, and of him being struck by some metal projection. Her imagination had pictured him being dragged along and mangled. She had an idea that engines had some sort of scoop in front of them to clear the line of obstructions and had thought this would have hit him.

Before Alistair could reply to Peter's voice came to her, "Here I am. I'm okay."

She looked up and saw movement in among the steel girders underneath the track. At that she sighed with relief. Somehow Peter had managed to get down through the sleepers and under the railway. Then her anger exploded.

"You silly boys! You scared the daylights out of us. What a stupid thing to be doing! What were you doing walking along the railway line anyway?"

"That's what I'd like to know," boomed a man's voice.

They all looked around. Standing at the end of the rail bridge was a big man in railway uniform. He was panting and looked very red in the face and angry. He pointed along the bridge and called, "You kids come here!"

Oh dear! Kylie thought, biting her lip with anxiety.

Graham had just found Peter's pack and he now lugged it ashore, splashing Margaret in the process and not even noticing. Margaret stood in the muddy water looking very unhappy. She waded ashore in Graham's wake. Graham dropped the pack and looked up the steep slope, concern wrinkling his brow.

"Your hat's just there!" Kylie snapped angrily, pointing to it. He nodded, mumbled thanks, and went to scoop it up. Jamming it on his head, he began climbing up a faint foot track in the long grass.

Kylie dismounted, as did Mrs Lucas. Margaret joined them. Up on the bridge Alistair and Peter could both be seen walking back towards the waiting train driver. A second man now joined him. Then Moira came into view, her horse walking slowly along. She appeared to be clinging tightly to the saddle and had lost her reins.

Margaret ran to grab the reins and then held the horse while Moira dismounted. She then held the reins out. "You hold the horses please Moira," she asked.

Moira did so. Kylie handed her Carbine's reins as well and set off up the slope after Graham. Margaret followed her. Moira was also handed Starblazer's reins and Mrs Lucas followed them up the slope.

It wasn't that far up but it was hot and unpleasant in the long grass. Kylie kept looking for snakes, even though her mind told her that Graham would have scared any away. The grass was so high that in places it met over her head. Seeds and sharp ends continually tickled or prickled her face.

By the time she reached the top all three boys were at the end of the bridge and the angry engine driver was well launched into a tirade about how stupid and irresponsible the boys had been.

"You might have been killed!" he shouted, "And how would that affect your parents eh? What would your mum and dad think then eh? You didn't think of that did you? And what about me and Walter? How do you think I would feel if I'd run you down and skittled you eh?"

The boys looked suitably abashed and hung their heads. None made any attempt to justify what they had done.

Mrs Lucas also joined in. "You silly boys!" she cried.

With that Kylie could only agree.

Chapter 5

CHANCE MEETING

As Margaret scrambled up the steep path, she swallowed several grass seeds. These made her cough and splutter. Her eyes began to water. Wiping away tears she struggled on upwards. There was a barbed wire fence to crawl under. Ignoring the dirt and prickles she crawled under it. On arriving at the top she stopped and looked anxiously at the angry scene. She was already very upset from the near fatal accident, and from Graham's causal reaction to her concern. Now he was in trouble again and it made her feel ill.

The train driver continued with his angry questioning. "What were you doing walking on the railway line anyway? Don't you know it is against the regulations?" he shouted.

A very shame-faced Alistair answered that. "Yes, we know that. We were walking along the road before we reached here."

"So why get off the road?" the driver demanded to know.

"Because... because...," Alistair began.

"It was my fault," Graham said. "When we saw how deep the valley was, I didn't feel like walking all the way down and then up that steep slope again. The railway bridge just goes straight across."

The driver stared hard at him, eyeing his wet and muddy clothes. "You are the kid that jumped?"

Graham nodded. The driver went on, "I thought you were dead for sure. That water doesn't look deep enough to jump into without hitting the bottom."

"It isn't," Graham admitted. "I hit the bottom real hard."

They all turned to look at the pool. From where they stood at the end of the bridge it looked very small and Margaret noted that she could see the bottom. She also saw several large logs and a couple of rocks in the water. It looked a long way down.

"Oh Graham! You could have been killed," she cried.

"Or broken your back," the driver added. "That would have been worse."

At that thought Margaret felt even sicker. She was now very anxious that the driver did not report them but, to her dismay, he next asked for their names. They gave them and he wrote them into a small pocket notebook. Then he stared hard at Graham.

"Kirk, eh? Who is your dad? What does he do?"

"He's a ship's master, a captain," Graham replied.

The driver rubbed his jaw. He now looked a lot less angry. "Yeah, I know your old man. He and I went to school together. When I see him next, I will tell him what a stupid little idiot you have been. You can tell him that Fred Forsayth said so."

"It was my fault," Alistair said. "I am the oldest."

"Yes, and you are damned lucky too. If that pack of yours had gotten caught on something, you would have been dragged to your death. I nearly had a bloody heart attack when I saw you running for that safety bay. I didn't reckon you would make it."

There was a moment's awkward silence. Alistair had gone a sickly, pale colour and Margaret felt very sorry for him. She stepped forward and looked up at the driver. "Please sir, don't get them into more trouble. They didn't mean any harm and I'm sure they have learned their lesson."

The driver looked at her and frowned, then said, "And who are you?"

"My name is Margaret Lake, and this is Kylie, Graham's sister."

"So how do you girls come into this?" the driver asked.

"We are spending the weekend horse riding," Margaret replied, gesturing down to where Moira held the horses. "The boys were doing a hike from Mareeba to Kuranda and had arranged to say hello as they went past."

"Where were you when this all happened?" the driver asked.

Kylie answered that, pointing through the trees. "We were riding along the road and were just at the top of the bank over there. We nearly died of fright when we saw what was going to happen," she said. She turned to Graham. "Didn't you hear us call out?"

Graham looked sheepish. "No. Sorry. We were discussing what would happen if a train came along, and bugger me! There was one!"

"No need to swear in the presence of ladies!" the driver snapped.

"Sorry sir," Graham replied.

The driver then looked at his mate who tapped his watch significantly. The driver said, "Yes, well, if we are late getting to Mareeba and get into trouble you are going to hear a lot more about this. Now get off the railway, and stay off!"

"Yes sir," they chorused.

As the driver and his mate turned to walk back to their train, Margaret felt a wave of relief that brought more tears to her eyes. She so much wanted to hug Graham but could only stand and watch.

"Come on," Alistair said.

He began pushing his way down through the long grass. The others followed. Margaret went last, wiping her cheeks as she did. Going down under the barbed wire fence and through the long grass again was unpleasant but she found it much easier as a track had been trampled by the time she followed.

At the bottom Moira wanted to know what had happened. She quizzed Alistair and that pleased Margaret. *She might think he is nice,* she hoped. *I think he is!*

Graham dragged Peter's pack out onto the track. "Here's your pack."

"Oh thanks! Bloody hell!" Peter cried, bending to roll the sodden object over.

"Where's yours, Graham?" Alistair asked.

Graham pointed out to the sandy island. "There."

Margaret wondered how she had missed seeing it earlier. The pack lay on the sand near some weeds. "You will get wet getting it," she said.

At that Graham laughed and indicated his muddy clothes. "Big deal! I think I'm wet already."

"What are you going to do now?" Kylie asked.

Peter straightened up, shaking his head. "I want to unpack all of this and try to dry it while I can," he said. He looked at his watch. "Nearly four. There are a couple of hours of daylight left."

"We had better camp here then," Alistair said.

"But we were going to camp another five kilometres further on," Graham protested.

"We have to help Pete dry out," Alistair replied. "We can just walk a bit faster tomorrow."

"Where will you camp?" Kylie asked.

Graham pointed to the island. "What about down at the far end of the island. That sandy area looks good. We can put up shelters under those trees if we have to."

Margaret looked at the place and thought it looked a lovely spot: white sandy beach, green grass, shady trees, and a pleasant view of the Barron River. Kylie did not agree. "What if there is a flood during the night?" she said.

Graham scoffed. "Oh fair go Sis! The wet season is over. There hasn't been any rain for weeks. It isn't going to flood."

Margaret hadn't thought of floods but now became anxious. Kylie tried to argue but the boys all howled her down. As a last argument she said, "But you will get wet just getting to the island."

"Oh piffle!" Graham snorted. "It is only ankle deep down there. We will just wade across. Anyway, we can take our boots off."

With that he waded back into the water heading for his pack. *Now he is showing off!* Margaret thought, but she still loved him for it. Peter picked up his pack and began lugging it along the track towards where the channel between the island and the shore was narrowest. Alistair followed.

Mrs Lucas turned to the girls. "You girls need to come home now."

"Oh Mrs Lucas, can we just talk to the boys for a few minutes," Margaret pleaded.

Mrs Lucas smiled. "Alright. But I want you home by five." With that she mounted Starblazer and trotted off back under the bridge towards the road. The girls took their horse's reins from Moira and began walking along behind the boys.

The water turned out to be knee deep. Peter and Alistair sat down and took off their boots and rolled their long trousers up above their knees. As they did, Margaret admired the river, which had now come into full view. At that point it was at least a hundred metres wide and was flowing smoothly. The water was slightly muddy and she could plainly see where the clearer water of Venture Creek mingled with the main flow. At that point, the river was making a sweeping curve to the left. Just visible through the trees downstream was the high bluff on which Corwa stood. The house was not visible but Margaret knew that the river was visible from the side veranda.

I might be able to see the boy's camp tonight, she thought hopefully.

The boys waded across to join Graham. For the girls it was simple. They mounted their horses, which forded the shallow stream easily. On the way the girls allowed them to stop and put their heads down to drink.

43

As they arrived at the end of the island where Graham had dropped his pack he asked, "What are you girls going to do?"

They hadn't thought of that. Kylie replied, "Help you set up camp?"

"That's done," Graham replied, indicating the soft sand and his pack.

"Aren't you going to put up tents?" Moira asked in surprise.

"Why?" Graham answered. He pointed up. "Not a cloud in the sky. It won't rain."

"Won't you get cold?" Kylie asked.

"We will light a fire," Graham replied. "Now, will you girls leave? I want to get out of these wet clothes."

"You can change in the bushes," Kylie replied, plainly miffed at being told to buzz off.

"I haven't got anything to change into," Graham answered.

Kylie was amazed. "You only brought one set of clothes!"

"It's only one weekend," Graham replied defensively.

"Oh phew! I'm glad I won't be sitting near you on the train home," she said.

Margaret was intrigued and very interested. "Are you going to wander around in the nuddy?" she asked Graham.

He shrugged and blushed. "Until my clothes dry," he replied.

"Oh poor Peter and Alistair," Kylie cried. "Having to look at anything so ugly."

Peter shrugged and grinned. "Nothing we haven't seen before. Not much to see anyway."

"Hoy!" Graham cried indignantly.

They all laughed. Graham then said, "Well, get going. I don't want to offend anyone."

"What if people come along?" Margaret asked.

"I will hide in the bush," Graham answered. "Now get going."

"Margaret would probably rather stay," Kylie commented.

"Oh I would not!" Margaret said, which she knew was not true at all. She blushed, then blushed again at her wicked thoughts, and at lying.

Peter grinned. "Be nothing she hasn't seen before from what I hear," he added, further embarrassing Margaret.

"What do you mean?" Moira asked, herself blushing bright red.

"Graham and Margaret have often been in the bath together," Kylie said. She giggled and went red.

44

"Oh that was when we were little!" Margaret cried.

In her embarrassment, she hauled Lucy's head around and tapped her flanks with her heels. The other girls followed, with much giggling and laughter.

"See you in the morning," Kylie called back to the boys as the horses waded back to the bank.

As Lucy walked up onto the bank Margaret urged her into a canter. She was still burning with embarrassment and feeling flustered. She really wanted to stay with Graham and knew she would have loved camping with him. In her haste she did not turn to go back along the track but instead followed a path that went on upstream along the bank of the Barron.

"Margaret! You are going the wrong way!" Kylie called from behind.

Margaret had realised that by then but, in her embarrassed mental state, did not want to admit this. Stubbornly she kept on. "I know," she called. "I just felt like exploring."

"But it is getting late," Moira added.

"We've got time," Margaret said. "I just want to ride along here a bit."

"We will have to come back past the boys then," Moira called from behind her.

"That's probably her plan," Kylie suggested.

It had been, and Margaret blushed fiercely, but she shook her head. "There must be other ways back up to the road."

She had now stopped and looked back at the other two. The riverbank they were on was a narrow shelf about ten metres wide. Up to their left it rose steeply for about ten metres to the plain above. Most of the flat area was overgrown with long grass and weeds. A thick line of trees grew along the water's edge. A clear track ran along the flat, winding around the bushes and trees.

"This track looks fairly well used. It must lead somewhere," Margaret said.

"Oh all right, but only for half an hour," Moira relented.

The girls urged their horses into a walk and set off. Now that the decision had been made Margaret actually did want to explore. It looked pretty enough, and it was only the thought of snakes that bothered her. She knew she was safe up on the horse but had heard that snakes even bit horses and she had no desire to cause Lucy any harm.

They did see one snake, or at least part of it. Kylie shrieked and pointed and Margaret glanced down just in time to glimpse the brown tail slither from view into the weeds. Lucy just kept on walking and the others followed, leaning over and looking anxiously down.

Then the incident was forgotten as they encountered an area with hundreds of large yellow and black butterflies. As the girls rode through the area the butterflies were disturbed. They rose in dozens to flutter around the clearing.

"Aren't they pretty!" Margaret cried, delighted by the bright colours.

"There are hundreds of them!" Moira called in amazement.

Luckily the horses ignored the fluttering creatures and just plodded on. The riverbank became more overgrown and they had to push through a small area of forest. Margaret was almost ready to give up and turn back when she saw sunlight ahead. With that to encourage her she kept on, pushing a couple of trailing vines aside. They came out on a long, grassy glade along which the track rain clear and wide.

During all this time the river had been curving continually to the right in a gentle sweep. From time to time the girls could see the river through gaps in the trees. Margaret noted that the riverbed was choked with rocks, trees and small scrub-covered islands. The far bank was closer and was now steep and rocky.

After rounding a large clump of bushes they came to a vehicle track and a steel pipe. The vehicle track was just the usual two-wheel ruts in the long grass and it led up the riverbank at an angle along a bench cut. The pipe ran beside it. Margaret was not surprised to see a large pump on the riverbank to her right. The track they had been following continued on along the bank.

"There must be a farm up there," she said, pointing up the track.

"Maybe, but they might not like people passing through," Kylie said.

"Won't hurt to try," Moira suggested. "I'm sick of pushing through all these weeds and long grass."

Margaret had wanted to go back past the boys, but she could not think of any convincing reason to give that Kylie would not see through at once. She did glance back the way they had come but then Moira took the lead and headed up the vehicle track with Kylie behind her. That left Margaret no option but to follow.

At the top of the slope was an open gate, a stand of mango trees and, as they had supposed, a farm. At the gate the track improved and changed direction to head past the cluster of buildings and on across flat country.

"This should take us straight to the railway and main road," Kylie observed as they paused at the gate.

Close on their left was a large steel shed. Beyond it was a dusty farmyard and another shed, then a second gate. More mango trees shaded what looked like a house beyond the second shed. On the right was a barbed wire fence, beyond which were open fields with some sort of crop growing in them. Long grass grew along the line of the fence. The vehicle track continued straight on out into open country.

Moira continued on so the others followed. Level with the end of the shed a gate offered a way through the fence into the field. As they passed the end of the shed Margaret looked around and saw that the farmyard was typical of many she had seen; pieces of machinery parked around the edges, several fowls scratching in the dirt, a battered old Land Rover parked near an open door. On the far side of the yard was a long, open-sided, machinery shed with several tractors parked in it. The usual clutter of tools, boxes and drums took up much of the open space.

Suddenly a dog barked and the horses shied. The girls halted and looked anxiously in the direction of the barking. Margaret saw a very large, black dog come into view. It growled and barked and looked savage. That made her feel anxious. Then, to her relief, she noted that it was chained up.

"We could go back," she suggested.

"The railway is just over there past the house," Moira replied, pointing to the line of trees a few hundred metres away.

At that moment, a youth came out of the shed next to them. He had a spanner in his hand and his forearms were covered in grease. All he wore were grimy blue shorts. He stopped in surprise, then called out, "Hoy! You can't go through here. This is private property."

The girls stopped and turned to face him. Moira went red, then said, "I'm sorry. We didn't mean to trespass. We were just riding along the riverbank and are looking for a way to get back to the main road."

The boy moved closer. Margaret saw that he was in his late teens. She also noted the muscles that rippled under the tanned skin. *He looks strong,* she thought. *And good looking.* The youth had a mop of curly black hair, and his squarish face contained a pair of bright brown eyes.

He stopped close to Moira's horse and looked at them. "I wondered what Ripper was barking at," he said.

"Can we go through please?" Moira asked.

The youth looked around then shook his head. "I don't mind but dad might go crook. He doesn't like trespassers."

The dog had continued barking all this while and the youth turned to yell at it, "Shut up, Ripper!"

As he did, a man appeared around the far end of the next shed, a big man in dark blue work clothes. He had another large dog, an Alsatian, on a leash. The Alsatian also began to bark, almost drowning out the man's shouted query.

"What's goin' on here? Who are these people?"

The youth shouted back, "Just some girls on horses, dad. They want to go through to the road." By his tone it was obvious to Margaret that he was scared of his father.

"No! This is private property. Get off my land you kids, before I set the dogs on you!" shouted the man angrily.

The sight of those dog's fangs was enough for Margaret. She began turning her horse. So did Kylie. Moira tried to as well but the barking had upset her horse and it began to shy and rear up. The youth reached out and grabbed the bridle and held it firmly, then led the horse around.

The man kept shouting angrily as he advanced towards them. "How did you people get in here?"

"We came along the riverbank," Kylie answered, her voice quavering.

Margaret was feeling very anxious too. The closer the man got the more frightening he looked, a big, burly version of the youth. The Alsatian continued to bark and snarl.

The youth had led Moira's horse around by this and he started walking quickly back along the lane leading it. Margaret and Kylie urged their horses into a fast walk and led the way back to the gate at the top of the bank. Margaret kept looking anxiously back over her shoulder. She saw the man stop at the end of the shed. He looked very nasty.

As they reached the gate, the youth said, "Where did you come from?"

"The Lucas's horse farm over the other side of Venture Creek," Moira replied.

"Do you live there?" the youth asked. He sounded quite nice, and Margaret looked at him with new interest.

"No. We are just up from Cairns for the weekend," Moira replied.

They were at the gate by then and Margaret went through and started down the bank. As she did, the man yelled, "Hurry up! Get a move on! And shut that bloody gate, Corey!"

The youth appeared to blush under his tan. "Sorry about that. It's just that... that we've had a few thieves come through and take things. Dad doesn't like strangers around the place."

By then Moira was through the gate. The youth let go of her bridle and went across to swing the gate shut. Moira muttered her thanks and added, "Don't worry, we won't be back."

"That's a pity," the youth said. "You are really pretty. What's your name?"

That got Margaret's interest. She turned in the saddle and noted the flush mottling Moira's neck and cheeks.

"Moira," she managed to utter.

"I'm Corey," the youth said.

"I know. I heard your dad call you that," Moira answered.

"See you then," Corey said, swinging the gate shut as he did.

Moira blushed but smiled. Then she started her horse walking down the bank after the others. As they went down Margaret could still hear the dogs barking. She kept turning to look and noted that Corey stood watching, leaning over the gate.

"He's nice," Kylie commented as they reached the bottom.

"His father is a coarse brute," Moira replied.

"He likes you," Margaret commented.

Moira blushed again. "Let's get out of here. I don't like this place."

"We will have to go back past the boys," Kylie said as they took the path they had come along.

"Oh goodie!" Margaret cried.

Chapter 6

NAUGHTY GIRL

Kylie giggled and shook her head. "You are a naughty girl, Margaret!" Margaret blushed happily and only smiled. The three girls rode quickly back along the riverbank. None said so but all wanted to be as far away from the farm and the horrible man as quickly as possible. They threaded their way back through the area of forest and hurried on along the riverbank.

Margaret was surprised at how far they had come. She had no real experience at estimating distance but guessed they had travelled over at least a kilometre. *Possibly more,* she thought as they rounded another curve and still could not see the island where the boys were camped.

The sound of boys laughing came to the girls. Margaret turned and grinned at Kylie. "There they are. They sound like they are having a good time."

"Sounds like they are swimming," Kylie replied.

Moira looked anxious. "I hope they have some clothes on," she said.

"I hope they don't," Margaret replied.

"Margaret! You naughty little girl," Moira cried.

But Margaret was disappointed. When the girls came in sight of the island the boys were swimming, but all were in the water, only their heads showing. As she reached the end of the vehicle track that led off under the railway bridge, Margaret kept straight on and urged Lucy to wade the stream across to the island.

"Margaret, where are you going? Here is the road," Kylie called.

"I know, but this track we have been following goes on along the riverbank. It must lead to the Lucas's," Margaret replied. She pointed across to where the faint trail could be seen on the far bank. At that moment, she glimpsed the roof of the Lucas farmhouse, confirming her idea.

"It might not," Kylie answered.

"Then we will just have to turn around and come back to here," Margaret replied.

"You just want an excuse to ride past the boys again," Kylie said.

"That's right," Margaret agreed.

She continued to urge Lucy into the water. The horse waded across and up onto the sand where the boy's belongings were scattered around.

Peter stood up in the shallow water. "Hey! Don't you girls wet our things," he called. Margaret looked and saw that he was wearing a pair of bathers. Alistair stood up as well and she noted he wore a pair of old shorts. Graham remained in the water.

Alistair and Peter waded ashore. "Where did you go?" Alistair asked, looking at Moira as he did.

"Just along the riverbank a bit," Moira replied.

"We came to a farm with savage dogs and a horrible man," Kylie added.

"And a really hunky boy," Margaret said, noting a faint blush mottle Moira's neck as she did. *She did think he was good looking too,* she decided.

"So we came back," Moira said.

"Why doesn't Graham come out?" Margaret asked. She knew she was blushing, and she giggled at her own naughtiness.

"He doesn't want you girls laughing at him," Peter replied.

Graham went red. "Oh poop! I don't want to offend anyone," he called.

"What about us?" Alistair said, but he smiled.

"You girls clear out," Graham called. "Leave us in peace."

"Why? We have as much right as you to be here," Kylie replied.

"Because I'm getting cold and I want to get out," Graham answered.

"Out you come then," Margaret called.

"Margaret, don't be naughty," Moira chided. She then looked at Alistair and said, "See you tomorrow. Come on, you two imps. We will be late."

She urged Tornado into motion and led off across the sand and into the water on the other side. Margaret and Kylie followed. As Lucy waded the next branch of the creek Margaret looked back and caught Graham's eye. He was watching so she gave him a mischievous wink. On the far bank they found the path continued, winding around trees and bushes. Twenty metres on it went close beside a nice, sandy beach before turning and going steeply uphill through long grass and lantana.

The vegetation closed in so much that Moira was about to turn back when she saw a gate ahead. It was half-hidden in long grass but beyond was a two-wheel vehicle track which ran along the top of the slope. After unlocking the gate she went through and waited till the other two had passed through. As they did, Margaret looked wistfully back, wishing she could have stayed down with the boys. She was just at that age when curiosity about life was of fascinating interest.

The vehicle track led through a clump of trees to an open pasture. On the far side was a fence so overgrown with long grass and weeds that it looked like a hedge. Standing clear above it were the roofs of the Lucas farm. Kylie led the way across to where another gate gave passage through the overgrown fence. They passed through this and found themselves at the back of the stables.

Turning right Moira led the way to the end of the buildings. Here they came to a large sandy yard with wooden railing fences around it. As they reached the middle of the yard Margaret reined in. Here she dismounted and began to unbuckle Lucy's saddle.

Kylie turned and called back to her, "What are you doing Margaret?"

"Just going to give Lucy a roll in the sand," Margaret replied. Then she felt guilty as that was not the truth.

"Don't be long. It will be teatime soon and we have to have a bath first," Moira replied. She and Kylie then dismounted and led their horses into the stables.

Margaret stood for a few moments thinking. "I'll make Graham notice me somehow!" she muttered. What she really wanted to do was go back to the river to be with Graham. Into her mind came a fantasy of her being nude on the riverbank with her horse and of Graham coming along and finding her. Those images got her body reacting and she became hot and excited. For several minutes she pictured and embellished this scenario and enjoyed it. Then another image came to her.

I could be riding along naked, like Lady Godiva, and could 'accidentally' meet him, she thought.

Driven by the urgent desire she stood and toyed with the idea. But then she shook her head. *The other girls will notice that I am not here, and the boys might not want me there.* The notion of thereby embarrassing and annoying Graham occurred to her. *I don't want to do that. I want him to like me and to want me around,* she told herself.

Giving a sigh of regret she abandoned the idea. With her heart still hammering from the excitement of the naughty thoughts she hauled off the saddle and saddle cloth and draped them over the fence, then led Lucy back around the rear of the stables. The horse was freed and allowed to roll. Then Margaret walked back to the fence and reached out to pick up her saddle. It had to be polished before being placed back in the harness room.

Suddenly, a movement on the fence near her hand caught her eye. A snake! Margaret let out an involuntary scream, snatched her hand back and jumped away. Only then did she study the reptile properly. It was about a metre long and was a bright green colour with yellow underneath. With her heart hammering from the fright she had received, she took several more steps back.

Girl's voices called anxiously, and Kylie and Moira came running around the corner of the stables. "Margaret, Margaret! What is it?" Kylie called.

"A snake," Margaret answered, pointing to where the snake was slowly sliding along the fence.

To her the shiny, sinuous creature while looking quite beautiful also gave the impression of being liquid evil. Then, from her Sunday School lessons, her mind made the connection of serpents and Satan. The idea made her shiver and then give a wry grin.

Serves me right for having wicked thoughts, she told herself.

But she said nothing of that to her friends who were now standing beside her and staring wide-eyed at the snake. Both Moira and Kylie yelled loudly for Mrs Lucas while Margaret just made sure that her horse was alright. She took her bridle and led her away from the fence.

Mrs Lucas arrived at the run, wearing a dressing gown and slippers. "What is it, girls?" she asked.

"Snake, Mrs Lucas," Kylie cried, pointing to it.

Mrs Lucas took one look and then nodded. "Oh yes. I see it. It's alright. It is only a harmless green tree snake. There are a few around here."

Moria frowned. "Are you sure it isn't dangerous Mrs Lucas?"

"Quite sure. But you are wise to treat all snakes as dangerous. There are some of the really poisonous ones in this area. We get lots of brown snakes and even Taipans along the riverbank and a lot of red-bellied and yellow-bellied black snakes. Don't you girls walk around outside without something on your feet and make sure you have a torch if you go outside at night."

Margaret was now feeling both relieved and silly. She managed a smile and said, "Sorry. I just got a fright. I didn't mean to scream."

Moira pointed to a nearby rake. "Kill it Mrs Lucas!" she cried.

Mrs Lucas shook her head. "Certainly not! It is quite harmless and is part of the natural ecosystem. Besides, it is against the law to kill snakes, unless a person is in danger. Now, come away girls and finish looking after the horses."

She walked forward and picked up Margaret's saddle and cloth and led the way around to the front of the stables. Margaret followed last with Lucy. There she joined the others rubbing and grooming the horses while Mrs Lucas returned to the house.

Kylie looked up from giving Tornado a vigorous rub. "That was a good scream, Margaret. The boys probably heard it down at their camp."

"Oh I hope not!" Margaret replied. "Sorry. It gave me such a fright. I nearly put my hand on it."

Kylie giggled. "Anyway Margaret, that isn't the sort of snake you need to worry about."

Moira blushed but laughed. "That is probably what she was thinking about," she added.

Margaret blushed fiercely and opened her mouth to deny this but before she could Kylie looked at her and cried, "Oh yes! Look at her blush."

"I was not!" Margaret cried, but not with much conviction as she knew it was a lie and she was already feeling guilty.

Moira suddenly added to this sense of guilt by saying, "It might have been Satan tempting her," she said.

Kylie looked puzzled. "Satan was a horrible dog next door," she said.

Moira shook her head. "No, Satan is Lucifer, the Devil. And snakes are the Devil's creatures. They are how Satan appears in the Bible when he comes to earth to tempt people."

Margaret was both shocked and surprised. *I didn't know that Moira was so religious,* she thought. But the notion that God was punishing her for being a naughty girl also flitted across her mind. A sharp stab of guilt added to her embarrassment.

"Stop it please," she whispered, tears starting to prickle in her eyes. *I am not a bad girl,* she told herself.

Kylie went over and put her arm around her shoulders. "It's alright. We are only teasing. I know you got a fright. I didn't mean to upset you."

Margaret sniffled and dried her eyes. "Thanks. Let's finish looking after these horses," she said.

She turned away and began combing Lucy, trying to pretend the incident hadn't upset her. But it had and she felt quite worried about what sort of person she really was.

* * *

The shower for visitors and guests at the Lucas homestead was built on a corner of the side veranda. There was only room for one person inside at a time and Kylie had waited till Moira finished. Then she went in and enjoyed a lovely warm shower. After shampooing her hair she wrapped herself in her dressing gown and went out onto the back veranda to towel her hair dry. As she did, a flushed looking Margaret came hurrying up the back steps with Mrs Lucas, followed by two of the dogs.

"You took a long time Marg. What were you doing?" Kylie asked.

"Just talking to Mrs Lucas," Margaret replied, indicating Mrs Lucas' departing back as she went in through the back door.

"What about?" Kylie asked. She had noted a blush mottling Margaret's neck and cheeks and her hesitant answer.

"Oh... er... er... about horses and things," Margaret answered.

"Where did you go?" Kylie asked. She was now intrigued and felt sure that Margaret was trying to hide something.

"Oh, just for a little walk," Margaret replied. Now she was obviously blushing, adding to Kylie's suspicions.

"Did you go back down to see Graham?" Kylie asked.

"No! I was with Mrs Lucas," Margaret relied. She bit her lip and lowered her eyes.

"So why are you blushing?" Kylie asked, unable to resist teasing her.

"Because... because... because I wanted to talk to Mrs Lucas," Margaret answered.

"What about?"

Margaret shrugged and went red. "Just some advice," she replied.

"About boys?"

Margaret went even redder. She nodded. Sensing a secret Kylie asked, "Was it about Graham?"

Margaret nodded again. "Yes," she whispered.

"What did you want to know?" Kylie queried. Then she wished she hadn't when Margaret looked up and met her eyes with a sort of desperation in them. "Just how I might get Graham to be interested in me," Margaret whispered.

"And what did she say?"

For a moment Margaret did not answer. Instead she shook her head and bit her lip. Finally she said, "That I was too young to be thinking about boys, and that the best thing I could do was just be his friend and help him."

To Kylie's dismay she saw a tear spring into the corner of Margaret's right eye. At that she relented. "Tell me about it later. You look cold. You had better hurry up and have a shower. It is nearly teatime."

Leaving an obviously relieved Margaret, Kylie walked off along the veranda to the French window giving access to her bedroom. As she did, she towelled her hair and hummed with happiness. *Oh, I hope he does notice her,* she thought. She really liked Margaret and badly wanted her dream of Graham loving her to come true.

The two dogs, a golden Labrador named Goldie and a black Labrador named Blackie both followed her in. Kylie really liked the two dogs as thy ewer friendly and playful. She patted them both and then had to spend a minute rubbing Blackie's stomach when that lazy hound rolled onto his back in an obvious beg for more attention.

"You are spoilt, Blackie, you hear me," she said with a laugh.

The dog's answer was to wag his tail so vigorously that his whole body slid from side to side on the polished timber floor. At that Goldie pushed in, also wanting to be fussed over. So Kylie patted and rubbed both for a minute more.

She dressed for dinner in clean slacks and a warm, flannel shirt, then sat in front of her mirror and brushed her hair. All the while she wondered about her own love life. *Or lack of it,* she mused. She did not begrudge Margaret her chance of romance, but she was reaching the age where she badly wanted some herself. But no boy seemed to be interested, or at least none she found sufficiently attractive as a personality.

Her dreaming was interrupted by Moira coming in to tell her that tea was on the table. Putting down her brush Kylie slipped on fluffy slippers and followed Moira along the corridor to the dining room. Eating in the dining room at Corwa was something Kylie really enjoyed. It was a long room, half dining room and half lounge. At the far end of the lounge area was a fireplace. Even though the area was only 16 degrees from the Equator it was also on a tableland nearly five hundred metres above sea level. In winter this often meant temperatures averaging about 10 degrees C at night, and sometimes dropping to zero and below. It was not a cold night but cool enough for logs to be burning in the grate. This gave the whole room a cheerful glow and contrasted markedly with Kylie's own 'tropical' style 'Old Queenslander' home down in Cairns.

The dinner was very enjoyable. The food was good, and Mr and Mrs Lucas were excellent hosts, making the girls feel very much at ease. This was the fourth weekend Kylie had spent there and she was coming to feel great affection for the place, quite apart from her love of the horses. But during this meal there was just an air of tension. Kylie was very conscious that Margaret was not herself.

I wonder if Margaret is fretting over something else? she worried.

However she made no attempt to find out and instead asked Mr Lucas about the next farm. "We rode along the riverbank upstream of Venture Creek for a kilometre or so and came to another farm," she said.

"There was a really grumpy man there with lots of big savage dogs. Is he always that unfriendly?"

Mr Lucas nodded. When he had finished chewing the slice of roast that he had in his mouth he said, "Yes, he is. That is the Duggan's place. They are really anti-social. We went to visit when they moved in last year and were virtually ordered off the property at gunpoint. I'd stay away from there if I was you."

Mrs Lucas nodded agreement. "They are not good neighbours. We even think that their dogs killed our dog 'Lassie'."

"Oh, that's horrible!" Kylie cried. "How did they do that?"

"We don't know, not for sure," Mrs Lucas replied. "It is just that one day we found two of their dogs attacking Lassie out on the road near our front gate and they had given her some awful bites. We had to take her to the vet."

"So why do you think that their dogs killed Lassie?" Moira asked.

"Just a suspicion," Mr Lucas answered. "She went missing one day and when I couldn't find her I went looking. I tracked her along the road as far as their gate and inside but when I went in and asked they told me they hadn't seen her. I don't know... it bothered me. I just had a feeling they were lying and that their dogs had done it."

"Oh, I wondered where Lassie had gone," Margaret said.

Kylie nodded, remembering the dog from a previous visit. As though in answer to the name a dog's cold nose touched her ankle. It was Blackie. He had been lying on the floor near her feet, hoping for any choice little off-cuts to come his way. She patted him and then found Goldie's muzzle push into her lap from the other side.

Mr Lucas saw this and called softly. "Down Goldie! Outside you dogs!"

Reluctantly Goldie did so, followed a moment later by Blackie. Blackie looked so anxious, his tail well down, and his eyes so sorrowful that Kylie burst into laughter.

Mr Lucas laughed too. "Yes, the great guard dogs! They would lick a burglar to death."

"Old Duchess would bite them." Margaret said. Duchess was the half-blind old mother of the two and was usually found slumbering on the back or front veranda. "I like your dogs, Mrs Lucas, they are nice, not like those ones we saw at the Duggan's."

"They certainly have a couple of big savage dogs," Moira commented.

"A couple!" Mr Lucas cried. "They must have a dozen. I've sometimes thought of telling the council. The Duggans not only have two or three big brutes of guard dogs but there is a pack of really vicious pig dogs."

Kylie shuddered at that. She had never seen pig hunting with dogs but she had heard about it and the thought of a pack of animals tearing another animal to bits made her stomach turn with revulsion. To change the subject off dogs, she said, "That boy, Corey, he seemed alright."

Mr Lucas shrugged. "Wouldn't know. I've never spoken to him."

"I have," Mrs Lucas said. "He dropped in one day to tell me that 'Prancer' was out on the road. It was very nice of him to do so and he was very polite."

"How old is he?" Margaret asked, glancing at Moira as she did.

"Not sure," Mr Lucas answered. "Sixteen or seventeen from the look of him."

"What school does he go to?" Kylie asked.

"Not sure if he goes to school," Mrs Lucas said. "The school bus goes past on its way to Mareeba, but their farm is closer to town, so I have never seen if he is on it."

The conversation now drifted on to the distances rural children had to travel to get to school and the long hours it caused, many children having to catch the bus at about 7am to be at school by 8:30.

After the meal, the girls all helped with the washing up, then settled themselves in the lounge room. There was also a sitting room with a TV, but Kylie found it a relaxing change not to sit and watch it at night. Margaret went out onto the side veranda for a few minutes, then came back in.

"Brr! Getting a bit chilly outside," she said.

"Can you see the boy's campfire?" Kylie asked, shrewdly guessing why Margaret had been outside.

She was rewarded by the sight of Margaret blushing and looking quite guilty. She hesitated, then shook her head. Rather than embarrass her further Kylie changed the subject to horses and what they would do the next day.

Kylie and Margaret shared a bedroom and later, as they went to bed, Kylie hoped that Margaret talk to her. But Margaret just seemed quieter than usual so she did not probe. By then it was cold, and Kylie found it a real pleasure to slip under flannel sheets with a feather quilt on top and snuggle down with her teddy. It was a lovely old bedroom with antique furniture of dark wood and an odd mixture of fittings and furnishings: an old oil lamp from the 19th Century and modern fluorescent reading lamps. It all seemed very homely but was sufficiently strange to give a real sense of being on holiday.

It was a great night for snuggling under the sheets and Kylie slept soundly right through the night, only waking when Moira jumped on her bed and began attacking her with her teddy. "Wake up you sleepy heads and get up," she cried.

Margaret was her next victim. "Go away!" she mumbled. "I was just having a nice dream."

"What was Graham about to do?" Kylie called as she slid out of bed and pulled on her slippers.

For a moment Margaret blushed so brightly that Kylie regretted asking. Then Margaret turned up her nose and poked her tongue. "He's not the only boy in the world!"

"Oh, so it was about a boy," Moira teased.

Margaret seemed to go even redder and then pretended to sniff as she reached for her dressing gown. There was then a race for the bathroom. Moira won so Kylie went to the toilet and then joined Margaret waiting on the side veranda out of the wind. From there they could see the river but not the boy's camp.

"Sorry, I didn't mean to tease," Kylie said.

"Yes, you did," Margaret replied, but she smiled. Then she added, "Anyway, I don't care what you say. I love Graham and one day he will realise he loves me."

Kylie had to smile at that, but it made her feel anxious for her friend. Recently Graham had become very interested in older girls and she was worried that Margaret might not succeed. Rather than dwell on it she changed the subject to talk about a bird she could see chirping away up in one of the Cook Trees along the side fence.

After a lovely big, cooked breakfast of eggs, toast and jam the girls changed into their riding clothes and made their way out to the stables. As they did, Kylie noted that Margaret was continually looking out towards the road and railway.

She wants to see Graham as the boys go past, she surmised.

She did, but the boys made it easier. They came walking into view at about 8:15am and Blackie started barking, followed soon after by Goldie and Duchess. The boys stopped outside until the girls each took hold of a dog and assured them that they were harmless. The boys then came in to say hello. They were introduced to Mr and Mrs Lucas. Mrs Lucas asked if they wanted some morning tea. Alistair answered that.

"Thank you very much for the offer, Mrs Lucas, but we've just had breakfast."

"Was it cold last night?" Margaret asked, looking at Peter.

"Not really. Did you think you needed Graham to warm you up?" he answered.

Margaret went really red and emphatically denied that any such idea had crossed her mind. Graham was embarrassed and annoyed as well but said nothing until Alistair added, "You wouldn't have wanted to be in his sleeping bag with him anyway, the way he farted last night."

"Oh I did not! No worse than you two!" Graham replied hotly.

Kylie blushed with embarrassment. "Graham!" she cried.

"Never mind that," Peter said. He held up his watch. "We camped about five kilometres short of our planned camp site, so we had better push on if we are going to reach Kuranda in time for that three o'clock train."

"Kuranda! Heavens, that's a long way," Mrs Lucas said.

"About twenty kilometres," Peter replied.

"Can you walk that far?" asked Mrs Lucas with concern.

The boys all smiled. Peter answered. "Of course we can. We go hiking a lot. We will do about four kilometres per hour so..." He consulted his watch and went on, "So we should get there by about two."

The boys took their leave and set off along the road. Kylie waved and then walked back towards the house. Margaret and Moira both lingered, Margaret watching and waving till the boys were out of sight. Kylie walked around to the horse yard and found that Mr Lucas had let the horses out. He had saddled a big stallion named 'Ranger' and went trotting off with Goldie and Blackie to check on some cattle in a paddock down the road.

With the boys gone the girls prepared for their riding session. Margaret enjoyed every minute of it but still wished she was with Graham.

I do love him, she told herself. Then she sighed. *If only he will notice me!*

Chapter 7

ONCE BITTEN

Two hours later Kylie was at home. Her mother had driven up to collect them and had dropped Moira and Margaret at their houses on the way back. Kylie had felt sad as they had driven away from Corwa but now, perversely, she was glad to be home. The almost frenetic greeting by Skip really made her feel good.

"Calm down, Skipper. I've only been away for two days, not two years," she said with a laugh, rumpling the puppy's ears as she did.

Graham was still not back so Kylie took it upon herself to do the rounds of the pets, feeding and playing with them. First the guinea pigs, then the budgerigars, next the tortoise and then the fish. Last of all was Claud the Cat, who had been hiding somewhere and who stalked in, looking grumpy and demanding his food.

The only sour note was when she was walking along the side lawn and a sudden hurrying scuffle made her look next door in alarm. It was Brute and the dog began to bark and run backwards and forwards along the fence. Then it stood up on its hind legs with its front paws on top of the palings and snarled at her. For a moment Kylie feared it was going to leap over and attack her and she hurried to the back stairs and up them.

It was only when she was safely upstairs and out of sight of Brute that the fear gave way to anger. *What right have they got to make me afraid to walk around my own home!* she thought. But there was no obvious solution and she felt ashamed at feeling anxious every time she went downstairs.

Graham arrived home just before 6pm. Kylie took some delight in reminding him he still had to mow the lawn. Then she returned to her homework. A very grumpy Graham, still in his sweaty, hiking clothes, got out the mower and did his chores. Then he went for a bath. Kylie had already had hers so she was able to sit and watch TV for a while till dinner was ready.

While she was sitting there, Kylie heard a knock at the front door. Curious to see who it was at that time of evening she walked through to look. It was a lady she had seen before. With her was an anxious, teary-eyed little girl of about seven or eight.

"Yes?" Kylie asked.

"We wondered if you had seen our dog?" the lady asked.

By then Skip had arrived and came bounding up the steps to sniff at the pair's ankles. The little girl looked down at Skip and then began crying again.

"What sort of dog?" Kylie asked. As she did, her mother came through to join her.

"A one-year-old Golden Labrador," the lady replied.

The little girl raised her tear-stained face and added, "Her name is Samantha. She's my pet."

Kylie's mother took over asking the questions. "When did you last see her?"

"This afternoon, about two o'clock. She was playing in the garden," the lady replied.

"Has she got a collar on?"

"Yes. And it has our name and address on it," the lady answered.

"We will certainly keep our eyes open for you," Mrs Kirk said. "How will we contact you if we find her?"

"I'm Mrs Dobbs. We live just along the street in the next block, at number sixty-eight," the lady answered.

She and her daughter turned and made their way back down the steps, Skip scampering around their ankles as they did. This seemed to increase the little girl's distress as she began weeping again. Kylie felt really sorry for her. She called, "Skip! Come back here, you naughty puppy!"

Skip obeyed reluctantly but finally trotted up the steps. Kylie bent down and picked her up so that the lady was able to open the front gate and go through. As the lady and her daughter walked on along the footpath in the twilight Kylie rumpled Skip's ears and felt very sorry for them.

"Poor things! I hope Skip never goes missing," she said.

"Yes," her mother agreed. "That's a good reason to always keep those gates shut, and to make sure she is on a lead when you go walking. Now come and have your tea."

The knowledge of the missing Labrador quite spoiled Kylie's tea. She could not help thinking about the poor little girl crying, and worrying about where the missing dog might be. However normal life soon reasserted itself and by the time she went to school the next morning she had forgotten about it.

School was ordinary. After a weekend of horse riding and fun, Kylie found it quite boring and while she sat at her desk, her thoughts were far away. During the breaks she sat with Margaret and they happily chatted about the weekend just gone and about plans for the future.

After school, Kylie made her way home. She really wanted Margaret to come over, but she had to work at home and was not allowed. As always, Skip was waiting at the gate, tail wagging and tongue hanging out. Kylie felt a great rush of affection for the puppy and scooped her up. She rumpled her ears and held her right up so she could look closely into Skip's eyes. The little dog wriggled so wildly that Kylie had trouble keeping a grip on her.

"Oh, you're a good doggy!" Kylie cried, rubbing her nose against Skip's. Skip's response was to lick her face. Kylie grimaced and held the dog away from her. "Ah, yuk! Oh Skip!" she cried. The dog was put down, to scamper happily around her.

Kylie's mother called to her from the kitchen as she went into her room, "You can come and help me clip the budgie's wings please, Kylie."

Kylie just wanted to lie down and read but had to agree. She put down her school bag and went with her mother down to the aviary. Her mother carefully opened the gate. "You get in and catch one," she instructed.

Having done this a dozen times before Kylie knew what to do. She slipped through the gate, pulling it closed behind her. Then she stood and softly chirped and whistled and allowed the excited birds time to become used to her presence. Step-by-step she approached Chirpy and slowly put out her hand. The bird became restless and suspicious but only tried to escape at the last moment. Kylie was able to corner her and get hold of her body. With her other hand she gently flattened the birds wings so that she could hold him in her closed hand. The other budgerigars all fluttered off to the far corners of the aviary and twittered nervously.

As she made her way back through the gate, Kylie was very careful not to crush the bird. She could feel its tiny heart beating and that made her quite anxious. *I would hate to injure one,* she thought.

Her mother got her to change her grip, then carefully extended the budgie's right wing. Using a pair of large scissors she then snipped off the ends of the wing feathers.

"Careful, Mum!" Kylie cried, amazed at how much her mother was snipping off.

"It's alright," her mother replied. "They are only feathers. I'm not cutting the bird."

Kylie knew that but still felt uneasy. "What about the other wing?" she asked when her mother told her to let the bird go on the lawn.

Her mother shook her head. "No, you only trim one side. That way they are unbalanced. If you cut both the bird can often still fly, although it takes them a lot more effort."

It seemed cruel to Kylie and she felt unhappy when, after placing Chirpy down, the budgie tried to take off but only fluttered over and crashed. After two more attempts the bird gave up. It then realised it was not in the cage and turned its attention to the lawn and the insects in it.

Kylie went back into the cage and brought out Misty. She was easy to catch, hopping onto Kylie's outstretched finger and allowing herself to be handled. Her right wing was also clipped and she was placed down. Lime followed, also without any trouble but Squawker did not want to be caught and fluttered around the cage so much Kylie was worried he would injure himself. At last she caught him and he was also trimmed and then released.

"You keep an eye on them now," Mrs Kirk said. "Make sure Skip and that horrible old Claud don't decide they would make a good meal. I will just check how my scones are doing."

She made her way to the back stairs. Kylie remained on the lawn watching the birds. She lifted Misty up to a branch in a small tree and the bird seemed happy for a minute or so, exploring this new place. But then she fluttered down to the grass again. In doing so she did a crash landing that brought Kylie's heart into her mouth. Misty stood up, ruffled her feathers and chirped with indignation, but then settled to happily hunting tiny insects among the grass stalks.

Squawker and Lime both made their way into the nearest garden bed and began scratching at the leaves and dirt with their claws. Kylie stood and watched with fascination as the birds pecked and explored.

Suddenly a noise made her turn. As she did, her heart leapt into her mouth. It was Brute! The huge dog had jumped the side fence and was bounding towards Misty. Kylie looked at the evil, yellow eyes, the slavering tongue and massive jaws and felt herself go cold with fear.

"Misty!" she cried.

The bird had seen the dog. Just in time it fluttered aside. Brute pounced and missed, then spun round and snapped again. By the narrowest of margins Misty escaped as the jaws went chomp. Kylie saw a feather flutter loose and a sense of urgent desperation welled up in her. *Oh what can I do?* she wondered.

Then she saw the lawn rake leaning against the small tree. She sprang to it, snatched it up and swung it.

Part of her mind told her she must hit as hard as she could but she could not bring herself to do that. The rake struck the dog just as it was about to pounce again. By now all the budgies were squawking and fluttering desperately around, crashing and tumbling over in flapping bundles of feathers in their frantic attempts to escape.

Brute was momentarily distracted. Lime was able to flutter clear. Then the dog turned again towards Misty. Kylie screamed and stepped between the dog and her pet.

"Go away you beast!" she shouted. "Mum! Mum! Help!"

She swung the rake again, but it was a poor swipe and only seemed to enrage the animal. It turned to snarl and snap at her, then lunged. Kylie could not believe the speed at which it moved. Only by a frantic whack was she able to block it from reaching Misty. She tried to hold the dog down with the rake handle but was unable to. She was appalled at how fast and how strong the creature was. Before she realised what was happening, it had turned and clamped onto her left ankle.

A wave of cold swept over her: shock and then fear. Kylie stared down in disbelief. Then the heat of outrage began to spurt. She cried out and hit at the dog with the rake handle. That made no impression on the huge black dog. Now fearful she would be really mauled, Kylie tried to wrench her leg free but Brute only dug his teeth in harder and snarled. The sound of sharp, rapid barks made Kylie look around. To her dismay, she saw Skip charging towards Brute.

"No Skip, no!" she screamed.

Skip ignored her and launched herself at the larger dog. Her jaws clamped onto Brute's left hind leg. Brute growled, released Kylie and turned. Before Kylie's horrified eyes Brute bit savagely at Skip. Skip looked so much smaller, only one third the size of the Doberman, that Kylie felt sick. Brute gripped the smaller dog around the neck and shoulders and began to worry her. Skip gamely kept hanging onto the larger dog's leg. Both dogs began to snarl and growl in a way that made Kylie feel nauseous.

Feeling sure that Brute would kill Skip, Kylie began kicking and hitting at the larger dog. "Let my puppy go! Let her go!" she screamed. "Mum! Help!"

Mrs Flawse arrived at the side fence. She began screaming, "Don't you hurt my dog, you cruel little girl!"

Kylie was really hurt by that but could only cry out for her to come and get Brute. She saw Mr Flawse heading along his garden path towards them as well.

There was Graham! He had just come in the front gate wheeling his bicycle. The bike was tossed on the lawn and he dashed across, straddled Brute and began trying to pull his jaws apart. His swearing was added to the din. Mrs Kirk then appeared. Her hand flew to her mouth in horror at what she saw but she then quickly acted. She dashed across to where the garden hose lay in a coil beside the house. As quickly as she could, she picked it up and turned the tap. She then hurried across, adjusting the nozzle as she came.

Mrs Kirk began to spray water on the dogs. In the process both Kylie and Graham got wet but neither cared. Brute snarled his dislike and shook his head but kept gripping Skip.

"Let go, you beast!" Mrs Kirk cried.

Brute did not. Graham now had his hands in the dog's jaws, trying to lever them apart. Mrs Kirk screwed the nozzle to increase the jet, then shoved the nozzle into Brute's mouth. Mrs Flawse screamed so angrily and so loudly that Kylie looked at her in fear. She saw that Mr Flawse was now clambering awkwardly over the fence, his face mottled with rage. The sight of him so scared her that she took several steps back.

The water did it. Brute coughed and released Skip. Graham at once scooped her up and ran clear. Mrs Kirk stepped back, still directing the stream of water on the enraged dog. Its almost equally enraged owner lumbered across the lawn and shouted at her, "Stop hurting my dog!"

"Grab hold of him before he really gets hurt," Mrs Kirk retorted.

To Kylie's relief, Mr Flawse seized Brute's collar. Despite that she took another couple of steps back and held the rake ready to protect herself. Brute kept snarling, barking and trying to lunge at them. Several times he almost broke free of Mr Flawse's grip. Mr Flawse began to hit at the dog's head.

"Sit still, yer mongrel!" he shouted. Then he turned to Mrs Kirk. "What's the idea of your kids hitting my dog?" he snarled.

"What was your dog doing in MY yard, attacking MY children?" Mrs Kirk snapped back. For a second Kylie thought she was going to direct the stream of water onto Mr Flawse.

"This naughty little girl was teasing it!" Mrs Flawse shrieked.

"How?"

"By putting those birds down near our fence," Mrs Flawse accused.

Kylie was even more outraged at the injustice of the accusation. Her temper boiled and she shouted back, "Oh, what nonsense! That's not fair!"

"Kylie! Stay out of this!" Mrs Kirk ordered. "Find the budgies and get them back into the aviary."

Kylie was now breathing so fast she felt dizzy. Her lips were pressed tightly together and she glared at Mr and Mrs Flawse. Then she huffed and stuck her tongue at them before turning to look for the budgies.

Indignation crossed Mrs Flawse's ugly face. "Rude, bad-mannered creature!" she yelled.

"Don't you call my daughter names you... you... you," Mrs Kirk replied. Then she turned towards Mr Flawse. "Get that vicious brute out of my yard before I wet the pair of you."

"You do and y'ell regret it!" Mr Flawse snarled but he began heaving Brute backwards.

"Don't threaten me!" Mrs Kirk cried. "You haven't heard the last of this. Look at the wounds on my children. You will be paying the doctor's bills for them to be treated, and the vets."

Only then did Kylie glance down at her leg. *Blood!*

It was streaming down her ankle in a red slick. There were several long gashes and a couple of deep puncture wounds. She suddenly felt faint and only her urgent need to find the budgies kept her up and moving.

Mr Flawse shook his head vigorously. "Wasn't our fault!" he shouted angrily.

"Yes, it was," Mrs Kirk replied "Your dog should not have been able to get into our yard! I don't know why you have such a dangerous creature here anyway."

"He's a guard dog," Mr Flawse replied. By then he had reached the front gate. Mrs Flawse moved around to the footpath.

Mrs Kirk sneered. "Huh! What have you got that's worth guarding?" she queried. It was such an obvious jibe at the fact that the Flawses were not as well off as the Kirks that Kylie felt both a spurt of malicious delight, and of guilt.

"We can't all be bloated capitalists!" Mr Flawse shouted back. "Some of us have to be honest workers."

Graham replied to that one. "You wouldn't know what work was, you fat slug! You're the boss of the Bludger's Union!"

"You insulting little pup!" Mr Flawse shrieked back. "You'll regret saying that!"

Kylie was vaguely aware that Mr Flawse was the leader of some sort of political party, and a union official, but up till now it had never meant anything to her. She could tell that her mother was deeply angry, however. She half expected her to start shouting insults back but instead she replied, "Graham, look after Skip, and keep your mouth closed."

She then turned back to face Mr Flawse and said, "I am going to report this attack to the council. And we will be demanding that you not only pay but that you either dispose of the dog, or have the fence made higher."

"Crap! It's high enough now, if your kids didn't tease and provoke our poor dog," Mr Flawse retorted angrily. At that he backed through the gate, held open by Mrs Flawse.

By then Kylie had found Misty. The budgie was huddled under a bush and she could see it was shaking with fright. She very carefully lifted her up and carried her to the aviary. Inside, she placed her up on the feeding platform in front of the bird house. Misty at once scuttled inside out of sight. Kylie went back to look for the others. By then Mr Flawse was out on the footpath, trying to drag Brute away. Brute was still enraged and kept growling and barking so much that Mr Flawse began to hit at it; hard, stinging blows to its head and back.

The beating was so savage that Kylie was appalled. "What a disgusting brute!" she cried, earning a baleful glare from Mrs Flawse at the front gate.

Mrs Kirk closed the gate and turned to Kylie. "Kylie, find the birds. Hurry up! Graham, keep holding Skip."

"Is Skip alright?" Kylie called as she bent to look in the garden beds.

"He's got a couple of deep wounds on his shoulder and back," Graham replied.

Kylie could see blood dripping from Graham's hands and dearly wanted to go and look at Skip, but her mother insisted she find the other budgerigars. She found Squawker and took him to the cage and her mother found Lime, but they could not see Chirpy.

After a few more minutes search, Mrs Kirk shook her head. "Never mind. We will find him later. We need to wash those wounds and get you to the doctor."

Kylie was shaking with shock by this, and tears were starting. She felt an urgent need to find Chirpy. "Please Mum! Just a bit longer."

"No! Animal bites can turn septic very quickly. We don't want poison or germs getting into your blood stream. You could get tetanus. Now come and let me clean those wounds."

Reluctantly, Kylie allowed herself to be led upstairs to the bathroom. Only then did the real impact of the attack make itself felt and she burst into tears and began trembling so badly she could not stand. She was appalled at how much blood there was. Then she cried some more as her mother made her sit on the side of the bath while she washed the bites and scratches. Vigorous rubbing to clean the wounds and to make them bleed some more added to Kylie's tears. Then the liberal application of antiseptic caused her to suck in her breath as the pain hit her.

"Aargh! Ow! Oh that hurts! It really stings!" she cried.

"Good! That means it is working," Mrs Kirk replied as she examined the injuries.

As the waves of stinging subsided and her tears dried, Kylie was able to look more closely. She saw that she had two really obvious puncture wounds on her lower calf and several deep scratches. Mrs Kirk handed her a pad to keep mopping up the trickles of blood. Then she went to call Graham.

By then Kylie's eldest brother Alex had arrived home. Graham was busy telling him the tale and he was able to hold Skip while Graham came upstairs to be treated. Graham had only a couple of bite marks to the sides of his fingers, but he got the same treatment. Mrs Kirk then bundled them all into the car, Skip now in a cardboard box on a piece of old cloth.

The next two hours were both unpleasant and boring. Kylie and Graham were dropped off at the doctors while Mrs Kirk and Alex took Skip to the vet. For over an hour and a half the brother and sister had to sit and wait. Kylie found this both boring and upsetting. She was anxious in case she had to have a needle as she was very squeamish about them. She was right. The doctor insisted she and Graham both have tetanus injections. That stung too, and then her arm throbbed and she felt so faint she had to be helped to a seat out in the waiting room.

Graham took it all with a great display of swagger and bravado but even he looked pale behind his freckles when he came back out. By then the bleeding had all stopped and Kylie was surprised at just how insignificant her wounds now looked. Graham's were even less obvious, just a couple of red marks under brownish dabs of antiseptic.

By then Mrs Kirk had returned and Kylie at once asked the question on the top of her mind, how was Skip?

"Not badly hurt," Mrs Kirk replied. "She will be alright."

That was a great relief to Kylie. She hurried out to the car, where Alex was minding Skip. All the way home she stroked Skip and spoke softly to him, telling him what a brave little dog she was, and what a good dog. It was only as they pulled up at the front gate that she remembered Chirpy.

Oh, I hope he is alright, she thought.

Chapter 8

CHIRPY

Kylie could hardly contain herself until the car was inside and parked under the house. As soon as it stopped, she clambered out and began looking. By then it was getting dark and that added to her anxiety. To her growing concern there was no sign of the budgerigar. She went to the aviary, hoping he might have made his way there, but he was nowhere in sight. With a growing sense of apprehension she resumed the search.

Her brothers helped. Mrs Kirk went upstairs to prepare the evening meal. With each passing minute Kylie became more and more anxious. "Oh, I hope nothing has happened to him!" she muttered repeatedly.

"He'll be up a tree somewhere," Alex reassured her.

Kylie fervently hoped so because they could find no sign of the bird. Then the search had to be called off while they had tea. Kylie felt so sick she had no appetite, but her mother insisted she eat. Then she felt Kylie's forehead.

"You are a bit hot, Boo," she said. "I think you should go to bed early."

Kylie was dismayed. "Oh Mum! We have to find Chirpy."

"The boys can look."

"Oh please, Mum! I won't be able to just lie there knowing he is missing, and I certainly won't sleep," Kylie replied.

"Oh, all right, but only for a little while," her mother relented.

Kylie and the boys returned to the search. It was dark outside by then and they needed to use torches. That made Kylie feel even worse. It also sparked a barking fit from Brute which persisted even after they had left the back yard. The boys called names at the dog until Mrs Kirk called down for them to stop it. The barking made Kylie feel distinctly apprehensive.

This is horrible, she thought. *Every time we come down into our own yard that animal barks at us.* Shaking her head she went on with the search.

A check of the cage showed no sign of Chirpy although Alex kept insisting that the bird would make his own way to the cage and spend the night there. The children kept looking, checking every garden bed and around the yard in the likely and then the unlikely places. Graham searched the Ship Room and the storeroom and Kylie went to the laundry. Alex even checked under the car.

After an hour, Alex lost interest and went upstairs. "The bird will be okay," he said. "It will just climb a tree and sleep there."

Kylie wasn't sure about that, but she went and looked in every tree, even ones the budgerigar could not possibly climb. Graham came with her, but she could tell he was losing interest. "I've got homework to finish," he muttered, by way of a lame excuse. Kylie knew that Graham rarely did his homework and knowing that her brother was losing heart depressed her even more.

After Graham had gone, Kylie went round the yard again, pointing the torch beam into every little corner and under every bush in the garden. As she searched, she became more and more apprehensive and sick. Finally tears came and she leaned over a bush and vomited.

That was how her mother found her and she held her for a while and patted her. "It will be alright, Boo," she said, stroking her hair. "Now come upstairs and clean up."

"But we've got to find Chirpy!" Kylie cried.

"Yes, but you are making yourself sick. Now come upstairs," her mother replied.

She led a sobbing Kylie up to the bathroom. After washing her face she made Kylie have a drink of cold Milo. Then she sent her to change and to get into bed. Kylie did not want to, but her mother was adamant. Later, when Kylie lay in bed, Graham came in to say goodnight.

"He will be alright, Hickety Boo," Graham said, using her family nickname. "He will be up a tree somewhere. We will find him in the morning."

But they didn't. Kylie had a miserable night. She tossed and turned and kept waking up. Several times she burst into tears and twice she heard noises outside and got up to shine her torch down. But no luck. When she woke in the morning, she ran downstairs in her pyjamas to check the aviary. She had been hoping to find Chirpy clinging to the wire mesh, but he was not there. Her spirits plummeted and she began a frantic search around the yard.

73

As she did, Brute rushed to the side fence and began to growl and bark at her. Kylie glared at the animal. "Bloody dog! I hate you!" she cried.

Her mother heard her and called from the kitchen window. "You mind your language young lady, and get dressed! No daughter of mine is going to prance around the yard in her nightie."

It wasn't a nightie and Kylie almost called back defiantly, but then felt her spirits drop and her resistance crumble. She bit back the comment that she was wearing cotton pyjamas and made her way reluctantly to the back steps. As she did, she saw Mr Flawse come out of his back door to investigate what Brute was barking at, so she poked her tongue at him.

He scowled back and muttered, "Rude little strumpet!" but too softly for Kylie's mother to hear. Kylie wasn't sure what a strumpet was but knew it was something horrible. She poked her tongue again and fled.

After breakfast and dressing, Kylie returned to the search. She even walked around the block. It was in her mind to do what the lady had done the day before and go in to each house and ask. When 8 o'clock came her mother called her upstairs.

"Time to go to school," she said.

"I don't want to go to school. I feel sick," Kylie replied. She did feel sick too.

"Nonsense! You are just upset," her mother replied. "You are going to school and that is that!"

So Kylie reluctantly went. At school she sought out Margaret and told her the story, bursting into weeping again while she did. Margaret was sympathetic and promised to come and help her look after school.

"You just want to see Graham," Kylie commented.

Margaret smiled. "That too," she agreed.

Kylie had to smile in return. But she had a miserable day at school. She was distracted and several times burst into tears. Some of the other girls teased her over that and that didn't help. She also got into trouble from the teacher for not paying attention. All she could think about was getting home to search for Chirpy.

I will go and ask at all the neighbours houses, she told herself.

After school she hurried home. Margaret walked with her and several times asked her to slow down. By the time they reached the house Kylie was in a real state. She was extremely apprehensive but also had built her hopes up. *Chirpy will be at the cage,* she told herself. From the front gate she hurried in under the front veranda.

No Chirpy. The other three budgies were safe in the aviary and twittered at her, but Chirpy was not there. Kylie was just about to say, 'No sign of him,' to Margaret as she joined her, when something on the concrete caught her eye.

It was a green feather. Kylie felt her heart turn with anxiety. She bent to pick it up. "Is this one of Lime's?" she asked, holding it up to the light.

Margaret shook her head. "Looks a darker green."

Kylie matched it to Lime, who came over to the side of the cage to beg for food. Normally Kylie would have fed the birds but now she was too distracted. By holding the feather against Lime she could see it was definitely darker. But was the feather lying there the previous day? She did not remember. Then she saw a second one ten paces away near the far corner and her heart seemed to stand still.

"Oh no!" she thought anxiously as she walked over to it.

Then she noticed some loose tufts of fluff on the side lawn and her suspicions deepened. Feeling sick with worry she walked along the narrow side lawn, her eyes scanning the grass for more feathers. She found none. But on arrival at the side entrance to the laundry she found what she dreaded: Chirpy, obviously dead.

Crouched over the dead bird and gripping it with one claw was Claud the cat.

"Oh Claud!" Kylie wailed as the reality broke on her.

Claud went to pick the dead bird up in his jaws, then blinked his yellow eyes at the upset and angry girl. His tail twitched as he changed his mind and he quickly turned and slunk in under the washtubs. Kylie knelt down and looked at the bird, unwilling to touch the tiny thing. She waved her hands at her side and felt the tears start.

"He's dead, isn't he?" she asked.

Margaret had joined her, and she also knelt and took hold of Kylie's shoulders. "Yes, I think so," she replied.

At last Kylie summoned up the courage to touch the bird and then she was sure. It was cold and stiff and its legs stuck straight out and did not move. Out of the corner of her eye she saw Claud slinking away around the washing machine. Grief turned to anger and she sprang up and shouted at him.

"Horrible cat! I hate you!"

She went to throw a broom, but Claud scampered through the back door in a flash of orange fur. In her anger Kylie swung the broom so far back that the handle hit Margaret. Margaret was able to grab it in time, but that made Kylie feel even worse.

"Sorry!" she sobbed.

"That's alright," Margaret said. She took the broom and stood it against the wall. "It wasn't the cat's fault. He was just doing what comes naturally," she said.

Kylie knew that but it still hurt. By this time her mother had heard the noise and came down the back stairs. Margaret did the explaining. All Kylie could do was stand and weep, staring through tear-misted eyes at the pathetic little body with its rumpled feathers.

Graham arrived home next, with his friend Max. "Bloody cat!" was his comment. "We should get rid of the mangy old mongrel. I saw him trying to get at my guinea pigs the other day."

"You leave the cat alone," his mum said. "And while we are on the subject of guinea pigs, their cage needs shifting. Do that straight away."

Graham sniffed. "Yes Mum."

Kylie wiped her eyes and asked, "What will we do with Chirpy?"

"Bury him in the garden, of course," Graham answered.

Mrs Kirk nodded. "Do that please, Graham."

That got Kylie more upset. "Can't we do something nicer?" she asked.

"Chuck him in the garbage bin," Graham suggested.

The callous way Graham said this upset Kylie more than the actual idea and she burst into tears again. Mrs Kirk looked pained. "Graham! Don't be horrible. Now go and get a shovel."

Graham did. He scooped the dead bird onto the shovel and carried it to the back garden. Here he quickly dug a hole in the soft loam. As he was about to scoop the bird up to drop it in, Kylie, who had walked down to watch, said, "You aren't just going to dump him in there are you?"

Graham looked puzzled. "Yeah, why?"

"But... but it's just dirt," Kylie cried, appalled at the thought of the sand going on Chirpy's still open eyes and up his beak.

"What do you expect?" Graham asked sarcastically. "A rosewood coffin? It's only a bloody budgie!"

"He was my pet!" Kylie wailed, bursting into tears again.

Margaret glared at Graham and moved to hug her. "Boys!" she muttered. Then she looked at Graham again and said, "You could at least wrap the poor little thing up."

"Oh alright!" Graham grumped.

He threw down the shovel and stumped back up the lawn to the house. A few minutes later he returned with an old newspaper and used that to roll the body up in. Kylie wasn't too happy about that, but she could not think of anything better. By now her thoughts had shifted to pondering her own mortality and puzzling over what death really was, and what it would be like. They were very uncomfortable thoughts and she tried to push them away.

The bundle was placed in the hole and Graham then shovelled the earth on top. At that Kylie began crying again. Graham opened his mouth to say something as he patted the soil down hard, then closed it again.

I'll bet he was going to make some smart remark about having a headstone, Kylie thought angrily.

Margaret saved her from saying anything by leading her away. She also commented that she had better telephone her own mother to tell her where she was. After washing her face and going to the kitchen, where her mother gave her a sympathetic hug, she felt better.

"Never mind dear," Mrs Kirk said. "We can get another budgie."

At that, Graham, who had followed her up the stairs, said, "We should get a bloody great eagle or falcon or something. It might catch that mongrel Brute then."

"And poor little Skip," his mother replied wryly.

"And the guinea pigs," Kylie added.

"Speaking of guinea pigs," their mother said. "I told you to shift their cage; and their water needs changing. Do it now, and take them the vegetable scraps from the sideboard too."

Kylie collected the scraps of cabbage, cauliflower and pumpkin and followed Graham down to the back yard. By the time she arrived he had dragged the cage another two metres along the lawn and was busy standing their hutch upright again.

As she dropped the food in the top hatch, Kylie said, "They must get very bored in there."

"Oh, I dunno," Graham answered. "They must get visits all day and night by things that want to eat them: dogs, cats, snakes."

That was an appalling thought to Kylie. "Oh, there aren't any snakes."

"Probably not, not since they filled in the swamp along the drain," Graham agreed, referring to the drain a block away that ran parallel to the railway line.

Seeing a broken length of clay pipe that had been dug up the last time the sewerage system had become blocked, and which had since lain discarded against the fence in a garden bed, she picked it up and lugged it to the cage.

"Do you think this might amuse them?" she asked.

Graham was enthusiastic. "I reckon it might," he agreed. He lifted one side of the cage and made sure the guinea pigs did not escape while Kylie rolled the metre long piece of pipe under the bottom edge. The guinea pigs retreated to their hutch for a few minutes but then emerged again and began sniffing at the pipe. In no time at all they began exploring it, scuttling through or jumping up on to it or over it.

"What a good idea," Graham said, making Kylie feel much better.

They stayed and watched the guinea pigs for a few more minutes before Graham mumbled about homework and went back to the house. Kylie stayed on, marvelling at how lively and cute the guinea pigs were. *Nature is wonderful,* she thought, amazed at how all the living creatures were so interesting and different.

For ten minutes she sat and watched, studying every fascinating detail. It all seemed wonderful to her: the way the tiny noses twitched as they ate or sniffed; the cute little dark eyes, the way they licked and groomed their fur; the surefootedness as they raced around the cage and over or through the pipe.

After that she transferred her interest to Skip. With loving gentleness she picked the dog up and carefully inspected his wounds. *They seem to be healing well,* she noted happily.

In fact the dog's injuries appeared to healing faster than her own inflamed scratches. Ruefully she examined the bite and scratch marks on her legs and arms and hoped that there would not be any permanent scarring.

Later she found Graham seated at his desk and working on a model sailing ship. It was a big one and looked like a ship-of-the-line. Recognising what type of ship the model was supposed to be caused her a wry grin. *I have learnt that much over the last few years,* she thought.

Inevitably she had been roped in to help make the game more interesting. As the little sister she had been forced into the subordinate role, having to accept ownership of the less favoured nations or groups.

She had set up her own country of 'Lucrania', a small kingdom in central Europe, and also had several other small counties to manage: the Dutch, Sardinians, and Spanish. While she was not at all interested in wars or soldiers, she had still made quite sizeable armies of little plasticine people simply to please her brothers. She particularly liked her Lucranians whose Napoleonic era uniforms were green coats and white trousers with various embellishments for the different regiments. They looked very attractive when all lined up.

She also very much enjoyed making buildings for the game. In particular she was very proud of her castle and her Spanish fort. Now she was working on a model of a cathedral. Her real intention was to use it for a school assignment, but she could also picture it as the beautiful centrepiece of her Lucranian capital city. Having done her homework she settled to make a bit more of the model, carefully painting each piece as she completed it.

The last incident for the night was at supper time. As Kylie, Graham and Alex sat drinking their Milo their mother walked to the back steps with a saucer of milk. Kylie turned and saw Claud the Cat looking around the doorpost at her. When the cat saw her looking it blinked and then quickly turned and slunk away downstairs.

Good thing too! she thought, remembering poor little Chirpy.

School the next day was nothing special. Kylie talked to Margaret and other friends and played games of chasey with the boys in her class (*Silly, immature creatures,* she thought them). After school she rode her bike home, to find Graham there with his friend Stephen. She did not like Stephen, considering him to be crude and not altogether trustworthy.

The two boys were standing at the fish tank, lowering something in. Kylie walked over to look and asked, "What are you doing?"

"Putting in a sunken wreck," Graham answered.

Kylie looked and saw that the 'wreck' was a plastic ship from a Lego kit. Many of the small, clip-on pieces had long since been lost so it seemed like a good idea. She saw that the fish were sheltering behind their rocks and weed while Graham's hands were in the water.

"Be careful," she cautioned.

"It'll be right," Stephen replied testily. He bent to look in the side of the tank, pushing his glasses further up the bridge of his freckled nose as he did.

Graham frowned. "You sure a fish can't swim inside and get trapped?"

"'Course not!" Stephen answered. "Besides, fish can't drown."

At that Kylie got anxious. "Oh yes they can!" she replied. "I read somewhere that fish have to keep moving so that the water passes through their gills."

"Oh bull!" Stephen snorted. "That is sharks. Some fish just go to sleep in one place."

"What about goldfish?" Graham asked.

"I think they are alright," Stephen answered.

By now both boys had removed their hands from the water. Graham slid the glass top back into place and they all stood back to watch. It took only a few seconds for the fish to emerge from hiding, and only a few more for them to nose forward to investigate the new objects in their environment. Kylie watched anxiously as Galleon nosed into the open hatchway. His tail flicked and he vanished down inside the 'wreck'.

Several anxious seconds followed. Kylie began to worry and opened her mouth to ask Graham to get the wreck out when Galleon swam lazily back into view. She closed her mouth and relaxed. Once one fish had been in the others all had to explore the wreck as well. It quickly became apparent that they liked the addition to their pool as they went in and out repeatedly and even stayed in there for minutes at a time.

Satisfied the fish were safe, Kylie said, "You make sure you change their water properly, Graham."

"Oh piffle! You just take Skip for his walk," Graham retorted.

Kylie left the boys to it and did just that. She gave Skip his afternoon tea and a good rub and tickle, then clipped on his leash. That was a signal to Skip, and she began running excitedly to and fro. That always made Kylie laugh, especially when she ran around and around her so that the lead wrapped itself around her legs, tripping her up.

Still chuckling with happiness she untangled herself and led Skip to the front gate. Once out on the grassy footpath there was the usual dilemma of which way to go.

I went right last time so this time I go left, she told herself.

It was a decision she almost immediately regretted.

Chapter 9

MORE TROUBLE

Within ten paces Kylie knew she had made a mistake. *I will have to walk past the Flawse's,* she thought.

Her misgivings were confirmed within another ten paces. By then Brute had appeared. The dog began barking and growling through the fence at them. Kylie eyed the fence apprehensively and hoped it was high enough. And Skip was no help. She barked sharply back and strained at her leash.

"Come on, Skip. Come away from that horrible place," Kylie called, tugging at Skip's lead and trying to drag her on along the grass footpath.

As they walked on, Brute kept pace with them inside the yard, snarling and barking, and jumping up to try to get over the fence. Then Mrs Flawse stuck her head out of an upstairs window and yelled angrily, "You keep that noisy little mongrel away from my dog, you horrible little girl. Stop causing trouble."

Kylie felt deeply hurt at being called such names and she had to restrain herself from calling back. Instead she walked on, hauling Skip along. "And you aren't a mongrel, Skip," she muttered, stung by the injustice of the accusations.

For the next fifty paces she felt very uncomfortable, and self-conscious, feeling sure that Mrs Flawse was watching her. It was a real relief to pass the dividing fence between the Flawse's house and the next property. That at least left Brute behind and eased the situation. Skip stopped barking and began to settle down to exploring.

Skip did this in her usual way, trotting happily from side to side of the foot path, sniffing at seemingly everything and looking with interest in all directions. After passing a few more houses, Kylie calmed down and began to relax. Her pleasure was increased just by watching how much fun Skip seemed to be having.

There was a brown Dachshund in the yard a few houses further along and the two dogs, old acquaintances, sniffed and yapped but without any heat. Kylie kept on walking with Skip, crossing the next side street and going on further than she usually did. Skip had to embarrass her by stopping to pee on several trees and fence posts. Kylie just looked away and hoped nobody was looking.

Halfway along the next block, Kylie saw a girl playing in the front yard of a house. The girl looked vaguely familiar and she puzzled where she knew her from. Then the girl looked up from chasing a ball thrown by a little brother and their eyes met. The girl gave a sad sort of smile. Then it came to Kylie.

She is the girl who lost her dog, she remembered.

"Hello, did you find your dog?" Kylie asked.

"No," the girl replied, her face crumpling up and tears forming instantly.

That embarrassed Kylie and she regretted having asked. To try to cheer the girl up she said, "It will turn up."

But she didn't believe that herself and was ashamed at herself for saying it. She hurried on, aware that the girl was looking resentfully after her, obviously jealous of her own good fortune. After that Kylie decided she had to go right around the next block as she did not want to walk back past the girl's house. As she walked, Kylie brooded on the possible fate of the missing dog and that depressed her. *Hit by a car probably,* she thought, thinking back to that horrible time when Bounce had been killed.

Thinking that she had walked far enough Kylie turned and set off home. She made her way back to her own street and started walking along the footpath. Only then, when she was one house from the Flawse's, did it occur to her that maybe she should have walked right around her own block to come home from the other direction. But thinking that just made her stubborn.

No. Why should I? It is a public street. I've got as much right to walk along here as anyone.

Even so she became mildly apprehensive and as she got closer to the Flawse's she looked up at the windows, hoping that Mrs Flawse was not watching. She also looked for signs of Brute, hoping he was at the back of the house and would not detect them passing.

But there he was!

With a gasp of dismay Kylie saw that Brute was pushing through the front gate. *Oh no!* she thought. *He is getting out!*

She stopped and pulled at Skip's leash. Before she could think what to do, Skip began barking and strained at the lead to try to get at Brute. Brute seemed to glare at them with his yellow eyes and then started to snarl. A moment later the big dog attacked.

Kylie cried out in fright and jumped forward. Just in time she snatched Skip up. As she lifted him clear, Brute sprang to get at him. Kylie held her as high as she could, but Brute's claws ripped down along the soft underside of her right forearm. Brute fell back and then sprang again. In near panic Kylie jumped back, swinging Skip away from the snapping jaws.

In doing so she stumbled on the concrete gutter. Only by risking a twisted ankle did she manage to regain her balance. Brute returned to the attack, jumping up and lunging repeatedly at Skip. To make things harder, Skip wriggled and squirmed while barking furiously back. It was only with difficulty that Kylie was able to hang on to her. The leash did not help, tangling around Kylie's left leg and threatening to trip her up.

In desperation she looked around for some way of escape. There, close behind her, was one of the ornamental hibiscus trees which had been planted in the grass verge along both sides of the street. As the only possible refuge, she ran the ten paces to it, still holding Skip high above her head. This was a mistake as Brute again sprang up and failed to reach Skip. As the big dog fell back its claws ripped down Kylie's side, tearing her blouse and drawing blood.

The scratch stung and a wave of shock swept through Kylie, almost paralysing her. But her survival instinct kicked in and she reacted by kicking at Brute as the dog again tried to reach Skip. Turning her back on the big dog, Kylie placed Skip in the fork of the tree. Then she sprang up to try to get away from Brute.

It did not work. An enraged Brute lunged, and his teeth became locked into Kylie's school skirt. As she swung herself up, the skirt, a 'wrap-around' secured by Velcro, ripped and tore off. Brute fell back but he scratched Kylie's left buttock in the process. That stung as well, and the pain spurred Kylie to haul herself up.

But before she could, things went wrong. To get leverage she had to use her left leg and Brute sprang forward and sank his fangs into her ankle. The attack was so sudden and so stunning that Kylie hung half in and half out of the tree in shock. Brute then began to 'worry' her, growling and shaking her leg. Kylie tried to wrench it free, but the dog was much stronger and just clamped on even tighter. She was able to lift herself and even get Brute almost off the ground but still the big dog did not let go.

His weight was too much for Kylie. She could not lift herself and her grip on the bark began to slip. She did not dare let go and ghastly thoughts of falling down on her back and being bitten on the face or throat sent her into a screaming panic.

And then Skip squirmed out of her grip and slipped out of the fork of the tree. To Kylie's dismay Skip fell out the other side of the tree. The leash suddenly went taut and Kylie was horrified to see that Skip was now hanging half way down, and was suspended by her collar.

It will break her neck, she thought in dismay, *or she will be strangled!*

But it was the saving of her. Brute saw Skip and let go of her leg. Kylie almost fell back out of the tree, inadvertently dragging at the leash as she did. This saved Skip, who was jerked upwards. In a flash, Kylie grabbed at her and held her in the fork of the tree again. Then she sprang up and tried to hoist herself clear.

Again she wasn't quite quick enough. Brute, baulked of his prey and now ferociously enraged, sprang and chomped onto her left ankle again. That hurt and Kylie screamed.

By this time Kylie was experiencing alternating waves of cold shock and hot outrage. There was something so elemental, so primeval, about being attacked by an animal that it caused her intense emotions. Fear, mounting towards panic, was one of these. When Brute would not let go, she became terrified and again screamed. In desperation she kicked at him with her right foot, even as she looked around, hoping to see her mother or someone.

Instead she saw an angry Mrs Flawse looking out of her front door. The woman's face was very red, and she shouted at Kylie, "Stop hurting my poor dog, you horrible, little girl!"

For a moment Kylie was stunned speechless by the injustice of the accusation. Then Brute snarled and tried to drag her down out of the tree. Kylie knew her arms were weakening and she became frantic, wondering how to keep Skip safe up in the tree. Once again, she screamed for help.

"Mum! Help! Mum!"

This time, to her intense relief, she saw help coming. Her big brother

Alex came racing out of the front gate carrying a rake. Then she saw her mother appear at the top of the front steps. Her mother's mouth opened in dismay and then she snatched up a broom and came hurrying down the stairs. By the time her mother was at the front gate Alex had arrived and Graham had appeared, vaulting the fence but empty handed.

Alex didn't hesitate. He whacked hard at Brute. "Let go, you bloody mongrel!" he shouted.

Mrs Flawse had reached her own front gate by then. Her face became even redder, and she screamed, "Don't you hit my dog, you vicious brute!"

Alex whacked Brute again, ignoring Mrs Flawse. The blow obviously hurt but the dog refused to let go and began to growl and savagely worry Kylie's ankle, sending sharp stabs of pain up her leg. Graham had also arrived by this. For a few seconds he stood there looking around for something to use as a weapon. Then he bent down and picked up some of the stones beside the edge of the bitumen. He flung one of these as hard as he could, striking Brute's flank with an audible thump.

Mrs Flawse screeched in fury and came hurrying out, shouting to leave her dog alone. She hurried up to Alex, waving her arms and screaming as she did. Alex had to turn to face her and waved the rake threateningly.

"Keep back, you old bag!" he shouted.

That just enraged Mrs Flawse even more, her face becoming a mottled purple and mauve. "How dare you! How... Don't you dare!" she shrieked.

By now Kylie's mother had arrived and she screamed, "Get that dog off my little girl!"

"Tell your boys to stop hitting him," Mrs Flawse countered.

Alex answered that by stepping forward and smashing the rake down hard on Brute's back. Kylie heard the smack and winced, fearing he would seriously injure the creature. Alex then reversed the rake and began to try to jam the end of the handle into Brute's jaws. Graham threw another stone, then dashed in and grabbed at Brute, ignoring his mother's cry to be careful.

Kylie could only scream and knew she was slipping. Her mortification was increased by the shameful knowledge that she had lost her skirt. Unable to hang on, she fell. As she did, she let go of Skip's leash, hoping that he would stay in the tree. But in this she was instantly disappointed, seeing him slither out of the fork and fall to the ground.

"Grab Skip!" she screamed. "Graham, grab Skip!"

To her relief, she saw Graham do this. But her fears returned at once as Brute let go of her ankle and sprung to try to get Skip. Graham jumped back, held Skip up high and kicked Brute in the chest, drawing another indignant shriek from Mrs Flawse. Alex added to this by wading in with the rake and ramming the tines against Brute's chest to knock him away. Kylie's mother swung the broom and then grabbed at Kylie, helping her to her feet.

Alex now whacked Brute on the nose, shouting to Mrs Flawse, "Grab your dog, you silly old bag or I will kill it."

"You do, you horrible boy, and you will regret it," Mrs Flawse shouted.

But she did step forward and try to grab the now enraged dog. By then Mr Edwards had run across from his house across the street and a man had stopped his car and climbed out. Other neighbours could be seen peering out of doors and windows or moving closer.

Knowing that they could all see her increased Kylie's sense of shame and distress. As quickly as she could she scrambled to her feet, helped by her mother.

Kylie's mother was now furiously angry. She placed herself between Kylie and Brute and confronted Mrs Flawse, even as that woman struggled to get a hold of the dog's collar. "You will be paying for this," Mrs Kirk snapped.

Mrs Flawse grabbed the savagely struggling Brute and snapped back, "Oh no I won't! It is you who will be paying. That nasty little girl of yours deliberately provoked my dog."

Kylie was really stung. Even as she tried to cover herself with her hands she shouted back, "That's not true! I was just walking along the footpath."

"Teasing my poor dog with that... that... that piddling little mutt!" Mrs Flawse retorted.

"I will be reporting your dog to the council again," Kylie's mother cried.

"You do, you stuck up bitch, and you will regret it," threatened Mrs Flawse.

"Don't threaten me you... you... ," Kylie's mother retorted. She then stepped forward and snatched up the torn remnants of Kylie's skirt. She shook this at Mrs Flawse. "You can pay compensation for this, and you can pay any doctor's bills."

Mrs Flawse snorted. "I will not! I'll... Ouch! Oooh, you bloody mongrel!"

This last because Brute had turned to snap at her right hand. Mrs Flawse belted Brute over the ears with her hand, then tightened her grip on the still furiously struggling dog. To Kylie it appeared that Brute could break free again at any moment.

Her mother obviously thought so too as she gestured and said, "Kylie, get back to the house, quickly! Alex, Graham, come away before that horrible creature breaks loose."

Satisfied that Graham had Skip safe, and that Alex was not in danger, Kylie started running for the front gate. Her mother hurried after her, holding Kylie's torn skirt and the broom as she did. Graham followed with Skip and Alex then began to retreat, keeping the rake ready to fend off any attack. Thankfully Kylie reached the front gate and hurried through. As she scuttled up the front steps, she looked back and experienced a spurt of malicious satisfaction by seeing Brute scratching at Mrs Flawse's legs, shredding her stockings and drawing blood. Once again Mrs Flawse belted the dog around the ears as she dragged it towards her own gate.

Once inside the house, Kylie ran to her room and burst into hysterical tears. She did not want to, tried not to, but could not stop herself. To her dismay, she found she was sobbing and shaking uncontrollably. Waves of shock swept through her, and she could only stand and howl. Her mother arrived and immediately flung her arms around her, hugging her tightly.

For a minute or so mother and daughter remained in a strong embrace. Then the sounds of Alex's voice calling taunts to Mrs Flawse caused Mrs Kirk to sigh and let Kylie go. "Into the bath with you," she ordered. Then she turned and called loudly, "Alex! Graham! Stop that! Stop that at once and come inside."

The boys reluctantly did so. Before they could see her Kylie dashed along the corridor to the bathroom, burning with shame and still sobbing with emotion. There followed the embarrassment of having her mother wash and clean the bites and scratches in her chest and buttocks, and then on her legs and ankle. As Kylie looked down at the wounds, she became more upset.

"I won't have scars, will I Mum?" she asked, fearful that her good looks might have been permanently spoiled.

Her mother's answer was not reassuring as she only muttered, "I hope not."

Then there was antiseptic and that stung. More tears trickled down Kylie's face. She was then told to run a warm bath. That done her mother said, "Now, you give yourself a good wash and then I will put some more antiseptic on."

Kylie was embarrassed at undressing in front of her mother but slowly did so. As she did, her mother said, "I will be back in a few minutes. I am just going to check on Skip."

Skip! Kylie thought. *Oh yes, how is she?*

Concern over her own injuries was swept out of her mind as she worried about her pet, or at least until she lowered herself into the warm soapy water. Then the stinging from her scratches quickly reminded her of her own problems.

As quickly as she reasonably could, Kylie washed herself. Then she climbed out and gingerly dried herself, noting that the bleeding had mostly stopped and that the scratches did not look as bad as they first had. Rather than have her mother doing it she carefully applied antiseptic cream and then dressed in the clean clothes her mother had placed ready. That done Kylie hurried downstairs.

On the way she met her mother coming up. "How is Skip, Mum?" Kylie asked.

"She will be alright. There is a bit of bruising, that's all. Now, we are taking you back to the doctor, and then to the council," her mother announced.

Kylie did not want that, but she had to go. So for the next three hours, she was out with her mother. First, they went to the doctor; luckily a lady doctor, as Kylie knew she would have felt very self-conscious if it had been a male examining the scratches in her chest and thighs. Then they went to the City Council and Mrs Kirk registered a formal complaint against Brute. The official there made them fill out a form and attach to it written statements and he also attached a photocopy of the doctor's certificate. That done they went home.

At home, Kylie had to get out of the car to open the main gate. As that was right next to the Flawse's house she felt very anxious. She kept glancing that way, partly watching for Brute, and partly scared of what the Flawses might do when they learned that a complaint had been made. Her fears and anxieties were put aside when Skip came scurrying out to greet her, tail wagging and tongue lolling. Kylie scooped her up and snuffled into her fur, glad the dog was not badly hurt.

And then she spotted Mrs Flawse scowling at her through an upstairs window. The woman had such a look of hate on her face that Kylie swallowed with dread and remember the threat: 'You do and you'll regret it!'

Oh dear! Kylie worried. *What will she do?*

Chapter 10

CLAUD THE CAT

By bedtime Kylie was feeling sick and worn out. Still upset over the dramas of the day she changed into her pyjamas, went to the toilet and then brushed her teeth in the bathroom. After a rueful examination of her face in the mirror she returned to her room, only to find Claud the Cat curled up asleep on her bed!

Normally Kylie would have been only mildly annoyed and would have shooed Claud off. Both the cat and the dog were allowed in the house when everyone was awake but during the night they were banished to the outside. Nor were either pet allowed to sleep on beds. But burning memories of poor little Chirpy's mutilated body now flooded Kylie's mind and she experienced a rush of rage.

"Get off there, you horrible cat!" she shouted, rushing forward.

Claud woke up and sprang instantly to his feet. By then Kylie had reached the bed and for a second she hesitated, looking for something to hit him with. She was loath to strike with her hands but then, as there was no potential weapon within reach, she swung her open hand to hit.

Claud didn't wait. By the time Kylie's hand came down he was gone. But his haste was almost his undoing as he sprang up and then tripped himself. Falling to the bed he scrabbled furiously at the bedclothes to get his balance and start running. In a flash he was off the bed, and before she could even turn around he had scampered through the doorway. All Kylie could do was call angrily after his departing tail, "And stay out, you horrible creature!"

The noise attracted mother, brothers, and Skip. Mrs Kirk raised her eyebrows quizzically. "What's the matter dear?"

"Claud. He was sleeping on my bed," Kylie cried. She was now ashamed of her outburst and feeling a bit fragile.

Alex didn't help. He commented, "Oh poor Claud! Sleeping on your bed! Now he will have fleas."

Graham chortled. Mrs Kirk frowned. Kylie felt hurt and her lower lip trembled. Mrs Kirk snapped, "Alex, you be nice to your sister."

"Yes Mum," Alex replied, but he kept grinning and obviously wasn't sorry at all.

That got Mrs Kirk angry. "You two boys go to bed!" she ordered.

They did, both still smirking. Kylie then went back into her room and her mother came in and gave her a hug. "Oh poor little petal! You haven't had a very good day, have you?"

"No Mum," Kylie sniffled.

She was helped into bed and tucked in and then, after a loving kiss, her mother hurried out to snap angrily at the boys, who were still chuckling out on the front veranda. Feeling slightly better Kylie snuggled into her pillow, hugged her teddy, and lay there brooding on life.

Then sleep was denied her and it was again Claud's fault. Just as she was drifting off, Kylie heard the pad of tiny footsteps on the roof. This was made of sheets of corrugated galvanized steel and the little feet sounded like tiny drumbeats.

"Oh go away Claud!" she muttered, pulling her bedclothes up over her ears to try to muffle the sounds.

Then it got worse. Claud snarled and began to spit and some other animal retaliated. At first Kylie thought it must be another cat. She knew it was easy to get on the roof. Just outside her end window was a lower roof over the back steps and this led up at a convenient slope to the main part of the roof just above the bathroom. Claud had often gone up there.

Now the sound of snarling and skittering feet kept her awake for at least ten minutes before the animals gave it up. It also annoyed Graham and Alex. Alex came through the house muttering and swearing and was of the opinion Claud was chasing a possum. Torch in hand he went out to investigate.

But the noises stopped and Kylie settled back, still a bit depressed, to drift quickly into sleep.

* * *

She was still feeling down the next morning and went to school feeling moody and depressed. Margaret was a comfort and provided a sympathetic audience for her scratches and the story of Brute.

She commented, "That dog is starting to give me the pip. He is a public menace."

"I hate him!" Kylie replied, images of Brute's slavering jaws and evil yellow eyes fuelling her dislike.

Brute again gave her more worries as soon as she arrived home again after school. Finding the doors wide open she assumed that one or both of the boys were also home. But there was no sign of them in the house. Having dropped her school bag in her room Kylie wandered through to the kitchen and poured herself a glass of fruit juice. She was just sipping this when movement in the back yard next door caught her eye.

Moving to the window she looked out, then sucked her breath in anxiously. Both Graham and Alex were in the Flawse's garden! It was immediately apparent to Kylie what they were up to.

They are trying to steal some mandarins from Mr Flawse's fruit trees, she thought.

She could see that the boys must have climbed in over the back fence and they were now creeping on hands and knees between the rows of cabbages and other vegetables. *Oh the silly boys!* she thought. Then she looked anxiously around. Where was Brute?

Even as she thought this, she saw the dog. Brute had been asleep near the back door of the Flawse's house but as she looked he suddenly sat up. His huge head swivelled to look in the direction of the boys and he sniffed the air. A surge of near panic swept through Kylie. Seeing the boys had not yet seen Brute and were still creeping closer to him she rushed to the window and leaned out.

"Graham! Alex! Brute!" she shouted, pointing as she did.

Both boys looked at her and then turned to look where she was pointing. Brute was also attracted by her cry and sprang to his feet facing her. He began snarling and then trotted towards the fence. This took him across one of the pathways that criss-crossed the garden. As he loped across the open space, he looked along it and it was instantly apparent that he saw the boys.

Kylie's heart seemed to stop as she gasped with anxiety. Both boys at once jumped to their feet and sprinted for the fence, leaping through the rows of cabbages, lettuces, and radishes as they went. Barking furiously, Brute was after them in a split second.

"Oh! They will never make it!" Kylie groaned as she watched Brute bound along the pathway in huge, swift leaps.

From the looks on the boy's faces it seemed that the two boys were of the same opinion. Both kept leaping garden beds, heedless of damage to carefully nurtured plants and of the effect of their desperate footsteps on the soft soil.

Then Brute tore into the growing plants with similar disregard for the niceties of cultivation. Within ten seconds, he had covered the distance and was snapping at the boy's heels, his savage barks rending the quietness. But the boys made it. Just as it seemed that Brute must latch on to one or the other with his ugly great teeth, both boys sprang at the fence. Each used a different method, but both were over in a single bound. Alex did a handstand and landed on his feet. Graham leapt onto the top of the palings on his chest and then swung his feet over while using his right arm to keep control against the other side of the fence.

Kylie gasped with relief but then worried that Brute would leap over the fence in pursuit. She knew he could easily do it, had seen him do it. To her relief, the dog stopped at the fence. There it stood on its hind legs and barked furiously over the top at the two boys, who were both now scampering away.

Even after the two boys had vanished around the far side of the house, Brute kept on barking. That caused Mr Flawse to appear at his back door. The man came out, muttering angrily and looking suspiciously around. Too late Kylie realised she should have hidden. As quickly as she could, she moved back from the window but Mr Flawse saw her and shouted angrily, demanding to know what was going on.

Kylie did not dare show herself at the window again, but skulking out of sight made her feel guilty and ashamed. Her bruised emotions fuelled her anger at the boys when they came hurrying through the house from the front door, having evidently run right around the far side of the house.

"You silly boys!" she snapped.

But then she saw Graham's chest and gulped. In crossing the fence he had torn the front of his shirt and something had scratched his chest, ripping a long gash which was bleeding profusely.

"Oh Graham! How did you do that?" she cried, knowing exactly how he had done it.

She was even more annoyed when he refused to make a fuss about it. She insisted he hurry to the bathroom and remove his shirt. Then she made him wash the scratch. As Kylie bathed it, all he could do was grumble and look at the rip in his school shirt.

"Aw, bugger!" he said. "How will I explain this to Mum?"

"The truth would make it easy," Kylie retorted.

Graham made a face at that and then grimaced in pain as Kylie daubed the still bleeding cut with antiseptic. "Serves you right!" she snapped. "That was a silly thing to do."

Alex curled his lip. "Anyway, we will settle with that bloody Brute."

A stab of worry hit Kylie, and she said, "What do you mean Alex? How will you settle with Brute?"

"You'll see," Alex answered.

The enigmatic answer worried Kylie even more. She said, "Don't you dare do anything to hurt that dog."

"I won't," Alex replied. Then he laughed and walked away, leaving a niggling worry that got Kylie questioning Graham. He obviously had an inkling of Alex's plan because he went red and got all stubborn, but all he would say was, "I hate the mongrel."

"So do I," Kylie agreed. "But that doesn't mean we can do anything harmful or illegal."

She had in mind that Alex might poison Brute, or something like that. Alex, she knew, could be very ruthless and heartless at times.

"It won't be illegal," Graham answered, and then he went off, allegedly to do his homework but actually to work on a model ship.

And to avoid my questions, Kylie thought.

But she could get no more out of them and soon forgot about the incident. She took Skip for a walk. This time she was careful to go the other way along the street to avoid any trouble with Brute or the Flawses. She walked for about five blocks, going south along the street until she was past Max's house. She then circled a few blocks. That calmed her and as she walked along, watching Skip happily sniffing and exploring this new part of town.

On arriving home, Kylie fed Skip and then went and fed her birds. That brought back the sadness over Chirpy's death. *That beastly Claud!* she thought. And it was Claud who gave her the next problem. After checking that the guinea pigs were alright, she went up to her room to do her homework. And there he was, sound asleep on her pillow!

"Claud!" she screeched angrily.

At that Claud jumped up, still half asleep. As Kylie yelled again the cat fled. But his haste was again his undoing and he misjudged his jump.

Instead of making the windowsill, he caught a curtain that was fluttering in the breeze. A second later Claud smacked into the wall just below the window. His claws managed to dig into the curtain material but it did not stop him falling. But only the claws on one back leg caught and he fell awkwardly, the claws ripping free so that he fell on his back.

By then Kylie's anger had changed to a mixture of amusement and concern. When she saw Claud fall heavily on the floor, she felt immediate anxiety that he might be hurt and hurried across to pick him up. Claud didn't wait. Still obviously fearing something he scrabbled on the timber floor and then went skittering in under the bed, to reappear a second later behind her. In a flash he was out the door and off along the corridor.

On the way Claud encountered Graham, who was coming in the other direction, clad only in a towel after having a bath. Graham whooped with amusement and jumped to block Claud's path. Ignoring Kylie's presence, Graham whipped off his towel and tried to make a curtain to block Claud's run. Claud swerved and slithered on the lino and slid into the wall, then scrabbled for a grip before scampering off around Graham and away down the back stair. Graham reached out a leg to try to stop him and slipped himself, falling on his back, giving Kylie and eyeful. This did not bother her particularly as she often saw the boys with little or nothing on and had even shared the bath with them until only a few years before.

By now Alex had appeared from his bedroom, which was next to hers, just in time to witness Graham's attempts. He hooted with laughter, "Go cat, go!" he yelled. Then he called loudly to Graham, "You want to watch out Little Brother. Remember the famous old book: *The Cat's Revenge* by Claude Balls. Ya get it? Clawed balls."

Kylie did get it. It was one of the silly jokes the boys often came up with like *The Yellow River* by I. P. Daily; or *The Camel Ride* by Major Bumsore. But she wasn't amused and now she blushed as Graham tried to cover himself and get up. He was now very red in the face and embarrassed.

"Sorry Kylie," he muttered.

Mrs Kirk wasn't amused and called from the kitchen, "Alex, stop that shouting? And you mind your mouth young man! I won't have language like that in this house."

"Yes Mum," Alex answered, but then he had to smother a giggle.

Mrs Kirk came through from the kitchen. "What's going on?"

By then Graham had his towel back around him. He answered, "Nothing Mum."

Alex added, "Just Kylie trying to kill that rotten cat,"

"Oh I was not!" cried Kylie, stung by the unjust accusation.

Alex snorted. "Wish you would, the mangy old rat-catcher. He is no use; just a nuisance," he replied angrily.

"Don't be horrible Alex," Kylie chided. "He can't help it. He's only an animal."

But at 2:00am that morning she found she agreed with Alex. Somewhere just outside her window Claud and another tom cat began a caterwauling session that sounded like it was right in her room. Worse still, the noise woke up Mr Flawse, who shouted angrily, "I wish you bad-mannered people would control your mangy pets so that ordinary folks could get some sleep!"

Both Alex and Graham went to call back but were forbidden to do so by their mother. Unfortunately, both Claud and the other tom did not stop for some time, each outburst of noise causing Mr Flawse to make angry threats about calling the council and complaining about the noise.

* * *

It was Claud who also provided the next minor drama in Kylie's life when she came home from school on Friday.

After dropping her school bag in her room she walked through the house to see who else was home, and arrived in the lounge room just in time to catch Claud in the act. He was up on top of the aquarium, scooping into the water with his paw in an attempt to get the fish!

"Claud!" Kylie shrieked.

Waving her arms she raced forward. Claud had cornered Galleon by this time and was reaching right in with one paw to pin the fish against the glass. On hearing Kylie he gave a startled jerk and went to spring away. Instead he slipped. To Kylie's mingled horror and amusement, the cat went plunging into the fish tank, water splashing out and bubbles streaming up. By then Kylie was at the fish tank but all she could do was stand and flap her arms as Claud went into a panic.

The cat came up but underneath part of the glass top that normally protected the tank. By then his legs were scrabbling for something to grip and the motions stirred up the sand and silt in the bottom. As the cat floundered and clawed frantically to get back out, the fish all dashed about in a panic and the weeds and toys were sent swirling around in the currents and turbulence he generated.

At last Claud got his head out and then his paws on the lip of the tank. Kylie tried to help, reaching out to grab him. Claud reacted by a sudden lunge, biting her hand. Shocked and hurt she let go, causing him to sink back in again.

Graham and his friend Roger arrived at the run from the front veranda. "What? What the…?" Graham cried.

By then Claud was in a real state. He got his head out and then his front paws and heaved himself over the edge, falling to the floor in a cascade of water and weeds. For a frantic second he writhed to get to his feet and then he was off. Around Graham's legs he went and out the front door, all sodden and frightened.

Graham burst into laughter. Kylie wanted to but she felt sorry for the cat and was concerned about the fish, which were still swimming rapidly around in the swirl of murk. Graham bent to look and asked, "What happened?"

"Claud. He was on top trying to catch the fish," she replied. "And he fell in."

Both Graham and Roger hooted with laughter again. This time Kylie managed a wry grin as she could see that all the fish were there and were slowing down. "He fell in through this hole in the top," she said accusingly. "I wonder who left it open?"

At that Graham went red but only shook his head. "Don't blame poor old Claud. He was just doing what comes naturally."

Kylie knew that and wasn't really angry. She bent and carefully studied the fish until satisfied they were all unharmed. Graham moved to put his arm in to replace all the rocks and weeds in their original places but she stopped him.

"The poor little fish have had enough of a scare. Leave that till tomorrow," she said.

Graham agreed. At that moment, Skip appeared, scampering along from the back of the house, yapping with excitement. "Oh, great guard dog!" Graham commented. He and Roger went back onto the veranda, still chuckling. Kylie bent to restrain Skip, who was sniffing and trotting around obviously puzzled by the water on the floor. "Let's clean that up little doggie and then you and I will go for a walk."

Once again Kylie took Skip to the right along the street so that she did not have to pass the Flawse's house. Doing that made her feel annoyed and guilty. *I'm a coward,* she berated herself. *And anyway, why should I have to detour on my own street?*

But she did. She walked for five or six blocks to work off her bad temper, ending up at the park. Skip was obviously enjoying the longer adventure, so she did not mind the walk. As she walked slowly along the side of the park, allowing Skip to investigate every tree and bush, she saw a girl of about her own age and in her school's uniform, walking a dog on the other side.

That's Emma from 6A, she thought. She waved and Emma waved back. Kylie watched her vanish around the corner. *Her dog's a wire-haired terrier I think,* she told herself. *I must ask her at school tomorrow.*

Later, at home, Kylie recounted the tale of Claud and his fishing to her mother. Mrs Kirk smiled and shook her head.

At that moment, Claud peeked around the doorpost at the top of the back stairs. He looked so cautious and scared that Kylie could only laugh. She got up to try to pick him up and comfort him but Claud would have none of it and dashed back down the stairs and out of sight. *Oh poor cat!* she thought, taking his food bowl down to the bottom of the stairs.

But she didn't think that at one in the morning when Claud was on the roof again, screeching and hissing and bounding around on the sheet metal. *Oh Claud!* she muttered, trying to muffle the sound with her pillow.

Alex thought the same when they met at breakfast. "Bloody cat!" he grumbled. "Keeping me awake half the night. I could strangle him!"

Kylie could only give a washed-out smile. She felt tired and would have liked to stay home but her mother insisted she go to school. After feeding Skip and rumpling his ears she did so. At school she met Emma.

"Hi Emma! That's a lovely dog you've got. What type is it?"

"A Scottish Terrier," Emma replied.

"Is it a boy or a girl?" Kylie asked.

"A girl," Emma answered. "Her name is Thistle."

Kylie smiled and said, "We should meet at the park and give the dogs a game."

"Good idea," Emma agreed.

Kylie liked Emma and she talked to her for most of the lunch break, to Margaret's mild annoyance. To make her point Margaret asked if she could come over after school.

"Of course Margaret. As long as your mum knows," Kylie replied. "It's Friday afternoon so those silly boys will just be reading comics."

Every Friday afternoon Mrs Kirk did the shopping and she nearly always brought home comics and a chocolate for each. Normally Kylie really enjoyed that, particularly as Friday night also meant 'Guides'.

After school she and Margaret walked home. When they got there Margaret telephoned her mother and was told she could stay for a little while. Skip came bounding in to meet them and had to be played with and her belly rubbed. The two girls then went to the kitchen to get afternoon tea. As they sat drinking cordial and munching biscuits, Kylie watched Margaret's face and knew she was getting anxious that Graham would not arrive home before she had to go.

But he did, coming in with Max and Peter. He saw Margaret and made a face, then called, "G'day Maggot. How are ya?"

"Fine thanks," Margaret replied. She smiled but Kylie could tell that she was hurt. *Stupid boy!* she thought angrily.

After wolfing down biscuits and several cold drinks the boys went downstairs. Skip went scampering down after them, nearly tripping Peter on the back stairs. The boys began running around the house playing 'brandy' with a tennis ball. Skip could be heard barking and joining in. Kylie did not feel like any sort of silly chasey game, particularly one that she knew could hurt. Instead she and Margaret sat and talked quietly.

Through the window on the Freeman's side of the house she heard muttered voices. These attracted her attention. The boys had stopped playing and were discussing something just below. *I wonder what they are up to?* she thought. Then she heard Max's voice very clearly say, "Is he dead?"

Is who dead? Kylie thought, her heart immediately beating faster with apprehension. Springing up she went to the window and leaned out. The boys were all grouped around something on the ground and her heart missed a beat. *Oh I hope it isn't Skip,* she thought.

Then Peter moved aside and she clearly saw the body.

It was Claud the cat.

Chapter 11

THE GUINEA PIGS

Margaret saw Kylie go pale and looked shocked. Quickly she moved over to look through the window beside her. "What's wrong Kylie?" she asked.

"Claud. He's dead," Kylie whispered.

Margaret looked down and saw the boys kneeling to look at the body of the cat. *Oh dear!* she thought. *Poor Kylie. Poor Claud.*

Kylie headed for the back steps. "We have to check," she said.

Margaret wasn't sure if that was a good idea or not but she followed. She did not really want to see a dead creature but knew this was an unpleasantness she could not avoid. Bracing herself to face the reality she made her way down to join Kylie and the boys.

Kylie knelt to look at Claud. "Is he really dead?" she asked.

Graham nodded. "Stone dead," he replied.

"Stiff as a board," Max added. "He's obviously been dead for a while."

Margaret stood and looked down, her hand on Kylie's shoulder. She could see the glassy stare on Claud's eyes and noted that ants were running in and out of the cat's nostrils and mouth. To her disgust and Kylie's evident distress Alex picked the cat up by its tail. It did not bend and confirmed that Max had said.

Rigor mortis has set in, Margaret thought, remembering something her mother had mentioned. "How did he die?" she asked.

"Not sure," Alex replied. He turned the cat over and then felt along the stiff body. "No obvious wounds."

Margaret had been thinking that perhaps a dog (Brute!) had attacked Claud but now she could see that there were no signs of torn flesh or ruffled fur. It made her feel nauseous to watch Alex actually handling the dead body. To her it looked as stiff as old cardboard.

Alex looked up and said, "I think his neck is broken. See here." He held the body up and pointed.

"How could that happen?" Graham asked.

Kylie looked up, then said between sniffles, "Fell off the roof maybe?"

Graham nodded. "Yeah, the old bugger's been running around up there fighting with the possums a lot these last few nights."

Alex put the body down and stood up. "That mongrel Flawse might have killed him," he suggested.

Kylie looked shocked. "Oh Alex! That's a horrible thing to say."

"Yeah, well, he's a horrible person," Alex replied defensively.

"But Mr Flawse lives over the other side of the house," Kylie said.

Alex gave a sneering grunt then said, "So what? He could have just brought the body here during the night, or today when we were all out."

At that moment, Skip arrived on the run and began to sniff at Claud's body. Graham picked the dog up and held him, rumpling her ears while he did.

"What will we do with him?" Kylie asked.

"Chuck him in the garbage bin," Alex replied callously.

Margaret could see that Kylie was shocked and upset at the suggestion. She said firmly, "I think you should give him a nice burial."

Graham nodded. "And we had better wait till Mum gets home and sees him."

"Where can we bury him?" Kylie asked.

"Down the back of the chook run," Alex answered.

Kylie now burst into tears, so Margaret put her arms around her and urged her to stand up. Once she had done so she led her away, leaving the boys to do the dirty work of digging the grave and wrapping the body up.

By chance Margaret led Kylie out onto the back lawn and they came to the guinea pig cage. That helped calm Kylie and both girls knelt to look at the guinea pigs, which mostly scuttled into their hutch to hide. As the guinea pigs scurried for cover Margaret could not help noticing that one looked very fat and walked with a distinct waddle.

"Is that guinea pig alright?" she asked.

Kylie wiped her tears and nodded. "That is Toffee. She is going to have babies soon."

"Pregnant!" Margaret cried. The idea fascinated her and she wanted to see more closely. "Has young Spike been naughty?" she suggested, seeing the young male poking his nose out to peek at them.

"Don't know which one," Kylie answered. Then she looked seriously at Margaret and added, "And you just remember that that is all any male wants. You watch how you tease Graham, or you might end up that way too."

"I will one day," Margaret replied. "But not till I'm good and ready."

"You just be careful please," Kylie replied. "We don't want any accidental slip ups."

That caused Margaret to blush and giggle. "I'll be careful," she promised.

"This cage needs moving," Kylie commented. So the two girls dragged the cage five metres onto afresh area of lawn. They then washed out the water bowls and refilled them and then added some fresh lettuce leaves. This enticed the guinea pigs out and Margaret was able to closely study Toffee and her distended belly.

I wonder how it will feel to have a baby squirming around inside me? she thought.

The now peaceful guinea pigs were easy to catch, and Margaret gently held Toffee and stroked her, then felt the quivering new life trembling through her belly. It was fascinating.

"Won't be long now, not by the size of her," she commented.

At that moment, Kylie heard a car drive in and park in the car port. She placed Blackie back in the cage and hurried to tell her mother about Claud. Margaret placed Toffee back in the hutch and made sure the latch on the small trap door was properly locked before following.

The retelling of the death of Claud reduced Kylie to tears again and Margaret had a little weep herself. She consoled herself by crouching to pat Skip, who had been tied up while the burial was undertaken. Mrs Kirk had a look at Claud's body, but Margaret did not go out to look. Nor did she or Kylie go when the boys took Claud, now wrapped in old cloth and newspaper, down to the back yard to bury him.

The girls went upstairs with Mrs Kirk who gave them both cups of strong, sweet tea. Margaret patted Kylie as she burst into tears again. "Sorry Kylie," she said.

Mrs Kirk sighed and said, "That is how life can be. So we will remember what fun old Claud gave us and then get on with things. In fact you can start by doing your homework young Miss. Margaret, it is getting late and you had better be getting along home."

Margaret looked at the wall clock and was surprised to see that it was already 5:30pm. "Oh yes! I will be late and in trouble," she cried.

"Ring your mother now and tell her where you are and why you are late," Mrs Kirk suggested.

Margaret did so, stressing to her own mother how she had stayed to comfort Kylie. She then promised to hurry home and at once said goodbye to Kylie and hurried out to her bike. She rode quickly back to her own house, arriving twenty minutes later.

As it was Friday night, Margaret had to hurry to wash and dress in her guide uniform. She loved being a guide and always looked forward to it. Her mother drove her to the Guide Hut, arriving just in time for their first parade. Kylie was there so she devoted more time to cheering her up. Being at Guides and playing games all obviously helped.

During their canteen break Margaret and Kylie made their way to the counter of the tiny canteen to buy a soft drink. As she stood there Moira arrived with a couple of Rangers.

Margaret smiled and said, "Hi Moira. How are things?"

"Okay," Moira answered.

One of the other Rangers, a girl named Tessa, chuckled and cried, "Better than okay. Don't fret Moira, he must really like you to do that."

"Who? Do what?" Margaret asked, her interest at once aroused.

"Some boy in the Venturers," Tessa replied. "He sent Moira a red rose and a letter asking for a date."

Margaret was thrilled. She saw Moira blush and said, "Alistair?"

Moira didn't answer but Tessa did. "That's the name," she agreed.

"Are you going Moira?" Margaret asked.

Moira nodded but said nothing. Again it was Tessa who supplied the information. "They are going to the movies tomorrow night. Moira's mum is driving them both there and back home."

"That's to stop any hanky-panky," added a third Ranger with a giggle.

Moira went very red and Margaret's mind conjured up lurid images of what hanky-panky might be. "Good luck Moira. I hope you have a good time."

"Thank you," Moira replied. Then she looked at Kylie and asked, "What's the matter Kylie?"

The story of the week's disasters with budgies, cats and dogs was told. Kylie got upset so Margaret did most of the talking. Tessa wasn't impressed. "You can always get another cat," he suggested.

That idea stuck in Margaret's mind. Later, at home, she considered buying a kitten to give to Kylie to make up for the loss but when she suggested this to her mother her mother shook her head. "That's a lovely idea dear," she said, "But you don't know if Mrs Kirk really wants another cat. Find out first."

Margaret, who loved cats and was busy rumpling the ears of her own tabby, Mischief, found the idea hard to accept but had to agree.

It was very cold that night (by North Queensland standards) and Margaret woke in the middle of the night to find she was curled up in a shivering ball. She climbed out of bed to get her quilt out of the cupboard. As she did, she discovered Mischief curled up on the foot of her bed. Her first reaction was to chase the cat outside but then she felt how cold the floor was and relented. Finding her quilt she flung it on the bed, covering the cat as she did. Mischief objected to this and hastily crawled out from underneath, giving her a resentful look as he did. He then vanished under her bed and curled up on her discarded clothes.

As Margaret snuggled back into her bed, she suddenly thought of Kylie's guinea pigs. *They will be cold,* she told herself. Then she had the worrying thought that any baby guinea pigs might freeze to death if they were born in such cold conditions. *We must do something,* she thought.

That was what she said to Kylie the following afternoon after school. Margaret went to Kylie's with her and was helping her collect eggs in the chook house when she remembered and mentioned it.

Kylie nodded and replied, "That's a great idea. What should we do?"

At that moment, Margaret was watching some newborn chicks scuttle in and out of their 'warm box'. Looking at that gave her an immediate idea. Pointing at it she said, "Something like that."

Both girls bent down to study the box. Kylie explained that it was just a warm box for chicks that had been incubated. "They keep themselves warm by huddling," she said.

Margaret studied the box, obviously homemade, and decided it was just the thing. The box was without a lid and had been placed on its side with strips of cloth nailed on the side that had become the roof. The cloth strips allowed the chicks to easily push in and out.

Only we will add cloth to the floor as well, she thought.

After taking the eggs upstairs, the girls went to the guinea pig hutch to say hello to the guinea pigs. Once again Margaret was fascinated by how bloated Toffee's body was.

"Won't be long now," she guessed.

"Might be tonight," Kylie suggested.

"Oh yes! So we had better make the warm hutch now," Margaret said.

Impelled by the horrible thought of the newborn baby guinea pigs dying of cold, the girls went searching for materials to construct the warm hutch. A small timber box was found. This had no lid but the other five sides were sound. "Just the thing," Margaret said.

Kylie then led the way to rummage through her mother's sewing room. In the process she discovered a length of felt. This, they both agreed, would make a fine carpet and wall coverings. After measuring the box the felt was cut up into four strips. These weren't quite wide enough, but Margaret could only shrug and say they would have to do.

How to secure the felt was the next problem. Margaret suggested glue but the only glue Kylie knew of was in tubes that Graham used for making his model ship. As he wasn't home they could not ask him, but Kylie took a tube of Tarzan's Grip anyway.

"When he finds out what it is for, he won't mind," she said. (But he did and the 'stolen' glue caused quite a ruckus later).

The glue wasn't ideal but while they had been looking for it Kylie had seen some small nails on Graham's work bench. She collected these, and a small hammer, and they proceeded to nail the felt on. When it was in place Margaret ran her hand over it and nodded with satisfaction.

"This will be great," she said.

The box was then turned on its top and twenty strips of cloth and felt were nailed to the underside of the roof so that when the box was turned back over the strips hung down with their ends just brushing the felt carpet on the floor. The girls weren't quite sure how many strips to nail on but copied the chicken hutch and left a clear space at the back of the box for the guinea pigs to lie.

Margaret picked the box up and peered in. "This is great!" she said.

"But will the guinea pigs go in?" Kylie replied.

That was a worrying thought. To test it the two girls carried the box downstairs and placed it in the guinea pigs' cage. The guinea pigs all dashed about and then cowered in the far corner of the cage as far from the warm hutch as they could get. Skip then joined the girls and proceeded to run around the hutch, causing the guinea pigs to rush from side to side and into a huddle behind the box.

"Skip! Stop that, you naughty dog!" Kylie cried.

Skip's response was to rush around some more, jumping up to lick both Kylie and Margaret as she did. The guinea pigs again went scampering around inside their cage.

Margaret could see their little chests heaving and their nervous eyes following Skip's every move. She particularly noted how Toffee lumbered and waddled with her distended belly wobbling from side to side.

Poor Toffee! This running could harm the babies, she worried.

She said this to Kylie and then suggested they take Skip and move away, to give the guinea pigs time to get used to the warm box.

Kylie nodded. "Good idea. Come here Skip. Ah, got ya, naughty little puppy!"

She scooped a squirming and wriggling Skip up and hurried away. Margaret followed, looking back to see what the guinea pigs did. The girls went up to Kylie's room to listen to music. To keep Skip there Margaret and Kylie took turns to rub her tummy and to ruffle her ears.

After half an hour Skip lost interest and wandered off towards the front of the house, where Graham and Alex could be heard arguing. Kylie pointed to the back. "Let's go and see if the guinea pigs have been brave enough to explore the warm box yet."

Margaret nodded and stood up but as she followed Kylie out of the room she looked towards the veranda, which was where she really wanted to go.

Kylie saw this and laughed. "Don't worry about my silly brother," she said. "He will still be there later."

"I wasn't worrying," Margaret replied defensively, drawing a laugh from Kylie.

The girls made their way back down to the guinea pig hutch. On arrival Margaret noted with alarm that the hutch appeared to be empty. *Oh no! We didn't leave the door open?* she wondered, thinking the guinea pigs had all escaped.

She hurried forward to check but found the door still firmly latched closed. "Where are they?" she wondered.

Then she saw a tiny nose poke through the hanging strips of cloth. "They are all inside!" she cried delightedly.

They were. A check through the small flap in the side of the new warm box revealed all the guinea pigs huddled in there. As the flap was opened, they scuttled away but tried to remain inside the cover of the hanging strips. Both girls were delighted. For ten minutes they tempted the guinea pigs to come out by placing pieces of lettuce on the far side of the cage.

After watching Toffee nibble at the lettuce, Margaret said, "You call me if Toffee starts having her babies, please Kylie."

"What if it happens in the middle of the night?" Kylie queried.

"Then text me so you don't wake up Mum or Dad," Margaret answered.

And that is what Kylie did. At daybreak the next morning, as Margaret lay in her bed on the edge of wakefulness, her mobile phone beeped. A quick glance revealed a message from Kylie.

'Come quick. Toffee giving birth,' the message read.

'On my way,' Margaret texted back.

Flinging off her pyjamas Margaret quickly dressed in shorts and T-shirt. Joggers were laced on and then her mobile phone was slipped into her pocket. As she made her way to the back door, she heard her mother snuffle in her bedroom.

I had better leave a note for Mum or she will get all worried, she thought.

Tearing a page from the notepad from beside the telephone she wrote, 'Have run away with my boyfriend. Will invite you to the wedding, love Margaret.' Stifling a giggle at her naughtiness she then added. 'PS: Have gone to Kylie's to see new baby guinea pigs. Back soon.'

The note was placed on the kitchen table. Margaret then tiptoed out of the house. Silently unlocking the underneath of the house she wheeled her bike out. By this time she was in a fever of impatience. She swung her leg over the bike and put her foot on the pedal. To her dismay, her father's voice came from behind her.

"Where are you off to young Miss?" he asked.

Margaret looked back and saw her father, still in his pyjamas, standing at the top of the steps with the newspaper in his hand. She called, "I am eloping with my boyfriend."

Her father nodded and his facial expression barely changed. "Oh yeah? Good. I hope the poor bugger has got plenty of money."

"Dad!"

"Well? Where are you really going?"

Margaret told him. As she was speaking her phone beeped again and the message read: 'Two out. Be quick.'

"I've got to go, or I will miss it," she cried.

In seconds she was pedalling rapidly down the street. Driven by a strong desire to be there for the birth she pushed herself to ride as fast as she could. Within minutes she was perspiring and gasping for breath, but she kept on trying.

As it was, she was too late for the birth of the third and only just made it in time for the fourth. Dumping her bike on the Kirk's side lawn she ran to the back yard and found Kylie siting watching intently. Panting heavily Margaret knelt down beside her. The two girls exchanged smiles and Margaret felt a strong sense of femaleness, of a bond with all female creatures.

We are the creators of life, she thought as she focused on what little she could see.

To help her Kylie reached in and shifted a few strands of cloth to one side. Margaret saw the first babies, all damp and tiny, their little eyes still closed and tiny pink tongues darting in and out. The mother gave them what she thought was an annoyed look but was obviously unable to move or do anything but let nature take its course. By leaning over Margaret was just able to see the rear end of the guinea pig.

At that moment, Graham appeared. He wore only shorts and a shirt and looked as though he had just woken up. He joined the girls, kneeling beside Margaret. Margaret felt a bit embarrassed at him being there, seeing such a thing. But she was also glad. "Isn't it wonderful," she said.

Without thinking she took his hand and he did not seem to notice. Instead he bent to study the mother as she strained to give birth. Margaret gave him a loving glance and then turned back to the hutch.

As she looked, she saw the guinea pigs rear swell and then a tiny bulge of wet fur appeared. Margaret glanced at the mother guinea pig and felt a surge of sympathy at the effort and probable pain she must be experiencing. Then the fourth baby began to slowly slide out. Fascinated, Margaret studied every detail.

Kylie was also enthralled. "It must hurt," she whispered in awe.

"Like trying to shit a watermelon my mum says," Margaret replied.

"Oh Margaret!" Kylie cried in a scandalised tone.

But she was not really listening, being engrossed in the real-life drama happening before her eyes. Graham looked at her and their eyes met, and Margaret blushed again as she knew what he was thinking about.

And I will have his babies if he wants, she thought. *Even if it does hurt.*

And then the fourth one was out. It slithered onto the damp felt, a small wriggling lump covered with a slimy coating. The mother guinea pig at once began to lick the sticky membrane off. Margaret felt her stomach heave.

That is disgusting! she thought. But then she shook her head. *No it isn't. It is true mother love.* She knew instinctively that if it was her baby she would not flinch from anything that helped it live.

Graham cried out and wrinkled his nose. "That is revolting!" he muttered.

The baby guinea pig began to snuffle and squirm and then the mother urged it towards her teats where the other three were now busily sucking. *It is going to live,* Margaret thought, her heart swelling with happiness.

As she fourth one began to suckle, she gripped Graham's arm and smiled at him. "Isn't nature wonderful!" she said.

Graham nodded and looked at her in a doubtful way. Then he seemed to realise they were holding hands and he let go. As he stood up, he said gruffly that Kylie had to come and have breakfast.

Margaret stood up. "I had better go home before Mum starts to fret. I'll see you at church," she said. But she did not want to leave. She wanted to watch the guinea pigs, and she wanted to be with Graham.

Kylie stood up with obvious reluctance. "Now we have to think of names for them all," she said.

Chapter 12

RIVALRY

Margaret and her family were late getting to church that next morning. As she walked into the church Margaret's eyes quickly scanned the congregation. She was looking for Graham but was disappointed not to see him. None of his family was there. Feeling quite deflated she sat down. It took an effort to concentrate on the service. Normally Margaret was very respectful and took her religion seriously. She took it seriously enough to feel severe pangs of guilt over her shameless behaviour.

She was just mulling over those words that said, 'The sinful desires of the flesh,' when she heard more people arriving late. Turning her head she saw that it was the Kirk family. Kylie met her eye and gave a smile and a tiny wave. Margaret smiled back, then almost frowned as she saw what Graham was doing. He was not looking at her, much less smiling. Instead he was smiling at a girl of his own age in the opposite row of pews.

That's Rowena in his class, Margaret thought.

A sharp stab of anxiety added to her jealousy. Rowena had a beautiful heart-shaped face framed by glossy black hair. Worse still her body had begun to develop into a very attractive shape. Margaret bit her lip and knew what fear was when Rowena returned the smile.

The Kirks sat in a pew behind Margaret, so she was unable to watch without being blatantly disrespectful. Not knowing whether Graham was making eyes at Rowena became a fine little torment for her.

Oh! How can I compete? she worried.

It was only after church that she got to talk to Graham. But he only said hello and wandered off to chat to Roger, who had been one of the altar boys. Kylie did not seem to notice. She said, "We were late because we moved the baby guinea pigs and their mother into a separate hutch of their own."

"What about the warm box?" Margaret asked.

"That too. The others can just get cold for a few nights," Kylie replied.

"Have you thought of any names yet?"

Kylie shook her head. "Not really. Come over and help after lunch."

Margaret nodded but then froze. Over Kylie's shoulder she saw Graham talking to Rowena. Both were smiling and laughing and at that moment Rowena placed her hand on Graham's arm and said something that made him beam with pleasure and nod vigorously.

Oh no! she thought. *What are they talking about?*

Once again, she imagined the worst and wondered how she could compete. She found it a great relief when Rowena headed off with her mother.

After lunch Margaret rode her bike over to Kylie's. She found Kylie with Moira down at the guinea pig hutch. Moira was cuddling one of the baby guinea pigs, a light brown and white one with the cutest little brown eyes. Margaret looked at the guinea pig and felt a tiny niggle of jealousy. That was the one she fancied best herself and she wanted to hold it.

"What are you doing?" she asked.

Kylie indicated the baby guinea pigs. "Trying to think of names. How does 'Fudge' sound for that brown one and 'Caramel' for this one?" she replied.

Margaret really liked the names and at once began to call the baby Caramel. "May I hold her?" she asked.

Moira handed the baby over and then reached into the cage to pick up another, a black and white one. "What about this one? How does 'Daisy' sound?"

"Daisy? Why?" Kylie queried.

"Because she looks like a black and white dairy cow," Moira answered.

Margaret shook her head. "Oh, I don't know," she said, not wanting to hurt Moira's feelings. What she really wanted to know was how the date with Alistair had gone but she did not know to ask.

Luckily Kylie asked for her. "Well, how was it?" she said.

Moira blushed and then said, "Oh, okay. Nice enough."

"Did he... did...," Kylie began, then stopped in blushing embarrassment.

"No he did not. He is a proper gentleman. He was very nice and never tried anything," Moira assured them.

"Not even a good night kiss?" Margaret asked.

Moira shook her head. "No. We just talked."

"What about?" Kylie asked.

"Animals mostly, and Scouts and Guides. He talked a lot about wanting to see a thylacine."

"A what?" Margaret cried.

"A thylacine. A Tasmanian Tiger," Moira explained.

"A Tasmanian Tiger! Here, in North Queensland!" Kylie cried with amazement.

Moira nodded. "Yes, apparently there have been lots of reports for the last hundred years of people seeing things that look like the Tasmanian Tiger up in this part of the world."

"Aren't they extinct, or is that the Tasmanian Devil?" Kylie asked.

"The Tasmanian Devil is alive and well. They are a pest," Moira answered. "It is the Tiger that is extinct. That's why Alistair wants to see one up here. He hopes they aren't."

"Is that all he talked about?" Margaret asked.

Moira nodded. "Mostly."

"Sounds a bit boring," Kylie commented.

"It was, but he was very polite and nice," Moira replied in a defensive tone.

Hmm, she isn't sure, Margaret thought. Personally she wanted a bit more love and passion on her first date, even though she knew it was not good form. *Except that it will be with Graham, and we have known each other for years,* she told herself. That made her ask, "Where's Graham?"

"He went over to Stephen's or Peter's," Kylie answered.

Margaret was disappointed but could only pretend it meant nothing much. She bent to study the baby guinea pigs. "This last one, he is all white. What about calling him 'Snowy'?"

"Margaret! That's a great name," Kylie said.

The compliment caused Margaret a glow of pleasure but there was still that niggling doubt that maybe Graham wasn't at Peter's or Stephen's. *He might be at Rowena's,* she thought. Having a potential rival that pretty was something she did not care for.

But there was nothing she could do about it so she made the best of being with her friends. That did not stop a few tears when she was alone in bed that night.

Monday was a normal school day. Margaret found school easy enough and was usually quite interested in what she learnt but it was still time she would rather have spent doing other things. When she was talking to Kylie at lunch time she suggested going to her house after school.

Kylie shook her head. "Graham won't be there. He said he was going to Roger's after school. Something to do with model trains," she explained.

Margaret was more disappointed than she cared to admit but she put on a bold front. "That's alright. I was coming to see you, not him," she replied.

"Oh yeah!" Kylie teased, but Margaret could see she was pleased.

At Kylie's the girls fed the pets and ended up at the guinea pig cage. Once again Margaret knelt and was thrilled and fascinated by nature. This time the mother guinea pig was suckling the babies and that got all her attention for a while. Watching the greedy little mouths sucking and gripping the teats got her wondering what it might be like to suckle her own babies. From that thought it was only a short step to lamenting that she had not yet developed any breasts herself. Knowing that Graham was very attracted to such things on older girls caused her quiet agonies.

Oh! I hope I grow some soon! she thought.

Kylie was also watching and after a while she shook her head. "They are very rough, aren't they?" she said, indicating where Fudge was pushing at his mother with his front legs while gripping tightly onto a teat.

"Poor little Snowy's not getting much of a chance," Margaret observed.

Kylie nodded and then shrugged. "He must be the runt of the litter. That's what Mum said."

The idea made Margaret feel quite sad. "Nature is very hard sometimes, isn't it?" she commented.

Kylie could only agree. The girls waited till the feeding was done, then lifted the babies out to cuddle them, watched by the anxious mother.

Chapter 13

BRUTE IN THE SHIPROOM

On Monday morning Kylie went happily to school. She was warmed by the knowledge that the newly born guinea pigs were doing well. They had all survived the night and when she had left home were feeding contentedly. At school she met up with Margaret and told her the good news. Margaret looked really pleased and said she wished that she could come over to see them after school.

"Can't you?" Kylie asked.

Margaret shook her head. "No. I have to go to Aunty Edith's with Mum," she explained.

That disappointed Kylie but she coped. *I will take Skip for a walk,* she decided. With that in mind she sought out Emma during the lunch break and suggested that they meet up at the park with their pets after school. Emma was obviously very pleased to be asked and agreed.

So that afternoon, as soon as Kylie had reached home and been greeted at the gate by Skip she told him the news. "Walkies Skip. Does that sound good?" she said, holding the puppy's ears and rumpling them. Skip obviously understood the word 'walkies' and she at once began to jump about and yap excitedly.

It was five blocks to the park and Skip appeared to enjoy every one of them. She continually zig-zagged to sniff at every bush and post and tree. Kylie was highly amused at the way Skip's tail wagged the whole way. Thus she was in a very relaxed and happy mood when she arrived at the park.

Seeing the large open stretches of lawn made Kylie wish she could let Skip off her leash, to run free. But she had been warned by her mother that the council by-laws about unrestrained dogs were very strict. So she resisted the temptation and kept her secure. Instead she ran with her. But not for far! After less than a hundred metres Kylie was puffed and gasping for breath while Skip was merely panting slightly and then proceeded to jump up and down and run around in circles, begging for another run.

"No Skip, no!" Kylie gasped, rumpling Skip's ears while she did.

Skip proceeded to try to lick her face. Kylie held her off but could not help laughing. Then she saw Emma and her happiness seemed to be complete. "Here's a friend for you Skip," she explained.

But the dogs did not agree. Both eyed each other and gave continual low growls. *Oh no!* Kylie thought. *I hope they aren't going to fight.*

To Emma she said, "Your dog's name is Thistle, isn't it?"

Emma smiled. "Yes, it is. Calm down Thistle. Skip is a friend."

The two dogs circled each other warily, held by their owner's leashes. When she was satisfied that Thistle was not going to attack Skip Kylie stepped closer so that Skip and Thistle could check each other out. The dogs proceed to do what dogs always do, causing Kylie to blush with embarrassment.

Emma embarrassed her even more by saying, "I hate it the way dogs sniff at each other's bums."

"I think they are checking for signs of good health or for diseases," Kylie commented.

Emma agreed and then bent to unclip Thistle's leash. "Go on girl, run!" she said.

Thistle went dashing off to explore a nearby garden bed. This caused Skip to whine and strain at her leash. Emma looked and said, "Go on Kylie. Let her have a bit of a run around."

Kylie felt awfully tempted but she shook her head. "I'd like to," she explained. "But Mum said I wasn't to let her off."

She wanted to mention the council laws but could not bring herself to make Emma feel bad. But she did cast a few anxious glances around, wondering if there might be a council employee watching. *Or the dog catcher,* she thought, wondering what the dog catcher might look like. The only vehicle nearby that Kylie could see was an old white van parked under a large shady tree and she was sure that wasn't it. *A council vehicle would have some sort of markings on it,* she reasoned.

To Kylie's relief, Emma did not press the issue. The two girls began walking around the garden area of the park. Skip strained at her leash and frequently tried to break free to follow Thistle, but Kylie held her firmly. Thistle dashed from place to place exploring the array of new smells and sights. She also ran out into the open part of the park to chase the ibis. The ibis lumbered into the air and flapped away, to settle at the far end of the park.

Emma had to call Thistle back and poor old Skip barked excitedly, also wanting to join in the fun. "Sorry Skip," Kylie said, wishing she could let her run free.

Kylie enjoyed the half hour at the park but was also slightly relieved when she said her goodbyes without anyone from the council arriving. The girls promised to meet again and set off on their separate ways home.

Once she was home, Kylie unleashed Skip and then fed the birds and the guinea pigs. For a few minutes she cuddled and stroked the baby guinea pigs, thereby earning jealous yaps and snuffles from Skip who had to be held back.

While she was doing this, Kylie saw Graham and his friend Stephen running around the house. Both had model aeroplanes which they were pretending to have 'dog fights' with. Both boys made so much noise with sound effects of roaring engines and stuttering machine guns that Skip began to bark and run excitedly around them in circles and the guinea pigs all fled into their warm box and other hiding places.

"Stop that silly noise, you boys!" Kylie cried angrily. "You are scaring the guinea pigs."

But that did not stop them. The two boys ran over and pretended that their small model fighter planes were busy strafing and bombing both the guinea pig cage and Skip. When Kylie scolded them again, they ran off laughing, to resume their game. *Silly creatures!* Kylie thought.

Tuesday was a repeat of Monday except that when Kylie got home from taking Skip to the park Graham and Stephen were busy throwing balsa gliders off the back stairs. That evening Kylie was able to organise with her mother something she had wanted to do for some time: take some pets to school for 'Show and Tell'. She opted to take the baby guinea pigs and their mother.

So on Wednesday morning Mrs Kirk drove her to school with a large cardboard box containing the guinea pigs. The 'Morning Talk' was a great success. The other girls in the class 'oohed' and 'aahed' and were obviously jealous while the boys, despite pretending not to be interested, in fact obviously were.

Mrs Kirk then took the guinea pigs home, and the school day resumed its normal course. Kylie enjoyed school. Most of the work she could do easily, but she did not try very hard to excel at academic things. Instead she focused her time and energy on social situations.

People are more important, she told herself.

After school Kylie walked home. She knew her mother would be at work and wasn't sure where Graham and Alex were. This was a normal situation for most afternoons so did not worry her. But as she opened the front gate she heard Skip barking frantically, the sounds overlaid onto a deeper growl and she suddenly wished that the boys were home.

Curious to know what the barking was all about Kylie did not go up the front steps but instead walked around to the side of the house. As she did, her heart began to hammer faster and she felt a spurt of fear. On the wide side lawn Skip was dashing back and forth and barking furiously at the Flawse's fence. Kylie instantly saw why: One of the wooden palings was loose and Brute had his head poking through the gap!

Oh no! Kylie thought.

She noted that Brute was struggling hard and appeared to be trying to push through to get at Skip. Even as Kylie started forward, she saw Brute thrust and shove the paling aside. Snarling and thrusting hard the big dog struggled furiously to get at Skip. Then, to Kylie's horror, Brute was through, his claws scrabbling for a foothold as did. Growling and snarling viciously the huge, savage dog leapt forward.

Kylie had thought to grab Skip and restrain her, but the situation changed too fast for that. On seeing Brute struggling to his feet, Skip turned and fled. All Kylie could do was stand open mouthed and fearful as the two dogs dashed off across the lawn.

"Stop! Oh, stop!" Kylie screamed. "Upstairs Skip, upstairs!"

But Skip paid no heed. She ran for her life for the nearest cover, which was under the house. In a flash of black fury, Brute was on her tail. Skip dashed into the car port and then did a sharp turn left, her claws skittering and slipping on the concrete as she did. The door to the Ship Room was open and Skip vanished through it at full speed, followed a second later by Brute.

"Oh no, not the Ship Room!" Kylie cried.

Thinking only of saving Skip, she was already running. But as she went in under the house, she was sick with anxiety. Not only was Skip in deadly danger but she could already hear the sounds of crashing and smashing as the dogs dashed around among the model ships.

Arriving at the open door a few seconds later, all Kylie could do was stand and look, appalled at what she was seeing. Skip was running for her life, leaping and yapping, while Brute lunged and dashed back and forth trying to corner her. In the process both dogs kept colliding with the model sailing ships, knocking them over and breaking masts and rigging with every bound. Kylie saw the foremast of Graham's favourite Ship-of-the-line, a model of the 100-gun HMS *Victory*, snap and crumple into a tangle of broken sticks, torn cloth and broken cotton.

Oh no! Graham will be heartbroken, she thought as she saw cardboard model houses and a castle go flying and tiny model trees being knocked in all directions by the savagely fighting dogs.

For Brute had now caught Skip and the two dogs were at each other with teeth and claws. The noise shifted to a primeval growling and snarling that made Kylie sick to the very pit of her stomach. And she could see that the battle was likely to have only one end.

Brute is too big and strong. He will kill Skip, she told herself.

Even as she thought this Brute lunged and gripped Skip by the throat. Skip yowled in pain and then clamped her jaws on to Brute's left front leg. The snarling and barking increased in intensity. The dogs began to roll over and over, snapping and scratching. To Kylie's added horror, she saw Brute change his grip, his huge slobbering jaws clamping onto the side of Skip's head, one yellow fang right next to her eye.

Skip will lose her eye! she thought.

Heedless of the risk to herself she ran across the Ship Room, trying hard to avoid stepping on all the tiny model houses, trees and tiny plasticine people as she did. She was not entirely successful, and she accidentally bumped a couple of small trees and a little house.

Worse immediately followed. As she reached the two violently struggling dogs and tried to reach for Skip, Kylie had to jump aside to avoid Brute's flailing hind legs. In the process she caught the bowsprit of an American 'clipper' model and sent it flying, the jib boom snapping in the process. In trying to avoid another lunge by Brute she had to jump. That was worse. Spread in a line at least five metres long was a huge column of tiny plasticine soldiers. They represented an army on the march and had tiny flags, officers on plasticine horses, little field guns and tiny wagons made of balsa wood and with tissue paper 'canvas' canopies; even small bands with miniature drums and trumpets.

'Napoleon's *Grande Armee*,' she thought as she hopped around. The tiny *tricolore* French flags told her that much.

Kylie tried desperately to avoid stepping on them but another lunge by Brute made her lose her balance and she could not help herself. One shoe came down hard directly on a company of infantry, squashing them instantly into an irretrievable flat mess. Even as her foot came down she noted that the company had the high bearskins and blue coats of the *Garde Imperiale*.

But she could only spare the flattened mass a quick glance. *Graham will be so upset!* she thought. Then she realised she had another problem. All of the tiny infantrymen had a pin to represent his musket and bayonet and half a dozen pins were now imbedded in the sole of her shoe. Some were driven so far through that the pinpoints were pricking the bottom of her foot.

However, there was no time to do anything but scrape the shoe hastily on the concrete as Brute was again gripping a frantically yelping Skip buy the throat. Kylie now dashed in, kicking another big sailing ship in the process. She seized Brute's collar and hauled, screaming as she did.

It was instantly apparent to Kylie that she lacked the strength to be able to break Brute's grip. But she tried. Ignoring how his hind legs were scrabbling and scratching at her own ankles, she straddled him and attempted to prize his jaws apart. Her hands were instantly covered in slime and saliva and she felt nauseous and terrified but she kept trying. Right next to her hands were Brute's eyes and for a few moments she was tempted to poke her fingers into them, but the very idea revolted her and she could not bring herself to do it. All she could do was cling, crying for help.

To make things worse, the fight kept moving, knocking over more model ships, scattering model buildings and trees and trampling armies and tiny people. Tears began to flow, and Kylie sensed she was on the edge of becoming hysterical.

"Help! Oh, help please! Somebody help!" she screamed.

To add to her distress, blood was showing on Skip's coat and she was making snuffling, whimpering sounds of pain. In desperation Kylie began hauling, dragging both dogs towards the door, heedless of the devastation to Graham's models.

I must save Skip, I must! she thought.

Another ship was knocked on its side. Some tiny red coat soldiers and a balsa cannon were scraped off the side of the half metre high rock that Graham had positioned to represent the Rock of Gibraltar. They went tumbling down and were trampled underfoot. Kylie felt balsa snapping and plasticine squishing under her shoes, but she hardened her heart and kept on dragging.

A small model fishing boat with a brown sail was shoved aside and a fisherman fell overboard. Then Kylie tried to avoid the model of a Spanish oared galley. In this she was only partly successful, and she heard the snapping, crunching sound as she trod on some of the tiny oars.

This is just awful, she thought. *Graham will be devastated.*

But she also knew that she would be emotionally shattered if she could not save Skip. So she continued dragging both dogs towards the door, and with each frantic heave the doorway was closer. Still Brute gripped Skip by the throat and Kylie was sure that Skip was weakening with every second.

Her neck might be broken, or she won't be able to breathe, she thought.

Struggling with the two animals was the most traumatic and primeval thing Kylie had ever done in her life and she was truly appalled at the ferocity of their struggles and sheer life-and-death nature of the battle. Feeling the rippling muscles and straining sinews and the moving flesh and fur was all too real and when the hot breath, drops of blood and dribbles of saliva were added it was so revolting she was almost paralysed with horror and disgust.

Despite her nausea and fear Kylie kept on and after another horrible minute she had both dogs out of the doorway and into the carport. But then she paused, and a feeling of almost overpowering helplessness gripped her.

I've got them out of the Ship Room, but how do I make Brute let go? she wondered. Then a more frightening thought came to her. *And when he has let go how to I save Skip and how do I stop him attacking me?*

Memories of being mauled and bitten by Brute on other occasions swirled in her mind to swamp her with paralysing terror. There was also the memory of hearing about a water meter reader being mauled to death by dogs. Very aware that the threat was real she stood there, gripping Brute with all her might but knowing, with dread in her heart, that she was rapidly weakening.

Oh, what can I do? she wondered.

Chapter 14

HORRIBLE NAMES

As Kylie struggled to release Skip from Brute's jaws, she also began to worry about herself. She was now straddling the big dog and was gripping his thrusting, squirming body with her legs. The thought came to her that after Skip was free Brute might turn on her. Into her mind came something she had read about how it was easy to get onto a tiger's back but hard to get off.

I will get really ripped, she thought miserably.

From past experience she knew that her legs and arms could be severely mauled. Already both her lower legs were stinging and streaming blood.

By now she was out of the Ship Room, and she was able to reach across with one arm and pull the door across. Using her right foot she shoved it hard, causing it to swing shut. That made her feel better. At least there would be no more devastation among the models!

But how to free Skip and get away from Brute? Kylie was at a loss. She was also becoming increasingly desperate as she could feel herself weakening. Once again, she began to scream for help.

There must be someone who can help me, she thought.

Then she remembered how her mother had used water from the hose to make Brute release Skip during a previous attack but to her dismay there was no hose in sight. Knowing that there would be one attached to a tap at the back of the house was no use.

I will never be able to drag Brute on the grass, she thought. She had now reached the grass of the side lawn and already the big dog was digging his claws in and making it hard to hold on.

Breathing, she thought. *The water cut off his air. Can I do that just for a minute, just enough to make him let go?* she wondered.

Having no other plan she tried it. Using her left hand she reached forward and covered Brute's nostrils. The action had an immediate reaction. Brute began to shake his head violently and Kylie's hand slipped on the mucous and saliva on his nose.

Frantic to save Skip, who now seemed to be just a limp rag doll in Brute's jaws, Kylie grabbed at Brute's nostrils again, this time clenching her hand to hold tightly to the top jaw. Once again Brute reacted with violent shaking. He also raised a leg to scratch at Kylie's hands and arm. She felt the pain but clung on.

Suddenly Skip fell free. But Kylie was given no time to rejoice as Brute snapped his jaws shut, catching Kylie's fingers in his teeth. He also jumped, struggled and twisted so strongly that he slipped from between her legs and was free.

Oh my God! Now I'm for it! Kylie thought.

Terror clutched at her heart and her throat as the huge dog began snapping and twisting. She pulled and was able to get her hand free, but it was numb and bleeding and she knew she was half stunned with shock.

I must keep fighting, she thought.

At the back of her terrified brain was the fear that Brute could maul her to death.

He certainly tried. He leapt at her throat, and it was only with a desperate jump and flailing arms that she fended him off. But in doing so she exposed her left arm and in and instant Brute snapped at it. His slobbering jaws clamped shut on her arm just above the wrist and waves of pain and fear shot through Kylie. She felt herself being twisted and pulled and realised that Brute was trying to drag her down.

I mustn't go down! she thought. *If I go down he will tear out my throat or my eyes.*

Fear gave her strength and she managed to dance around and keep her feet while whacking frantically at Brute's head. But he was strong, too strong, and she sobbed in terror.

Suddenly Brute let go and whirled to snap at something white which had darted in to latch onto his hind leg. Through a mist of tears Kylie saw that it was Skip. She had attacked to help her.

"Oh good girl Skip! But no Skip, no! Run! Get away while you can!" she cried.

Then the whole situation changed again. Kylie heard a man bellowing angrily and she looked around. To her mingled dismay and relief she saw it was Mr Flawse. He had come out into his back garden and was shouting angrily over the fence.

"You horrible little girl, leave my dog alone!" he yelled.

The unfairness of his statement made Kylie's blood boil. "You get him off me!" she screamed.

She held up her left arm, noting that it was streaming with blood and sweat. *I hope I'm not scarred for life,* she worried.

Mr Flawse swore foully and went to clamber over the picket fence. But as he straddled the top of it there was a loud *crack!* and he fell hard onto the pointed tops. The sharp point of a paling drove up into his crutch and he let out a bellow of agony. Kylie did not know whether to laugh or cry at the way his face contorted with pain and anger.

But worse instantly followed. Mr Flawse's weight was too much for the fence and two palings broke loose and he fell heavily onto the Kirk's lawn. As he rolled on the grass he swore in a most disgusting way, deeply offending Kylie.

Kylie turned her attention back to Skip and was relieved to see that Skip had let go of Brute and was jumping around, barking and growling and just managing to avoid the bigger dog's lunges.

Seeing her chance, Kylie ran to the back of the house, turned on the hose and hurried back, dragging it behind her. As she adjusted the nozzle, she saw that Skip had retreated to join her and she was just in time to deflect Brute's next attack with a high pressure jet of cold water. Brute withdrew, shaking and snarling and looking baffled.

By then Mr Flawse had struggled to his knees. He was obviously still in pain and was clutching himself, all the while swearing and shouting threats. Nevertheless, the sight gave her a spurt of malicious glee.

"Stop swearing and get your horrible dog out of our yard," she shouted, hosing wildly to keep Brute at bay.

The big dog ran back and forth snarling and yapping but clearly unwilling to suffer the water treatment again. Skip dashed back and forth, matching him for yaps and growls. The speed at which she moved eased some of Kylie's worries but that was offset by the streaks of blood in her fur.

Mr Flawse struggled to his feet, still gripping his groin. With his other hand he shook his fist. "Don't you tell me what to do you horrible little creature! You stop hurting my dog."

Once again, the injustice of the statement rendered Kylie temporarily speechless. All she could do was shake her head and keep hosing to prevent another attack.

At that moment, movement at the front of the house attracted Kylie's interest. She glanced and saw that it was Margaret. Relief at the arrival of a friend was instantly offset by anxiety lest Brute turn on her.

"Watch out, Margaret. This vicious mongrel might attack," she called.

Mr Flawse exploded with wrath. "Don't you call my dog a mongrel, you little bitch!" he screamed, adding some disgusting swear words.

Kylie was shocked by the crudity of his speech, but Margaret ran forward, scooping up a garden rake as she did. "And don't you call Kylie horrible names, you bad mannered brute," she shouted.

"Lookout!" Kylie cried, jumping aside as Brute lunged again. Margaret fended the dog off and Kylie directed the stream onto his head. "Go away!" she cried. "Oh Margaret, take the hose so I can grab Skip."

Margaret nodded but then swung the rake and used the prongs to fend off another attack by Brute. But it was Skip Kylie was more worried about. Skip had let go of Brute's leg and was now barking furiously at his heels. The big dog spun to face Skip and pounced. But Skip was quicker and managed to evade the snapping jaws. Kylie sobbed and hosed both dogs, reaching out with her left hand to try to grab Skip. Margaret shoved at Brute with the rake, drawing more angry bellows from Mr Flawse, who was still bent double and holding himself.

"What's wrong with Mister Brute?" Margaret asked.

"He fell on the fence and hurt his nuts," Kylie answered. This drew a scowl and a grimace from Mr Flawse, which both frightened and cheered Kylie.

Margaret gave a short, harsh laugh, then snapped, "Good! Serves him right." Her eyes flashed with anger. She faced Mr Flawse and shouted, "You catch your horrible dog and get it out of here."

At that Mr Flawse straightened up, still in obvious pain. He then advanced towards the battling group. "Don't talk to me like that, Missie! You don't live here so mind your own business!" he snarled.

At that moment, Kylie got her chance. She had the nozzle set to make a jet and had the hose turned full on. The water squirted ten metres out and she aimed it at Brute's mouth. The water blasted into his mouth and nostrils. The dog reacted instantly, jumping back. Skip went to charge in, but Kylie reached down and scooped her up.

Mr Flawse stepped forward and seized Brute's collar. "Stop hurting my dog you nasty girlie!" he yelled.

At that moment, Alex and Graham both arrived at the run. Dumping bicycles and school bags on the side lawn they raced over to join the girls. "What's going on here?" Alex demanded to know. "What are you and your dog doing in our yard?" he yelled at Mr Flawse.

For a few moments Kylie could not speak as the relief washed through her. Keeping the jet of water directed between her and Brute, she said, "Brute broke through the fence and was chasing Skip."

"Is Skip alright?" Graham asked.

"I think so," Kylie replied, keeping a tight grip as Skip began to squirm in greeting to the boys. "But Brute chased her into the Ship Room."

"The Ship Room!" Graham gasped. He turned and quickly made his way to the Ship Room door. Mr Flawse backed across to the broken section of fence, dragging a furiously struggling Brute with him. Alex followed, fists raised.

A moment later, Kylie heard Graham's cry of distress and her heart went out to him. He came running back and snatched the rake from Margaret. "You bloody dog!" he screamed at Brute. "I'll kill you!"

At that Brute turned and fled, causing Mr Flawse to twist and fall onto the broken fence. "Ow! Argh!" he screamed as he fell onto the exposed nails. The dog broke free and dashed away into the neighbour's garden.

Kylie felt a surge of real fear. "Graham! No!" she screamed, fearing he would strike Mr Flawse with the rake. Mr Flawse struggled to get up, his face a mask of pain, fear and rage. "You hit me boy and I'll see you in court," he threatened.

To Kylie's relief, Graham came to a halt, his chest heaving with exertion and emotion. Then he swore horribly and hurled the rake. The rake struck a side window of Mr Flawse's house. The glass shattered and Graham shouted, "Rotten bloody dog! If it comes into our yard again, I will kill it."

Mr Flawse struggled to his feet on his own property. Gasping and face red with anger he shouted, "You'll pay for that boy!"

"And you can pay for all my broken models!" Graham screamed back. Kylie could see he was almost beside himself, so she stepped forward and said, "Margaret, take the hose. Graham, come back please."

Alex now stepped forward and pulled Graham back but took his place, glaring at Mr Flawse with clenched fists on hips. Margaret did as she was told, freeing one hand so she could take hold of Graham's arm.

Suddenly Graham turned and hurried away. Kylie saw that he had tears streaming down his face. Margaret turned to follow but Kylie met her eyes and shook her head.

"He's upset. Let him go," she said, knowing that Graham would not want them to see him crying.

Alex now took charge. He instructed Margaret to keep the hose ready, then said, "Kylie, tie Skip up out of sight and then go and wash your arm."

Kylie glanced down and was horrified to see that her left arm was now smeared with blood and that it was dripping off her fingers onto her clothes and the lawn. There were even smears on Skip's coat. For a moment she felt nauseous, and she feared she would faint but she managed to make her legs work.

Then, as she was tying Skip up, she heard her mother's car at the front gate. Alex went to open it and the car came driving into the carport as Kylie made her way to the washtubs in the laundry. By the time she got there both Alex and Margaret were busy telling her their versions of events.

Kylie's mother was horrified and then very angry, but she quickly took charge. She hurried over to Kylie and switched on a light to see better. As Mrs Kirk spoke, asking Kylie how she was, Kylie could not contain herself any longer. Tears misted her eyes and she began to shake and sob.

There followed half an hour of rapid action. Kylie's mother washed her arm and then hurried her upstairs to use antiseptic and to bandage the larger bites. To Kylie's relief, these were not as bad as she had feared. In fact, once they were washed and the blood stopped flowing, most were mere scratches and only a couple were obvious tooth incisions. Alex was sent to repair the fence with hammer, nails, planks of wood, and chicken wire netting. Margaret went from one to the other helping. She also took the opportunity to look into the Ship Room.

"Oh no! Poor Graham! He must be really hurt," she said when she rejoined Kylie and her mother.

Mrs Kirk's face darkened with anger, and she made her way downstairs to the Ship Room. By then Kylie had calmed down and she and Margaret followed. As Mrs Kirk surveyed the wreckage of the ship models, she shook her head and said, "This is the last straw! I am going to lodge another official complaint with the council and get that horrible dog removed. It shouldn't be allowed in a suburban area."

At that moment, Kylie heard Alex, who was out on the side yard, begin shouting abuse at Mr Flawse. "Ya fat slug! Keep that mongrel out of our yard."

Mrs Kirk turned and snapped, "Alex! That is enough of that sort of talk! Now just fix the fence so that the vicious creature can't get through while I phone the council."

Mr Flawse obviously heard her as he shouted from an upstairs window. "You keep your brats under control lady, or I will call the police."

Alex at once called back, "And I'll give you good reason to, ya great fat turd!"

"Alex!"

"Sorry Mum."

Graham now re-joined them and stood at the door of the Ship Room, dejection all over his face. Kylie wanted to hug him, but Margaret moved first and put her arms around him. Graham appeared not to notice but just stood there, shaking his head in apparent disbelief and muttering, "All that work!"

Chapter 15

TEMPTATION

Margaret moved instinctively to hold Graham. Only after she had put her arms around him did she realise what she had done and she tensed, anxious lest he resent her actions. To her relief, he seemed to accept her embrace so she hugged him again. "Oh Graham, I'm sorry," she whispered.

To her joy he gave her a return hug and said, "What a mess! All that work, wasted!"

"No it wasn't. It gave you hours of pleasure making them," Margaret replied.

"But it will take years to repair all the damage," Graham answered. She felt him tremble and heard a catch in his voice. A glance showed his face to be drawn and his eyes prickling with tears.

To try to cheer him up she said, "It might not be as bad as it looks."

Graham tensed and shrugged, then eased her arms from around him. For a moment Margaret feared that her words had upset him but he gave a wry grin and said, "Maybe."

In an attempt to be positive Margaret suggested they work their way slowly in, tidying up as they went. To her relief, Graham nodded and stepped forward. Both knelt down and she watched anxiously as he picked up a small cardboard house that lay on its side. This was placed back beside a chalk 'road'.

Next to the house was a squashed piece of coloured plasticine. Graham muttered and shook his head and then used his fingers to pry up on edge. The plasticine came up in a flat layer and he looked at it and shook his head. "The farmer," he explained.

Only then did Margaret realise that there more of the flat plasticine objects in other places. *They are squashed little people,* she thought.

Graham stood up and walked over to where there was a large and now very obvious gap in a long column of plasticine people. Amongst the column were tiny balsa wagons with canopies made from tissue paper glued over wire frames. There were also tiny cannons made from balsa wood. *An army on the march,* Margaret realised, noting that the tiny people wore uniforms and were meant to be soldiers.

Graham knelt and gently poked at where about twenty little soldiers had been squashed flat. "Napoleon's *Grande Armee,*" Graham explained. "There were his best troops, the elite *Garde Imperiale,* the Imperial Guard," he explained.

Margaret had seen them before and had even played the game with him and Kylie so knew that, but she knelt and studied the surviving twenty or thirty. She saw the blue coats with white facings and red cuffs, the white cross straps and white trousers, black bearskins decked with a gold badge, braiding and red plume. Each tiny soldier even had a drooping moustache made from black plasticine.

They actually look very good, she thought, knowing that it took about ten minutes to make each one of the tiny figures.

Then Graham gave a cry of distress and reached down to another squashed figure, much larger than the others. "Oh no! Marshal Ney!"

"You can make another one," Margaret suggested.

Graham shook his head. "No, it wouldn't be... wouldn't be right. He is dead and... well..."

He could not explain but Margaret knew what he meant. In his mind the tiny figures were alive, by the virtue of imagination and magic, and he could not make another plasticine person and give him the same name. For a few seconds she struggled for the right thing to say, then asked, "Didn't Napoleon have more than one marshal?"

"He did; a dozen or so at least," Graham answered. "But Ney was my favourite. The bravest of the brave Napoleon called him."

"I'm sorry," Margaret said, feeling Graham's pain.

Graham made no answer but instead moved to look at a fort that had been kicked. The soldiers and little cannons had been scattered far and wide but, apart from a crumple in one cardboard wall the fort looked undamaged. Graham placed it back in position and began picking up the gunners and guns. Margaret knelt to help him. As she did, she glanced to her right, to the area of concrete that was Kylie's county of Lucrania. She saw that part of a forest had been trampled but that the 'capital city' and the white castle that was the Princesses' residence were unharmed.

"Not much broken here," she said, standing up a couple of the small trees.

These were two dimensional, made from pieces of green cardboard cut roughly to shape and stuck to pieces of twig about 10 centimetre's long. The base of each tree trunk was merely stuck into a blob of brown plasticine to hold them upright.

A pack of small plastic wolves and a bear lurked in the forest, which Kylie had made as a barrier right along her border. There were also a couple of border guards, plasticine riflemen, *jaegers*, in grey and green uniforms. None had been damaged.

While Margaret was tidying up the forest Kylie came to the door. "Mum is taking me to the doctors again, and we are taking Skip to the vet," Kylie explained.

"Are you alright?" Margaret asked.

Kylie nodded. "Just a few scratches."

"What about Skip?" Margaret asked.

"He seems okay, but he might have internal injuries," Kylie answered.

"We will tidy up," Margaret answered. "Your Lucranians didn't get damaged."

"No, but the poor old Spanish got trampled a bit," Kylie said, indicating the patch of concrete that was Spain.

As Kylie got in the car Graham and Margaret moved to where a line of football sized rocks three metres long marked the Pyrenees Mountains. Two narrow gaps were named the Pass of Rosconvales and the Andorra Pass. Beyond, on the 'Plain in Spain', were a few groups of wood blocks representing buildings as villages and towns and a dozen ship models in the chalked in harbours.

The galleon *Santa Anna* had been kicked over but after Margaret righted it she only found one cotton thread in the rigging broken and a few balsa cannon barrels and gun port lids broken off. "This isn't too bad. You can call it battle damage for a while," she suggested.

Graham grunted and picked up the galley with its broken oars. Once again Margaret tried to be positive. "Only five broken. You can easily replace them," she said.

"Kylie can," Graham replied. "She owns the Spanish."

The next place that took their attention was the Rock of Gibraltar. Scattered around the base were a dozen redcoats. Graham shook his head, but Margaret knelt and saw that only two had been stepped on. "This one is only half squashed," she said, picking up the tiny figure and trying to squeeze him back into shape. This was not entirely successful, but she placed him up on one of the rock ledges anyway.

No-one will notice he is a bit misshapen, she thought.

Graham knelt with her and began picking up the redcoats and placing them back in their guard posts. As they worked, Margaret sneezed and noted how grimy her hands and knees were getting.

"This place is getting really dusty again," she observed. "It needs another clean out."

As she said that, she had a vivid flashback to the previous year when all the models had been packed up to make room for Graham's birthday party. The concrete had been swept and then hosed and scrubbed.

"We need to clean this up," Graham said, pointing to some wrecks.

That wasn't what Margaret wanted but she agreed and they moved to where several big ships lay on their sides. One was the pride and joy of Graham's fleet, the 100-gun HMS *Victory*. Seeing the tangle of broken masts and rigging upset Graham, but Margaret looked and said, "Is there much actually broken?"

Graham teased at the tangle and then shook his head. "No, only one spar, the topmast. But it will take a couple of hours to re-rig it all."

The same applied to the American Clipper with the broken bowsprit. Other things would not be so easy to fix. There were more trampled plasticine people and several crumpled cardboard houses that had been squashed flat. But an hour's steady work had most of the disarray tidied up and the extent of the damage quantified.

Graham picked up the *Victory*, something which needed both hands the model was so big. "Could you please bring the 'clipper'," he asked.

Margaret picked up the sailing ship and followed Graham upstairs and out to the front veranda. As she went up the stairs behind him, she wondered if she should make another suggestion to share a bath but then shook her head.

No, I don't want to risk getting him into trouble, she told herself. But she had to admit that she was sharply disappointed. That notion led her to feeling ashamed of herself and wondering just what sort of person she really was.

Once the two model ships were safely stowed in the shipyards beside his worktable, Graham turned to her and looked her earnestly in the eyes. "You have a bath first. I will work on the models. Then I will have a bath. That will remove temptation and also save us from being teased by Kylie," he said.

"Oh, she won't find out. I wouldn't tell," Margaret replied.

Graham laughed and shook his head. "Yes, she would. We would get caught or something. Now off you go and don't be long."

Margaret could only nod. The sudden thudding of her heart sounded so loud she was sure he could hear it. Once in the bathroom she undressed, all the while wishing that Graham was there with her. When she was finished, she returned to the front veranda. Graham was busily repairing the broken rigging.

"Your turn now," Margaret told him.

He nodded and left her to it. To fill in time, Margaret lay back on his bed and began to spin lovely daydreams of romance and adventure. She fantasised that she was a princess and that Graham was the handsome prince come to rescue her. And then she changed it.

I don't want to be a useless weak person. I will rescue him instead.

She pictured herself picking up a sword and deflecting the Black Knight's descending axe just in time...

It was the sound of voices that woke Margaret. She sat up and looked around, then realised where she was. *They are home. Where is Graham?* she wondered. She did not remember hearing a car. Quickly she sat up and hurried through the house to the back stairs. She stopped at the bathroom door to listen. There was no sound from inside. Tentatively she knocked.

"Graham, are you still in there?" she called softly.

"Yes," was the muffled reply.

"You'd better get out. Your mum and Kylie are home."

Suddenly Kylie appeared at the bottom of the steps. Margaret saw her eyes widen in surprise even as she noted that her arm was bandaged differently. All Margaret could do was shake her head in a silent plea to her friend not to say anything.

Kylie gave her an odd look, a half-smile on her face. "Hello Margaret. Where's Mister Wonderful?" she asked.

"Hi Kylie. How is Skip?" Margaret said, quickly changing the subject.

"Bruised and scratched and very sore but otherwise fine," Kylie said as she started up the stairs. There was a pause as the two girls met, then Kylie said, "Have you and Graham been in the bath together?"

"No!" Margaret replied in instant denial.

She regretted this immediately as she knew it made her sound guilty and she was also aware that she was blushing as images from her naughty thoughts swirled in her mind.

"Look at the colour of you! You have so," Kylie cried, her eyes twinkling with excitement.

Margaret felt hurt at not being believed. "We haven't, truly. Please don't say that. I don't want your mum to hear and Graham get into trouble," she pleaded.

Kylie glanced back down the steps to where sounds indicated her mother was closing car doors. Turning back to Margaret, she nodded. "Okay. It's just that you look so guilty, that's all."

"Well we didn't," Margaret insisted.

"But you wanted to," Kylie added shrewdly.

A denial sprang to Margaret's lips but the idea of lying about something so obvious and fundamental seemed to choke her up, so she changed the shake to a nod. Gulping for air as though she had run a race she said, "Yes."

At that moment, Margaret saw Mrs Kirk arrive at the bottom of the back steps. To Margaret's relief she turned the other way and went into the laundry. Margaret flamed with embarrassment but curiously did not feel ashamed. She said, "Oh please Kylie, we didn't do anything. Please don't say anything. I don't want Graham to get into trouble."

Kylie's face split into a mischievous grin. "Oh Margaret! It will be you who will get into trouble."

Margaret blushed fiercely. To change the subject, she said, "What did the doctor say?"

"I will be fine," Kylie answered.

At that moment, Graham emerged fully dressed from the bathroom. He glanced towards them and said, "Well Ki, how are your fang marks?"

Kylie showed him her bandages and antiseptic daubed scratches. "The doctor says I will be okay," she replied.

"Not without brain surgery," Graham replied. Then he turned and walked into the kitchen. Margaret heard him ask his mother about Skip and then saw him make his way downstairs.

"Let's go and see Skip," Margaret suggested.

"No. Let Graham be for a while," Kylie said. "Come and talk to Mum and tell her about the models."

So Margaret did that, her heart hammering with guilt. It took an effort to act cool and relaxed, while hoping Mrs Kirk didn't notice her damp hair or fresh appearance. If she did, she said nothing and after afternoon tea was served and taken Margaret relaxed.

Only when it was time for Margaret to leave did she relent and whisper to him, "It's alright. Kylie knows we didn't do anything."

"What made you say that?" Graham asked.

Margaret had to bite her lip and could not stop a blush mottling her neck and cheeks. "She saw me at the door and asked. Sorry, she knows we both had separate baths but don't worry."

Relief and annoyance mingled on Graham's face. "Oh bugger! Now she will trot it out and hold it over me every time we have an argument for years," he muttered.

"So don't argue with her. She is the most wonderful sister, and you should be grateful," Margaret said.

She then said goodbye to Alex and Mrs Kirk, who was on the telephone to the City Council complaining about Brute. After that she had a look at a sick looking Skip who lay snoozing in a comfortable box, then walked with Kylie to the front to get her bike.

"See you tomorrow then at school," she said.

"Yes, at school," Kylie answered without enthusiasm.

Chapter 16

PIGS MIGHT FLY

Kylie lay awake far into the night. Partly she was feeling her wounds and reliving those terrifying minutes. After a restless night, tossing and turning half awake and very aware of the itching pains of her bites, wounds and scratches, she woke feeling washed out and sore.

Maybe I should stay home sick? she wondered. But then rejected that idea. *No, then Mum will have to stay home to look after me.*

Angry shouting in the side yard broke into her thoughts and she hurried to see what was happening. But before she could look out, she heard her mother calling angrily, "Alex! Graham! Stop that you boys and come upstairs."

Mr Flawse's voice came clearly to Kylie. "And you keep out of my yard, or I will have you prosecuted for trespass!" he shouted. "You are just spoilt little troublemakers."

Alex began an insulting retort but was cut short by his mother. Kylie looked out and watched the two boys, both in their school clothes, reluctantly turning away from facing an angry Mr Flawse.

As the boys came up the back stairs, Kylie joined them. Her mother was angry and demanded to know what was going on. Alex did the talking, shrugging and saying, "Just a bit of psychological warfare and letting that mongrel Flawse know that we have reported his dog to the council again."

"Psychological warfare indeed! Stop stirring the situation up!" Mrs Kirk snapped. "There is enough unpleasantness now without you making it worse."

"Yes Mum," both boys answered, but Kylie could see that they did not really mean it.

Seeing her mother so upset and angry decided Kylie. *I won't stress her anymore. I will say I am fine and go to school.*

So she did. It was a decision she several times regretted because she really did feel sick for much of the time, but she coped. Talking to her friends helped but she also spent a lot of time fretting about how Skip was. She had seen her briefly before coming to school and Skip had looked very feeble and miserable, merely looking up with big brown eyes and giving her tail a listless wag.

So as soon a school was over, Kylie hurried home. She was first there and instantly regretted it as she found both Mr Flawse and Mrs Flawse in their back yard. As Kylie walked past to where Skip had her basket under the back of the house, Mrs Flawse hissed, causing Kylie's hair to stand up in sudden fright. She felt her skin come out in goose bumps. But she managed to keep control and not turn her head.

I am home alone, she told herself. *I don't want any trouble.*

But Mrs Flawse snarled some swear words and then added, "You will regret giving us trouble, you spoilt little minx!"

The threat made Kylie feel as though someone had suddenly gripped her heart with a cold hand and she hurried in under the house to get out of their sight. *I hope Skip is safe,* she worried.

Skip was. And she seemed much better. This time she lifted her head and panted, and her tail wagged enthusiastically. Kylie's spirits at once rose and she knelt to pat Skip. Skip struggled to her feet and Kylie very gingerly stroked her but remembering the bites and bruises she must have she did not try to pick her up. Skip seemed content with that and after a time lay down again.

Kylie went upstairs to get Skip some 'chewies' and then changed her drinking water. By then Graham was home and she heard him also endure a gauntlet of threats and insults from the Flawses. To her relief, he did not respond but once he had placed his bike under the house and joined her, he said, "I see the Wicked Witch and the Troll are in fine form."

"They made threats, saying we would be sorry," Kylie said, stroking Skip gently as she did so.

"Threats! What sort of threats?" Graham asked.

"They didn't say. They just said we would regret having complained to the council," Kylie said.

"They'd better not do anything to Skip, or it will be them that have regrets," Graham vowed. He then looked around and said, "Anyway, I doubt if the council will do anything. They didn't last time."

But no sooner had the two gone upstairs to get afternoon tea than a knock at the front door revealed a council official. He showed his ID and then said, "Are you the people who made the complaint about a dog?"

"Yes, we are," Kylie answered. Holding up her bandaged left arm she said, "The dog attacked me and in our own yard."

"Did you see a doctor?" the man asked, making notes on his clipboard.

"Yes," Kylie replied, naming the doctor.

Graham now spoke, saying, "I hope you are going to do something. This is the third time that mongrel has attacked Kylie."

"Third time? I only have a record of one other attack."

Graham explained when Kylie had been attacked and the man wrote notes in his notebook. But then he said, "That first incident wasn't reported."

"But it happened. What are you going to do?"

"Well, I'm not sure. There is no dog registered as being owned by the people next door."

"But they have got a dog; a bloody great black mongrel named Brute," Graham said.

The council official looked puzzled. "Well, I have just come from there and they assured me they do not have a dog and they let me look around. There is no dog there."

"They are lying!" Graham cried angrily.

Kylie was shocked. She said, "But there is a dog, a big, savage dog. It bit me and mauled me three times."

The official looked puzzled. "Is there an adult here I can speak to?" he asked.

Both shook their heads. Kylie answered, "Mum works. She won't be home until after five."

"I need to speak to her. Where does she work?" the official asked.

Kylie told him and he wrote it down then left, leaving two unhappy children standing at the top of the steps.

Graham looked across towards the Flawse's and then said, "So Brute is not there. I wonder what they have done with the mongrel?"

"Hidden him probably. You shouldn't have told them that we had complained," Kylie said.

She joined Graham at the door and also looked next door. As she did, she saw Mrs Flawse's face at a window and when Mrs Flawse smirked it made Kylie's emotions boil. *She thinks she has won,* Kylie thought, even more sure that Brute had been hidden somewhere. Knowing that they had been outsmarted hurt her more than she cared to admit.

To take their mind off this, she insisted they have afternoon tea and then urged Graham to start repairs on his models. She got him busy cutting away all the pieces of cotton rigging with a razor sharp, craft knife. To keep him focused, she sat beside him and worked at making new oars for the model Spanish galley. Thus, by the time their mother came home, the galley was back downstairs and as good as new. Even the *Victory* had its new topmast lashed in position and a start made in re-rigging the topgallant mast and the yardarms for the topsail and topgallant sail.

As soon as Mrs Kirk was home, Kylie rushed to tell her the news and to find out if the council official had spoken to her. Mrs Kirk shook her head and said she had been out of the office most of the afternoon.

"He might contact me tomorrow," she said.

On hearing that Kylie became even more dejected. She had a feeling that the complaint might not succeed and that annoyed her. She went to bed feeling both sick and depressed.

Next morning, Skip was much better and was up running around when Kylie got out of bed. That cheered her up a lot and she went to school in a much happier frame of mind. School was much happier as well and she and Margaret did a lot of giggling over the memory of Mr Flawse hurting himself.

After school Margaret asked if she could come over. Kylie nodded. "Yes, of course you can. You can help me repair some of my models," she said.

"And feed the pets," Margaret replied, adding, "I will go home first and ask Mum."

"Okay, see you there," Kylie replied.

Kylie walked home. As she turned into her own street, she noted three people standing at the top of the front steps of her house. *Who are they? And what on earth are they doing?* she wondered.

The sight of arms moving upwards and then a small white object floating down had her puzzled. It was only when she got closer that she saw it was Alex, Graham and the boy with the glasses, Stephen, and they were tossing a toy parachute into the air.

Kylie lost interest until she reached the front gate. As she opened it, Graham ran past on his way back up the steps from picking up the parachute he had just thrown. "G'day Kylie," he called.

Kylie opened her mouth to reply and then stopped, open mouthed.

Alex had a much bigger toy parachute, and he was tying the shrouds to one of the guinea pigs!

"Alex! Don't you dare!" she shrieked, recognising young Spike as the guinea pig.

Alex sneered. "He won't mind. Hold him still Steve," he replied.

"Alex, please!" Kylie cried, hurrying up the front steps.

"Why not? It will give him a thrill," Alex answered.

Kylie was appalled. "But I read that guinea pigs have really weak hearts and bad fright can give them a heart attack and kill them."

"Oh poop!" Alex replied. He took the parachute from Stephen.

Kylie was desperate by this, and she pushed at Graham. "Stop it, Alex! Graham, don't let him. Stop it!" She reached past Graham.

Before Kylie's hand could close, Alex threw the guinea pig into the air. Kylie came to a stop, sick with anxiety. She watched the fluttering bundle rise up almost as high as the electricity wires leading in from nearby pole. The guinea pig squirmed and twisted and the parachute flapped and fluttered. Then the bundle reached its highest point and began falling.

"Oh no! The parachute isn't going to open!" she shrieked.

But it did, just in time. The white cloth opened with a loud flap a metre from the grass and the guinea pig landed safely on the lawn. Kylie sighed with relief, then realised that Alex was going to try again as he started down the stairs. To forestall him, she cast her school bag over the other side and ran back down the steps. Alex shoved Graham aside and dashed after her.

She reached the guinea pig first and reached down to scoop him up. Spike was huddled in a shivering ball, half tangled in the strings and cloth. As she did, Alex pushed her and she missed, tumbling onto the lawn beside the bundle. As she fell, she cried out in pain, emotional rather than physical. She also noted a very large model aeroplane standing on the lawn near the garden beds.

"Alex! Don't be a bully," she cried angrily as she rolled over and struggled to her feet, hotly aware that her skirt had flown up and shown Stephen her knickers.

Alex just laughed and picked Spike up. "He'll be right. He enjoyed it, didn't you boy?" he said. He held the guinea pig up near his face and laughed.

Kylie tried to step in and stop him, but Alex fended her off and made his way back to the steps. Kylie shook her head and felt both angry and ill. "Alex, don't be cruel," she said. "Please don't."

Alex made his way back up the steps and laughed again. "He needs to do three jumps at least if he is to qualify for his parachute wings."

Such a selfish attitude really annoyed Kylie and she hurried after him, determined to stop him throwing the guinea pig up again. To Kylie's disappointment, Graham made no attempt to stop Alex. But he did offer words of caution.

"You nearly hit the electricity wires that time Alex," he said.

Alex laughed and said, "Fzzz. Frazzle… zap! Exit one guinea pig."

"Roast pig," Stephen added.

Kylie was appalled. She was even more disgusted when Alex said, "We could eat him for afternoon tea then. Didn't the Incas in Peru eat fried guinea pigs?"

Stephen nodded. "They still do, I think," he said.

"Alex, please!" Kylie pleaded, pushing past Graham again.

But Alex ignored her and leaned over the railing to toss the guinea pig high into the air again. Kylie could only watch with apprehensive disgust as he did. This time Alex heeded the wires and threw the guinea pig further away. To Kylie's relief, the parachute opened even before Spike had reached the top of the throw. He floated down, his body hanging quite still.

He is either dead or scared stiff, Kylie thought.

This time she acted faster. Even before Spike had landed, she had turned and scuttled back down the steps.

But she was still not fast enough. As soon as Spike landed his legs began moving, reminding Kylie of how cartoon character's legs rotated in a blur, like in *The Flintstones*. Spike dashed away, trailing the parachute behind him. The nearest cover was the large model aeroplane and to Kylie's astonishment he scampered across to it and then squirmed in through an open door in the side of the fuselage.

Kylie crouched beside the model and peered in the door. This was mostly stuffed with parachute and cords but through small windows she saw movement. Then Spike's head appeared behind the plastic windows of the cockpit. The guinea pig peered up at her and then looked down and began to explore the interior of the model. Only then did Kylie pay it much attention. She saw that it was at least a metre long and that the wingspan was even bigger. It was painted a dark green on top and a pale blue underneath and had black crosses with white edging painted on the wings and the sides of the fuselage.

Having two brothers who read war stories and who watched war movies gave Kylie sufficient knowledge to recognise the markings as World War 2 German, and a glance at the swastika on the tail fin confirmed that. The model appeared to have three motors, one at the front of the fuselage and one on the leading edge of each wing.

Stephen joined her. "It's a model of a German Junkers 52 transport plane," he said, kneeling beside her and looking in at Spike.

Kylie's initial reaction was dislike. She sniffed and went to look away, but Stephen said, "I made it. It flies really well."

"Oh yeah? Well get my guinea pig out and don't hurt him," Kylie replied as coldly as she could.

But how? Stephen pulled gently at the end of the parachute but Spike would not budge, and when they heard his claws scrabbling to get a grip Stephen stopped pulling. "I don't want to wreck the model. It is only made of balsa wood."

"Take him back to his cage and I will try to tempt him out with a piece of pumpkin," Kylie said.

Alex at once bent and picked the model aircraft up. "Come on little pig. Let's go for a fly," he said.

Kylie also stood up and her anxiety once again went up. "Alex, be careful. He might jump out."

Alex laughed. "So what? He's got a parachute."

The boys thought that very funny and Alex proceeded to fly the model by moving it up and down and even did a circle and then some diving and climbing. He ignored Kylie's protests, and she was even more annoyed when Graham said, "He is in the right plane if he is a paratrooper. They were JU 52s that the Germans used for parachute drops."

But she had no choice but to run upstairs to get some pumpkin. She also tore off a leaf of lettuce, just in case the pumpkin did not work. She came down the back stairs just in time to see Alex with his right arm back, obviously intending to throw the model aircraft.

"No Alex! Don't!" she cried.

Alex fended her off with his left arm and yelled, "Let's see if pigs can fly!"

Chapter 17

SPIKE OR SNOOPY?

To Kylie's horror and annoyance, Alex ignored her and threw the model plane. Heart in mouth Kylie watched it as it first flew downwards, then zoomed up in a gentle climb. As it lost speed the model also lost lift until it stalled. The nose dropped sharply and the model plane went into a steep dive. Kylie gasped, but at the last second the aircraft levelled out and swooped upwards, only to stall again ten metres further along the back yard. But now it was only half a metre off the grass and it dropped and came to an abrupt stop, standing on its nose and wheels.

They all ran forward, Stephen anxious about his model and Kylie and Graham anxious about the guinea pig. To her relief, he appeared to be uninjured, his dark little eyes shining at her through the windows, his nose and whiskers twitching with apparent curiosity.

"Come out, Spike. Come out, little boy," she called, holding the pumpkin and lettuce where he could see them.

But he wouldn't. They all tried but finally Kylie said, "All you boys go away. I will move him to near his cage and then he might come out when there isn't such a crowd. Now, where is Skip?"

"Tied up," Graham answered.

"That's something at least," Kylie said. "Now, you boys go away."

To her surprise and relief they did. Very gingerly she picked up the model aircraft, surprised at how light it was for its size. She then walked around to the guinea pig pen at the back of the house. As she carried the plane she kept one hand over the doorway, just in case. But she noted that Spike was still looking around with apparent curiosity.

I hope he hasn't been hurt, she thought.

Spike did not appear to have suffered any harm when he emerged five minutes later. Kylie placed the model on the grass a couple of paces from the pen, where Spike could see the other guinea pigs. Then she gently teased the parachute back out and lightly pulled until Spike's nose appeared. He then sniffed at the lettuce and happily jumped out and began nibbling at it.

Kylie took hold of him and was apparently ignored while he ate. Carefully she untied the strings and tossed the parachute aside. That done she lifted Spike and his piece of lettuce and put him back in his cage. The other guinea pigs scuttled in to join in the feast. This led to a chase and a tussle.

"Oh, good manners little pigs! Share!" Kylie cried, noting with dismay how Toffee leapt up and abandoned her babies to join in.

At that moment, Margaret arrived. She watched for a while, then gestured to the model aircraft. "Whose is that?"

"Some rude boy in Graham's class called Stephen," Kylie explained.

"He will be the one with the glasses," Margaret said. "I tried coming in the front door but there were about four of five boys there and they told me to go away."

That annoyed Kylie. "I'm a bit disappointed by Graham. He could have helped me try to stop it all," she said, explaining what had happened.

"Peer pressure," Margaret commented sagely.

"Weak and cruel I call it," Kylie snapped.

She left the model aircraft where it was and led Margaret up to the kitchen for afternoon tea. Later the girls made their way to her room, and they talked and listened to music, the sounds of the boy's raucous laughter and crude jokes drifting in to irritate and annoy. It was obvious that more boys had arrived, and Kylie had no intention of joining them. A glance showed her that Andrew Collins was there, but also several of Alex's rougher and older friends.

Kylie was even more annoyed the following afternoon after lunch to find another similar gathering of boys, one of whom was Stephen. To add to Kylie's annoyance and concern, he had once again brought his large aircraft model. Being a Saturday, the group had gathered and begun to play rough boy's games: tiggy, which quickly degenerated into 'Red Rover'; and then 'Moriarty' (with rolled up newspapers and blindfolds).

To add to her irritation was the discovery of another dog in the Flawse's yard. While the boys were rushing up and down the side yard, with Skip yapping and barking with them, a large Alsatian had appeared at the Flawse's fence and started snarling and barking. The noise drew Mr and Mrs Flawse out to see what the cause was.

Kylie had only just poked her head out of her window when yet another incident began. Mrs Flawse shouted angrily for the boys to 'cut that racket or I will phone the police,' and Mr Flawse had yelled angrily for the boys to stop teasing and provoking his dog.

Alex at once shouted back, "Mind yer own business."

This led to more abuse from both Flawses. Alex retorted by jeering and calling the Alsatian a 'piddling poodle'. But as Mr and Mrs Flawse began shouting angry threats, Mrs Kirk appeared and told Alex to stop. Alex reluctantly turned away, but not before yelling, "I hope that mangy looking mutt is registered with the council!"

In reply, Mr Flawse glowered and yelled, "You'll get yours boy!"

Kylie saw Mrs Flawse glaring at her, so she poked her tongue at her and withdrew to her room. Here she read magazine stories, mended models, and listened to music, all the while wishing some of her friends would come over.

Or maybe I could go to visit them?

Then she heard Alex call, "Bring your plane Steve, and we will show them how well Snoopy can fly."

Oh no! she thought. *They are going to frighten poor little Spike again.*

She put her book down and hurried down the back steps, just in time to see Stephen placing his model on the back lawn near the guinea pig cage. There were six boys there she counted: Alex, Graham, Stephen, and three of Alex's Year 10 friends.

"Alex, don't please," she called as she hurried across the lawn.

"Go away, Kylie!" Alex retorted. "We won't hurt him. We are just playing. We aren't going to do any more parachute drops."

He leaned into the cage and caught Spike. Spike, being a thoroughly tame pet allowed himself to be picked up and stroked.

Skip now began barking and jumping up towards Spike. Alex held Spike higher and said, "Skip, go away! Graham, grab her and tie her up."

"She's just jealous," Kylie said, trying to reach out for Spike without causing a tussle which could hurt him.

"I know that!" Alex sneered. "Now tie her up."

Kylie did not want to, hoping that would stop Alex, but Graham moved to do so. She protested, but to no avail. Alex then said, "Righto you mob, all move back and we will see if Snoopy goes to his plane."

"His name is Spike, not Snoopy. He's a guinea pig, not a beagle," Kylie argued, standing her ground.

"If I say it is Snoopy, then Snoopy it is," Alex said.

He then ignored Kylie and, after checking that Graham had Skip, and that the others had moved back, he bent and placed Spike on the grass. Kylie was hoping Spike would not move, or that he would run away but, to her dismay and amazement, he stood quivering and looking around for a few moments, then dashed across to the open door of the model aircraft and climbed inside.

"See!" Alex crowed. "He is Snoopy, and he likes flying. Snoopy, the world's only flying pig!"

That got Kylie angry. "You are the pig! Stop being cruel, Alex."

Alex was stung but the anger just made him stubborn. "Don't call me names little sister. We are just having some fun."

"Fun! The poor little thing must be scared stiff," Kylie cried. She was close to tears now but could only think of running to tell her mother as a means of stopping Alex. Clearly Graham was not going to.

"He's not scared!" Alex jeered. "He likes it. Look!"

Alex picked up the plane and, after peering in at Spike, began walking around pretending the aircraft was flying. As he did, he made aero engine noises and made the model swoop gently up and down. Then he gave the model a gentle toss. Kylie felt tears prickle as she watched anxiously. But the model just swooped down and landed gently five metres away. It did not even tip up on its nose. Spike could still be seen in the cockpit, peering out through the windows.

The boys cheered and called on Alex to do it again. Alex picked the model up, ignoring Kylie's pleas to stop. This time he threw the model hard and high. Again Kylie watched with beating heart. But once again the model flew well. It climbed, then went into a long, gentle glide that ended right near the side fence.

This brought a frenzy of snarling and barking from the Alsatian, but Alex just walked over and kicked at the fence. "Shut up yer mongrel!" he shouted.

Kylie looked around, fearing another bout of unpleasantness but there was no sign of either Flawse.

One of Alex's friends now called out, "That was great, Alex. But you need more height. I reckon it would go the whole length of the yard if you were higher."

"Off the roof," suggested another boy, a loutish looking lad Kylie thought was named Howard.

Kylie was appalled at the suggestions and then dismayed when Alex nodded and agreed. "I will get up on the roof of the back steps," he said.

He passed the model to Stephen as he walked in that direction. Now Kylie was in tears and her begging just seemed to make Alex angrier and more determined. Graham looked upset but still did nothing.

The back stairs came down sideways facing down onto the side lawn. They led down from the passageway outside the toilet and bathroom with the kitchen on the left and Alex's room on the right. A corrugated iron roof ran down above them, held up by a timber framework. It was the work of seconds for Alex to climb onto the railings and then up onto the roof. It was something the boys often did, particularly when playing hide and seek. Alex then told Stephen to pass the model up.

Again Kylie pleaded with him to stop, her fingers itching to grab the model but not daring to in case Spike got injured in the resulting tussle.

If Mum is in the kitchen she must hear this, she thought.

But her mother did not appear and Alex stood up, then threw the model plane back along the side yard. Kylie again watched in a turmoil of apprehension. But the prediction had been correct, the model flew straight and well and glided for about twenty metres. It landed with a bump that threw it up on its nose, but Spike did not appear and Stephen rushed to it and picked it up.

"He's okay," Stephen called.

"Bring him here. That was really good," Alex called.

Again Kylie pleaded for Stephen not to but was ignored. Stephen passed the model up and Kylie could only wail, "Oh Graham! How could you? Stop him, please."

Graham looked embarrassed and said, "What happens of the guinea pig moves and shifts the balance? The plane could really crash then. Don't Alex."

Graham stepped forward and Kylie called, "Stop him, Graham!"

Alex just sneered and snapped at Graham, "You try you little wart and I'll thump ya!" He then started walking up the covered roof. To her dismay, Kylie heard him say, "I will try from the roof. That should really get some distance. We can go for a long distance, flying record."

The roof was out of bounds according to both parents. That knowledge, plus the fear of what might happen to Spike, now sent Kylie racing upstairs. *I must stop this,* she thought.

"Mum! Mum!" she yelled. She was crying now and on the edge of becoming hysterical. "Mum! Mum, Alex is on the roof, and he is going to throw Spike off!"

To her relief, she heard her mother's voice. It was out the front. Kylie dashed through the house and met her mother as she came up the front steps, gardening gloves and secateurs explaining why she hadn't heard the earlier ruckus. "What's wrong dear?"

"Alex!" Kylie gasped. "He's on the roof with Spike in that model airplane and he's going to throw it."

Mrs Kirk shook her head and muttered something about children and then began hurrying through the house. Kylie turned and ran ahead of her. She reached the back steps just as a shout from the boys told her she was too late. All she could do was scamper down the steps and look out.

Into view came the model, gliding smoothly down across the side yard. *Oh, I hope it lands safely!* she thought.

But even as she thought this the model banked sharply, whether from a gust of wind or from Spike shifting the balance she never knew, and it swerved towards the Flawse's yard.

"Oh no!" she cried, this time hoping it would crash into the fence.

But it didn't. In a mesmerising slow motion the model aircraft lifted slightly and skimmed over the top of the paling fence with centimetres to spare.

Then it crash-landed into the Flawse's vegetable gardens.

Chapter 18

SKIP THE IMP

Margaret ran around the side of the Kirk's house just as the model aircraft flew over the fence. Two minutes earlier she had ridden past the vehicle gate and seen Alex on the roof and the boys on the side yard. She had then heard Kylie's cries for her mum and had seen Mrs Kirk go hurrying up the front steps. By then Margaret was at the front gate. She had opened it and pushed her bike through, then tossed it onto the front lawn and run to see what was going on.

As she ran along the side yard, she saw Graham dash across the lawn and then vault up so that he landed across the pointed wooden pickets on his front. Seeing that caused Margaret to dry out in dismay, sure that he would be impaled but before her amazed eyes he flicked his legs up and over, pushing with his hands so that he landed on his feet in the Flawse's garden.

Oh, I hope he isn't hurt, she thought. This was immediately replaced by worry about Brute. Then she shook her head. *No, Kylie said that Brute was gone.* But just as she thought this, she heard the bark of a savage dog.

Her heart leapt into her throat. Anxiously she watched as Graham jumped across a vegetable garden and then bent to pick up the large model aircraft. She saw him glance over his shoulder, then hurl the model as hard as he could. It flew back over the fence into the Kirk's yard, crashing heavily on one wing and cartwheeling along the lawn. But Margaret had no eyes for the model aircraft. Her attention was focused on Graham as he jumped back over the vegetables and dashed to the fence. The sound of loud barking indicated that a large dog must be close on his heels.

Once again, Graham sprang front first onto the fence then used his arms and a flick of his legs to vault across. His feet just cleared the top of the fence as the snapping jaws of a large Alsatian appeared just near them. The dog's jaws snapped shut, just missing Graham's right ankle. He landed on his feet and turned to let out an exultant whoop.

"Beat you, you mangy mongrel!" he cried.

By then Margaret had reached him and Mrs Kirk had come down

the back steps. Margaret was upset at the risk. "Graham, that was silly, taking a risk like that just for a silly model," she said.

Graham grinned and looked at her in puzzlement. Then he shook his head. "I wasn't trying to save the model. Spike is in it. I was saving him."

"Spike?" Margaret asked, glancing towards the model.

She was distracted by noting that Graham's shirt was torn and that there was blood showing on his chest. Then she noted that Kylie had dashed to the model and had pushed a boy aside so she could get at it. To add to the scene, the Alsatian was now standing up on its hind legs and barking furiously. It appeared to Margaret that it could leap over the fence at any moment. Worse still, both Mr and Mrs Flawse had come out of their back door and were yelling angrily.

Graham pointed to the model aircraft. "Spike is one of the guinea pigs. We have been giving him flights. He is the pilot."

"Guinea pig! Oh Graham, how could you? The poor little thing must be terrified." She turned and hurried across to where Kylie was easing a quivering Spike out of the door on the model.

Mrs Kirk joined them. "Is he alright, Kylie?" she asked.

Kylie held Spike very gently and examined him. "Yes, I think so. He's just had a bad fright."

A boy with glasses and freckles bent down and picked up the model aircraft. "You've broken my plane," he wailed.

"Too bad! Serves you right, Stephen," Kylie snapped.

Margaret saw that one wing was now splintered and half torn off. But she felt no sympathy now that she knew the boys had been using it for such a cruel game.

Kylie turned to Margaret and said, "I'm glad you are here, Margaret. Help me put poor little Spike back in his cage."

Margaret now wanted to see how badly Graham was hurt but his mother moved to do that, so she went with Kylie. As the two girls walked away, an argument began over the fence. Mr Flawse belted the Alsatian around the head and told it to shut up while Mrs Flawse shrieked, "You have been trespassing! Someone has been in my garden."

Graham sneered and scornfully yelled, "Your stupid dog did that."

As the Alsatian was even then jumping around on a bed of lettuces and radish, this was a good answer, but Mrs Flawse just got angrier. She snapped at her husband, "Tie that useless thing up!" Then she turned back and yelled, "You stop annoying my pets, and keep out of our yard or I'll set the dog on you!"

From up on the roof Alex shouted, "And you keep it out of our yard, you old bag!"

Mrs Kirk went red and turned, calling, "Alex, get down off that roof! And don't you get up there again."

"No Mum," Alex replied, adding, "Good, I don't have to clean the leaves out of the gutters anymore."

"Don't you be a smart alec!" Mrs Kirk cried.

Mrs Flawse crowed and called, "Hah, hoh! Bad mannered brats who are cheeky to their own mother! They need a good spanking."

Mr Flawse, still struggling to haul the snarling Alsatian away without trampling more garden beds, added, "Just what you'd expect from such badly brought up and neglected children!"

Margaret saw Graham open his mouth to retort but he caught his mother's eye and closed it again. Mrs Kirk went very red, and Margaret seethed with anger at the injustice of the remark, well knowing how much Mrs Kirk loved her children and how well she looked after them.

At that moment, Mr Flawse let out a loud yelp of pain. Margaret turned from watching Kylie put the guinea pig back in its cage to see Mr Flawse hit at the Alsatian.

"Ouch! Bloody mongrel bit me!" he snarled. He then kicked the animal.

From the roof of the back landing, Alex let out a loud laugh but his mother said, "Alex!" and he did not add whatever he had been going to say. Mrs Kirk then turned and said, "All you children get away from here. Go inside or upstairs or go home. Graham, go and wash those scratches."

There was a general scattering. Some of the boys went to the front and left. These included a sulky Stephen with his broken model. Graham went into the bathroom (to Margaret's disappointment) while Alex and one friend went upstairs. Kylie led Margaret to the back steps and up them. Mrs Kirk came last, followed by unpleasant muttering from the Flawses. She went to fix up Graham's injuries. Margaret wanted to see these and to help but was taken to the Kylie's room instead.

Five minutes later, she saw Graham go past, shirtless and whistling. Margaret called out to him, "Are you alright?"

Graham turned and showed a couple of small scratches on his chest.

"Yeah, of course I am. Just a few scrapes. But Mum's mad about me tearing my shirt."

Margaret was relieved. Graham continued on to the front of the house, then went downstairs. Kylie and Margaret talked until Mrs Kirk called them to come to the kitchen for afternoon tea.

No sooner had they reached the kitchen than knocking came from the front door. Kylie went to see who it was and came back with four more children: Andrew and Carmen Collins plus Moira and Alistair. Seeing Alistair and Moira together really made Margaret feel happy.

Kylie said, "Good. I'm glad you guys have arrived. We need some civilised company here."

Mrs Kirk smiled. "You are just in time for afternoon tea. I have just cooked some pumpkin scones."

Carmen held up her hands and cried, "Oh Mrs Kirk! We didn't come here to eat you out of house and home. We came to see Kylie and her pets."

Mrs Kirk laughed and said, "You are more than welcome. I cooked them for children to eat. You can eat them with butter and honey."

On hearing that Alex came into the corridor. "What about with syrup?"

Mrs Kirk looked fierce. "None for you Alex, not after that disgusting exhibition. You can go to your room and think about not harming animals."

Alex scowled and said, "We were only giving the guinea pig a thrill."

"Terrifying it more like!" Kylie snapped.

Alex shrugged. "It only got a bit of a fright."

Mrs Kirk intervened, "Kylie, stay out of this. Alex, I don't want to see you hurting any animals again. They are all God's creatures, and I don't care how big or small they are."

"Okay, I won't swat any more mosquitoes," Alex retorted.

Mrs Kirk's face suffused with embarrassment and anger. "That is enough cheek! Now go to your room this minute!"

Reluctantly Alex did so. Margaret saw his embarrassed friend say goodbye and quickly leave. The others were all ushered into the kitchen and the story had to be told. Graham heard the voices and came upstairs to investigate. After a snack and a drink of cordial, he and Andrew made their way down to the Ship Room to repair more of the damaged models.

Once again Margaret wanted to follow but she did not want to be teased either, so she stayed and talked to Moira, Alistair, Carmen, and Kylie. The group sat on the front veranda, Moira and Alistair on chairs and Kylie and Margaret on Graham's bed. While they talked Margaret surreptitiously studied Moira and Alistair. *Alistair is trying very hard to impress her,* Margaret decided, noting Alistair's slightly anxious expression and the way his eyes continually flicked towards Moira. But Moira wasn't responding the same way. She smiled often but seemed a little bit tense to Margaret and there was something else she couldn't be sure of.

I wish Graham would treat me that way, she thought. Then she sighed.

A few minutes later Graham and Andrew came up, each carrying a damaged model ship. Graham placed his carefully on his table, wedging it upright with thick books. Then he turned and said, "Make room for me, Maggot."

Margaret poked her tongue and deliberately spread her legs and arms to take up more of the bed. Graham came over and grabbed her legs and tried to drag her off the bed. When this failed because she gripped the bed frame, he let go of her legs and reached forward to grab her wrists. He got her left wrist, but Margaret squirmed and giggled and called on Kylie to help her.

Kylie just laughed and moved aside. Graham leaned over and wrenched her hand loose. In doing so he had to get half on top of her. An impish idea immediately came to Margaret, and she quickly wrapped her legs around his waist, locking her ankles behind his back. Graham grunted and frowned but then tried to grab her other wrist. The moment he broke the grip of her left wrist she grabbed the bed frame with it. That annoyed him and he gripped her right wrist and pulled.

What was apparent to Margaret was that, even though he was annoyed, Graham was being careful not to hurt her. Instead he said, "Let go Margaret or I will tickle you."

"You tickle me, and I will kiss you," she threatened.

Graham's hand at once went to her ribs and she could only squirm and writhe as he touched. "Stop it!" she shrieked, amid muffled giggles. He didn't so she put her threat into action, reaching up to put her arms around his neck and then lifting herself to try to kiss him. Graham stopped tickling and tried to stop her. His reaction amused her even more and she managed to kiss him on the side of the face (rather than on the lips as she had intended).

"Urk! Yuk! Girl germs!" Graham cried, pulling back and wiping his face with his free arm. "Let go Margaret!"

Kylie gave a shrill laugh and said, "Behave yourselves."

Margaret blushed and also saw Graham go bright red. "Kylie!" she muttered accusingly.

"What's this?" Moira asked, obviously amused and curious.

"Kylie, don't you say anything!" Margaret cried.

Kylie nodded. "Okay, but only if Graham lets Margaret sit up."

"I will," Graham instantly agreed.

He let her arm go and tried to move away. Margaret let go with her legs and struggled to a sitting position. She glared at Kylie and blushed some more. Graham went red and Andrew and Carmen both chuckled. Margaret tidied her hair and then, to change the subject, said, "Let's feed the pets."

They did. This took half an hour, fish first, then the birds, next guinea pigs and finally Skip. Skip was still tied up, so Kylie let her free. She immediately ran over to the side fence and began to bark at the Alsatian, which was tied up at the Flawse's back door.

Kylie ran after her. "Naughty Skip! Stop that Skip or you will be tied up again," she scolded.

Skip obviously understood this as she reluctantly retreated, growling and giving a half-hearted bark as she did. To distract Skip Kylie got a tennis ball and organised a throwing game in which she could join in. Half an hour of chasing the ball around the house, with the children trying to hide from her led to a lot of fun and made them all forget the earlier unpleasantness.

Later Margaret watched Moira and Alistair ride off on their bikes. "I hope they fall in love," she said. "They are just made for each other."

"You are just being romantic, Margaret," Carmen said with a laugh.

"I am too. Everyone should have someone to love," she said, glancing at Graham as she said this.

He made a face and muttered about girl germs again and said, "Come on Andrew. Let's repair those ships."

Margaret did not want him to leave but could not think of any ploy to get him to stay. Nor did she want to go home to her own home when the afternoon drew to a close. But she did, her mind filled with romantic hopes and love.

* * *

The following day at church she saw Graham again glancing at several other pretty girls and then he ignored her afterwards. Nor could she visit him during the day as her family went for a picnic with her cousins at the Mulgrave River near Gordonvale.

There was a different type of jealousy on Monday when she spoke to Kylie at school. "Can I come over after school?" she asked.

Kylie shrugged. "If you like, but I have arranged with Emma to take Skip to the park," she answered.

It hurt a bit to think that Emma might be edging her out from the position of being Kylie's best friend. It also hurt to not have her own dog. But she knew it was no good asking her parents again. Every time she had raised the subject over the last year they had said no and pointed out that she had a cat. Margaret sighed. She loved Mischief, but a cat wasn't as much fun as a dog!

After school, Margaret rode home and asked her mother if she could go to the park. Her mother agreed so she had some afternoon tea and then pedalled to the park, aware that her envy was making her anxious and irritable. It was a very nice park. Bounded on four sides by streets and with a line of mango trees around its outer edge it was divided into two distinct parts by a large pond. The pond was only knee deep and was peanut shaped and had been used before by Graham to test some of his model ships. One half of the park was open lawns, and the other half was covered by gardens and trees. Footpaths wound through the gardens and there were seats, many set in semi-secluded alcoves of shrubbery.

Kylie and Emma were there. Both had their dogs. Margaret placed her bike against a nearby tree and went to join them. She noted that both dogs had been let off their leashes and were running free.

"Is that allowed?" she asked.

Kylie shook her head and Emma said, "No, but it will be alright. We have never seen any council workers here."

"Aren't there council dog inspectors who go round and catch dogs that are running loose?" Margaret asked anxiously.

"Dog catchers," Kylie agreed. "They take them to the pound and you have to pay to get them back."

Margaret looked anxiously around but, as Emma had said, there were no council workers in sight. In fact they were the only people visible in the park. She was still a bit uneasy about it but could only decide to keep a sharp lookout. Emma introduced her dog, Thistle. Secretly Margaret thought Skip a much nicer dog, but she made all the right noises and patted Thistle and rumpled her ears. Skip got all jealous at that and began yapping and jumping up, so she had to do the same for her.

For the next twenty minutes the girls played happily, throwing sticks for the dogs to chase, and then running to try to hide from them. In this they were always unsuccessful because the dogs traced them by scent.

"One more go," Emma said. "I will throw this ball and you throw the stick Kylie, and then we run. Ready? One, two, three, throw!"

Margaret was already facing away and as soon as the dogs ran, she dashed off in the opposite direction. This time she went a different way, running fast through one garden bed and then continuing on to a second. Kylie and Emma both followed. Picking a gap in the crotons, Margaret pushed quickly through the wall of shrubbery and found herself on another pathway. Thinking to get even further away she turned and started running.

Ten paces further on, Margaret came to one of the little bays in the garden beds. Under a nice shady tree was a bench seat and sitting on it were a young man in work clothes and a girl in a Trinity Bay State High School uniform. They had their arms around each other and were kissing. Not wanting to be rude, Margaret skidded to a stop and began to turn away. But as she did her eyes met those of the surprised girl. Recognition was instant. It was Moira! Margaret stood and gaped. Then the young man stopped kissing and turned his head and Margaret was even more surprised. It was Corey!

As Kylie came to a panting halt beside her, Margaret saw both Moira and Corey go red and release each other. It was Kylie who spoke first.

"Moira! What are you doing here?"

Neither Moira nor Corey answered, and Margaret had to stifle an embarrassed laugh at the absurdity of Kylie's question. But she was also a bit hurt about Alistair, though resisted asking. By then Emma had joined them, looking from one pair to the other with evident curiosity.

As Margaret struggled to think of something to say that might ease the embarrassment, the two dogs arrived. That changed the situation. "We are giving the dogs some exercise," Margaret explained.

Moira sat up and Skip ran over to her, and she managed a smile and patted her. "Hello Skip. Hello doggy."

This was to Thistle, who had also gone over to her after dropping his ball. Emma said, "He is my dog. His name is Thistle."

"He's very nice," Moira said, ruffling his ears and fur. Then she looked anxiously at Margaret and Kylie. "Please don't tell... don't tell anyone you have seen me here."

Hearing her say that hurt Margaret because it seemed to imply that Moira was being a sneak. *Is she two-timing Alistair?* she wondered. She badly wanted to ask and was tempted to say Alistair's name but didn't. She was also intrigued to notice that both Skip and Thistle had sniffed at Corey but then kept well away from him.

Kylie said to Corey, "She is my dog. Her name is Skip. She is a little imp."

Corey was obviously in a bad mood as he just nodded and said gruffly: "Good."

It was obvious to Margaret that both Corey and Moira wanted them to go away, but Kylie said, "Are you down here for school, Corey?"

Corey shook his head. "Nah. I'm doing a job for dad."

There was another embarrassing silence which Margaret broke by saying, "Oh well, we'd better be going. See you later!"

Only Moira answered. "Bye, and please don't tell," she called.

The three girls and the two dogs hurried back the way they had come. Only when they were out of earshot did Kylie speak. "Well, that was surprise! I wonder how she organised that?" she said.

"And when," Margaret added. It made her sad. "Poor Alistair!" she said.

"What should we do?" Kylie asked.

Margaret sighed. "Mind our own business I guess," she answered.

Emma wanted to know who they were so while the trio made their way back to the more open part of the park Margaret and Kylie told her. She agreed it was up to Moira who else knew about it. Sadly Margaret agreed. She went home later wondering just what had gone wrong between Moira and Alistair.

It's a shame though, I think Alistair is much nicer, she thought. But the whole situation niggled at her as she wondered whether Moira and Alistair had broken up, or whether Moira was two-timing.

To her surprise, she got the chance to ask Moira the next afternoon. Once again, the girls had agreed to take the dogs to the park to play and they found Moira waiting there, her bicycle leaning on a nearby tree.

Margaret blushed but said, "Hi Moira! Are you waiting for someone?"

Moira went very red and looked from one girl to the other. "Yes. For Corey."

"Does your mum know you are here?" Kylie asked.

Margaret thought that was a bit catty but noted Moira blush even redder. Moira shook her head. "No," she replied. "And please don't tell anyone. Corey and I aren't doing anything wrong."

"It looked naughty to me," Kylie said.

That gave Margaret the clue that Kylie did not approve either, so she said, "What about Alistair? I thought you were going out with him."

"We went on a couple of dates," Moira admitted.

There was a tense silence and Moira looked even more uncomfortable. "Oh please! I'm not really two-timing! Alistair and I aren't boyfriend and girlfriend. We haven't sworn to be true to each other or anything."

At that moment, an old blue utility stopped beside the road and Corey got out. He waved to Moira and walked towards them. Margaret could see he was frowning. Luckily, the arrival of Emma and Thistle gave them an excuse to leave. This was spoilt by Thistle. He was already off his leash and went running over and yapped at Corey until he yelled angrily at him to go away.

The girls and dogs withdrew to the other side of the park, Margaret feeling even sorrier for Alistair. Emma obviously felt the same way as she said, "I don't like that Corey. He looks a bit rough to me."

Both Margaret and Kylie made no answer, so they turned their attention to playing with the dogs. Once again both dogs were set free. Skip at once began sniffing in all the garden beds and then started digging up some flowers.

"Skip! Naughty dog! Stop that!" Kylie cried.

She moved to catch Skip. Skip thought that a good game and dodged around and began scampering through the garden beds, sniffing and digging.

Kylie called and pointed, "Margaret, you go that way and I will go the other way. We must catch her before she makes a mess."

Margaret nodded and ran along to her left, very conscious that only a couple of garden beds away were Moira and Corey and they were probably kissing again. *Now where did Skip go?* she wondered. As quietly as she could, she pushed through a gap between two stands of shrubbery and peeked right and left.

What she saw horrified her. Skip was over at the next garden bed and she was digging up some yellow and orange flowers, geraniums, but hurrying towards her from the left was a man in an orange council work shirt and the man was carrying a long pole with a net on it.

Oh no! The dog catcher! Margaret thought.

Chapter 19

SNATCHED

Kylie came hurrying around the end of the garden bed then stopped in surprise. In a single glance she took in the situation and her heart leapt and began to hammer.

The dog catcher, a tubby man in his forties wearing a long-sleeved orange council work shirt and grubby blue shorts, was holding out something in his left hand and calling softly to Skip, saying, "Here nice doggy! Here doggy!"

Kylie began running. As she did, her mind did automatic calculations. She was twenty or thirty paces from Skip and the dog catcher about the same. Skip started to walk towards the dog catcher and was sniffing at whatever it was he held in his left hand. Then he heard Kylie and looked around. The dog catcher raised his net and stepped closer.

Kylie screamed: "Skip! Run!"

But Skip hesitated and began jumping around, looking from one person to the other. The dog catcher stepped closer and held his net ready. Kylie kept running.

Oh no! I will be too late! she thought.

At that moment, Margaret burst out of the bushes only five paces from Skip. She darted forward and reached for Skip, even as the dog catcher swept his net down. Skip began to jump and bark. To Kylie's relief, the net missed, but so did Margaret. Skip obviously thought this a great game. She began yapping and running around excitedly.

"Skip! Come here Skip!" Kylie called.

By now she was only a couple of paces from her and within reach of the dog catcher's net. So was Margaret. Skip dashed around behind Margaret and then towards the dog catcher. This brought her inside the reach of the net, but the pole was too long and the man could not scoop her up. Instead he dropped whatever was in his left hand and reached down to grab her.

To Kylie's dismay, Skip swerved towards the thing the man had dropped. A lure of some sort, she presumed. The dog catcher snatched at her and for a second his fingers gripped Skip's fur. But she was too quick. In a flash she was between his legs and running away, gripping the lure in her mouth.

The dog catcher yelled angrily and spun around to lunge at Skip as she scampered away. "Come here, you bloody mutt!" he shouted.

The pole almost hit Margaret and Kylie had to stop running to avoid it. The dog catcher looked angrily at her and said, "You bring that dog here girlie!" he ordered.

Kylie made no answer but dashed past him and after Skip. The dog catcher began running as well. Skip suddenly turned and vanished through a garden bed on their left. Margaret also turned and crashed her way through some ferns and shrubs. This brought another angry bellow from the dog catcher. Kylie saw a gap in the flower beds and also went left. The dog catcher followed, so close on her heels that she could see his net just out of the corner of her eye.

Oh no! This is terrible! Kylie thought, imagining all sorts of trouble with the law. But she was determined not to stop and felt sure she could outrun the man. *If only he doesn't catch Skip!*

The chase went racing past a surprised Moira and Corey. They had been kissing and sat up so suddenly that Kylie felt like laughing.

"Sorry!" Kylie gasped as she sped past.

Skip had run into another garden bed, obviously determined not to be caught. Kylie and Margaret pushed into the bushes and flower beds, ignoring the angry shouts of the dog catcher as he tried to find a gap. As she ran, Kylie kept calling for Skip, but she ignored her and Kylie realised that calling out was using up valuable breath. So she stopped calling and concentrated on running.

They raced through another gap and Kylie saw that Skip had doubled back and was heading towards the pond and the open part of the park. She also saw that she had no chance of catching Skip if the dog did not want to be caught. Then she saw Thistle. Thistle was racing across the open lawn, yapping and running towards Skip.

Kylie had to use some of her wind to yell. "Emma! Emma! Grab Thistle and put his leash on! The dog catcher is coming," she cried.

The effort winded her but she saw Emma turn a startled face to look towards her. Another glance behind showed that the dog catcher had fallen behind and was now about twenty paces back.

But Thistle had caught up with Skip and the two dogs began snarling and running around in circles, both fighting over the lure in Skip's mouth. That was even worse.

Oh no! Now the dog catcher will catch both! she thought.

Luckily Margaret reached the two dogs first. Without hesitation she scooped Skip up and kept running, ignoring the fact that Thistle was dangling by his teeth and scrabbling against her legs. Emma raced in and grabbed Thistle and held him up, the two girls running side by side. Kylie was close behind by this and could see that neither dog would let go of the lure. After another glance back showed the dog catcher even further behind, she called on the other two girls to slow down.

They did and Kylie reached forward and gripped the lure. It was a piece of cloth and she tore at it. *Must have a scent that dogs find irresistible,* she thought. But the cloth was tough and she began to sob with frustration and anxiety as she tried to rip it. The girls kept running but it was hard to do with them all in a tight group and Kylie feared they might stumble. The dog catcher began catching up, calling loudly for them to stop.

Suddenly, the lure tore in two and they were able to sprint again. Kylie had Skip's leash in her hand, so she now ran along beside Margaret and clipped the snap catch to the collar. Emma just held Thistle and ran. By this time Kylie was starting to run out of breath and that got her panicky.

I'm not fit enough! she thought unhappily.

She gasped, "Emma, you go to the left. Margaret, you get your bike. Meet at my place. Go!"

They did. As the girls split up, the dog catcher let out another angry yell. Kylie glanced back and saw that he was very red in the face and puffing loudly. *He is less fit than us,* she thought. That gave her hope, so she slowed down and kept glancing around to check that her friends were alright.

They were. Emma and Thistle vanished across the road and around the next corner, Thistle now on his leash and scampering happily along. Margaret reached her bicycle and jumped on. In a few seconds she was half the length of the park away and was able to slow down and wait for Kylie. Kylie put Skip down and she ran happily along beside her, snuffling loudly because she still gripped part of the lure in her mouth.

Another glance showed the dog catcher had stopped running. He shouted angrily for her to come back, then turned and began walking back the way he had come. In the far corner of the park, Kylie saw a parked council vehicle and that got her all anxious again.

He might follow me in his vehicle, she thought.

When Margaret joined her, she suggested this. Margaret agreed and suggested she give Kylie a double. They tried this but Kylie found it very uncomfortable and awkward, especially as she tried to hold Skip's leash.

"No good. We will have an accident," she said as the bike wobbled along the side of the road.

At that moment, a police car came around the corner. *Oh no!* Kylie thought in dismay. She felt sure the dog catcher had called them. To her dismay, the police car slowed and pulled up next to them. A young, handsome police officer in his twenties leaned out.

He pointed down and said, "That is unsafe, and it's against the law. You girls stop being silly and stop doubling."

By then Margaret had brought her bike to a wobbling standstill and Kylie sprang down. "Yes officer," she said.

Skip hurried to the car and stood on her hind legs to look at the young policeman. He looked down and then reached out to rumple her ears.

"Good doggy! And it's good to see you girls have him on a leash."

"Her. She's a her," Kylie said, relief washing through her.

As Skip's mouth opened, she took the opportunity to snatch the lure from her mouth and tossed it aside, apparently unnoticed. Skip wagged her tail happily and licked at the policeman's hand.

"Sorry doggy. We can't stay to play. Okay Frank, let's go," the policeman said to his companion. The car accelerated into the traffic and was soon gone.

"Oh phew! I was sure we were done," Kylie said.

"Me too!" Margaret agreed. "But the dog catcher might still catch us. Let's get moving."

The two girls hurried on as fast as Kylie could trot. As soon as they reached the corner, they crossed the street and kept going. Every few paces one or the other glanced back. At every moment Kylie expected the dog catcher's vehicle to appear. By then Kylie was puffed and the pace had to slow to a walk. Even Skip was panting hard, her tongue hanging out and dripping sweat.

To escape from the dog catcher, the girls zig-zagged around several blocks, walking nearly twice the distance they needed to. But they saw no sign of the dog catcher and arrived thankfully at Kylie's.

Once safe inside the yard, Skip was let off her leash. To Kylie's annoyance she immediately dashed to the side fence and returned the snarls and barks which had started coming from the Alsatian. Kylie hurried over and grabbed Skip, clipping on her leash as she did. While she was doing this, the Alsatian stood up on its hind legs and she feared it would spring over the fence and attack her. As it was the big dog's paws were on the top rail and the animals head was level with the tops of the palings.

Kylie led a barking, struggling Skip away and secured her to her post under the house out of sight of the other dog. "Just you calm down Skip. You've caused enough trouble today," she admonished.

Margaret brought Skip fresh water while Kylie got some dog food. The girls then went upstairs. Here they found Graham sitting at his desk. He was busy repairing the rigging of a model ship-of-the-line.

"What was all that barking?" he queried.

Kylie explained. Graham nodded, placed a dob of glue to hold the knot in the cotton, and said, "If Skip and that mongrel Alsatian are going to fight, we might have to tie Skip up when we aren't at home."

Kylie was appalled. "Oh, we can't! That would be cruel," she cried.

But it was what her mother said also, adding that it was the second time the dogs had started to fight at the fence. That made Kylie angrier than she could remember and she fumed at the unfairness of life.

Why do we have to have neighbours like the Flawses? she brooded.

Kylie and Margaret related Skip's narrow escape from the dog catcher to Graham and Alex, but were careful not to let Mrs Kirk know. "We had better not go to the park for a while," Kylie said to Margaret.

So there was no visit to the park the next day, and no walk for Skip either. As before, Skip and the Alsatian immediately started to fight if Skip went into the side yard at all. She had to be tied up while they were at school and then kept upstairs or with them at other times.

* * *

At school on Thursday, Emma joined Margaret and Kylie and asked if they were going to take the dogs to play. "Where?" Kylie asked.

"The park," Emma replied.

"What about the dog catcher?" Kylie said.

Emma snorted and said, "He can't catch us. We will just be more careful."

"Oh, I don't know. Couldn't we go somewhere else?" Kylie said.

"We could, but the park is closest and best. Anyway, I am going. You can come if you like," Emma answered.

After Emma had gone, Kylie said to Margaret, "What do you think?"

Margaret shook her head. "I think you should go somewhere else. But I can't come anyway. Mum said I have to help her clean the storeroom."

So Kylie took Skip for a walk on her own. To begin with she just walked the streets but after half an hour she found herself only two blocks from the park. *I wonder if Emma did go to the park?* she thought.

Curiosity led her to go and look. As soon as Kylie rounded the corner near the open end of the park, she saw Thistle running free out on the lawn. Emma was running after him and laughing. They were playing some sort of chasey game.

Oh, silly girl! Kylie thought. *I hope the dog catcher doesn't come.*

She waited for a gap in the traffic and led Skip across the road, then stopped and ruffled her ears. "Sorry Skip, but you are staying on your leash today," she said.

Emma saw her coming but didn't wait. She threw a tennis ball as hard as she could across the park towards the far side. Kylie looked anxiously in all directions for the dog catcher or his vehicle. But the only vehicle she could see was an old white delivery van parked under a mango tree on the far side of the park. The only other people visible were three small boys throwing things up into another mango tree.

Thistle retrieved the ball and came running back. Skip started to yap and tug at her leash, trying to break loose. Emma saw this and called, "Let her go Kylie. The dog catcher won't catch us."

Kylie badly wanted to and was very tempted but finally she shook her head. "No. Sorry Skip."

"Scaredy cat!" Emma teased, which was what Kylie had feared. She now regretted having come to the park. But rather than argue she looked away.

"What are those boys doing?" she said, noting that one of the small boys was climbing up into the mango tree.

To ease the situation with Emma, she walked towards them. As she got closer, she recognised them. *They are those three little monsters from 3C,* she thought.

When she was about 25 metres from the tree, she realised the boys were trying to knock down a bird's nest. Instant anger flared. "What are you three doing?" she demanded.

The boys looked guilty, then defiant. "Mind your own business," replied one.

Adam, Kylie remembered. *And the other two are Shaun and Troy.* "Don't knock the bird's nest down please."

The boy up the tree, Shaun, called down, "But it's got eggs in it, and we want them."

That idea really upset Kylie and made her angry. "What about the mother bird? She will be very hurt," she said.

"Haw! So what? If I want them then I'm going to have them," Shaun retorted. To show he meant business he began to shake the branch he was kneeling on.

"Oh please don't, Shaun!" Kylie pleaded. By this time she had reached them and stood looking up. The other two boys both looked sulky but also worried.

Not Shaun. His first attempt to shake the branch having failed because it was too thick where he was, he moved out along it, reaching out to grip a second branch to give him better balance.

"I am going to get them," he insisted.

By this time Kylie was almost in tears. She hated bullies and she hated people who harmed innocent and helpless creatures and she was determined. She also knew she must not cry. *If I do, they will jeer and think I am weak,* she told herself.

"Please don't. If you destroy the eggs, there will be no young birds. If enough people do that the species will die out."

"Die out! What crap!" Shaun retorted. He edged a bit further out and again began to shake the branches.

Kylie bit her lip and tried to think of some argument that might soften Shaun's heart. She was now sure that the other two were sorry and would agree but she could also see they were weak and would not go against

Shaun. For a moment she wondered if she could threaten them with Skip. But she knew that idea was ridiculous.

She will just lick them and want to play, she thought. *What about Emma? Maybe she can help?*

She looked around and saw that Emma was looking her way. But at that moment the problem solved itself. There was a loud crack. The lower branch Shaun was standing on had broken. Shaun let out a cry of alarm and Kylie was only just in time to jump back and drag Skip aside as a branch came crashing down, Shaun with it. He landed heavily on his back and lay there.

For a few seconds Kylie feared that Shaun had really hurt himself as he lay on his back gasping, his mouth open and his eyes wide. "Are you alright?" she enquired anxiously.

Shaun made no reply, but his mouth worked and she could see his chest heaving in spasmodic twitches that really worried her. Now she tried to remember her First Aid training from Guides.

I hope he hasn't broken his back or something, she thought. *Maybe I had better call the ambulance.*

Then, to her great relief, Shaun gasped and sucked in air. "J... j... just... w... wind... winded," he croaked. For the next minute he lay and gasped in air. Then he groaned and reached to feel his arm and shoulder. "Ow! I hope I haven't broken something," he groaned.

He hadn't. Kylie badly wanted to say, 'Serves you right' but instead she said, "Adam, you and Troy had better take Shaun home to see that he is alright."

To her relief, they agreed. All she wanted was for them to leave because she had noted that the broken branch was not the one that held the bird's nest. The pair helped a groaning and dizzy Shaun to his feet and the three boys headed off, having apparently forgotten the bird's nest. As they went, Kylie looked up and was pleased to see that the bird's nest was still there, apparently unharmed.

"Good!" she muttered.

At that moment, Emma joined her. "What was that all about Kylie?" she asked.

Kylie explained the incident to her. As she did, she held Skip and then glanced around with a niggling worry. "Emma, where is Thistle?"

Emma pointed back along the park, then gasped. Even as the two girls looked Thistle ran to a thin man who was standing near the white van. The man was bending down and holding something. Having seen the council dog catcher do something like that the previous day Kylie immediately thought 'lure'.

"Emma, that man! He's got a lure."

Emma gasped again, then shrieked, "Thistle. Here boy!"

But she was just too late. As Thistle turned to look back, the man pounced and grabbed him. He then hurried to the white van, glancing towards the girls but ignoring Emma's shouts to let her dog go. Kylie watched in stunned disbelief as the man opened the back and threw Thistle inside. As he slammed the back door, she at last found her voice.

"Hey! Let that dog go!" she yelled.

The man went quickly out of sight around the driver's side of the van and a moment later the van's engine started and it drove off.

Emma screamed and shouted and as the van vanished from sight around the next corner she turned to Kylie and grabbed her.

"Kylie! Kylie! That man. He... he took Thistle! Stop him!"

Chapter 20

RAW EMOTION

Kylie felt stunned. It had all happened so quickly. And it was so unexpected. Emma continued to grip both her upper arms while screaming.

"Kylie! Kylie! That man has taken Thistle! Stop him! Oh do something! Stop him!"

Emma began to sob hysterically, quite unnerving Kylie and making her cry as well. *What can I do?* she wondered, almost frantic with worry. The vehicle was already out of sight.

"We must phone the police," she said.

Emma stared at her. "How? I haven't got a mobile phone."

"Nor have I. Come on, let's go to your place," Kylie replied.

"But we must get after that man!" Emma shrieked.

Now Kylie got a bit annoyed. "He is in car Emma. We need to call the police. Now come on!" she said. She was feeling very fragile but could also see that she had to do something to help Emma.

Emma lived only two blocks away but it still took more than ten minutes to hurry there. Along the way they passed several shops and a petrol station but Kylie rejected the idea of calling the police from them. *Emma needs her mum,* she reasoned, looking around for any sight of the white van. She also kept a very tight grip on Skip's leash.

The resulting scene at Emma's she found very distressing. Emma had a younger brother in Year 3 and a baby sister who looked like she was Year 1 or Preschool. When they understood that their dog was gone, they also dissolved into tears. Kylie joined in. She could not help it and felt the need.

When they calmed down a little Emma's mum said, "This man, did he try to do anything to you?"

"No Mum. He just grabbed Thistle and drove off," Emma replied, her face red and tear stained.

Emma's mother went to the phone and called the police, adding that the man had been watching the girls at the park. *Is that true?* Kylie worried. She had not noticed. Her mother had often warned her about perverts and 'stranger danger', so she now felt a chill of real fear.

After putting the phone down Emma's mother came back and said, "So how did Thistle come to be near this man? What were you doing?"

Emma sniffled and another tear trickled down her cheek. "We... we... sniff. Were. j... j... j... just... sniff... playing with a ball," she said.

"Was Thistle on his leash?" Emma's mother asked.

Emma went even redder and shook her head. "No Mum," she whispered.

At that Emma's mother became very angry. "You silly little girl! How many times have I told you to keep him on his lead?"

Kylie felt very sorry for Emma so she spoke up, hoping to ease some of her mother's anger. "It was my fault Mrs Pearce. If I hadn't gone over to those boys Emma would not have followed me."

"What boys?" Emma's mother demanded to know.

Kylie told the story of the boys and the bird's nest. By the time she finished she was feeling very guilty, sure it had been her fault that Emma was distracted. But Emma's mother shook her head.

"Nonsense! It wasn't your fault, Kylie. If Thistle had been on his leash he would have been with Emma, not dashing all over the park. Where was your dog?"

"On her leash," Kylie whispered, not daring to meet Emma's eyes. She still felt guilty though. *I should have been more aware*, she told herself.

She felt even more guilty and upset after the police arrived. Kylie was surprised and slightly pleased to see that one was the handsome young constable who had spoken to her the previous Tuesday. But the other was a female senior constable with a very severe face and hair pulled tightly back into a bun.

Notebook in hand she said, "Describe this man please."

Kylie and Emma looked at each other. To Kylie's frustration and dismay, she could not form a clear image of the man. "Thin, about twenty or thirty I suppose. Er..."

Emma was even less help. All she could add was that he wore brown long trousers.

"Colour of hair? Colour of eyes? Skin complexion?" the senior constable asked.

Kylie could only shake her head and ask, "What is complexion?"

"His skin, the shade, tone, colour," the senior constable explained.

Kylie felt very ignorant and embarrassed. "Sort of sun-tanned," she said.

"Indigenous?"

"No."

"Did he have a hat? A beard? Anything odd about him?"

The girls could not think of anything, so the senior constable turned her attention to the vehicle. "White van. What make?"

All Kylie could do was shrug. Cars didn't interest her and she had no idea. Nor could Emma say, and she began to sniffle and sob again.

The senior constable pursed her lips to show her opinion and said, "What about the registration number?"

Kylie felt a surge of shame and guilt as she realised it had not even occurred to her to note such a thing. It was obvious that Emma had the same reaction as she had not thought to look and then burst into tears.

"Was there anything about the van?" the young constable asked.

Kylie thought hard, trying to picture the vehicle. "Dirty white, with smears of red mud on it," she said. "It had no side windows but there were two tiny windows on the back. Yes, the back door was double, and one of the little windows had been broken and had grey plastic tape across it."

The young constable noted this and Kylie felt better. Emma stopped sniffling and smiled, and both the senior constable and Emma's mother nodded approval. But that was all she could remember. She was left feeling fairly useless.

Emma still sniffled and wailed, "But why would that man take my dog? Thistle isn't any sort of pedigree. He is just an ordinary mutt. He couldn't sell him."

The senior constable started speaking, "Because, er… well, there have been quite a few dogs stolen recently. We are looking into this and hope to get to the bottom of it quickly."

Kylie noted the way the senior constable hesitated and that worried her. *What is she not saying?* she wondered. Not knowing made her even more anxious.

Emma obviously did not notice this as she looked hopeful and said, "Do you think you will be able to get my dog back?"

"I can't say," the senior constable replied.

Emma's dad arrived home from work at that moment. He was understandably concerned to find a police car outside his house. After he had been told the story he shook his head.

"This is terrible. I have heard about this dog snatching gang. They are suspected of taking them for dog baiting and fights, aren't they?"

The senior constable nodded. Kylie wasn't sure what dog baiting was but she had heard of people making dogs fight. She was appalled. Emma began to sob and wail and that set all the younger children off again. Mr Pearce then realised he should have been more careful what he said. The police then took their leave and drove off.

By this time Kylie was feeling quite battered emotionally. She said, "I had better be going home."

Emma's mother at once said no. "You are not walking, not with that creepy man out there. George will drive you."

Kylie tried to insist she would be alright, but Emma's mother rang her mum. The upshot was that Kylie's mother drove there on her way home from work. While the adults talked Kylie tried to cheer Emma up but had no success. Emma was so distressed she was almost distraught and kept bursting into tears. This would set the younger children off and Emma's mum would have to come and comfort them. Kylie helped by hugging and stroking Emma, but she was feeling very fragile herself.

On the drive home, her mother said, "Well, I think there will be no more afternoon walks with Skip until this horrible business is sorted out."

"Oh Mum!" Kylie cried. "Poor Skip! She needs her exercise."

"She will have to get it running around the yard," her mother replied.

"But Mum, then that horrible Alsatian will keep barking at her and they will fight," Kylie said.

They drove in silence for a couple of minutes. Then Kylie asked a question that had begun to gnaw at her. "Mum, what is dog baiting?" she asked.

Her mother looked very thoughtful, then said, "I think it is when people put two dogs into a ring and then torment them until they fight each other. Like cock fighting," she explained.

Kylie tried to imagine this and was appalled. *How could people do things like that?* she wondered. "Do the dogs get hurt?" she asked. She had seen a TV program showing cock fighting in Southeast Asia and in that the roosters had been terribly injured or killed.

171

Her mother sighed and said, "I think you are too young to talk about things like this."

"Mum! I need to know!" Kylie cried.

"Yes, they do. I think they fight to the death," her mother said.

That disgusted and horrified Kylie. "How could people do that? Why would they do it?" she cried.

Her mother shrugged. "Some do it for money. They bet on which dog will win. I have heard they even mix the type of animals to make it more interesting. But sadly, there are some horrible humans who watch things like that for pleasure."

That appalled and saddened Kylie even more. For a minute or so she tried to imagine this. Then she shook her head in disgust and asked, "What types of animals?"

Her mother clearly did not want to answer but as they parked the car under the house Kylie insisted. So Mrs Kirk said, "I have heard of dogs against cats, and dogs against roosters. I am told that a dog against a lot of rats used to be popular."

"Oh Mum! That is awful!" Kylie cried.

She climbed out, shaking her head, to be immediately confronted with another problem. As soon as Skip hopped out of the car the Alsatian in the Flawse's back yard began barking and lumping up against the fence. Skip responded with furious barking and tried to rush over to fight. It took a real effort for Kylie to hold her. She then had to lead Skip into the laundry and tied her up out of sight.

It was a very sad and worried Kylie who sat at the dinner table that night. She told Alex and Graham what had happened and they were also concerned. That night Kylie did not sleep well. She lay in her bed reliving the incident in the park and wondering what she could have done to prevent it. Guilt made her feel sick and ashamed. There were also fears of bad men sneaking into the house at night. From that thought on every tiny sound caused her to stiffen in fear and she lay rigid for minutes at a time until nothing happened and sleep finally overtook her.

The next day, Friday, usually one of Kylie's more enjoyable days, she found very upsetting. It began after breakfast when her mother insisted that Skip be tied up during the day so that there were no fights with the Alsatian next door. Kylie thought that very unfair and she went to school in a gloomy mood.

At school there was more unhappiness. Emma wasn't there but Kylie told Margaret and her other friends what had happened. They were horrified and anxious. Then Margaret hurt Kylie's feelings by saying, "She should have kept her dog on its leash. I told her that, and after the dog catcher tried to catch Skip you'd think she would have."

Kylie secretly agreed with that, but as Emma wasn't there to defend herself she tried to. That resulted in an argument with Margaret which left both girls eyeing each other unhappily. It also made Kylie glimpse the fact that Margaret was feeling anxious and jealous of Emma.

'Show and Tell' made things worse. It was quite common for kids to bring something to show the class, and these were often pets. This time Brianna had two really cute and fluffy white puppies. The students all 'oohed' and 'aahed' and wanted to pat them but it just made Kylie feel a deeper regret over what had happened to Emma.

Billy did not help. Billy was a typical urchin with a mischievous grin. He put his hand up as the puppies were put back in a cage. "Please Miss, can I show the class my pet?"

The teacher, Miss Wallis, smiled and nodded, distracted by the need to make sure one of the puppies did not escape. Billy quickly left the room and came back in with his school bag. He unzipped it and looked in, then put his hand down inside. "Here it is. It is an... Ow! Bugger! Bloody thing's bit me!"

Miss Wallis frowned. "Billy, don't use language like... eeeek!"

The whole class, Kylie included, jumped with fright as Miss Wallis screamed. Then Kylie (and most of the others) screamed as well. Out of Billy's bag slid a snake.

"Snake! Snake!" thirty voices shrieked.

Kylie was sitting in the front row and the snake flopped onto the carpet only a metre from her and began to slither towards her. In a frightful panic she tried to spring to her feet but was pushed over and fell, other children tripping over her and falling in a struggling heap. Sheer terror impelled Kylie to move and she clawed, kicked and pushed to get free.

Driving Kylie's terror was the fact that she had lost sight of the snake and had no idea how close to her it was. Almost blind with panic she tried to struggle free to get to her feet. A piecing scream of mortal terror spurred her on.

That was Brittany, she thought, wondering if the snake had bitten her.

Finding herself able to stand Kylie scuttled across the classroom. On all sides of her were other students also fleeing. Behind her were more shrieks and screams. One of them was Margaret and Kylie, who had reached the far wall, turned and glanced back. All she could see were scared kids running or climbing up onto desks. Anastasia, the prettiest girl in the class, was standing on a chair and holding her skirt tight around her knees while she screamed and stared with wide-eyed horror at the floor. Miss Wallis was standing over near the door, yelling and waving her arms.

But still Kylie could not see the snake. She paused to get her breath and then saw it. It was slithering in her direction under the desks. Another spasm of panic coursed through her, and she screamed again and began to run, crashing into desks and chairs. This time she fled into the other half of the room where the other Year 6 class was now also all standing and looking frightened. Their teacher, Mr Davis, was moving to see what the drama was.

To add to Kylie's emotional state was the sight of half a dozen boys, all laughing and jumping from desk to desk. Then she saw Billy scrambling along the carpet on hands and knees yelling, "Don't worry. He won't bite you. He's only a green tree snake. Here Greeny! Good boy Greeny!"

Then Aaron tried to scramble over a desk and lost his balance. The desk and Aaron both went down. Aaron let out a wail of fear as he crashed to the carpet. Billy let out a shout of anger.

"Hoy! Watch out! Don't hurt my poor little snake!"

Poor Brianna had also fallen and had her skirt up around her waist. "Pink knickers!" shouted Toby, making her go red with shame as she tried to simultaneously escape and pull her skirt back down.

"Aaah! Got ya, ya slippery little bugger!" shouted Billy. He stood up, his face a mask of triumph and in his right hand the wriggling, writhing snake. He then turned and walked towards a nearly hysterical Miss Wallis and said, "It's alright, Miss, I got him."

"Take it away! Get it away from me!" screamed Miss Wallis. She hastily backed off and so did a dozen others.

Billy laughed. "It's alright Miss. He only eats little frogs and mice and things, not people."

Miss Wallis stared at the snake with eyes wide with fear. "Take it away! Put it in your bag! And get to the office at once!"

"Aw Miss!" Billy complained, obviously not aware of what he had done.

Kylie now had to smile, even though her heart was still hammering and she was almost hyperventilating. She realised that the snake, about a metre long, was actually a thing of great beauty. It was a bright green on top and a bold yellow underneath and her rational mind now told her it really was a harmless tree snake.

Just like the one that scared Margaret at Corwa, she thought.

By now Mr Davis had intervened. He picked up Billy's bag and held it open. "Put the snake in the bag!"

"But sir, some of the kids might like to hold him," Billy replied, stroking the snake and allowing it to slide up his arm and entwine itself around it.

Mr Davis shook the open bag and said in a very determined tone, "Put the snake in the bag Billy!"

"Yes sir." Reluctantly Billy did so. He then zipped it up.

Mr Davis pointed in the direction of the office. "To the principal Billy."

But there was no need for Billy to go. At that moment, Mr Worcester, the principal, arrived at the door, having obviously heard the screams at the office. He listened to Miss Wallis and Mr Davis describing the incident while the students were set to work restoring the room. Kylie stood her chair up and pushed her desk back into place, then helped Margaret pick up her pencils and papers that had been scattered on the carpet.

By then Kylie had calmed down and was starting to feel sorry for Billy. He was a cheeky brat at times but was usually very kindhearted. She and Margaret began to giggle with relief as they recalled the scenes of panic.

Compared to that, the remainder of the day was boring and ordinary. Billy only returned after his parents had been rung and had come to collect the snake. He apologized to Miss Wallis but was obviously still puzzled at what the fuss had been all about.

At dismissal time Miss Wallis said, "In future, do not bring any pets without first checking with me if it is alright."

That led to a great gust of laughter and Kylie went home happy. Once there she took Skip off her leash and led her upstairs. Later she played with Skip on the other side of the house. But that side lawn, the south side, was much narrower and not as nice to play on. It made her resentment at the Flawses return.

Being Friday night Kylie went to Guides. While she was there, she met up with Margaret and they both had a good laugh about the day and enjoyed telling the other guides about it. Later Kylie saw Moira with the Rangers in their room.

She wasn't sure if she wanted to speak to Moira, but Margaret said, "We must ask her if she is going horse riding next weekend."

* * *

The following weekend was a long weekend, and they had a booking at Corwa. Kylie thought for a moment, then said, "Do you still want to?"

Margaret nodded. "Yes, I do. And the boys are doing another hike that will take them there on Saturday night."

Kylie knew that so she nodded. But thinking about Moira with Corey made her feel uncomfortable and she felt embarrassed.

Margaret followed her gaze and then said, "Never mind Moira's love life. At least she has one. Let's find out if she will come. I don't know if Mum will let me go if she isn't there."

That was a compelling argument as Kylie knew she would not be allowed to go on her own and she wanted to go. So the two girls went to speak to Moira. When she saw them coming Moira smiled but Kylie also noted her go red.

She's ashamed, she decided.

"Have you two come to ask about horse riding?" Moira asked.

Margaret answered. "We have. Do you still want to go?"

"I do," Moira answered.

Kylie said, "You just want to see Corey."

Moira smiled. "Yes, I do. And I am seeing him tomorrow night."

Margaret looked surprised. "Do you have a date with him?"

Moira nodded. Kylie felt embarrassed. To change the subject she said, "Whose car are we going in?"

For the next few minutes the girls discussed the details of their planned trip and agreed on times to contact each other and on other details. Then the Guide Leader called all the younger girls together and Kylie and Margaret had to hurry off.

Later Margaret said, "I feel sorry for Alistair. I think he is in love with Moira."

"I agree," Kylie said. "There's something about that Corey that I just don't like."

"You are just jealous," Margaret suggested.

"I am not! Anyway, he's too old for me," Kylie hotly denied.

The girls were saved from an argument by the arrival of Carmen, who gave them rope work to do.

For Kylie it was a long but mostly boring weekend. On Saturday morning she had to do chores with her brothers. In the afternoon the family drove to Mareeba to see their grandmother. They took Skip and were able to take her for a walk. But Kylie also found that there were very few places for dogs. When she suggested they go to Davies Creek or to Emerald Creek for a swim her mother pointed out that dogs were not allowed in National Parks or State Forests. Nor were they allowed off their leashes in almost any park or on beaches.

Saturday night was spent at home watching TV or reading. Graham worked on repairing another model ship and Alex played computer games. From time-to-time Kylie would speculate about Moira and her date with Corey and wonder how she might feel when she was allowed to go on dates.

If some boy will ever ask me! she thought.

Sunday morning was taken up with church and pets. She saw Margaret at church, but she wasn't allowed to come over because she also had chores to do and her family were going to a flower show in Innisfail that afternoon. So during the afternoon Kylie did her homework and played with Skip in the south side yard. But both her brothers had gone out to be with friends and that left Kylie feeling quite lonely and left out.

She was particularly annoyed by the Alsatian next door. Not only did it break into a frenzy of barking every time it saw Skip in the back yard, but it even growled and barked at Kylie or her mother. It also kept jumping up on its hind legs, making Kylie frightened and worried that it might spring over the fence and then attack her.

It was the problem of the Alsatian that led to Skip being tied up under the house again when she went to school on Monday morning. Kylie wanted to protest but she could see that there would be trouble and dog fights all day long if Skip was left free to roam the yard.

It is so unfair! she thought. She determined to take Skip for a walk after school regardless of strange men.

At school she was again reminded of the threat of strange men because Emma was back in class. Kylie saw she looked very tired and down, so she hurried over and said a cheerful hello, then asked, "Have the police found your dog yet?"

"No!" Emma replied, then burst into tears.

Kylie comforted her as best she could but felt both scared and depressed herself. It made for an uncomfortable and gloomy day. Even the story of Billy and his snake did little to cheer Emma up.

After school Kylie hurried home, determined to take Skip for a walk. She walked as quickly as she could. This soon raised a sweat, so she stopped for a minute and took off her pullover. As her school bag was full, she draped it over her back and tied the empty sleeves loosely around her neck. Then she continued walking.

But as she came in the front gate, she heard dogs barking in what sounded like a furious battle. One of the dogs was certainly Skip but the other was the Alsatian and she felt a spasm of alarm.

That sounds like the Alsatian is in our back yard, she thought.

She started running, taking off her school bag as she did. As she ran, she felt a growing sense of alarm when the sounds of the Alsatian changed to snarling and growling and then died away, but Skip kept up a frantic barking. By then she was certain that the Alsatian was definitely at the back of the house, not in the Flawse's yard.

Worry about Skip sent Kylie dashing in under the back of the house. Here she found Skip safe but straining at her leash trying to break free, all the while barking madly.

Oh no! The Alsatian has jumped the fence and is in our yard! Kylie thought, tossing her bag aside and hurrying through the laundry to the back entrance. As she came out into the backyard her eyes were instantly drawn towards savage dog sounds and what she saw made her heart stand still. The Alsatian was inside the guinea pigs cage and was dashing to and fro in an attempt to catch one of the guinea pigs. Two dirty and crumpled little bodies on the grass indicated that the Alsatian had already been successful twice.

Oh no! I must save them, Kylie thought.

She broke into a run and dashed towards the cage.

Chapter 21

UTTER DISTRESS

As she ran Kylie screamed. Her scream was a mixture of rage and dismay and was torn from her by the sight of the Alsatian clamping its jaws around the neck of another guinea pig. The dog gave the guinea pig a savage shake and then bit hard. Kylie was sure she heard the tiny bones go crunch and her emotions boiled. The Alsatian then dropped the body and dashed across the cage and began to snarl and scrabble in the warm box.

Oh no! The babies! Kylie thought.

By then she had reached the cage but was baffled for a moment as to what to do next. She saw that the Alsatian had ripped part of the chicken wire loose from the heavy wooden frame and had been able to crawl in through the opening. But it was also obvious that the opening was much too small for her.

And the cage isn't big enough. I won't be able to stand up, she thought.

While she dithered the Alsatian stuck its front legs and snout into the hangings of the warm box and began scraping and barking furiously. Kylie saw a tiny white form come scampering out. In a flash the Alsatian turned and pounced, the tiny baby guinea pig almost vanishing inside the dog's huge jaws.

The sight so aroused Kylie that she seized the side of the cage and heaved upwards with all her might. The cage rose up and fell away from her, to end up upside down on the lawn. But by then the Alsatian had dropped an obviously dead baby guinea pig and snapped its jaws onto another little creature.

Fudge, Kylie thought as she rushed to help.

She was so upset and angry that she did not think but grabbed the neck of the Alsatian with both hands and tried to drag it away. Instantly she had the sickening revelation that the dog had no collar and all she could do was twist her fingers into its fur to try to get a grip. She was also appalled to discover that she lacked the physical strength to pull the dog away. But she tried, hauling so hard she felt sure she must choke the dog.

She did make it drop the now mangled and broken baby guinea pig, but she could not prevent it from seizing yet another baby guinea pig as it emerged from its hiding place.

As Kylie struggled desperately to make the Alsatian break its grip she screamed and swore, shouting at the top of her voice. Many of the words were ones she would not have wanted her mother to hear but she was so incensed and distressed that she did not care. But her efforts were in vain. The third baby guinea pig fell dead and the last one, and Toffee, the mother, both appeared, darting to and fro in terror.

The Alsatian lunged at Toffee, dragging Kylie with it as it tried to catch the guinea pig. To her dismay, Kylie saw that Toffee was already bleeding and that her sides were heaving in and out as she took frantic breaths. In her distress, Kylie began to hit at the Alsatian's face with her clenched right hand.

That did not seem to work, so she reached forward in a desperate attempt to hold the dog's jaws shut. But the animal's snout was all a slippery mess of blood and dribbling saliva and Kylie could not get a grip. After failing three times she gripped the dog's nostrils. All the while she was dimly aware that she was screaming and crying and that the dog's claws were scratching at her legs.

But she had the Alsatian's attention now. It twisted and broke free and then stood barking savagely at her. Kylie's relief that she had saved Toffee and the last baby guinea pig instantly turned to fear.

It is going to attack me! she thought.

It did. She tried to back off but found her escape blocked by the upturned cage. The Alsatian gave a vicious growl which chilled Kylie. Then it sprang. The jump was so fast and from such a distance that Kylie was stunned and caught by surprise. She flung out her arm in a frantic attempt to fend it off, but the dog's front legs and sheer weight smashed her arm aside. To Kylie's utter horror, the dog's face appeared right next to hers and slammed into her. The dog attacked with such weight and fury that Kylie was knocked over. As she fell backwards under the impetus of its attack her, shocked mind told her that the animal had her by the throat!

I am going to die! she thought.

Panic sent her into a frenzy of struggling as she landed on her back. She tried to scream but the pressure on her windpipe was so strong that the noise only came out as a choking gurgle. The whole situation was so real and so primeval that her entire body seethed with a mix of emotions. Dominant was terror but there was also disbelief and rage. She was also very aware that her life was at stake.

I must break his grip, she told herself.

By now she was lying on her back on the lawn and the dog's paws were tearing and scratching at her body and legs and a claw even jagged the corner of her eye. She felt hot, smelly breath and disgusting odours. Worse still, she could feel warm liquid trickling on her face and neck. Frantically she tried to roll over in a desperate attempt to get to her feet. But she needed to use both hands to try to prize the dog's jaws apart.

Suddenly, there was a heavy *thump!* which shook Kylie and smashed the dog's snout against her jaw. Then she saw a moving shape against the sky and heard Graham's voice.

"Let her go, you mongrel!" Graham shouted.

Thump!

Graham struck the dog again. Kylie felt a surge of relief and tried to focus her eyes.

Thump!

Graham struck the dog a third time. Kylie got a fleeting glimpse of a dark shape, a board or plank, swish across her vision and then smash down onto the Alsatian. Her mind told her that Graham was hitting the dog very hard with a heavy piece of timber and even in her own peril a part of her felt sorry for the dog.

Suddenly, the Alsatian released Kylie and scrabbled to turn. Kylie seized the opportunity and rolled away. She heard Graham shout, "Get up, Kylie! Run!", but she was too distressed and frightened to react fast. All she could do was struggle onto her hands and knees. As she did, she saw the Alsatian launch itself at Graham.

"Look out Graham!" she screamed.

What happened next was so fast that Kylie only got a fleeting glimpse. What she was sure of was that Graham, instead of trying to get away, actually took a step forward. As he did, he swung the plank, an old fence paling, in a scything swipe. The plank and the dog met in mid-air. There was a ghastly sounding *thunk!* and the dog spun around and fell heavily onto the ground.

Graham at once dashed over to her and reached out with his left hand and gripped her arm. "Get up Kylie! Quick, get upstairs!" he cried.

Kylie staggered to her feet and tried to run. But she was so distressed and winded that she knew she was on the edge of hysteria and collapse. She stumbled and nearly fell, and Graham held her up and hurried her a few paces. She could feel his muscles straining to hold her up and she tried to help him, but her own muscles were now trembling in fits of almost uncontrollable shivering.

Suddenly Graham stopped and Kylie saw him looking back. She heard him gasp and mutter, "Oh bloody hell!"

Then he trembled and she felt his breathing come in great gulps. Despite her fear and upset she made herself look back. When she saw what he was looking at she gasped in horror. The Alsatian lay in a crumpled heap and was so still she knew instantly that it was dead.

Then emotion engulfed her, and her eyes went out of focus and she fainted.

* * *

Kylie came to a minute later. As she did, she found herself looking into the concerned faces of Margaret, Moira, and Carmen. Then Graham knelt beside her and reached down to her neck.

"The bloody dog had her by the throat," he cried, obviously deeply distressed.

Carmen and Margaret both pushed Graham aside. Carmen said very firmly, "Phone the ambulance, Graham. Go on. Do it! We will look after Kylie."

Ambulance! Am I that badly hurt? Kylie wondered, her heart rate shooting up again with anxiety. She saw Graham's worried face and then he bit his lip, nodded and dashed away.

"It's alright, Kylie," Carmen said. "Just relax. I don't think it's as bad as it looks. Just lie there and let me untie this pullover from around your neck."

My pullover! Kylie thought.

She remembered tying the sleeves around her neck. She struggled to sit up and managed to look at her front before Moira and Margaret made her lie down.

"There's a lot of blood!" she wailed in dismay.

Carmen shook her head. "It looks worse than it is. Most of it is just from a few scratches. Now hold still while I look at your neck." She gripped Kylie's head firmly and bent to study Kylie's throat. "Hmm. Just one deep bite, here. Boy, if you hadn't been wearing that pullover, I reckon your throat would have been ripped open."

Margaret agreed. "I nearly died of fright when I saw the dog spring."

"Did you see the attack?" Kylie asked.

"Yes. We were just coming to visit you. We yelled like anything. Didn't you hear us?" Margaret answered.

Kylie tried to shake her head, but a sharp stab of pain made her wince and lie still. "No. I suppose I was screaming too loud myself."

"You were earlier," Moira agreed. "We could hear you right at the end of the street."

"Do you think I will die?" Kylie whispered, aware that her heart was fluttering very fast.

Both Margaret and Carmen laughed aloud. Carmen shook her head and answered, "No chance! Only the good die young. No, Kylie, the bites are not deep and most of the bleeding has already stopped."

That made Kylie feel very relieved, but a new worry immediately took its place. "Will I be badly scarred?"

Again Carmen answered. "I don't think you will even notice most of them in a week's time. They are just scratches."

Margaret nodded. "Anyway, you are so pretty that a few little scars won't matter," she said.

The comment sent a pulse of gratitude through Kylie, but she was still worried. She began to tremble again and burst into tears. While the girls comforted her Alex arrived and demanded to know what had happened. The girls were still explaining it when Graham came back to report that he had telephoned the ambulance and their mother.

When Alex understood that the Alsatian had done the attacking his face darkened with anger and he strode over to where it lay, then gave the body a savage kick.

That upset Kylie even more. "Stop it, Alex!" she cried.

Then Kylie saw Graham's face and she was even more upset. His face was a mask of misery. He called to Alex and asked, "Is it dead?"

Alex nudged the dog's body again with his shoe and then bent to look more closely. Then he straightened up and nodded. "Yep, dead as a doornail."

On hearing that Graham let out a sob and tears began to stream down his cheeks. "I... I... I did... didn't mean to... to k... kill it," he wailed. "I j... just wanted to save K... Kylie!"

Kylie began to cry as well and all the girls joined in. Margaret moved and hugged Graham and he did not resist. That was the only good thing that Kylie could find in the situation. Then she saw Alex walk over to the guinea pigs and their cage.

She felt sick with misery and dread but had to know. "Are the guinea pigs all dead?" she asked.

Alex knelt and began feeling the torn and dirty little bodies that were strewn around the lawn. Then he turned and nodded, his face moving with anger. "Yes, they are. Sorry," he said.

There were more tears, but they were cut short by Alex suddenly shouting and waving his clenched fist in the direction of the Flawse's house. "Look what your bloody dog has done you old hag! It has nearly killed Kylie and has killed all our guinea pigs."

Kylie glanced towards the Flawse's house and was just in time to see Mrs Flawse pull her head back in a back window. That fleeting glimpse showed that the woman was frightened.

I expected her to be angry because we have killed her dog, Kylie thought.

Alex did some more angry shouting, adding, "I will report you, you old bag!" With that he turned to the friends and said, "I am going to ring the council. Graham, stop blubbing and get your camera."

Moira and Margaret went with the boys as they hurried upstairs. Kylie was left on the lawn but now felt she had to sit up. With an effort she brushed Carmen's protests aside and heaved herself into as sitting position. For the next minute or so all she could do was sit and brace herself as her eyes went blurry and her head spun. Nausea swilled in her stomach. "I want to check the guinea pigs, just in case," she insisted.

Carmen shook her head vigorously. "No Kylie! No! It will just upset you more. Leave that to us."

She was able to stop Kylie. The fact that Kylie kept having shivering fits as the shock hit her helped. Then Margaret and Moira returned with hot water and antiseptic and cloths and began to bathe her wounds very gently. A pillow was placed on a towel for her to lie on and she felt so unwell that she gladly lay back down again.

Then Mrs Kirk arrived. She was almost frantic with worry, and as soon as she had parked the car under the house she raced out to join them. Graham and Alex re-joined them a few minutes later and the whole story had to be told again. As she explained what had happened, Kylie kept trembling and her voice quavered so much she could hardly make herself understood. There were lots of tears and comforting hugs. Graham was as bad. As he explained how he had battled the dog to save Kylie, his face crumpled into a mask of misery and he burst into tears again.

Seeing that upset Kylie more than anything else. *Poor Graham!* she thought. *He loves dogs. Now he has killed one, and only because he was trying to save me!* The thought that her brother might suffer from a guilty conscience on her behalf really distressed her. *He must feel awful!* she told herself.

Then the ambulance arrived. There was a lot of fuss and the paramedics quickly placed Kylie on a stretcher and lifted her into the ambulance. As the stretcher was slid in, Kylie glanced at the Flawse's house and caught a fleeting glimpse of a face at a side window.

Mrs Flawse, and she is a worried woman alright, she decided. The thought gave her some satisfaction.

Her mother spoke to the others for a few minutes then joined her in the ambulance and they set off for the hospital. For Kylie the next three hours were very unpleasant. At the hospital she was quickly checked and told there were no serious injuries. Then she and her mother were put in a room and they had to wait for nearly two hours before another doctor attended to her. During all of this she kept having bouts of shivering and tears as the shock hit her.

As she trembled and relived the moments of horror, there were vivid flashbacks of fear and dismay. But as she calmed down there were also flashes of anger. She found being attacked by an animal an intensely disturbing experience, but she also felt deeply wronged. When she thought about the attack on the guinea pigs, she felt spasms of rage that made her clench her teeth.

When the doctor had inspected and cleaned the wounds Kylie was relieved to find that most of the scratches had long since stopped bleeding and that only a couple were deep enough to cause any trouble. Two were long scratches on her right thigh and another was the fang wound in her neck.

There was the usual sting of antiseptic and all the hospital smells and bustle. None of the medical staff seemed worried, and when one said she was lucky that the dog had not mauled her face, Kylie could only agree. *I didn't think of that,* she told herself.

But what about the claw marks in her thigh? She pictured ugly scars which would mar her good looks when she wanted to cut a figure in her bathers at the swimming pool.

When she asked about the scars the doctor shook his head. "They will heal very quickly and at worst might leave a very faint line. You have been very lucky."

Kylie saw her mother's face relax and realised she had been worrying as well. That made her feel a warm glow of love for her mum. She reached up and touched her arm. "I will be alright Mum. It was the pets I am upset over."

"Pets!" her mother cried. "The house is overrun with the creatures!" But she clasped Kylie to her and hugged her tightly.

"Can I have more guinea pigs, Mum?" Kylie asked after she was released.

"Hmm. I will see. Now let's get home and see how things are," her mother answered.

Chapter 22

By the time Kylie and her mother got home it was dark and the others had gone home. The boys had eaten snacks and were watching TV. Both immediately made a fuss over Kylie, Graham more than Alex.

Mrs Kirk asked them, "Did you do those jobs?"

"Yes Mum," Alex answered.

"Did the council man come?"

"Yes Mum," Alex answered.

Mrs Kirk nodded. "Good. What did he do?"

Alex answered. "He took some photos and then he went next door to talk to Mrs Flawse. We don't know what he said but we heard her doing a lot of angry shouting. When he came back, he said that Mrs Flawse denied that the dog was hers."

That jerked Kylie out of her misery. "What! But it's been in her yard for a week or more," she cried angrily.

Alex nodded. "We said that, but the council man said she claimed she had never seen it before in her life."

"Oh the lying b...!" Kylie cried. *Bitch!* she thought, but did not say.

Graham now spoke. "He said that the dog was not registered and that we would have to prove it was hers before he could take any legal action."

Mrs Kirk shook her head sadly. "That means we have to hire a lawyer, I suppose. What happened to the dog?"

"He told us to dispose of it," Alex answered.

That also horrified Kylie. "Did you?" she demanded to know.

"No fear! We argued and he finally had us put it in a plastic garbage bag and he took it away in his van," Alex answered.

Again Mrs Kirk shook her head. "This is all getting very messy and distressing. I wish your father was here," she said.

"We can handle it, Mum," Alex replied.

Mrs Kirk looked unhappy and snapped, "You can't. This is serious adult stuff. And don't you do anything to those people next door, you hear!"

"Yes, Mum," Alex replied with obvious reluctance.

"I mean it, Alex. Don't you even glance sideways at them. And none of your tricks like tossing dead toads into their yard," Mrs Kirk snapped.

Her mother's anger told Kylie just how worried she was. She asked, "Where is Dad, Mum?"

"He is at Weipa and won't be back for a week," Mrs Kirk replied. Anyway, enough talk. Let's have tea."

But Kylie did not want to eat. She felt too sick and kept breaking into fits of shivering. However her mother insisted she have some soup and toast. While it was being prepared Kylie sat on a stool in the kitchen. She turned to Graham. "All the guinea pigs were dead, weren't they?"

Graham looked miserable. He nodded and said, "Yes."

"What did you do with them?"

"Buried them under the mulberry tree against the back fence," Graham answered. Then he reached out and patted Kylie's arm. "Sorry Kylie. If I'd come home earlier we might have been in time."

All Kylie could do was shrug. There was no sensible answer to that sort of 'what if?'. She said, "Thank you for saving me. I'm really sorry you had to hit that dog."

Graham's face crumpled but he managed not to cry. "I'd fight anything to save you," he said. "You are worth it."

That made Kylie feel so loved and cared for that she burst into tears again. It was only when the telephone rang, and she was told it was for her that she managed to get her snuffles under control.

It was Margaret, wanting to know how she was. Kylie assured her she was alright, and the girls discussed the incident until her mother called her to eat. Later Kylie went to bed early and lay thinking. From time to time she trembled with shock. What hit her the hardest was the sheer 'reality' of it all. The speed and savageness of the attack and her feelings of utter helplessness when seized by a strong wild animal all swamped her mind with terrible images and feelings of horror and fear.

I suppose I am lucky, she mused. *I am living in a nice, civilized country where horrible things don't happen much. If I had been born in Africa or the Amazon jungle, I would have to face such threats every day.*

It got her pondering on what life for primitive humans might have been like and of what it might have been like to grapple with real wild animals like lions and tigers.

She slipped into a fitful but exhausted sleep. Several times horrible nightmares swirled in her mind, and she twice woke up in a sweat of fear, even though the night was cold. The second time she realised she must have made a noise as light came on and her mother came into her room to calm her.

"Sorry Mum," Kylie said as her mother soothed her trembles. "But it was just so awful."

"Real life sometimes is," her mother agreed. "The thing to do is learn positive lessons from the experience and not let it weaken you."

Positive, Kylie thought, wondering whether she would now be frightened of all the big dogs she met.

The next morning she was drained and feverish and her mother would not let her go to school. Even when Kylie complained she did not want her mother to lose a day's work her mother insisted on staying home with her. Kylie was glad of that. She did not want to be alone in the house, knowing that the Flawses lived next door.

This is horrible, she thought. *Now I am scared of the neighbours!*

But at least she had Skip to keep her company and that helped pass the time. So did doing homework and reading. She also slept for several hours and then watched TV. There was a phone call from her anxious Gran in Mareeba and another from her father. Both cheered her up, knowing that she was so loved.

After school, Margaret and Carmen came to visit. They soon had her laughing again, this time with the story of Billy and the great escape of the white mice.

"It got Miss Wallis screaming again and poor Billy in trouble," Margaret explained with a giggle.

"Did you scream and climb on the desk like last time?" Kylie asked.

Margaret went red and tried to deny she had ever done any such thing but then giggled and nodded. The girls had afternoon tea and then went to feed the other pets. That was bit sad but Skip was happy and dashed around jumping and licking. While the girls walked around to the back yard with Skip Kylie glanced over at the Flawse's house. Then she wished she hadn't as she clearly saw Mrs Flawse glaring at her from an upstairs window.

The sight of the woman's hate-filled face sent a shiver of fear through Kylie and she felt quite sick and apprehensive. It was a relief to walk around to the back of the house and out of sight.

The girls looked at the guinea pig cage and Kylie was moved to anger and tears again. For a few seconds she shivered as images of the brutal mauling swirled in her mind. Then she had a good cry and led the way across to the mulberry tree. The newly disturbed soil was easy to find and seeing the little grave upset her even more. For a few minutes she had morbid thoughts about death, picturing the tiny bodies with dirt in their eyes and up their nostrils.

Then they will rot and the worms will eat them, she thought.

That made her shudder, and when she contemplated her own mortality she was even more disturbed. *If that Alsatian had ripped my throat open, I would be dead too,* she thought. It was all horrible stuff and upset her so much she turned and hurried away. She led her friends back around the other side of the house to see the budgerigars.

Margaret and Carmen both made a determined effort to cheer her up and Kylie could see that they were concerned. Knowing that they were trying and they cared about her caused a warm glow through her.

That night Kylie still felt feverish and sick, but she slept better. There was only one nightmare in which a huge black dog kept chasing her around the house.

Just as it sprang and clamped its jaws onto her neck she woke up.

* * *

On Wednesday morning Kylie felt light-headed and very hungry. Her muscles felt so weak that she had trouble dragging herself out of bed. But she did not want to stay home another day, so she hid this from her mother and pretend she was well. She ate a big breakfast and actually felt better.

Before leaving for school she had an argument with her mother about Skip. Her mother insisted that Skip be tied up under the house. "I don't want Skip running loose to annoy the Flawses while we aren't home," she said.

"But Mum, that's not fair!" Kylie cried.

"No, it probably isn't. But for a week or two until your father is home and all this unpleasantness is over she can stay tied up during the day. Now go and make sure she had plenty of water and chewies," her mother said.

So Kylie tied Skip up, making sure she had a full water bowl and a bowl of dry food. "Sorry Skip," she said, ruffling Skip's fur and ears. "I will play with you this afternoon."

Feeling inexplicably anxious Kylie went to school. When she got there all the girls fussed over her bite marks and scratches. Kylie liked the attention but not the memories. She also worried about scars marring her looks when she was older. Margaret helped ease these fears by commenting that most of the scratches were healing nicely and were hardly noticeable. Kylie knew that from the mirror and because they itched. Even the bite on her neck was smaller and not weeping as much pus.

School was made easier by Emma pouring sympathy over Kylie and then telling her that her mother had given her a new puppy. "His name is Scamp," she said. "He is a lovely little beagle and is just so cute. Would you like to see him?"

Kylie said she would, so after school she hurried home. Partly this was out of anxiety in case something else had gone wrong while the family were away. But as she reached the front gate everything seemed normal. The only sour patch was after she untied Skip and led her out onto the side lawn. As she did, she saw Mr Flawse working in his garden. He did not say anything but gave her a nasty look that made her stomach turn with apprehension.

As quickly as she could, Kylie walked with Skip to the front gate and out of sight. She then walked to Emma's. Skip obviously enjoyed being out and about again and Kylie felt the happiest she had for days. At Emma's she was bitten by jealousy because Scamp was just the cutest little bundle of energy she had ever seen. She did not want to admit this but did say nice things and pat the puppy. That got Skip jealous and she had to hold her.

"I am so happy for you Emma," Kylie said.

And she was. But she also worried about what had become of Thistle. However she did not mention this in case it upset Emma again. Nor could she stay long as she wanted to be back home by the time her mother got home so she said goodbye and walked Skip home, going a different way for variety. She did not really enjoy that because the route took her past a number of houses where there were big, savage dogs. While the dogs could not get out to attack her or Skip, their growls and barking caused her to shudder with anxiety and to have searing flashbacks to the Alsatian's attack that left her sweating and feeling sick in the stomach. Skip, of course, enjoyed the barking matches.

When she got home, Kylie found Graham busy sorting out his hiking gear. His pack and its contents were spread right along the front veranda, along with his webbing and all the items he intended to take. His obvious enthusiasm for his planned hike infected her and she began to look forward to the horse riding.

"Where are you planning to hike?" she asked him.

"We are getting dropped off at Kamerunga and are going to climb up Douglas's Track to Glacier Rock. Then we are going to walk through the Speewah area to the Kennedy Highway and along some old timber tracks to the Kambah Road. We plan to camp where the Kambah Road crosses Venture Creek," Graham explained.

Kylie knew the area just well enough to picture where he meant, and it sounded like a very long way to her. She said, "Are you coming to see us at Corwa?"

Graham nodded. "Yes. We are going to explore some old gold mines in the hills at the top of Venture Creek and will camp beside the Barron where we camped last time. That will be Sunday night."

"Margaret is hoping to see you," Kylie said, noting the blush mottle his neck and ears.

"Yeah," Graham answered casually and turned back to sorting tins of food.

Kylie went to her room and then studied her scars and scratches in the mirror. She was pleased to see that they were mostly healing well and most were not even obvious any more.

Good, she told herself. *Maybe I won't be scarred.*

On Thursday morning the wounds had healed even more. The one she was most worried about, the fang bite on her neck, had almost closed up and had stopped weeping pus. That cheered her up and she dressed for school in a happy mood. *Two more days to the long weekend,* she told herself, imagining herself astride Carbine and happily cantering through the bush.

Once again, she tied Skip up under the house and made sure she had plenty of food and water. Seeing Skip's mournful face and hearing her sad whine upset Kylie a bit.

"It's alright Skip. It won't be for much longer," she said. Then she hurried off before she started to cry.

At school, Kylie talked to Margaret about the weekend. Margaret wanted to know all the details of the boy's planned hike. Kylie could only remember some of the detail but she was able to assure Margaret that the boys would be camping beside the Barron River at Corwa on the Sunday night. Talking about horse riding lifted Kylie's spirits and she became quite excited. This peeved Emma, who obviously felt excluded from the conversation.

School was a bit tedious, even though it was Thursday and they had art after lunch. Kylie was happy enough making a woven mat out of coloured cardboard strips, but she also wanted to the day to end.

"I will take Skip for another walk," she told Margaret.

"Are you allowed? I thought your mum didn't want you going walking while that creepy man in the white van is still driving around," Margaret said.

"She doesn't want me to, but Skip needs the exercise. But I will go a different way today," Kylie answered. She then explained the problems with savage dogs as she walked past along the footpath. "They really scare me now," she confessed.

"Can I come?" Margaret asked.

Kylie nodded. "That would be good. Mum won't mind if there are two of us."

So after school the two girls rode their bicycles to Kylie's. When they got there, they left their bikes under the front of the house and went up the front steps and through to Kylie's room, where they dumped their school bags. They then made their way to the kitchen for a glass of cordial and a biscuit. While they had afternoon tea Kylie noted Margaret glancing towards the front of the house. That caused her to smile.

"I don't know if Graham is coming home straight away," she said. "I heard him say something about going to Peter's."

Margaret shrugged but smiled. "Oh well," she said. "I will just phone my mum to tell her where I am, if that is alright?"

Kylie said yes. Margaret went to the phone in the hallway while Kylie tidied up. She then went to the back door. "I will just get Skip ready," she called as she went out. Humming happily she went down the back stairs and in under the house.

And stopped.

Skip was not there.

Her heart at once leapt and began to beat fast. A sudden sense of dread gripped Kylie and she hurried over to the post that his leash had been fastened to. But there was no sign of it, or of Skip. With a feeling of mounting alarm she looked around.

Did Graham or Alex beat us home and take her? she wondered.

Margaret came down the back steps and joined her. At once she saw the worried look on Kylie's face. "Kylie, what's wrong?"

Kylie gestured to the post. "Skip isn't here. I don't know where she is."

Chapter 23

WHERE IS SKIP?

Margaret felt a sudden stab of worry. She looked quickly around and said, "Skip gone? Where?"

Kylie shook her head. "I don't know. This is where I tied her up this morning. Here are her water and food bowls." She shook her head and began to walk around the laundry.

"Are you sure that neither Alex nor Graham has come home and taken her for a walk?" Margaret asked.

By this time she was feeling terribly apprehensive and the sick feeling in her stomach threatened to break out in tears.

Again Kylie shook her head. "No, I don't think so. Oh, I don't know!" she wailed. She began to cry, and Margaret's eyes became moist in sympathy.

"She might have got loose somehow and be here in the yard," Margaret suggested.

"Oh yes! Let's look," Kylie cried. She dashed out to the back yard, calling loudly, "Skip! Skip! Where are you Skip?"

Margaret followed, her heart pitter-pattering with anxiety. For the next five minutes both girls hurried around the back and side yards, but there was no sign of Skip. Kylie's cries became more and more heartrending as her concern increased. That got Margaret more upset as well and she found she could hardly see for tears. "She must be somewhere," she said, trying to sound hopeful. "Let's look upstairs."

"But how could she get into the house? Both doors were locked," Kylie answered.

She shook her head in obvious distress and disbelief. Then she hurried up the front steps and began searching from room to room, calling loudly as she went.

Margaret followed, kneeling to look under beds or other hiding places where a sick or frightened dog might try to conceal itself. As they reached the phone she pointed to it and said, "Why don't we call Peter's and see if Graham is there?"

"Good idea," Kylie sobbed. She snatched up the phone and tried to punch the numbers, then burst into tears and held the phone out to Margaret. "You do it please... sob!... I am too upset."

Margaret quickly rang Peter's. Peter's mother answered. Margaret said, "Hello Mrs Bronsky. This is Margaret Lake. Is Graham Kirk there please?"

He was. A minute later Graham came on the phone. "Margaret? What do you want?" he asked, obviously puzzled as Margaret had never rung him at a friend's place before.

"Have you got Skip with you?" Margaret asked. As she did, she felt her lip quaver and she had to swallow, and it became a struggle for her to keep control of her voice.

"Skip? No, why?" Graham answered.

"She's not here, at your place I mean," Margaret answered. Then she said, "Might she be with Alex?"

"With Alex? No chance. He has gone over to Davo's. Maybe Kylie's got her and gone for a walk," he said.

"No," Margaret croaked, tears misting her eyes as hopes crumbled and Kylie dissolved in tears as he understood that neither Graham not Alex had her. "K... K... Kylie's here... sniff, wit... sniffle... with m... me! We can't f... find her."

"I'll be home as quick as I can. Better call Mum," Graham said.

"Y... Y.. Y... sob!.." replied Margaret. She hung up and then phoned Kylie's mother and gave her the news. Then she turned to a weeping Kylie. "M... M... maybe she has got out of the... sob... yard?"

"Let's look," Kylie said. She set off running, clearly impelled by a terrible sense of urgency.

The two girls ran to the front of the house and looked both ways along the street. By now Margaret was biting her lip with anxiety and she could see that Kyle was becoming more and more distressed. There was no sign of Skip so she said, "Could she have got out of the yard?"

Kylie shook her head. "Not easily. Both front gates were closed, weren't they? Quick, we must check the fence for loose palings, and then the back gate. Come on!" So saying she hurried down the front stairs, taking them two or three steps at a time.

Margaret hurried after her, calling out, "Careful Kylie! If you miss your step and hurt yourself, it won't help Skip."

Kylie either did not hear her or just ignored her and kept running. She went to the right and along the southern side fence, looking at the palings as she went. But there were no obviously loose ones so she kept going at a trot. Margaret kept up with her, also scanning the fence and garden beds. She could see no sign of any holes dug under the fence either.

The Kirk's property extended right through to a wide 'laneway' at the rear. The back part of the yard was all vegetable gardens and fruit trees, including a large mango tree. A wide gateway led out onto the grassy laneway. That gate was also closed and had not been opened for a long time, weeds growing along the fence. Both girls stopped at the fence and looked both ways along the lane. The lane was a gravel road with ten metres of grass on either side, making quite a wide space which ran the whole length of the block.

A single glance revealed no sign of Skip, or any other dog. Kylie sobbed then cried, "She might be out wandering the streets."

"She doesn't normally do that does she?" Margaret queried, now as worried about Kylie as about Skip.

"No," Kylie admitted. "But she might be. Let's look."

She went to climb the fence, but Margaret grabbed her arm. "Wait. Be sensible, Kylie. We can do this quicker on our bikes."

Reluctantly Kylie agreed so both girls hurried to the front of the house. Kylie went so fast that Margaret had trouble keeping up, and by the time she got there Kylie was already wheeling her bike out the front gate. She jumped on and began pedalling, not waiting for Margaret.

Margaret pushed her bike out onto the grass footpath and yelled after Kylie, "I will go the other way. Just go round the block."

She saw Kylie nod but wasn't sure if she had understood. Acting on her own advice Margaret jumped on her bike and started off in the opposite direction, going to the right. By this time she was puffing and perspiring and had a horrible sinking feeling inside her.

Three minutes later she met Kylie coming the other way on the far side of the block. Kylie's drawn face and distressed manner told their own story, and all Margaret could do was shake her head. Kylie pointed and said, "You go that way for three blocks. Go round each block and then come back to my place. I will go the other way."

"Okay," Margaret agreed. She swung her bike around and resumed pedalling as fast as she could.

Despite quickly becoming puffed, Margaret rode around block after block. She saw one dog, a Dalmatian, but there was no sign of Skip. By the time she had circled the next three blocks along the street with no result she feared the worst. In her mind she ran over the possibilities and half expected to find a battered and crumpled body beside the road. But she saw no sign of Skip and felt awful as she rode back to report to Kylie.

She found Kylie already there, sitting astride her bike and sobbing outside the front gate. It only took one glance from Kylie to establish that Margaret had bad news. The sight of her tear-stained face and obvious misery caused more anguish for Margaret.

Then Kylie pointed and said, "We go the other way this time. Four blocks."

"Shouldn't we wait for Graham and for your mum?" Margaret asked.

"We must find Skip!" Kylie cried, her torment clearly etched on her face. Without waiting she set off again.

Margaret could only do the same. She was feeling tired and sick and was perspiring despite the evening chill that was setting in but she forced herself to search. It took her about 5 minutes to go around each block and at the end of each she felt ever more depressed. There was no sign of any dogs. Sadly she turned around and began pedalling back towards Kylie's.

Even before she got there, she heard Kylie's voice shouting angrily. As she rode along the last hundred metres Margaret saw that Kylie was up at the front door of the Flawse's house. The door was closed, and Kylie was pounding on it with her fists and yelling.

The sight quite alarmed Margaret. *Have those horrible Flawses got Skip?* she wondered. To find out she pedalled as fast as she could.

From the sound of things Kylie certainly seemed to think so. She screamed, "Where is my dog! Come out and talk to me! Tell me what you have done with Skip!"

Margaret jumped off her bike outside Kylie's house and ran to the front gate of the Flawses. As she ran, she saw Graham and Peter riding their bikes towards her. All she could do was point and then hurry up the steps to where Kylie was banging loudly on the closed front door. Through Margaret's mind flitted all sorts of awful worries: the nasty Flawses coming out to have a confrontation; Kylie hurting herself by breaking the coloured glass in the door; another savage dog appearing to attack her.

And me! Where is that horrible Brute? she wondered as she reached the small landing at the top of the wooden steps.

By then Kylie was becoming hysterical. Her words were hard to understand as she was now sobbing so much. Her face was all screwed up and tears were trickling down her face. The word 'distraught' flitted across Margaret's mind. She took gentle hold of Kylie and called to her, "Kylie, Kylie, stop it! Stop it! You will hurt yourself. Please stop it!"

But Kylie kept shouting and hammering on the door. Margaret looked anxiously around, noting heads poking out of neighbouring houses and several people standing on the footpath staring.

To her enormous relief, Graham had arrived. He came racing up the steps, calling as he did, "Is Skip in there?"

"I don't know," Margaret replied. She was now so upset herself that she was sobbing loudly.

Graham grabbed Kylie and spun her round. "Kylie! Kylie! What is going on?" he shouted.

Kylie looked at him through tear-misted eyes and opened her mouth, then seemed to crumple into his arms. Graham grabbed her and held her up, looking from her to Margaret. Then he said, "Has Flawse got Skip?"

Kylie shook her head, more tears streaming down her face. "I... d... d... don't know."

"Did you see him take Skip?" Graham asked.

Again Kylie shook her head. "No!" she sobbed.

"So why are you here?" Graham asked.

"Who else could have taken her?" Kylie cried.

Margaret found Kylie's distress very upsetting to see and feeling her trembling body as she held her added to her own awful feelings. She looked at the closed louvres and windows along the front of the house, half expecting to see a glaring face. But there was no-one visible.

She met Graham's eyes and said, "I don't think anyone is home."

Graham glanced at the louvres and then nodded. "I reckon. If there had been I think they would have been out here abusing us by now. Come on Kylie, come home."

At that Kylie broke down and began to sob and her chest to heave. "Oh no! No!" she wailed between sobs.

But she did allow Margaret and Graham to turn her and help her down the steps. Margaret kept a tight grip on Kylie's left arm, worried that she might miss her step or faint and fall. As they made their way slowly down the stairs, she saw that even more people had appeared on the footpath and in the front yards or front doors of other houses. Strangely she did not feel the embarrassment she would usually have experienced. All she cared about was getting Kylie to safety.

As she and Graham helped Kylie to the front gate, Mrs Kirk arrived in her car. Graham left Kylie and hurried to open the vehicle gate for his mother. She gave Kylie and Margaret a searching and anxious look before driving her car inside. The children followed. By the time they reached Mrs Kirk in the car port Kylie had calmed down a bit but was still sobbing.

Margaret found she was the one who did most of the talking. As the tale unfolded, Kylie began to weep again and her mother hugged her and soothed her. Kylie then said, "I think that those horrible Flawses have taken her."

"Why do you say that? Did you see them do anything?" Mrs Kirk asked, glancing anxiously at the Flawse's house.

Kylie shook her head. "N... n... no. B... but it... sniff... stands to r... r... reason... sob. We k... k... killed their d... d... dog so they... sniff... have taken ours," she said.

Knowing the neighbours as she did, Margaret thought that was very likely but she also felt uneasy at making accusations without any proof. So did Mrs Kirk. She pursed her lips and said, "That may be right, but if you have no proof then we had better not make any accusations. We could end up in court on a defamation charge. There's enough unpleasantness as it is. Now, are you sure you tied Skip up before you went to school?"

Kylie nodded. "Yes Mum. I remember giving her a pat."

The group moved a few paces to the post where Skip had been secured. Margaret could see that there was no sign of the chain that was normally fastened around the concrete post. She bent and studied the post, then said, "Maybe Skip broke the chain or something?"

Graham grunted scornfully, making Margaret feel silly. He said, "No chance. It was a new steel chain. It would take an elephant to break that."

"Perhaps the catch came undone?" Mrs Kirk suggested.

Graham shook his head. "No Mum. It was a good quality snap catch. Skip has often been tied up here. If she broke free at all it would have been the catch that attached to her collar."

Mrs Kirk stood and studied the post and the matt and bowls. Then she shook her head and said, "I agree. That chain was too strong. Now, come upstairs you children."

Kylie shook her head. "No, we have to keep searching. We must find Skip!"

Mrs Kirk tightened her grip on her arm. "Now be sensible, Kylie. You have already done that. Now we must contact the police and the council. And you look like you need to wash your face and have something to pick you up."

With that she took Kylie up to the bathroom. Margaret was relieved that Kylie gave in as she was now worrying that she might do something silly. She and Graham followed, exchanging anxious glances as they did.

Upstairs they had some refreshments. Margaret took the opportunity to go to the toilet. When she came out, she found Alex there with one of his friends. The story had to be retold. Alex at once insisted they keep searching. This time Kylie ignored her mother's protests.

"You phone the police, Mum. We will just have another quick look around," she said.

Margaret went downstairs with the others. Once again, they searched along all the fences for any sign of a breakout. But there was none. The group ended up at the back fence.

Graham gestured to it and said, "Perhaps she jumped the fence?"

Alex pooh-poohed that idea. "Skip isn't big enough. That mongrel Brute was, and the Alsatian, but not Skip."

"So where is Skip?" asked Kylie, fresh tears watering in her eyes.

Chapter 24

EVEN MORE MISERY

For Kylie the whole thing was now a nightmare of anxiety. What had become of Skip? Had she been taken by someone, or had she just broken free? And if she had been taken by whom? And why?

Have the Flawses taken her in revenge for us killing their Alsatian? she wondered. *And what might they do to her?*

Just thinking about the possibilities made Kylie sick to the pit of her stomach. As she walked back along the side lawn with the others, she kept glancing at the Flawse's house, hoping for some clue. But it looked all closed up and she gathered nothing.

Alex suggested that they get on their bikes and look around the neighbourhood. Margaret explained that she and Kylie had already done that, but Alex insisted. Graham came up with a plan so that each had a group of streets to search. This meant a much wider search than previously and the idea gripped Kylie with renewed hope. Without waiting to ask for permission they set off.

But once again Kylie was cruelly disappointed. By the time she had circled four more blocks and found no sign of Skip she was deeply depressed. The misery so upset her she had difficulty seeing and her breathing was fast and shallow.

After half an hour she was home again, and her final hopes were dashed when all other others reported negative results. There was no sign of Skip on any of the streets within about two kilometres of the house. Both boys were upset and angry and Margaret looked as dejected to Kylie as she felt.

Kylie's mother was waiting for them in the kitchen and said that she had telephoned the council and the police but the tone in her voice did not suggest much hope that either authority would do much.

"I'm not sure there is much they can do anyway," Mrs Kirk added.

"Oh Mum! There must be something we can do!" she cried.

"I will call the radio stations and ask them to put a request in their community information bulletins," Mrs Kirk said.

That gave Kylie another straw of hope to clutch at and she nodded eagerly. Mrs Kirk then turned to Margaret. "You had better get home Margaret. It is getting late. And you be careful. Watch out for... for strange men."

That thought chilled Kylie too and she saw Margaret go pale and look anxious. Then Graham annoyed her even more by saying, "Huh! You'll be right, Maggot. Even deviates have some taste."

Kylie saw the hurt look on Margaret's face and at once turned on her brother. "Graham, that was a horrible thing to say."

Mrs Kirk agreed. She snapped, "There is no need to be bad mannered or to hurt people's feelings."

Graham looked ashamed and bit his lip. "Sorry Margaret. Sorry Mum. It's just that I am feeling really upset over Skip."

Kylie saw a tear trickle down Margaret's cheek, and she felt a spurt of anger at Graham's selfish insensitivity. *I am so lucky to have a good friend like Margaret,* she thought as she moved to give her a hug.

"Thank you, Margaret. And don't worry. One day he will realise that he does love you and will value you for your true worth."

Margaret nodded and wiped her tears, then whispered. "I hope you find Skip. Goodbye. Goodbye Graham. See you on the weekend."

At that Mrs Kirk said, "The weekend? Oh, I don't know. Not after what has just happened."

Kylie felt another stab of dejection. "Oh Mum! Please! We must go horse riding. I couldn't possibly let my friends down," she cried.

Mrs Kirk frowned. "But this business over Skip is making you sick. I can see it. You are going to bed as soon as you have had a bath and tea."

"Oh please, Mum! If I stay home all weekend while Margaret and Moira go horse riding, I will just feel jealous and will lie around and be miserable. Besides, they may not be allowed to go if I don't," Kylie said.

Margaret nodded. "That's right, Mrs Kirk. Please let Kylie come. She will be better off being busy and trying to enjoy herself than she will be brooding and getting upset all the time."

Mrs Kirk frowned again. "Hmmm! I will think about it. We will discuss it again tomorrow afternoon. I will talk to your Mum. Now you get along home Margaret," she said.

"Thank you, Mrs Kirk. Goodbye Kylie. I hope you find Skip." With that she poked her tongue at Graham and hurried away.

Kylie was hurried into the bath and then given tea. By then she was having frequent fits of shivering and felt sick in the stomach and utterly miserable. She did not feel she could eat anything, but her mother insisted. Then she was put in front of the TV, wrapped up warmly as the night was quickly growing chilly. It was a very sad household that evening and even Graham wept a few quiet tears.

* * *

Later, snug in her bed, Kylie cried herself to sleep. What particularly distressed her was the thought that Skip might have been taken by people who would use her in a dog fight. Ghastly images of what she imagined went on at a dog baiting match seemed to flood her mind with horror. Several times during the night she woke, sweating and shaking after nightmares. All of these involved terrifying images of a giant black dog (Brute?) which was not only savaging a bleeding and crumpled Skip, but which then turned to leap at her.

Next morning Kylie felt exhausted and miserable. There was some debate as to whether she should stay home sick. Finally her mother decided that she would be better off at school with other things to do and to think about.

"You are right," she said. "If you stay and home you are likely to just lie there brooding and getting even more miserable."

"Does that mean we can go horse riding tomorrow?" Kylie asked.

"We will see. I will phone the other parents during the day and we can discuss it this afternoon. Now you get dressed and get to school," Mrs Kirk said.

Kylie was already peeved that there had been no suggestion that either of her brothers stay home, or that Graham not go on his hike. She said, "What about Graham?"

"What about him?" Mrs Kirk asked.

"Is he allowed to go hiking?"

"Yes."

"So I can go horse riding," Kylie said. "Otherwise it is not fair."

"Yes Miss. Now you get moving," her mother answered sharply.

Kylie did get moving, feeling she had scored a small victory. But she was still utterly miserable and went to school feeling sick and unhappy.

Her mother drove her. All the way Kylie kept looking out for Skip but the only dogs she saw were a mangy looking Blue Heeler and a tubby Labrador. Not finding Skip cast her hopes down again. Once at school her mother went in with her to talk to Miss Wallis about how Kylie might be feeling. Kylie was feeling awful and as soon as she saw Emma she choked up and burst into tears and was unable to speak for a while.

After she had been comforted by her mother and by Miss Wallis and Emma, Kylie was able to tell the story. Emma was appalled and very sympathetic. "Kylie, that is terrible! Oh poor little Skip! I did so like her."

All Kylie could do was weep some more. Margaret joined them and hugged her, and then other girls came to find out what the problem was and to fuss. Her mother soothed her again but had to leave for work. It took nearly half an hour for Kylie to calm down.

Margaret said, "Maybe Skip will turn up. Someone might find her."

"Maybe," Kylie sniffled, but secretly she did not hold much hope.

"Has your mum placed adverts in the 'Lost and Found' in the paper and on the radio?" Emma asked.

"She is going to do that now," Kylie replied. It was one of the straws she was now clinging to.

She had trouble settling to schoolwork but actually found it a relief when she did as the mental discipline of doing mathematics at least took her mind off Skip and her own misery for a while. Somehow, she got through the first half of the day without breaking into tears too much but she felt tired and sick by lunchtime.

Her friends tried to cheer her up and she was included in their games. This at least got her out in the open and active and she began to recover slightly. The girls began a game of hopscotch under the trees near the side fence of the school. It was a game Kylie was good at because of her dancing training so she joined in and began to relax and enjoy herself.

She finished another game and moved aside to allow Sophie to have a go. This put her near the fence and she looked sadly out in both directions, with the vague hope of seeing Skip. Then she realised what she was seeing and gasped.

"The white van!" she cried.

There it was, driving past along the road. It was the same one, she was sure. In the fleeting glimpse she was granted the driver looked the same and then she was able to concentrate on the side and back.

Yes, there is the cracked window that is taped up with grey packing tape, she noted.

Then another thought came to her, the number. "What is the number plate? Oh, quick!" she muttered, as the van was moving quickly away. "F. I... and is that a Q... or an O? And is that first number an 8 or a 3? Oh, blast!" she muttered. But she could not see the last two numbers clearly. "It is getting away!" she cried.

In desperation she vaulted up onto the fence and over and then started running. The other girls looked at her in astonishment but all she did was yell, "The white van!" and keep going. She felt doubly scared doing it. Not only was it very much against the school rules but there was anxiety about what might happen if the man driving the van saw her. But she was determined to get that number and kept running.

But the van accelerated and quickly drew away. Kylie strained her eyes and thought the first numeral was definitely a 3 and the second numeral either a 1 or a 7. In desperation, she strained to make out the last two letters but could only cry with frustration as the van turned at the next corner and went out of sight.

For the next minute she just stood, staring at where the van had vanished from view while she mumbled the registration letters to herself. Only when she turned and started walking back towards her friends did it dawn on her that she had done something wrong. She saw Emma, Margaret and some others all leaning over the fence looking towards her but behind them stood Mrs Birch, the dreaded Mrs Birch!

I guess I am in trouble for leaving the school grounds without permission, she thought.

But she didn't care. And she was in trouble but all she insisted on was that she go directly to the office. Her willingness to do so astonished Mrs Birch. The teacher wrote a note explaining her behaviour and told her to go.

Kylie was so impatient to get the police on the tail of the white van that she almost jiggled with impatience while the teacher wrote the note. Then she hurried off towards the office, leaving her friends trailing in her wake.

"Slow down Kylie!" Margaret called.

"No! I saw the white van, the one that took Emma's dog. He might have taken Skip. I must get the police," Kylie answered.

That got both Emma and Margaret trotting to catch up and Emma began to sob when she realised what Kylie meant. "I might get Thistle back," she said hopefully.

Kylie glanced at her eager face and thought of the dog fighting stories and bit her lip. "You might," she said. But inside she did not believe that. Instead she felt a sickening sense of dread over Skip's possible fate.

But things just seemed to get worse. The Principal, Mr Worcester, did not want to hear about the van and began to lecture her about breaking the school rules. "It is for your own safety young lady," he said. "You could be kidnapped by bad strangers."

"My dog was, and so was Emma's, and by the man in that white van I told you about," Kylie replied. "Now please call the police."

"The police! Oh, that's a bit drastic," the principal replied.

"Please!" Kylie cried. Tears began to flow.

The principal looked anxious then said he would ring her mother first. He did this and while he talked Kylie found she could not hold back the sniffles. When Mr Worcester held the phone out to her and said, "Your mother wants to talk to you," she burst into tears.

For a couple of minutes Kylie was unable to speak coherently but then she managed to stifle her sobs and explain the outline. "It was the white van, Mum. Please call the police," she said.

"I'll be right there. Please put the principal back on," her mother said.

Kylie was sent to sit in the sick room while she waited. She found the waiting horrible. Every second she fretted that the man in the van would get away and then Skip would die a ghastly death. It took her mother half an hour to get there and for all of that Kylie was distressed.

Then it took another half hour for her to convince her mother and the principal to call the police. By the time they turned up it was almost 3 o'clock. Then Kylie had the awful experience of the police not seeming to believe her and not even being particularly interested. They were polite enough and one of them wrote down the details she was able to give them but they merely said they would look into it and then took their leave.

Kylie's mother then drove her home, only to find herself in the midst of what became a difficult social situation. Graham had previously arranged for Peter, Stephen, Roger and Alistair to come over to finalize arrangements for the weekend. While Kylie was changing in her room, they began their discussions on the front veranda. Afternoon tea was postponed by agreement because Margaret and Moira were both due as well.

When both girls had arrived the whole group was called into the dining room for cordial and scones. Mrs Kirk got Kylie to do the fetching and carrying and to act as hostess.

Moira poured herself a glass of orange cordial and said, "Are you boys all organised?"

Alistair answered, assuring her that they had all their timings and distances worked out and that they even had a Plan B if things did not work out.

"What's that?" Moira asked.

"Instead of walking all the way back to Kuranda, we will cross the river and look for the old gold mines in the hills there, then phone our parents to pick us up from Corwa," Alistair answered.

As he said this there was a knock at the front door. Mrs Kirk called from the kitchen saying, "Kylie, would you get that please?"

Kylie stood up and went to the front door, wondering who the visitor was. When she saw who it was she stopped in surprise and she was sure that her jaw dropped open.

It was Corey! "Hi," he said. "I was told that Moira was here. May I come in?"

Kylie's brain raced and she wanted to say 'No', thinking of Alistair, but no valid reason came to mind. Instead, she mumbled and led the way inside.

When the two of them walked into the dining room Moira's face registered real surprise and her mouth opened and closed a couple of times before she could reply to Corey's greeting.

"Corey! What brings you here?" she cried, her face mottling with embarrassment.

"Just passing by and I thought I'd drop in to check if you were still going horse riding on the weekend," Corey replied.

"Yes, we are," Moira answered, her face and neck now flushed red. Kylie saw her eyes flick nervously from Corey to Alistair and back.

"Good. I might see you then," Corey answered. For the first time he appeared to notice all the others, who sat in silence studying him. "Hello! I'm Corey," he added.

Kylie saw Alistair's face darken and set in a hostile glare. The other boys just looked at Corey with relative indifference and returned his greeting. Margaret had a tight little smile on her face, but her eyes were also swivelling back and forth as she assessed the reactions of Moira and Alistair. Alistair made no attempt to be nice and gave a curt nod in reply to Corey's greeting.

Oh dear! Kylie thought. *I hope there isn't going to be a fight.* She wondered how much Alistair knew about Moira meeting with Corey and even going out with him.

Corey seemed to be unconscious of the tension and then raised it dramatically by saying to Moira, "Could I talk to you for a minute?"

Moira seemed to go even redder and nodded. After an anxious glance at Kylie and Margaret she got up and followed Corey outside.

Chapter 25

LONG WEEKEND

Margaret watched Alistair's face as Moira followed Corey outside. She could see that Alistair was struggling hard to hide the hurt, but she was sure it was there. *Oh, how sad!* she thought. She liked Alistair and felt a bit annoyed with Moira for hurting him. Instinctively she felt that Alistair had more in common with her. A vague sense of unease made her unsure about Corey.

After they had gone outside there was a minute or two of silence. Then Graham said, "Who's that joker?"

Margaret saw that Kylie looked very upset so after a pause she shrugged and answered, "He lives on a farm near Corwa."

Stephen asked, "Is that the place we are hiking to this weekend?"

That was news to Margaret. "I didn't know you were going too."

It wasn't an idea that appealed to her. She had discovered that Stephen could be charming when he chose but still felt slightly uneasy about him.

Stephen nodded. "Mum said I could go if Alistair would be there. I have to get my hiking badge too. Then we can start on our Duke of Edinburgh Bronze award," he explained.

"Are you a scout?" Margaret queried.

"Yes. I'm in the Kookaburra patrol," Stephen answered.

This brought a burst of jibes from Peter and Graham. Peter was in the Platypus patrol and Graham in the Crocodiles. That set people laughing, and the good-natured banter kept them talking until Moira reappeared at the door. As she came in, Margaret glanced from her to Alistair, and she noted that Alistair appeared to be ignoring her. Thinking about how painful love could be at times made her glance at Graham. He met her eyes and gave her a quizzical smile in return.

Oh, I wish! Margaret thought.

She looked across at Kylie and saw that she was also watching the by-play (or lack of it) between Moira and Alistair. For something to say, Margaret asked Moira if she was going to Guides that night. Moira nodded and smiled but did not reply in words. That bothered Margaret a bit, but it wasn't till that evening when she was at Guides that her feelings shifted to annoyance and regret.

There was no sign of Moira at Guides and when Margaret asked her friend Sally if she was coming, Sally shook her head and said, "No. She said she was going out with this wonderful guy."

"Going out?" Margaret queried. "A date you mean?"

Sally nodded. "Yeah."

"With a boy named Alistair?"

This time Sally shook her head. "No, I don't think that was the name."

She has gone out with Corey, Margaret thought. The idea that Moira had, if not actually lied to her had at least misled her, made her feel both annoyed and hurt. It also made her feel sad. *I wonder if she has asked her parents?* she wondered.

Margaret at once sought out Kylie and discussed the gossip with her. Kylie looked sad and shook her head and said, "I hope not. I don't really like Corey and I think Alistair is very nice."

"Yeah, but if Moira is going to cheat then I'd rather Alistair didn't get involved with her," Margaret said.

Kylie agreed. The girls were then called away to take part in a game, so the subject was dropped. It did not resurface until the next morning when Kylie arrived in her mother's car. After Margaret had loaded her gear into the car, said farewell to her parents and little sister and settled herself in the back seat she thought, *I will have Moira next to me.* That idea made her feel somewhat uncomfortable.

Mrs Kirk drove the two girls to Moira's to pick her up as well. Along the way Mrs Kirk chatted happily and Kylie tried to join in, but Margaret could see that she had been crying and had not slept well. She wondered if she should mention Skip and even framed a question as to whether she had been found or not. But it was very obvious she had not, so she left the question unuttered.

Poor Kylie, she looks really down, she thought. That decided her not to mention Moira's date. It also occurred to her that Mrs Kirk might not be too happy for them to go off for the weekend if Moira was up to mischief. *And I do want to go horse riding,* Margaret thought. She had been looking forward to that for weeks and did not want to spoil it.

But it all made for a tense hour or so as they travelled up the Kuranda Range and west along the Kennedy Highway, then north along the Kambah Road. From Kambah to Corwa was a gravel road and the corrugations and potholes gave Margaret something else to think about. Then, as they got closer to Corwa, the excitement of arriving caused her to forget about Moira and her love life.

Mrs Lucas met them at the house and there were warm greetings and dogs to pat. There was then a distressing few minutes while Mrs Lucas was told about how Skip had gone missing. Kylie burst into tears again and had to be comforted by her mum. It was very obvious to Margaret that Kylie's mum was worried about leaving her, but Mrs Lucas patted Kylie and said, "She will be alright. A few days with the horses will help her a lot. Don't worry, Mrs Kirk. We will look after her and make sure she is happy."

Mrs Kirk gave a sad smile and nodded, then said, "I know you will. Anyway, it isn't Kylie who causes the problems. It is that youngest son of mine and his friends. They always seem to be getting into scrapes."

Kylie sparked up a bit at that. "Oh Mum! All the boys are doing is going on a hike. Anyway, we will see them on Sunday."

During all this Margaret found herself torn by the urge to run to the stables to see the horses so as soon as she had unloaded her belongings and thanked Mrs Kirk for the ride she said, "May I?"

Mrs Lucas smiled and nodded, and Margaret set off at the run. She was followed by Goldie and Blackie, the dogs. Kylie followed. A minute later both girls were happily rubbing horses' noses and patting their flanks. To Margaret it was obvious that Lucy remembered her as she gave a soft whinny and came eagerly to rub against her. Margaret hugged the horse's neck and pressed her face into her hair, savouring the odour of horse and leather that she exuded.

"What a good horse you are Lucy!" she cried, stroking her neck.

Lucy seemed to nod her head and Margaret wished she had a little something to give her. But she knew Mrs Lucas' rules. The riders could only give the rewards she gave them, and then only on meeting for the first time, or after a special event.

Margaret then noted Kylie patting Carbine and saw that she had smiled for the first time that day. *Good!* she thought. *Something to take her mind off Skip.*

A few minutes later, Moira appeared and said that Mrs Lucas wanted them. The girls walked back to where Mrs Kirk and Mrs Lucas stood beside the car. Mrs Kirk said, "I will be off now. You children be good now and don't give Mrs Lucas any cause for worry."

Kylie was indignant. "On Mum! We never give you any cause for concern, not like those brothers of mine."

Mrs Kirk smiled and gave her a farewell kiss before getting into the car and driving off. As she did, Margaret noted Kylie's bottom lip pucker and tremble and saw her eyes go moist. *Oh poor Kylie! I hope she is alright,* she worried.

To help divert Kylie's thoughts from home, she said, "Which rooms are we in, Mrs Lucas?"

"The same as last time, Margaret. Moira is on her own and you and Kylie are sharing," Mrs Lucas answered. She indicated their bags and said, "Come on, let's take you things in and then have morning tea."

Margaret really wanted to go for a ride but was happy enough to do as she was asked. She was glad she was sharing with Kylie and not with Moira. The girls collected their belongings and made their way to the rooms on the west side of the house. Having been there four times before they knew the layout of the house well and to Margaret it was almost like coming home. She particularly enjoyed going into the lovely old room with its quaint furniture and fittings.

"I love the smell in this room," she said to Kylie as she placed her bag on the floor beside her bed.

"So do I," Kylie agreed, flopping onto the bed and sighing.

There was then a delay of several minutes while they patted and rubbed the dogs. Goldie gave most of her attention to Margaret, so Kylie patted Blackie. Even old Duchess waddled in for a bit of attention. The girls then shooed the dogs out and Margaret brushed the dog hairs off her clothes.

"Aren't they lovely dogs?" she said, then could have bitten off her tongue when she saw Kylie nod and then her eyes water. *Poor Kylie,* she thought. Then she shook her head sadly, wondering what had become of Skip.

The girls quickly unpacked. Kylie made her way to the toilet and Margaret carefully arranged her toilet things on her bedside table. While she was doing this Moira appeared at the door.

"How is it? Okay?" Moira asked.

Margaret nodded. "Fine. I love this place."

Moira also nodded and there was a short pause. Margaret then asked the question that had been nagging at her all morning. "Did you go out with Corey last night?"

Moira nodded and Margaret saw her blush. When Moira made no reply Margaret said, "Well? What was he like? Is he nice?"

Moira blushed even redder and paused before answering. "He... er... he was very... very fresh."

"Fresh?" Margaret queried, her interest quickened.

"He... er kissed me a lot and his hands would have been all over me if I'd let him," Moira replied.

Margaret blushed too. "Are you planning to see him while we are here?" she asked.

"We might," Moira answered defensively.

That bothered Margaret and she wanted to ask Moira if she intended meeting Corey without telling Mrs Lucas. But she hesitated, knowing the question could make things very awkward between them. Kylie's return caused her to change the subject to horse riding and the moment passed.

Morning tea followed. This was in the back veranda. Margaret loved the view from there. It took in a long stretch of the river and the hills on the other side. In all that view there wasn't another house to be seen. Thinking about the boys possibly going hiking there, she asked, "Mrs Lucas, are there any farms or houses on the other side of the river?"

"Not in this area dearie. There are back towards Bilwon and Biboohra but none near us. The nearest downstream are all the way down at Oak Forest," Mrs Lucas replied.

"The boys talked about old gold mines," Margaret explained. "Are they near here?"

It was Mr Lucas who answered, after first giving a snort of disbelief. "Huh! Gold mines! There were a few miserable little scratchings back in the old days, but they were just a couple of old fossickers living in shacks. There'd be nothing much to see now. Just a few bits of rusty corrugated iron and some holes in the ground. You girls keep away from places like that. Old mines are dangerous places. You could fall down a shaft or the ground could collapse under you."

"And don't take the horses over there either please," Mrs Lucas added.

After hearing that Margaret became quite anxious about the possibility of the boys going there. As the girls went to their rooms to change, she said to Kylie, "I must warn Graham about the mine shafts."

Kylie's face broke into a grin. "Is that all you want to see him for?" she asked teasingly.

Margaret blushed but grinned. "No, but it is a good excuse."

"Okay, so let's ask if we can ride out along the road they are hiking on," Margaret suggested.

After changing into riding clothes they put this idea to Mrs Lucas. She smiled and nodded and said that was alright. "But you are not to travel for more than two hours out; and that at the walk, trot, canter and no galloping. And you are to dismount and walk for ten minutes in the hour."

"Walk!" Moira cried in horror.

Mr Lucas answered. "Aye, that is the best for horses on a long march. That is how the cavalry did it in the old days."

"Were you in the cavalry, Mr Lucas?" Margaret asked.

Mr Lucas nodded. "Aye, that I were. I spent six years in the Horse Guards in the British Army when I were younger. They are part of the Royal Bodyguard."

Margaret nodded. "I've sent them on TV. They have red coats and lovely, shiny silver armour and ride the most gorgeous big black horses. They guard the King and Queen when they travel in a coach."

Mr Lucas grinned. "Aye. That's them. That's where I learned about horses. But we were really an armoured regiment. We actually did our fighting in tracked armoured fighting vehicles."

Margaret was impressed. She had known that Mr and Mrs Lucas were migrants from England, but she had not known he had been a soldier. "Did you fight in a war?" she asked.

"Aye, but never mind that. It was a long time ago. You young girls don't want to hear about things like that. You go off and have a good ride," he said.

"And don't get lost," Mrs Lucas added as the girls made their way to the door.

Half an hour later the girls were wondering if they were. They had saddled their horses and ridden off in high spirits. At Moira's suggestion they had turned right once they reached the main gravel road.

"You just want to see Corey," Kylie had commented.

Moira had laughed and said nothing. But she had led them in the direction of Corey's farm. They had trotted to the bank of Venture Creek and then walked down to the bridge and across. As they crossed the road bridge, Margaret kept glancing right, remembering the boy's 'leap of death' off the rail bridge. She had been able to get glimpses of the rail bridge through the trees.

Once up on the west bank, they were still separated from the railway by a hundred metres of bush. The road then trended left until two hundred metres further west they had come to a road junction. A graded dirt road of noticeably lower quality led off to the left and went southwards.

"This must be the Kambah Road that the boys are going to hike along," Kylie suggested.

So the girls turned left and followed it. Margaret noted that it wound through open savannah woodland and that it ran roughly parallel to Venture Creek. To confuse matters more the road forked again after another half a kilometre. At that junction a road went off back to the right at a sharp angle, heading northwest. Margaret assumed it went back to join the main gravel road. At that point both roads deteriorated dramatically, and the grading ended. Both roads were just two-wheel ruts which wound off among the trees. The road that went south parallel to the river looked well used so they took that one.

But after a couple of kilometres the road forked again. They took the one to the right as it looked better used. But this road came out into cleared fields and went to a farmhouse. Dogs came out to bark, making the horses skittish. Rather than have a possibly unpleasant encounter the girls turned their horses around and rode back the way they had come.

After reaching the closest road junction at the Kambah Road, they went left and trotted back to the next road junction. At this Moira went left, instead of taking the graded road. Margaret wondered where she was going but assumed she knew and followed. Only when the track branched again at a Y-junction, the second road going off at a sharp angle to the left, did Moira stop and look around.

"Is this the road we came along," she said.

Margaret was astonished at the comment. *How could she not notice?* she wondered.

Kylie also looked surprised. "No, we were on the graded road."

"Graded?" Moira queried.

Again Kylie looked surprised. "Yes. You know, a grader has been along and smoothed the dirt."

Margaret could see that Moira still wasn't sure what Kylie was talking about, but she knew. Having played numerous games involving toy cars and earthmoving machinery with Graham and Alex she knew very well what a grader was.

"So which way do we go?" Moira asked anxiously.

Once again Margaret was astonished. Not once had she lost her sense of direction and she could even see the hills on the east side of Venture Creek from where they were. "Follow me," she said. Turning Lucy around she set off back at a fast walk.

Five minutes of trotting and cantering had them back at the graded Kambah Road. Turning left Margaret led the way back to the main gravel road. Once there they reined in and Moira looked around. "So which way is it to Corey's?" she asked.

"Left, to the west," Margaret answered, pointing. That puzzled her because she was sure the road Moira had taken by mistake actually joined the main gravel road somewhere that way.

"Then we will go that way," Moira answered.

"Nearly lunch time," Kylie reminded.

"It isn't far, is it?" Moira asked.

"A kilometre or so I think," Margaret answered.

Never having seen Corey's farm from the road she wasn't sure, and she tried to visualise the ride along the riverbank and convert it to distance.

Without further discussion Moira started riding west. Margaret exchanged a wry grin with Kylie and followed. The road curved to the left and then back to the right. Five hundred metres further along and still in bushland they came to a low ridge covered with savannah woodland. The road crossed this at a saddle. To the right was a small rocky knoll and Margaret got glimpses of the railway and open fields out beyond it. Right on the crest yet another side road went off to the left. This went south.

After a moment's thought Margaret said, "I bet this road joins up with that other one we were on a while ago, where we turned back."

Kylie agreed but Moira looked doubtful, so they rode on down the slope. The main road curved to the right and came back to the railway. Here it curved left and then ran parallel to the railway. A hundred metres further along the girls came to yet another road junction going off to the left. This junction was very similar to the first one they had come to, even down to the big tree beside the side of the road and the types of scrub beside the road.

Again Moira stopped and pointed along the side road. "Does Corey live down that way?" she asked.

Once again Margaret found it hard to believe anyone could be so disoriented. "No," she said. "He lives to the north, on the other side of the railway line, near the river."

Moira looked puzzled and said, "River? Isn't it that way?"

"No, the other way," Margaret said. "Come on, we had better hurry or we will be late for lunch."

She set Lucy moving and trotted on westwards along the main gravel road. This continued on parallel to the railway, the belt of bush getting narrower and narrower until there was only a single line of trees between road and train track. Beyond the railway were open fields and half a kilometre to her right front Margaret saw a cluster of buildings.

"That is Corey's farm," she said. "Now let's get back to Corwa before Mrs Lucas starts to worry."

The girls were only a few minutes late for lunch. The main delay had been in persuading Moira she needed to off-saddle and look after her horse first.

"But we will be riding again straight after lunch," she had argued.

But Margaret would not hear of it and was secretly a bit disappointed in Moira. Kylie supported her so Moira grumpily agreed.

Over lunch they discussed what to do during the afternoon. Margaret knew what she wanted. "Can we do jumps, please?" she asked Mrs Lucas.

"Yes, but only the low log jumps," Mrs Lucas answered. "And make sure you walk the horses around the jumps first to let them see them. And stay together in case of an accident."

So after lunch the horses were saddled again, and the girls rode out the front gate and across the road to the bush paddock. Having been there a dozen times before they knew all the tracks and mowed areas, but Margaret still made sure they obeyed Mrs Lucas and walked the horses around the track that had the log jumps.

The log jumps were old tree trunks of various thicknesses that had been placed across a mowed trail five metres wide. The trail wound through the savannah woodland and in most places was shady and reasonably cool. Some of the logs were only 10 or 15 centimetres thick but others were so big that Margaret would have had difficulty stepping over them. Even so they were quite small really. Margaret thought them pretty tame and thirsted for the day that Mrs Lucas considered her good enough to start training on the high slip rail jumps.

The girls began riding around trotting or cantering, taking the jumps in a follow-the-leader game. Moira led the way. As always, Margaret found the first jump a bit of a challenge, with faster heart beats and sweaty palms. But she soon settled to the sheer enjoyment of staying firmly on the horse as she took flight over each log.

"This is just so much fun!" she cried to Kylie.

Kylie grinned back and urged her horse to a canter to take the next jump. Margaret watched and waited. As she did, she saw Moira vanish around the next bend in the track. As this had been going on for nearly an hour, she gave it no more thought. It was only after she had completed another complete circuit and not seen Moira that she began to wonder. So she stopped in the shade and waited until Kylie arrived, hot and cheerful after the biggest jump.

Kylie wiped perspiration from her face and said, "Have you had enough?" she asked.

"No, but I think the horses need a drink and so do we," Margaret said.

The girls started towards the gate, their horses moving at a walk. As they approached the main road Kylie looked around. "Where is Moira? Are we waiting for her?"

Margaret shook her head. "I don't know where she is. I last saw her heading this way. That was nearly twenty minutes ago," she replied.

Kylie looked anxious. "We had better go round the circuit just to make sure she hasn't had an accident."

Margaret hadn't thought of that and felt quite guilty. So she kept her suspicions to herself and set off at a canter behind Kylie. It took them less than ten minutes to ride around the circuit and return to the gate, still without seeing any sign of Moira.

"Maybe she is still ahead of us," Margaret suggested. "You know, like a dog chasing its tail."

No sooner had she said this and seen Kylie's face cloud with misery at the word 'dog' than she felt she could have bitten off her tongue. *Oh, you thoughtless girl!* she berated herself.

Kylie shook her head sadly and said, "Okay, so one of goes one way and the other does the other way around and we meet back up here."

They did that and once again there was no sign of Moira. "Where can she be?" Kylie wondered aloud.

Margaret thought she had a pretty good idea, but she did not want to voice her suspicions in case she was wrong. "Let's go and find her," she said, urging Lucy into a walk towards the gate.

Chapter 26

RED FACES

Kylie was also thinking suspicious thoughts about Moira. For most of the time she had been consciously enjoying the horse riding, using the pleasure to push out the misery that engulfed her over Skip's disappearance. But now she was feeling annoyed.

Moira should not be sneaking off, she thought. *She is supposed to be looking after us.*

Moira's actions in dating Corey and not telling the truth also offended her own very strict code of what was right and what was wrong. To Kylie honesty was paramount.

I hope Moira has not snuck off to meet Corey, she thought unhappily, knowing that could spoil the weekend.

By then Kylie was near the gate leading into the bush paddock. The first thing she noted was that the gate was ajar. *I'm sure we closed that properly,* she thought. An image of Margaret doing so came to her and added to her suspicions. Then she looked down and saw the horseshoe marks in the sand of the entrance track leading to the main road.

She pointed to these and said, "These hoof prints are going the other way. They aren't ours."

Margaret nodded and looked both sad and annoyed, which was how Kylie felt. "Which way do they go out on the road?" Margaret asked.

Kylie walked Carbine through the gate and looked down. In her heart she was hoping to see the hoof prints cross directly over to the front gate of Corwa but instantly those hopes were dashed. The hoof prints were clear to see in the dust of the main gravel road and they turned left.

"They are going west," she said.

A tight feeling gripped her stomach and she began to feel slightly sick. *This could be unpleasant,* she thought. She stopped and waited till Margaret had come through the gate and swung it shut.

"Should we follow her?" she asked.

Margaret did up the gate catch and straightened up, then nodded. "Yes. We need to know, for our own sake."

"I think she has gone to meet Corey," Kylie said as they set off west along the road at a steady walk.

"So do I," Margaret agreed.

The girls lapsed into silence and rode on without speaking. A passing car forced them to the side of the road and after that they rode in single file, Kylie leading. Five minutes later they reached the top of the high bank overlooking Venture Creek. The hoof prints continued on down into the creek bed along the road, so Kylie kept following them.

As she went down, she kept glancing to the right to look at the railway bridge. Her mind filled with the awful memory of seeing the boys caught by the train and she broke into a cold sweat as she relieved the horrible seconds during which she had feared that her brother and his friends were dead.

I hope they are safe this time and not taking any silly risks, she thought.

With her mind full of anxious concerns and past worries she rode across the ten metres of road bridge, barely seeing the dark water that flowed beneath. But at the far side her thoughts shifted instantly back to the present. All the way she had been noting the hoof prints in the dust. There had even been enough sand and dust on the deck of the bridge to leave clear imprints, and to muffle the sound of her horse's own hoofs. Now she saw that the hoof prints turned right off the main gravel road and onto the rough vehicle track that ran along the lower bank from the turn-off at the far end of the bridge.

Kylie pointed to the tracks and turned Carbine to go that way. But almost at once she wished she hadn't. Not twenty metres ahead was a parked vehicle, a battered white utility. The ute was parked with its nose into the bushes beside the stream so that it was invisible from the main gravel road. It was in a small, grassed area beside a tiny sandy beach. On the far side of the grassy clearing was a horse. Kylie at once recognised it as Moira's and she noted that it was still saddled.

Maybe we should turn back? she thought.

But by the time that Kylie had realised that coming there was probably not a good idea it was too late. She was past the back of the ute and could see all of the small clearing. Her shocked gaze took in the blanket spread on the grass and the two people lying on it, writhing in each other's arms.

Kylie reined in and stared in shocked surprise. She saw that Corey was half lying on top of Moira and that he wore a pair of jeans but no shirt. Muscles rippled under tanned skin and caused her a surge of admiration and an emotion she had never experienced before but dimly recognised as physical desire. But it was where Corey's left hand was that riveted her gaze. It was inside the open front of Moira's shirt.

Even as Kylie took all this in, she heard Margaret give a shocked gasp from behind her and the pair stopped kissing and both turned their heads to stare at them. A look of horror flashed across Moira's face, to be instantly replaced by the crimson of embarrassment. Corey snatched his hand out and moved so that he was half lying, half crouching. His face flushed as well, but more with annoyance than shame.

Then anger flared in his eyes and he rose, chest heaving and hands clenching and unclenching. Seeing his physical lust and anger caused Kylie to recoil in fear.

Corey glared at her and Margaret, then gestured to go away with his clenched left hand. "Piss off you kids! Get out of here and mind your own business," he snarled.

One of Kylie's first reactions had been concern for Moira, fearing that perhaps Corey was forcing himself on her, but now she saw Moira also flashing angry looks through her bright red shame. She hastily started buttoning up the front of her shirt but said nothing.

Even so Kylie asked, "Are you alright Moira?"

Moira merely nodded and looked down.

That made Corey flare with even greater anger. "Of course she is! Now clear off and leave us in peace," he shouted.

His yelling and threatening posture caused Kylie a shiver of fear. It also upset Carbine and the mare began to fidget and high step. To keep control she held tightly on the reins. By now she was very embarrassed herself and she just wanted to get away, but Margaret and her horse were blocking in behind her.

Turning she called, "Let's go, Margaret."

Margaret, her face alive with interest and scarlet with embarrassment, could only nod and saw at Lucy's reins. The horse backed up and was turned away. Kylie was then able to turn Carbine around and as soon as she had a clear run she kicked back and urged her into a trot.

Back at the bridge, Margaret turned left and Kylie followed. Her thoughts were in a whirl and she was burning with embarrassment. To her own shame, she was also very excited about what she had seen. As soon as they were across the bridge and on the upslope, she slowed and looked back, her face red but her eyes alight.

"They were kissing," Margaret said. "And did you see what he was doing?"

"Yes!" Kylie cried, blushing even more fiercely.

Margaret shocked her some more by discussing the scene. "It's only natural," she added.

Part of Kylie knew that was true, but another part was still shocked. By then they were at the top of the bank. She said, "Corey must have arranged to meet her there," she suggested.

Margaret slowed to allow her to ride alongside. "Yes," she agreed. "I am sure they did. And didn't Corey lose his temper! He was horrible."

Kylie nodded and felt quite uneasy about Corey's reaction. "I thought he was going to hit us. I don't like him," she replied.

"He was certainly worked up," she said seriously. Then she giggled again and added, "Poor boy! Now we have spoiled their little pash."

Kylie went red again. "I hope that is all they were going to do," she said.

"Oh I think so," Margaret replied. "They are much too young to be doing anything more serious. But weren't their faces a picture?"

Kylie blushed again. "Oh, how will we ever face her again?" she asked.

Margaret just shrugged. "Easily. I'm more annoyed that she snuck off and didn't tell us."

"And that Mrs Lucas doesn't know," Kylie added.

That was what was really bothering her. The thought that Moira was a sneak made her feel very uncomfortable and she knew that the friendship would never be the same again.

Margaret looked serious and nodded. "Do you think we should tell her?" she asked.

That thought had just occurred to Kylie and it tormented her. She bit her lip as she thought hard. Then she shook her head. "No, not yet. But we must say to Moira that she has to stop sneaking off or we will. It isn't fair to Mrs Lucas."

Kylie knew that talking to Moira like that was going to be very embarrassing and awkward, but she was sure it had to be done.

The opportunity to do so came sooner than she expected. From behind her Kylie heard the thud of horses' hooves and, looking back, she saw Moira on Tornado galloping after them.

We have to face this now, Kylie told herself.

With sinking heart she reined Carbine to a halt and she and Margaret sat waiting. Even during the few seconds it took Moira to reach them she felt her face burning with embarrassment and she felt sick inside.

When Moira reined in facing them, Kylie saw that she was also red in the face. Moira looked very anxious and several times licked her lips with embarrassment. She glanced from one to the other and then said, "Please don't tell on me."

To her own surprise, Kylie found it easy to reply and she let her anger show. "Why not? You snuck off and left us to worry that something had happened to you," she said.

Moira had the grace to blush even redder. "I'm sorry. It's just that I didn't think you would approve."

"Not of you sneaking off if Mrs Lucas didn't know," Kylie replied coldly.

Again Moira blushed. "I thought you didn't like Corey very much."

"I don't," Kylie answered. "And I like him even less if he is going to be a sneak too."

Tears formed in Moira's eyes, and she bit her lip and looked hurt. "We didn't mean it like that. We just... just wanted to be... to be together. Please don't tell."

Margaret now spoke. "Only if you promise to us that you won't sneak off again."

Moira hesitated, then nodded. "Yes. Thank you. I promise."

Kylie did not feel very happy about the situation but also did not want to make it worse. She said, "Then let's go and do a few more jumps and then maybe go back to the homestead."

That eased the situation. The girls rode in silence back to the bush paddock and spent the next hour riding around doing jumps and then walked their horses back to Corwa. By then relatively normal conversation had been resumed and the situation had eased a little. But Kylie still felt resentful and sad.

Being greeted at the front gate by the dogs did not help. It reminded her of Skip, and she suddenly found herself with tears streaming down her face. Margaret and Moira both came to comfort her, and when Mrs Lucas saw them she also hurried over to see what was wrong.

"J... j... just think (sob!) thinking of... of... sniffle... of Sk... Skip," Kylie cried, indicating Goldie, who was jumping up and trying to lick her hands.

There was little the others could say to reassure her and Kylie wiped her face and said, "I will put Carbine away."

The girls led their horses to the stable yard and took off saddles, cloths and bridles and gave the horses a good brush and rub down. Seeing the obvious pleasure Carbine was getting from this attention made Kylie feel a lot better and she calmed down again. But she was still dejected.

Poor Skip. I hope she doesn't suffer, she thought.

Once the horses had been looked after and released to the home paddock the girls went into the house. It was still only mid-afternoon, but Kylie felt quite drained, and she could see that both Margaret and Moira looked tired.

"I am going to have a quiet afternoon," she said. "I think I will have a shower and then sit and read."

Both of the other girls thought this a good plan. Margaret added, "It has been a very stressful week. I feel like a good lie down."

Mrs Lucas also thought this a good idea. "You don't want to tire yourselves out," she agreed. "While you get changed, I will organise a nice afternoon tea."

Kylie and Margaret went to their room and from there Kylie went to be first in the shower. The hot water eased her tension a bit and she came out refreshed and also very aware that the air temperature had dropped noticeably in the last half hour. At the door she met Margaret and commented on this.

Margaret went into the shower and Kylie returned to the bedroom and brushed her hair. For a while she studied her wounds in the mirror, fretting over being permanently disfigured and relieved to see that most of the scratches were healing well. Once she had set herself to rights, she slipped her feet into her fluffy pink slippers and made her way to the back veranda. Mr and Mrs Lucas were both seated there with Moira. All three dogs were sprawled on the timber floor nearby. The winter sun was shining along the length of the veranda and Kylie sat so that her legs were in it, grateful for its warmth.

"It is getting quite cool," she commented.

"Yes, the weather report said there could be a frost tonight," Mrs Lucas answered.

As she said this Margaret appeared, dressed in flannel pyjamas, wrapped in a dressing gown and also with fluffy slippers on her feet. Margaret let out a squeak and cried, "Oh! The poor boys! They will freeze."

Moira gave a short laugh and said, "Would you like to go and warm them up?"

Margaret went red and gave an embarrassed giggle. But before she could answer Mrs Lucas said, "No talk like that thank you."

There was a strained silence and Kylie saw Moira go red as well. To save the situation she said, "The boys won't be here until tomorrow night anyway."

"Where are they camping tonight?" Mr Lucas asked.

"Somewhere along the Kambah Road I think," Kylie answered.

Mr Lucas nodded. "They will find it a bit chilly if they don't have the right camping gear. It can get very cold here. We had a minus four last week."

Kylie poured herself a cup of tea and sat stirring and sipping, her gaze looking out across the treetops to the hills across the river but her thoughts on Skip. *I wonder where she is?* she worried. Her brooding thoughts were not helped by two of the dogs coming to lick at her fingers and then to lie at her feet wanting a pat and a tummy rub.

The dogs then provided Kylie with another reminder of Skip when Blackie lifted his head and looked towards the front of the house. Next, he emitted a low growl, then a sudden outburst of barking as he scrabbled to his feet. With a clicking of claws on polished timber he dashed through towards the front of the house. Goldie squirmed in alarm, rolling onto her stomach, then followed, also barking. Old Duchess also got up and went growling into the house.

Mr Lucas stood up and laughed. "The great guard dogs have detected an intruder," he said. "It is probably only Mrs Thompson from down the road."

By then the barking at the front had already started to subside and it ended abruptly. Mr Lucas called from the front that it was Mrs Thompson and Mrs Lucas heaved herself up and hurried through.

Kylie sat back and relaxed, regretting the shadow of resentment and distrust that Moira's actions had caused, and which now stood between them like an invisible wall. She tried to overcome it by pretending everything was normal and by chatting about horses and the weather. It was a relief when all three dogs returned and again begged for attention.

By teatime the temperature had plummeted. Dinner was eaten inside in the gracious old dining room. The food was excellent, roast beef, baked potatoes, peas, and gravy. Kylie enjoyed it and felt slightly better.

After dinner the girls did the washing up. Kylie washed and Margaret dried, and Moira put the clean items away. When that was done, they joined Mr and Mrs Lucas in the lounge and sat watching TV. The programs did not particularly interest Kylie, but she was tired and did not feel like talking so she sat and watched and dozed.

After about an hour, Moira stood up and said, "I am just going to my room to write my diary."

She left the room. Margaret went and picked up a woman's magazine from the coffee table and set flicking through it and watching the TV. Kylie closed her eyes and tried to be positive. In spite of these efforts thoughts of Skip kept creeping in and she became quite dejected. These were in part prompted by two of the dogs raising their heads and looking towards the front and then getting up and going out. A minute later there were a couple of barks at the front of the house. Mr Lucas frowned and glanced that way but the barking stopped so he settled back to watching the TV.

Ten minutes later the need to go to the toilet caused Kylie to walk along the corridor. As she went past Moira's room, she noted that the door was closed. The sound of soft music came from inside. Kylie thought no more about it until after she had returned from the toilet.

As she sat down, Margaret whispered to her, "Is Moira in her room?"

"I think so. I'm not sure, the door is closed," Kylie replied. Only then did a niggling suspicion worm its way into her mind.

But obviously Margaret had been thinking the same thoughts as she whispered, "I wonder if she has snuck out to meet that Corey?"

Kylie was a bit shocked at the thought and said, "Margaret! You have a very suspicious mind."

Margaret nodded. "I have too. I can be as devious as the best of them if I want to be. But I don't sneak. Anyway, I am going to check."

"Margaret! Don't upset her," Kylie hissed.

Margaret nodded and went along the corridor. A few minutes later she came in from out on the back veranda. She gave Mrs Lucas a smile as she walked past. Then when she was sure the Lucases could not see her, she grimaced and shook her head.

"Not there," she whispered.

Kylie felt a spasm of alarm. "Where can she be?" she hissed back as Margaret settled beside her.

"Out the front at that big mango tree beside the railway line. That's where I'd arrange to have a secret rendezvous," Margaret replied.

Kylie stood up and said, "Let's go to our room and discuss this."

As the two girls walked across the room, Mrs Lucas turned and said, "Are you girls going to bed now?"

An instant surge of guilt heated Kylie's neck and cheeks and she hoped it wasn't obvious. "No Mrs Lucas, we are just going to our room to talk for a while. We will be back for supper."

"Good. We will have cocoa if you like," Mrs Lucas replied.

Feeling slightly ashamed of her answer Kylie led the way to her room. As soon as they were there she said, "What should we do?"

"Go and find her," Margaret said.

That made Kylie feel quite anxious. "It could be embarrassing, like this afternoon. What if... if they are... you know?"

Margaret pressed her lips together and then said, "No. Doesn't matter. It will be worse if Mrs Lucas finds her. We will all get a bad name then."

Kylie could only agree. She bit her lip and shook her head but stood up. "Lets' go around outside the house to the front."

"What about snakes?" Margaret asked.

For a moment a chill of fear surged through Kylie. But then she shook her head. "Too cold for them. They will all be curled up hibernating. Come on," she said. She led the way out through the far door onto the side veranda and then down the short flight of steps to the lawn. Outside it was quite dark. There was no moon and no cloud, so the sky was brilliant with stars. In spite of her confident assertion that the snakes would all be hibernating she still stared hard at the lawn and felt her heart tighten with anxiety.

The girls went around to the front of the house then detoured left into the front garden. "We will check the stables later," Kylie said.

As they walked slowly along the front driveway, both girls looked carefully in all directions. Kylie found she was breathing fast and knew she was anxious. Anticipating an embarrassing scene she bit her lip several times.

Then, as the girls neared the front fence, Kylie heard Moira's voice. It was raised in alarm, and she cried, "No! Please don't! Stop it! Stop or I will scream."

Kylie felt her heart skip a beat and she clenched her fists. *Margaret was right,* she thought. The voice came from over behind the big mango tree where there was a garden seat.

"Come on!" she hissed to Margaret and set off at the run.

Chapter 27

MOIRA

Margaret broke into a run to follow Kylie. As she dashed past the rose garden and headed for the mango tree she heard Moira again call out, "No! Stop! Please don't!"

In reply came Corey's voice, an angry and threatening voice. "Don't give me that, you teasing bitch! You can't lead me on like that and then not give."

"No! Stop!" Moira cried. Then she obviously saw Kylie as she gasped, "Oh!"

Margaret skidded to a stop beside Kylie and stared down. Moira was lying on her back on the grass with Corey lying half across her. He had both her wrists in his and was wrestling with her and Margaret noted that he had his left knee in between Moira's thighs. Luckily, she wore jeans.

As he became aware of their arrival, Corey jerked his head around to look and then rolled off Moira and sprang to his feet. He was breathing fast, almost panting and Margaret saw that he had clenched his fists and raised them. Then he snarled and hissed, "Go away, you girls. Mind your own business!"

"It is our business," Kylie replied coldly. "Moira is our friend, and she should not be out here."

Corey swore and again said, "Clear off! And don't you dob on us."

By then Moira had rolled over. She got to her feet and brushed at her clothing. Even in the starlight Margaret could see that she was blushing and looking very angry. But she spoke very quietly when she said to Corey, "I think you had better go."

Corey swore again and looked from one to the other. For a second Margaret feared that he would make a scene but the arrival of the three dogs forestalled that. Goldie and Blackie arrived first, barking with excitement. Old Duchess followed, coughing and wheezing.

Corey swore again and snarled, "Keep the bloody dogs under control. If they bite me, I will make them regret it!"

The threat sent a shiver through Margaret, and she decided that she really did not like Corey at all. *He is just a brute, out for what he can get,* she thought. But for the sake of the dogs she grabbed at Goldie's collar and patted her.

"Shhh Goldie! Quiet girl," she said.

Kylie took hold of Blackie but said, "Don't you dare hurt these dogs. They are just doing their duty as guard dogs. What a horrible thing to say!"

Corey sneered and said, "Guard dogs! Some guard dogs! I was here for half an hour before they realised it."

Moira took hold of Duchess and said, "Maybe, but they only stopped barking because I told them to."

"Don't you turn on me too!" Corey snapped at Moira.

Moira shook her head and said, "You had better go, Corey."

Corey glared at them, but at that moment the front door of the house opened and a light came on over the front veranda. Mr Lucas appeared. In the faint light from the veranda Margaret saw Corey's face twist into a scowl and he hissed, "Don't tell on us you two. Make sure Moira doesn't get into trouble."

Having said that he slipped out through the partly open front gate and hurried across the railway line. Margaret saw his shadowy form in the starlight for a few seconds and then he vanished. Even the soft pad of his boots on the dirt road was lost in the sighing of the wind.

But by then another minor crisis had begun as Mrs Lucas joined her husband on the veranda and he called out, "Are you girls there? Are you alright?"

Kylie called back, "We are all here, Mr Lucas. It is alright."

Mrs Lucas answered, "You had better come back in. It is getting cold, and it is getting late."

Margaret realised she was shivering without a coat. But as the three girls began walking back along the garden path Moira placed them all in a dilemma by whispering, "Please don't say anything about Corey."

That really put Margaret on the spot. "But he was... was trying to force you... He was..."

Moira shook her head. "No. It was my fault. No, please don't say anything."

"You want us to lie to the Lucases," Kylie hissed accusingly.

There was an embarrassed silence and Margaret knew that Kylie had said the exact truth. And she agreed with her, but wasn't sure what to do. But there was no time to discuss it in private as the Lucases were standing waiting and were now too close for the girls to have a secret conversation without raising suspicions.

Reluctantly, Margaret nodded and hissed, "Okay." But she blushed with shame as she did it as she knew it was wrong. But having acquiesced in the plan she set out to make it work. As she reached the front steps she said to Mrs Lucas, "I love the way you can see all the stars here. When you live in big city you don't see them like this."

Mrs Lucas nodded and agreed but said, "I would prefer that you girls don't go outside at night, and that if you want to go somewhere you let us know."

"Sorry, Mrs Lucas," Kylie answered.

As they went back inside, Margaret met Kylie's eye and gave wry grin. She noted that Moira was hanging back to come last and that she did not look happy. *Oh dear! This is really going to spoil things,* she thought.

As they got to the dining room, Moira said, "I will just go to the toilet."

She hurried off and Margaret saw that the back of her shirt and jeans was dirty and that she had some grass and twigs adhering to the cloth. *I hope Mrs Lucas doesn't notice them,* she thought. Suspecting that Moira was not aware of the state of her clothes, she followed her along the corridor.

As Moira went to enter the bathroom, Margaret called softly, "Moira!"

"Yes, what?" Moira answered. She looked angry but ashamed.

"Let me brush you down. You have some grass and dirt on your clothes," Margaret replied.

Moira blushed bright red and for a moment Margaret thought she was going to say no, but then she bit her lip and nodded. Margaret followed her into the bathroom and immediately brushed Moira's back. This was mildly embarrassing as she had to brush down Moira's bottom. As she did, she wondered if she should say anything about the incident but decided to hold her tongue. All she said was, "That looks okay now. See you in a minute."

She hurried back to the dining room to find that Mrs Lucas had set out small plates and bowls and was placing a cheesecake on the table. "Would you prefer cheesecake or ice-cream?" she asked.

Kylie answered first, asking for ice-cream. Margaret shook her head. "Cheesecake for me please. It is too cold for ice-cream."

The food was served and they sat down. Margaret had been hoping that Moira would have re-joined them by then but she hadn't. In an attempt to cover the social situation she began to chatter happily about the day's horse riding. But when Moira hadn't reappeared after another five minutes Mrs Lucas frowned and said, "Is Moira alright?"

"I think she is feeling a bit sunburnt," Margaret answered.

Kylie stood up. "I will just check," she said.

Margaret gave her a grateful smile. Facing Moira again was something she wasn't looking forward to. Kylie went off along the corridor and Margaret tried to pretend everything was alright. She began eating the cheesecake with a teaspoon. As she did, she tried to listen to what was being said at the bathroom while at the same time talking to the Lucases. But all she heard was Kylie very firmly saying, "I think you should."

A few seconds later, Kylie reappeared with an unhappy looking Moira behind her. Moira gave a half smile and said, "Sorry. I've got a bit of a headache."

She and Kylie sat and were given desert. Margaret kept up her cheerful chatter but soon found it a strain. What was particularly nagging at her was Moira having said that she did not want them to say anything about what Corey was trying to do.

If Corey is like that and nothing happens to him, he could force some other girls to do things, she thought.

This was the issue she raised when the three girls made their way to their bedrooms fifteen minutes later. "You must complain, Moira," Margaret said. It had taken her an effort of will power to summon up the courage to say this and her anxiety made her more abrupt than she normally was.

Moira shook her head. "No. Please, I don't want to talk about it."

"But he might hurt some other girl," Margaret said.

Moira looked doubtful and very unhappy, but she still shook her head. "No, he is alright. I just led him on."

Kylie snorted and said, "Oh you did not! He was trying to... to force you. You were scared."

"No... I... I... Oh please drop it! I love him!" Moira cried. Tears began to trickle down her cheeks and she sniffled.

Hearing that really annoyed Margaret. *How can she be so blind?* she wondered. In exasperation she said, "But you don't really know him."

"I do! And I do love him! And I am going to see him again," Moira cried.

Kylie shook her head and snapped, "Not by sneaking off while you are here!"

Moira glared at Kylie. Kylie held her stare and compressed her lips. Margaret felt ill at the thought of a fight and the resulting ill-will. But she was also sure that Kylie was right.

She said, "Moira, he is just using you!"

Moira turned on her and almost shouted, "What would you know? Mind your own business."

Margaret was about to retort that it was her business when Mrs Lucas called along the corridor, "Are you girls all right? What's the problem?"

Margaret called back, "Just a little disagreement, Mrs Lucas. It is settled now. Goodnight."

Mrs Lucas appeared and looked doubtful, but Margaret managed a smile and Kylie said goodnight. Moira turned and walked off to her room, her back stiff with anger. She went in and closed the door without looking back.

Kylie led the way along the corridor to their room and Margaret followed. Once inside the friends looked at each other and shook their heads. "He is just using her," Margaret whispered, aware that Moira was just in the next room.

"I agree, and I think he is a real coarse brute and a bully," Kylie replied.

"Oh dear, this has spoiled the whole weekend," Margaret sighed.

Kylie shrugged. "No it hasn't. We will just make sure Moira doesn't get up to mischief. Anyway, the boys will arrive tomorrow. That should cheer you up."

Margaret gave a little giggle and her mood changed instantly. She said, "Oh yes! And then it is me you will have to keep an eye on."

Kylie grinned and said, "Margaret!" but there was no heat in it. She collected her pyjamas and toothbrush and went off to the bathroom. While she was gone Margaret changed into her own pyjamas, nice thick flannel ones; pale blue with little dancing bears all over them.

When Kylie came back a few minutes later she said, "It is really cold outside. The temperature must have gone down ten degrees in the last half hour. Mr Lucas might be right. There might be a frost tonight."

The two girls walked out onto the side veranda. The moment they stepped out of the door Margaret felt the chill bite at her. Almost immediately she began to shiver. "Oh yes! It is freezing! The poor boys are camping out in this. They will really suffer."

Kylie laughed. "They will survive. If I know them, they will have a really big camp fire and be sitting around it as warm as toast."

Margaret looked out into the darkness and imagined the boy's camp. Into her mind came the image from where they had camped down at the mouth of Venture Creek, but she knew they were somewhere else tonight.

I hope Graham is alright, she thought.

But it was cold; too cold to stay outdoors for long, so the girls went back in. Margaret cleaned her teeth and then hurried to bed, glad she had warm fluffy slippers and a good dressing gown. After saying goodnight to Kylie and then turning out the light, she slid into bed.

But she did not go to sleep for a long time. She kept thinking about Graham and fantasising about snuggling up with him, and about Moira and Corey. The saddest thing she found was that her respect for Moira had gone down. It was all very confusing, but she knew she would be a hypocrite if she was too critical of Moira. It also came to her that women in love could be very blind and very foolish.

Oh, I hope I don't make terrible choices and mistakes in my relationships, she mused. That got her thinking about her ideal man, her 'Mr Right'.

From that it was a short step to fantasising about Graham again and she got herself very heated and soppy by imagining a whole range of romantic situations in which he was her hero.

Chapter 28

SUNDAY MORNING

Kylie was in a very deep sleep when Mrs Lucas shook her awake on Sunday morning. Mrs Lucas smiled and said, "Wake up sleepy heads! It is nearly seven o'clock and breakfast will be on soon."

Kylie opened her eyes and realised she was curled into a snug little ball with only her nose poking out from under the quilt. As soon as she went to throw the quilt off, she realised it was very cold.

"Oooh Mrs Lucas, it is freezing!" she cried.

Mrs Lucas smiled and said, "It is. The thermometer reads four degrees in the kitchen so it will be much colder outside. There is frost on the grass."

Margaret had been sitting up and rubbing her eyes during this, but she now cried, "Oh, the poor boys! I hope they are alright." She hopped out of bed and immediately sprang back up and let out a little squeal. "Oooh! The floor is like ice!"

She quickly slipped on her slippers and dressing gown and hurried out onto the veranda to look. Kylie reluctantly sat up and then wished she was back under the blankets as a draught of icy cold air came in through the open door.

"Margaret! Close the door!" she wailed.

Margaret laughed and called from outside, "Don't be a big sook! Come and look at the frost."

Kylie did so, but without much enthusiasm and only after slipping on her own slippers and dressing gown. But when she stepped out into the bracing air, she at once perked up and felt better.

"It is really fresh," she said.

Revealed to her amazed eyes was a shimmering white world. It was almost as though it had snowed. A coating of frost covered the lawn and the leaves on the trees and even formed in little clumps on some of the fruit and bigger objects. Several spider webs stood out in quite startling patterns. As the first rays of the sun glinted on the frost it seemed to sparkle and shimmer.

In spite of herself, Kylie was impressed. She was also astonished. "But we are in the tropics! We are only sixteen degrees from the equator!" she said.

Mrs Lucas had joined them and said, "Don't forget you are up on the Tablelands and are also a fair way inland. It is always colder away from the sea."

Margaret looked enraptured. "Isn't it pretty!" she cried, clapping her hands and hopping up and down.

"Graham won't think so," Kylie replied.

"Oh yes! I hope they are alright," Margaret said. Her face changed to a look of concern. Then she said, "You are steaming Kylie."

"So are you" Kylie answered.

They both were. Their breath came in very obvious puffs of condensation. She was fascinated as it was a phenomenon that she rarely saw in Cairns.

Mrs Lucas said, "The frost will be gone in an hour or so. And the radio said there is a change in the weather coming so it will be quite hot today and tonight should not be as cold. Now you girls wake Moira and get ready for breakfast in fifteen minutes."

She left them staring at each other. Kylie felt her insides tighten up as she remembered the previous night's incident. *Moira! What can we say?* she wondered. But she saw the anxious look on Margaret's face so said, "I will wake her. You go first to the bathroom."

Margaret gave her a grateful little smile and hurried off. Kylie went to Moira's door and then paused to take several deep breaths before knocking. There was no response and for a dreadful moment Kylie feared that Moira had snuck away during the night. So she knocked again.

This time a muffled, "Yes, who is it?" answered.

Feeling a wave of relief, Kylie said, "Me, Kylie. It is breakfast time. Mrs Lucas has called us."

"I don't want any. Please go away," Moira replied.

"No," Kylie replied. In a flash of insight she knew that it all had to be settled at once or everything would be spoiled so she said, "Moira, please come and join us."

"I don't feel well," Moira replied.

"Please, you need some food," Kylie replied. She was determined now and quite surprised that she didn't feel more scared. She went on,

"Moira, we still want you to be our friend and we want to enjoy the weekend. Please help us."

To her relief, she heard Moira's bed creak and Moira said, "Oh very well!"

"Thank you. See you in the dining room," Kylie answered. She then hurried to her own room to collect her towel and toilet bag.

At the door of the bathroom she met Margaret coming the other way and now dressed. Margaret raised an eyebrow and Kylie nodded. "She says she is coming," she said.

As quickly as she could, Kylie washed her face and brushed her hair and dressed. Feeling much better she pulled on a jumper and went back to her room. Margaret was waiting for her, and the two girls went to the dining room together. When they got there, Kylie let out a little cry of delight. Mr Lucas had lit a fire in the fireplace and the room was already warming up. The cheerful crackle of the flames made the whole room seem very welcoming and the smell of fried bacon and fresh toast added to the sense of pleasure.

The two girls sat and began eating. Kylie discovered that she had a real appetite, and she savoured the taste and aroma of the food. But after a few minutes she began to worry that Moira might have changed her mind. She was very relieved when Moira appeared a few minutes later. Moira was dressed for riding and was rubbing her hands vigorously together. She said good morning and made a comment about the cold before sitting down. Kylie could see that she was very unhappy, even though she was trying to smile. Her appearance shocked Kylie. Moira looked very pale and had dark rings under her eyes.

She has had a bad night, Kylie surmised.

To cover this she began a cheerful chatter about the boys and their camping trip. Then she realised that this probably wasn't a popular topic with Moira because Alistair was one of the group. So she was very careful not to mention his name and led the conversation on to the weather forecast.

Moira hardly spoke during the meal and when asked by Mrs Lucas if she was alright she just said she felt a bit tired as she hadn't slept well. That got Kylie worrying that she might want to stay at the house but to her relief she made no request to do so.

Margaret said, "What shall we do today?"

Mr Lucas said, "I am shoeing a horse named 'Lively Lad'. You can watch and help if you like."

Kylie at once agreed. Shoeing was something she knew the theory of and had seen it done from a distance, but she had never watched the whole process. Margaret was equally enthusiastic, but Moira just shrugged and nodded. Mrs Lucas then said she would like to introduce the girls to show riding and dressage. Kylie wasn't as keen on that, but Margaret was really happy about it and said so.

After cleaning and washing up and then brushing their teeth, the three girls went out to the stables. By then the frost had all melted and everything looked normal. Kylie was surprised at how quickly the air had warmed up and wondered if she needed her pullover on. When they made their way into the workshop at the end of the stables she knew she didn't as it was quite warm inside. Mr Lucas had a fire going in a brazier of coals and that heated the room as well.

Mr Lucas was busy using a hand powered bellows to make the fire even hotter. He looked up and said, "One of you girls can take over here if you like."

Both Margaret and Kylie offered to do so at once. Mr Lucas told them to take turns so Kylie allowed Margaret to take the handles of the bellows. Margaret began pumping with a strong, steady movement.

She said, "What is this for, Mr Lucas?"

"The bellows give a forced draught to increase the flow of oxygen into the fire. That makes it hotter. The fire is to heat the metal horseshoe so it can be shaped exactly to the horse's foot," Mr Lucas explained.

While Margaret pumped the bellows Mr Lucas asked Kylie to help him bring Lively Lad in. The horse was tethered outside and was a lovely chestnut yearling. Kylie thought him a beautiful horse and could not resist going to say hello. The horse twitched his ears and looked at her with equal interest. Mr Lucas nodded with approval.

"You are a good hand with horses, Kylie. I might get you to hold his head while I work, if you don't mind?"

"That will be fine, Mr Lucas," Kylie answered. She was happy to help and did not mind what job she was given.

They led the horse inside and positioned it. As they did, Kylie noted that Moira was standing to one side looking bored. Margaret on the other hand was panting and her face had taken on a cheery reddish colour, both from the glow of the fire and from her exertion. She stopped and wiped perspiration from her brow and said, "You take over for a minute Kylie while I take off this pullover."

Kylie did so. Within a minute she was also panting and understood exactly why Margaret had done so. She also quickly discovered that her arm muscles were not used to such work. The speed at which the muscles began to tire and weaken surprised her, and she decided she must do more physical exercise. The exertion quickly heated her up and she began to sweat inside her pullover.

Thinking to involve Moira, she turned to her and said, "Would you like to have a go, Moira?"

Moira shook her head and folded her arms. That disappointed Kylie but Margaret had taken off her pullover by then and moved back to take over from Kylie. Kylie gave her a grateful grin and returned to holding Lively Lad's bridle.

For the next half hour, Kylie took turns at pumping the bellows and at holding the horse. During all of it she watched fascinated as Mr Lucas trimmed and then shaped the horse's hooves with a file. Moira was surprised when Mr Lucas began filing away at the front nearside hoof.

"Won't it hurt him?" she asked anxiously.

Mr Lucas shook his head. "No. It is just a giant toenail. For the same reason it won't cause him any pain when I place a red-hot horseshoe against it; although the smell and hammering might bother him. That's when you have to hold him steady and keep him calm," he explained.

Kylie saw exactly what he meant when he took a horseshoe and then held the fetlock between his knees and tested the shoe for fit. It was slightly too big, so it was then placed in the charcoal to heat while he moved on to work on the next hoof.

As he worked, Mr Lucas said, "And you girls always remember not to walk behind a horse. If he lashes out with his hind legs and kicks you in the head, it could kill you. The poor old horse won't mean it. It is just instinct. So be very wary of his back legs. Now, Moira, will you please help me hold this hind leg while I check the shoe size, please."

For a moment Kylie feared that Moira would refuse but she nodded and moved to help. That seemed to break her mood as she had to concentrate and then became obviously interested in the work. Seeing that made Kylie feel much happier and she relaxed. But she did wonder if Mr Lucas had not noticed that something was amiss and was working to fix it.

One at a time red hot horseshoes were taken out of the brazier using long tongs. Mr Lucas held them in position on the hoof they were to go on while Kylie held the horse's head and Moira his fetlock while Margaret patted and stroked it and Mr Lucas checked the fit.

Mr Lucas then held the horseshoe on the steel anvil and picked up a heavy, short-handled hammer. After a couple of solid strokes with the hammer Mr Lucas again placed the horseshoe against the bottom of the hoof. Nodding with satisfaction he dipped it into a bucket of water. When it was cool, he put down the tongs and took the shoe in one hand and a hammer in the other. Taking a long and wicked-looking steel nail from a nearby box he positioned it at one of the holes in the horseshoe.

Moira looked horrified. "Oh Mr Lucas, you can't hammer that in!" she cried.

Mr Lucas looked up at her and shook his head. "It won't hurt him, Lass. There are no nerves in the hoof. You just hold him firm like."

When he was satisfied that Moira was doing as she was told he drove the nail in with four deft strokes. Kylie winced at the first couple, but the horse only turned to watch and did not otherwise react. To help keep him calm Kylie stroked his cheek and spoke softly to him.

"Won't be long now, boy. You will have nice new shoes and then you can gallop on the rough ground without splitting your hooves," she said. The horse bucked his head a couple of times and Kylie felt sure he had understood and was nodding. "Good boy!" she said, patting him some more.

It actually took about another twenty minutes and Mr Lucas had some trouble with the third shoe, having to reshape it twice before he was satisfied. By then Moira was also talking, both to them and to the horse. That really pleased Kylie and she hoped the day would be enjoyable.

Once Lively Lad was shoed and returned to his yard the girls went to saddle their horses. Mrs Lucas joined them and insisted they put on their riding caps.

"I don't want any broken heads," she said.

The four of them then rode across the railway and road to the practice paddock. After warming up the horses Mrs Lucas got each girl in turn to demonstrate to her that they could walk, trot, canter and gallop. The whole time she called encouragement and advice. Mostly this consisted of reminders to keep their backs straight, their heads up and their elbows in.

Then Mrs Lucas introduced a whole new level of challenge, riding over low jumps while keeping their arms folded or with their hands on their heads. The jumps were only small logs or a single plank in height, and when Kylie first looked at them she thought it would be easy. But when she came to have her first go with her hands on her head, she experienced a real rush of anxiety. Her self-confidence evaporated and she bit her lip and knew her heart was hammering fast.

Her confidence was not helped by watching Margaret. She looked perfectly composed and sat on her horse as though glued to it. At every jump Margaret grinned and looked as though she was thoroughly enjoying herself. She took every jump easily and trotted back to join them smiling and patting her horse's neck.

Kylie went next, swallowing to clear her suddenly dry and choked up throat. The first jump was only about 20 centimetres high and looked to be nothing but when Carbine's motion suddenly changed as she stepped lightly over it Kylie felt herself sway backwards and then forwards far more then she thought she would. To stay on she gripped tightly with her knees and thighs and that turned out to be a mistake as the pressure urged Carbine to go faster.

The pony took the next jump, still only about 25 centimetres high, at a good canter and before Kylie had recovered her balance. Suddenly Kylie felt herself sway back so far that she was looking at the sky. In an attempt to keep upright she used her stomach muscles to pull her upper body forward. She managed this, but too far and too late. By then Carbine was coming down on the other side and Kylie fell forward. Her face was flicked forward so that she bumped her nose on Carbine's neck. Before she realised what was happening, Kylie felt herself falling forward over Carbine's left shoulder. She tried to get her hands down to grab hold of the bridle or the mane but was unable to do so in time.

Suddenly Kylie found herself looking at the horse's chest and his legs and she knew she was coming off. To make sure she was not dragged, she had the presence of mind to flick her right foot out of the stirrup and to curl herself into a ball. She hit the ground on her left shoulder and rolled. Thankfully this was to the side of the hooves and she was not struck.

For a few seconds Kylie lay on her back wondering if she was hurt. But there was no obvious pain. Instead a wave of embarrassment surged through her. Margaret arrived first, leaping from her horse even before it had stopped.

"Kylie, are you alright?" she cried, kneeling to hold her.

Kylie nodded and sat up. "Yes, I think so. Only my pride has been hurt."

"Oh piffle!" Margaret replied. "Everyone falls off at some time or other."

"You don't seem to," Kylie replied.

She felt annoyed at herself and also jealous of Margaret's obviously superior ability. But she stood up and dusted herself down then began walking towards where Carbine was now standing looking at her. Through her mind ran the old adage about getting straight back on and she was quietly determined not to let the jumps beat her.

This attitude was reinforced by Mrs Lucas who, after she had checked that Kylie was unhurt, also said she should have another go.

"I'm going to, Mrs Lucas. I won't let it beat me," Kylie replied. Clenching her jaw with determination she took hold of Carbine's bridle and then gently patted the horse's neck. "Not your fault old boy. We will do better next time," she said.

She swung herself back into the saddle and trotted back to the start of the run, her mind full of anxiety and determination.

Chapter 29

MOIRA'S MOODS

Margaret watched carefully as Kylie rode forward. Because she really cared for her friend she felt considerable anxiety that she do it right. To her relief, Kylie did and Margaret clapped and cried, "Well done!"

That caused Moira to make a wry face and seeing it sent a stab of worry through Margaret. *Moira is not enjoying today,* she thought. But she was determined not to let the previous night's unpleasantness spoil the day, so she also cheered and clapped when Moira made a successful jump.

That seemed to ease the atmosphere and Moira manage a smile in return. The girls began riding around in a circle, jumping and cantering and soon Moira was laughing and smiling all the time. Margaret noted her change of mood and cheered up. The morning then seemed to fly past, with the girls becoming quite sweaty and even saddle sore.

Mrs Lucas was pleased with their efforts and said so. She led them back to the homestead for lunch and again insisted that the horses be unsaddled and rubbed down.

"But Mrs Lucas we want to go riding after lunch," Moira protested.

"Too bad. It is not fair to the horse to leave it standing in saddle and bridle for hours. So please looked after your horse now," Mrs Lucas replied firmly.

Margaret saw Moira nod but look sulky and that did not please her. *It is just laziness not to take the saddle off,* she thought. So the animals were looked after and then the girls hurried in to wash before going to the dining room.

Moira still seemed to be in a bad mood during the meal, but Margaret tried to ignore it. *The boys will be here this afternoon,* she thought. That thought cheered her up and helped to make the situation easier.

After lunch, the girls made their way to the stables and again saddled and bridled their horses. As she tightened and tested her girth strap, Margaret asked, "Where shall we ride this afternoon?"

"Where would you like to go?" Kylie countered.

"A bit further along the tracks we were on yesterday afternoon," Margaret answered.

At that Kylie grinned. "You just want to see Graham."

"I do too!" Margaret answered, blushing but happy. To change the topic she said, "What about you, Moira, which way do you want to go?"

"The same way will do," Moira replied.

Margaret suspected that Moira wanted to see Corey and for a second she held Kylie's eye, sure that her friend was thinking the same thing. However, she said nothing, not wanting to upset the fragile mood. Instead, she nodded and bent to check the buckles of the strap.

A few minutes later, the girls trotted out the front gate after telling Mrs Lucas where they were going. As they turned right after crossing the railway line, Margaret experienced a real mix of emotions. There was happy anticipation at possibly seeing the boys (especially Graham); but also some apprehension lest Moira caused more tension by trying to sneak off. There was also embarrassment as they rode down across the bridge in Venture Creek. Margaret had vivid flashbacks to seeing Moira and Corey in their heated embrace on the creek bank and by her blush and the way Moira pretended not to look she suspected she was having the same reaction.

For the sake of harmony, Margaret made no comments about the previous day and Kylie rode stiff backed and silent ahead of them until they were up on top of the other bank. Here Kylie cantered ahead and waited at the road junction, then turned left and walked her horse along the Kambah Road.

Margaret worried that Moira might just ride straight on along the main road but to her relief she didn't. She followed Kylie. That eased the tension a bit and the girls began to chatter. Their mood was lightened even more by seeing a large goanna which went scuttling off up a tree as they approached it. After circling the tree to study the huge lizard, the girls continued on. A few minutes later they came to the next road junction, where the other road went off back to the right. Once again, they halted.

All the while Margaret had been hoping to meet the boys, but her watch told her it was only 2pm. The girls sat there on their horses and debated riding on southwards.

Moira looked anxious and tense. "What time are these boys due here?"

Kylie answered. "Not sure. They were supposed to camp last night at where this road crosses over Venture Creek. Today they were taking some side track over the hills to some old gold mine and then hiking to here."

"So we don't really have any idea?" said Moira.

"No, but they must get here before dark as they are camping here," Kylie replied.

Margaret felt the tension and noted Moira's mood change again. To calm things she said, "Maybe the boys have had an accident or are delayed? We could ride that way to meet them."

"They have a mobile phone. They will be alright," Moira said.

Kylie shook her head. "Mobile phones don't work very well in among all these hills," she pointed out.

"Why don't you check?" Margaret suggested. She really wanted to know where the boys were and how they were.

"Okay, I will," Moira answered curtly. She took out her mobile phone and looked at it, then frowned and shook her head. "No, you are right. We haven't got any reception here."

Seeing that confirmed to Margaret that Moira had tried using her mobile phone to contact Corey. Moira then looked at her watch and then bit her lip before glancing along the other fork in the gravel road. That made Margaret tense up even more.

Moira is thinking of going to see Corey, she thought.

She was right as Moira pointed along the other road and said, "That road leads to the main road doesn't it?"

"I think so. I think it joins the main road on the ridge we crossed the other day. That was over near Corey's place," Margaret answered.

"Then I am going to see him," Moira stated.

"Moira, don't!" Margaret cried.

"Why not? I'm not sneaking off this time. You lot can come and check that I am being a good little girl if you like. I just want to tell him something," she said.

Her tone of voice was challenging and curt, but Margaret nodded and said yes rather than precipitate an argument. Kylie looked doubtful but when Moira pulled Tornado's head around and set off along the other road she followed with Margaret.

"I don't like this," she hissed to Margaret as they rode side by side along the other dirt road.

"Nor do I, but it is better than her going off on her own," Margaret replied.

She could only shake her head and bite her lip as her anxiety about what the meeting might be like built up. It was obvious that nothing she or Kylie might say would dissuade Moira from going.

It turned out that Margaret's suppositions were correct: the road did join the main road at the crest of the ridge near the small rocky knoll. But once again Moira went the wrong way when she got to it. For a few seconds Margaret hesitated.

Will I tell her? she wondered, seeing that Moira was now heading for Corwa.

Then Kylie settled it for her by calling out. Moira stopped and looked back. "What?" she called, irritation and defiance in every line of her face.

Kylie pointed back to the west. "Corey lives over that way."

"He does not! You are just trying to trick me," Moira replied angrily.

"We are not," Kylie answered, going red and obviously put out that she was not believed.

"You are. You don't like Corey and you don't want me to see him," Moira answered. With that she turned and continued on.

Kylie shook her head angrily and muttered, "Well, suit yourself then!"

Margaret looked at her friend and said, "What do we do? Do we wait here till she finds out she is wrong, or do we follow her and try to persuade her to go home?"

"Follow her," Kylie replied. With that she tapped her heels against Carbine's flanks and set off down the hill after Moira.

It was just as well they did because when they caught up with Moira she had reached the first road junction and ridden around in a circle with a puzzled look in her face and was then starting up the other road again.

Margaret could not believe what she was seeing. "Moira!" she called.

Moira stopped, reefing angrily at the reins as she did. "What?"

Seeing the way Moira was treating her horse annoyed Margaret, but she tried to restrain her temper. "That is the way we first went."

Moira looked along the other road and looked doubtful. "It isn't. You are just saying that."

"It is Moira. Look, you can see the hoof prints of our horses in the dust," Margaret replied, pointing down. Then she added, "Anyway, why should we bother to lie?"

"Because you are jealous and don't want me to see Corey," Moira replied.

For a moment Margaret was struck speechless by the accusation. Then she snapped back. "I am not! I love Graham and... and..." Just in time she bit off the rest of the sentence. She was glad of that because in her mind were the words calling Corey a coarse bully and a brute.

Kylie also looked astonished. "Don't be ridiculous, Moira!" she snapped. "We just care for you and don't want you to get hurt. Now let's please go home."

"No! I want to see Corey. Which way do I go?" Moira replied.

Seeing that Moira was determined Margaret pointed back up the slope to the west. "That way."

Moira turned and kicked her horse into a canter. Within seconds she was almost out of sight. As she turned her own horse to follow, Margaret noted that tears were streaming down Kylie's cheeks.

"Why Ki, what's the matter Boo?"

"Just a bit... sniffle... bit...up... upset sob," Kylie answered.

Margaret felt a surge of annoyance at Moira's moodiness and said, "Is Moira upsetting you?"

"Yes... No. sniff... I was just thinking about Skip and... and... sob."

Kylie burst into tears and Margaret moved to reach across to touch her arm. The two friends stopped and Margaret waited until Kylie stopped sobbing. Then she handed her a handkerchief and said, "We had better keep up with Moira to stop her doing something silly. I don't trust that Corey."

"You... sniffle... are sniff... right. He is a real thug," Kylie answered. She blew her nose and then handed the hankie back before urging her horse into motion again.

The two girls trotted down the dusty slope until the railway and open fields became visible. They passed the next road junction and rode on. As they came to the long straight that ran west Margaret felt a twinge of anxiety. There was no sign of Moira.

"Where is she?" she commented.

Worried that they might lose her she urged her horse into a canter. Kylie followed. As she rode Margaret looked to her right front, trying to see out across the open fields through the gaps in the trees. But even though she could see the buildings of Corey's farm in the distance there was still no sign of Moira.

Where can she be? she wondered. Then, remembering Moira's difficulty with geography she glanced down at the road. *Did she turn off at that last side road?*

But she hadn't. A line of fresh hoof prints showed clearly in the dust on the side of the road. But still no sign of Moira. So Margaret continued riding, until an approaching vehicle caused her to rein in and move into the long grass beside the road. The vehicle, a station wagon coming from the west, raced past at high-speed leaving a billowing trail of dust. Margaret waited till the dust had drifted away before proceeding lest another vehicle be traveling behind the first.

Then she moved back onto the road and trotted on. A sneezing Kylie followed 25 metres back. Margaret studied her friend and noted that she was still looking unhappy, but she could only shrug and ride on. Then, as she turned to face the front again, Margaret saw Moira.

She was standing at a closed gate on the side road leading to the Corey's farm. The gate was on the far side of the railway. Margaret reached the turnoff and slowed to allow Lucy to pick her way across the railway tracks. As she crossed, Margaret glanced both ways along the line, noting how the rails shone in the sun and in the distance appeared distorted in the heat shimmer.

Reaching Moira, she saw that the gate was locked. Moira was angrily trying her mobile phone but gave an exasperated snort and snapped, "There isn't any service here. What a stupid system."

"We are a long way out in the bush," Margaret pointed out. She was quite irritated by Moira's behaviour and not in any mood to placate her.

"Humpf! I will walk in," Moira replied, moving to climb the gate.

Margaret glanced along the road leading to the farm. It was ruler straight and led to the side of the cluster of buildings. These also appeared to shimmer in the heat mirage. Nobody was visible and she estimated the distance at about 500 metres.

"Don't do that Moira. That sign there says 'Trespassers will be prosecuted'," Margaret pointed out.

An anxious looking Kylie added, "And that other sign says, 'Beware of the dogs'. I think they mean it."

"But Corey will look after me!" Moira cried.

That got Margaret really anxious. "But he may not be there. They were pretty savage looking dogs we saw."

Kylie agreed, calling, "Oh Moira, please don't!"

To Margaret's relief, Moira hesitated and then reluctantly climbed back down from the gate. Margaret wiped perspiration from her brow and said, "Oh please let's go home. You can contact him on the Lucas's phone maybe."

That idea caused Moira to brighten and after a last wistful glance towards the farm she untied Tornado and remounted. Margaret glanced at Kylie and sighed with relief, then turned and began walking her horse back across the railway.

But Moira didn't wait. She was obviously angry and upset and she kicked Tornado into movement and clattered across the railway and then reefed his head around to face east and kicked him into a canter. Margaret was both surprised and annoyed but urged Lucy to follow.

Moira had a fifty-metre lead but Margaret didn't worry as she was heading back towards Corwa. But within another two hundred metres, just as the road curved into the bush, she had to urge Lucy into a gallop when she saw Moira turn right along the dirt side road.

"Moira! Moira! Stop! Stop! That is the wrong road," Margaret yelled.

But Moira did not hear her and kept on riding. Margaret turned onto the side road and followed, marvelling that Moira could make such a mistake as this road was grey sand and not even graded. Again she yelled. By then Moira was just visible through the trees as the side road wound among them.

Luckily, Moira heard her and reined in. "What's wrong?" she called, her face a mask of annoyance.

"This is the wrong road. We need to stay on the main gravel road to get home," Margaret explained, reining in near her and pointing back.

"Are you sure?" Moira queried in a peevish tone.

"Yes, I am, but you can keep following this road if you like!" Margaret snapped back, nettled by not being believed.

With that she turned Lucy around and set off back along the side road. Kylie met her and also turned her horse around. "Is she coming?" she asked.

Margaret glanced back and then nodded. "Yes."

By then the two girls were back near the junction with the main gravel road. As she went to express her opinion of Moira's ability to navigate Margaret heard a vehicle approaching at high speed. It was coming from their right along the main road. Fearing for the horse's safety she looked that way and relaxed when she glimpsed the vehicle. It was going much too fast to turn into the side road.

As it got closer the vehicle became visible in a series of flickering images between the trees. A cloud of dust billowed up behind it. Then it roared past the junction, rattling and juddering over the corrugations and potholes. It was a white van.

Suddenly Kylie's hand seized Margaret's wrist and she cried, "The white van!"

Chapter 30

THE WHITE VAN

Kylie stared at the white van as it raced past but it took a few seconds for the meaning of the image to register in her mind. *A white van,* she thought. Then it struck her, as she noted the streaks of red mud and the broken back window.

"THE white van!" she shrieked, grasping Margaret's wrist as she did. Then dust obscured the scene and hid the van from view. Kylie coughed but barely noticed it. "The white van!" she cried again, still gripping Margaret's wrist.

"Are you sure?" Margaret replied, staring into the dust cloud.

"Positive. Come on!" Kylie yelled.

She let go of Margaret and urged Carbine into motion and even used her heels to drum on his flanks to get him to canter. Through her mind surged a rush of emotions: hope, fear, revenge. Images of Skip swamped her thoughts, and she rode with determination, bent on following the van. And then she thought of needing to see the van's number plate. Angry at herself for not thinking of that before the dust hid it, she urged her horse to go faster.

But the horse was no match for the machine and the dust began to settle ahead of her. *Oh no! I mustn't lose it now!* she thought, anguish twisting her hopes. Then she saw that the dust cloud led off along the side road towards Corey's farm. That puzzled her but also gave her hope because she knew it was a dead-end road. *I will catch it now*, she thought.

Through the trees she spotted the van again and noted that it had stopped at the gate on the other side of the railway lines. *I will catch it!* she thought. But then another, more sobering thought came to her: what would she do when she did catch it?

What can a young girl like me do against a grown man? she worried.

But she kept on, only glancing back to check that Margaret and Moira were both following. They were. Then Kylie saw that a man, the thin man she had seen take Emma's dog, Thistle, had climbed out and was unlocking the gate.

That is the man! she thought exultantly. Then she frowned.

But what is he doing? Why is he going to Corey's?

The fact that the thin man obviously had a key gave her pause and it came to her that charging up to challenge the man might not be the best tactic. So she slowed down and then reined Carbine to a halt while still a hundred metres back. From there she urged Carbine in among the trees beside the road. That gave Kylie a view along the railway line clearing and she was able to watch the man. It also revealed to her that another man, a big, burly man, was driving the van.

As Margaret caught up and joined her among the trees, the thin man swung the gate open and the van drove through. The thin man then swung the gate shut. Margaret leaned forward and peered through the trees.

"What is it? What's going on?" she hissed, catching the need for silence from Kylie's actions.

"They have closed the gate and the thin man is locking it. Oh, I'm sure that is the man who stole Emma's dog that day at the park," Kylie answered.

Then Moira arrived. "What on earth are you doing?" she called from the edge of the road.

Luckily her voice was drowned out by the van accelerating as soon as the thin man had climbed back in. Kylie pointed to the van and then explained that she was sure it was the same van she had seen when Emma's dog had been stolen. Moira looked doubtful.

"Oh it is not! It is just a van," she replied.

But Kylie was certain. "It is, Moira, I am sure of it," she insisted.

"So what?" Moira asked.

"So we need to call the police," Kylie answered.

That made Moira frown even more. "But you can't be that positive."

"No, but I still think it is worth calling the police. I am certain that man who opened the gate was the same one who stole Thistle," Kylie replied.

"The police won't be impressed if it is just a false alarm and they drive all this way for nothing," Moira said.

"I don't care! I won't ever forgive myself if I don't try to find out," Kylie replied fiercely.

Margaret backed her up. "We must Moira. I won't ever sleep soundly again if we don't. I will lie awake at night wondering," she said.

"But you won't catch it," Moira said.

"Yes, we will. That is a dead-end road. The van must come back this way," Margaret answered.

"Are you sure?" Moira queried.

"Moira! You've been there. That is Corey's farm. The road just runs down onto the riverbank and ends. There aren't any side roads, just gates into paddocks," Margaret said, shaking her head as she did.

Kylie also shook her head and wondered how Moira ever got around without always being lost. "One of us can stay here and one go for help," she said.

"Why stay here?" Moira asked, obviously puzzled and worried.

Kylie again shook her head. "To note the registration numbers and to tell the police which way the van goes if it drives back out again before they arrive," she explained.

Moira said, "Oh!" and nodded as comprehension dawned. Then she frowned again and said, "And what will you be doing?"

"I am going to ride around to the back of Corey's farm to check that the van has gone there and to get its number," Kylie replied. The plan had come to her ready formed and she felt the urgent need to act.

But not Moira. "But... but shouldn't we check first?" she suggested. "I mean, if it is the wrong van, it might cause a lot of upset to Corey and his family. That wouldn't be fair."

Kylie had already been having some dark thoughts about what the van might be doing at Corey's, but she did not want to hurt Moira by voicing her suspicions. Also she did feel the justice of her argument. *Maybe we had better not just rush in,* she thought.

Reluctantly, she said, "Alright, we will check first. Margaret and I will ride around to the back and look and if it is the van we will come back and get you. How about that?"

"That will be better. But shouldn't we all go?" Moira replied.

"No. Someone needs to be here to watch which way the van goes and to get its number," Kylie repeated. "But you don't have to stay. Margaret can."

"No, I will," Moira answered.

A niggling worry made Kylie bite her lip and she made herself say, "You must hide. And don't let Corey see you. We will put your horse back up that side road out of sight."

"Why shouldn't Corey see me?" Moira asked, shocked.

"Because... because the van has gone to his house and h… his family might be involved," Kylie replied. She had been going to say, 'he and his family' but had bitten it off just in time.

"Oh Kylie! That is an awful thing to say! How dare you! What right have you got to suggest such a horrible thing," Moira cried angrily.

Kylie could think of several things she had seen Corey do that made her doubt his character, but she did not answer. It was Margaret who spoke. "I will stay here if you like," she offered.

Moira shook her head. "No! I will stay here. You two go and look at this van, then come back and get me."

"Promise you won't speak to Corey please," Kylie asked, knowing she was pushing things but wanting to be sure.

"No. I will speak to him if he comes along. But I won't mention you two or what you are doing," Moira answered.

"We will take your horse," Kylie said.

"No. I will just be able to say that I am out riding; and I can run away better on a horse too," Moira replied.

Kylie wasn't entirely happy with that answer but felt that any further argument could lead to Moira refusing to co-operate. She glanced at her watch and saw that it was 3:30pm. "We will try to be back by 4:30. That is an hour. If we aren't back by 5 o'clock then go back to Corwa and tell the Lucases please."

"Alright," Moira agreed. She then sat and stared towards Corey's farm, looking very thoughtful.

Kylie did not wait. She turned Carbine and gee-upped him out to the road. Margaret followed and the two girls set off at a canter back along the road.

By this time Kylie was in a ferment of impatience. Now that she had a straw of hope to cling to she was gripped by fierce determination to investigate. Pushing the niggling worries about Moira to the back of her mind she urged Carbine into a gallop.

This only lasted for a short distance as the road went up over the low ridge. On the downslope Kylie eased back to a steady trot after Carbine slipped and almost fell.

"Sorry boy," she said, patting his neck and feeling guilty that her impatience might have injured the animal.

256

A glance behind showed Margaret trotting along behind her. They passed the two turn-offs to the south and then came to Venture Creek. At the bottom Kylie reined in and waited for Margaret.

As soon as she had caught up, Kylie turned Carbine left onto the vehicle track along the creek bank. As she trotted along it she noted the grassy clearing where they had caught Moira and Corey in their heated embrace and the memory caused her mouth to twist into a sour grin. Then the railway bridge brought back other unpleasant memories but also hope.

The boys might be here, she thought. That would make everything easier. *Graham loves to play commandos. He will be good at sneaking up.*

But as she passed under the railway bridge and was able to see the small island at the junction her hopes crashed. The place was deserted and there were no boot prints to indicate anyone had been there for some time. Biting her lip and shaking her head, she rode on, turning Carbine left again to follow the trail along the riverbank.

Having been along it before she barely noticed the overhanging branches, prickly bushes, and long grass. Only once did she really focus on where she was and that was when Carbine suddenly shied and reared back.

"Whoa! Whoa boy!" Kylie cried, managing with difficulty to stay in the saddle. As Carbine backed up Kylie looked anxiously around. Margaret was close behind on Lucy, so Kylie called, "What was that? Why did Carbine shy?"

"A snake. A big brown one," Margaret replied, pointing to the left ahead of Kylie. "It was all coiled up and Carbine must have nearly stepped on it. I only saw it when it uncoiled and took off."

"Is it gone?" Kyle asked, peering anxiously at the long grass and weeds that bordered the narrow foot trail.

"It went into that long grass. I saw its tail," Margaret replied, pointing again.

"Thanks. Come on Carbine," Kylie said. She urged the horse to move but it baulked and stood firm, trembling and with legs locked. Again Kylie tried but the horse would not move. Irritated and impatient Kylie dismounted and grabbed Carbine's reins. "Come on horse!" she commanded.

But Carbine was still reluctant. That got Kylie all in a lather. It also caused her to look over her shoulder. There was no sign of the snake, but the possible danger finally sank in and Kylie stopped pulling and stood, thinking hard.

Margaret helped by saying, "We are halfway. Why don't we leave the horses back there in that little clearing? We can do the rest on foot."

That made good sense to Kylie. She wasn't sure how far they had come but thought they didn't have far to go. She nodded and said, "Good idea. Besides, we don't want the horses too close in case they whinny or get discovered by those horrible guard dogs."

"Oh yes!" Margaret replied, obviously appalled at the thought of the savage guard dogs attacking the horses.

So the girls led the horses back 50 metres to a small grassy clearing and tethered them to saplings. "Sorry boy," Kylie said when Carbine gave her a worried look.

Kylie now led the way along the narrow track. There were a few anxious moments as she passed the clump of bushes where the snake had vanished but once past the bushes she went faster. Even so she kept a wary eye on the ground in case of other snakes. Margaret followed, also casting frequent anxious glances at the long grass and weeds on both sides of the track.

After five minutes of walking, Kylie began to worry. *I didn't think it was so far,* she thought.

But she admitted to herself that she hadn't been paying much attention when they had ridden along the trail previously. At least it all looked familiar to her and she continued on, feeling sure that they would come to the vehicle track leading up to the farm at any moment.

It took another seven minutes of fast walking before they reached it and when they did Kylie experienced both a sense of relief and then a prickling of anxiety. Glancing back, she placed her finger to her lips to caution Margaret to keep quiet. Margaret nodded and followed her. Knowing that Margaret was there gave Kylie more confidence and also caused a surge of affection.

Good old Margaret! She is very game, she thought. *I am very lucky to have such a good friend.*

The vehicle track that led up the steep slope of the riverbank was just two-wheel ruts with a water pipe beside it. On either side was a tangle of weeds, lantana and tall grass. The road angled up to the left, and as they walked up it Kylie glimpsed the back of the large steel shed they had seen on their previous visit.

As she approached the top of the bank Kylie slowed down. Her caution was driven by memories of the savage dogs that had barked at them last time.

"We don't want any dogs to smell us," she whispered to Margaret.

Margaret nodded and then licked her finger and held it up. "Better stay upwind if we can," she replied.

Kylie hadn't thought of that but immediately saw the importance in what Margaret suggested. She knew that dogs had a quite remarkable sense of smell. That thought made her change her plan. Directly in front of her were a locked gate and the vehicle track which ran straight for a kilometre out to the railway. On the right of the track was a fence and beyond that an open field. The bottom of the fence was hidden by long grass and weeds, and she had thought to creep along the edge of the field to where she could see past the end of the big shed and into the farmyard beyond. Now she realised that the wind was blowing gently from that direction and that would make such a course risky.

"We had better go the other way," she whispered, pointing to the left along the rear of the big shed.

She knew that beyond it was the farmyard with buildings on three sides. All she could hope was that there would be gaps between the buildings through which they might be able to observe the white van. The back of the big shed was close to the top of the riverbank and was covered in tall grass, weeds, and lantana. That promised to be very unpleasant to creep through and also conjured up images of snakes.

Snakes must live in that tangle, she thought.

But fierce determination to obtain justice (or was it vengeance?) allowed her to grit her teeth and start pushing into the thicket. She went slowly, both to make the minimum of noise and to allow time for any snakes to slither out of her way. Margaret studied the tangle of vegetation and grimaced but then followed without argument.

It was as horrible as Kylie thought it might be. Lantana crackled underfoot and scratched her exposed skin and leaves fell down the back of her collar to irritate and prickle. The long grass caused her to itch, and she had to frequently suppress the urge to sneeze. Not being able to see clearly where she was putting her boots was the worst aspect as each step was an effort of willpower and courage.

Now I know what it must be like to walk through a minefield, she thought.

Even though the air was now cooling she was in a lather of sweat and that made it worse as grass seeds and dead leaves stuck to her bare skin, adding to the irritation.

It took nearly ten minutes of slow and painful creeping and pushing to reach the far end of the shed. Kylie peeked around and saw that a fence continued on along the riverbank and a second fence went off inland at right angles. Beyond the fences was another open field, this one dotted with beef cattle. Luckily these were in the distance but the sight of them still got Kylie anxious lest the beasts detect their presence and betray it by looking or stampeding.

The only choice was to crawl under the back fence and then along the side of the shed on the outside of the second fence. Luckily it also had a screen of long grass and weeds growing along it so it offered some cover from both the cattle and the buildings. As she crept along on hands and knees Kylie noted that there were no windows in the end of the big shed, nor in the back of the long shed that took up that side of the farmyard.

Margaret followed, looking grubby but determined. The grass and prickles were both irritating and painful, but Kylie persisted. And her efforts were rewarded. At the end of the big shed there was a gap of about five metres between it and the long shed. Through the gap she was able to look into the farmyard, and there was the white van!

Kylie lay in the long grass and studied the van. "It is definitely the one," she whispered to Margaret, who crept up beside her.

"What will we do now?" Margaret asked.

"Memorise its registration number and get the police," Kylie replied.

Both girls began to do so, muttering the numbers quietly over and over to fix them in their memory. Then, just as Kylie was gesturing to creep away, a dog began to bark in the yard beyond the van. The sound sent a thrill of fear through Kylie and she froze in anxiety.

Have we been detected? she worried.

Then, to her surprise, Moira appeared at the back of the white van. She was on foot and had walked across the yard from the other side.

Margaret gripped Kylie's arm and hissed, "What is she doing here?"

Chapter 31

HIDE!

Margaret stared in astonished dismay at Moira. *What is she doing here?* she wondered. She met Kylie's eyes and thought to call out.

Moira stopped and looked around, then moved to the back of the white van. She looked worried and was biting her lip. First, she bent forward to peer into the small windows. Then she shook her head with annoyance or disbelief and reached for the door handles and opened the doors. As she opened them, she let out a gasp and then leaned forward into the interior.

As she did, more dogs joined in the barking. Margaret thought to call to Moira to tell her to get away from the van but even as she opened her mouth to call out a man stepped through an open door in the front wall of the big shed. The door was near Margaret and she had not noticed it until then.

Corey's father, Margaret noted.

As she did, she was torn by the desire to call out to warn Moira and fear. Corey's father was carrying a stock whip and looked anxious and angry. He was followed by a thin man, the same man who had taken Thistle.

Fear held Margaret silent although her mind told her it was better to stay hidden. Corey's father strode the three paces to Moira and grabbed her shoulder even as she heard him and started to turn.

"What are you doin'? Who the bloody hell are you?" Corey's father snarled.

Moira recoiled in shock, mouth agape. Worry showed on her face, but she quickly mastered it. "Keep your hands off me! I'm looking for Corey," she said, shaking herself free.

"Corey! Looking for Corey! Who the hell are you? Hey Corey!" Corey's father replied, the last in a loud shout.

Corey appeared through the same door, wiping his hands on a piece of cloth and looking puzzled. Then he gaped and cried, "Moira! What the hell are you doing here?"

"I came to see you," Moira answered. By now she was looking scared. Margaret saw her eyes flicker to the van and then to the driver and then back to the van.

"How did you get in?" Corey asked. He did not sound very friendly or glad to see her.

Moira pointed and said, "I climbed the gate." Again she glanced at the driver and the van.

The driver spoke first, cutting Corey off. "What are you looking at? Who are you?"

"I'm not looking at anything. I came to see Corey," Moira answered.

Corey's father frowned and said, "Where did you come from? How did you get here?"

"On a horse, from Corwa," Moira replied.

"With your friends?" Corey asked, looking around.

At that Margaret felt a chill of fear and crouched lower in the weeds. Moira shook her head. "No. On my own. They... they don't know I am here," she explained.

"Friends?" Corey's father queried.

Corey answered. "Yeah, two little girls, a good looker with dark hair and a tubby little one built like an egg."

Hearing that caused Margaret to burn with jealousy and embarrassed hurt.

Corey continued, "Where are they?"

"Gone home. They rode back towards Corwa," Moira replied. Once again, she glanced at the van and then at the driver.

"And you didn't tell them where you were going?" Corey's father demanded to know.

"No," Moira answered. By this time she looked really scared. She turned to go and said, "Sorry. I didn't mean to cause any trouble. I'll go now."

The driver obviously did not believe her as he said, "She was looking in the van. I don't believe her. What were you looking at girl?"

"Nothing," Moira cried, but even to Margaret it did not sound very convincing.

The driver shook his head angrily and swore. "Don't lie to me, you stupid bitch! You were looking at them." He pointed into the back of the van, making Margaret intensely curious about what was inside.

She learned the answer immediately when Moira defiantly pointed into the back of the van and said, "Are they your dogs? That dog there looks like my friend's."

Margaret felt Kylie stiffen and their eyes met. *Skip! Is he in there?* Margaret wondered.

Corey's father swore and the driver snarled, "She knows something, Cass. Who are you? Who sent you girl?"

"Nobody. I came to see Corey," Moira replied. She looked very scared now and turned to try to walk away.

She got no more than two steps. The driver sprang forward and grabbed her arm. "Oh no you don't! You know something."

"Let me go!" Moira cried, the fear showing in her eyes.

Margaret tensed ready to try to help but Kylie gripped her and hissed, "Sssh! We can't do anything against three men."

Corey's father stepped closer and snarled, "What's your game, girlie? What are you doing here?"

"I came to see Corey. Let me go! Corey, tell him to let me go," Moira cried, anger and shock alternating in her voice.

Corey's father turned to Corey. "Were you expecting to see her boy?"

Corey shook his head. "No, Dad. I told her not to come here."

Corey's father curled his lip into an ugly sneer and placed his face close to Moira's. "What's the game? Why are you here sneaking about?"

Moira tried to move away and showed her distaste on her face. Then she again pointed into the back of the van. "They aren't your dogs, are they? You stole them."

Cass snarled, "She knows something alright. Don't let her go."

"But what will we do with her?" Corey's father asked.

Cass looked around, causing Margaret to cringe in fear. Then he said, "We better lock her up and see if she will tell us what she knows."

"But what if she won't talk?" Corey's father queried.

Cass chewed his lip and said, "Then we leave her here. We obviously have to get out of here now. If she knows something, then others might also." He turned to Moira again. "Tell us what you know, or you will regret it," he threatened.

"I don't know anything," Moira cried, tears now starting to trickle down her cheeks. "I just came to see Corey."

"How do you know Corey? Is this true Corey?"

Corey now spoke and he explained how he had met Moira. "I took her out when I was down in Cairns."

"Is she the girl you snuck off to see last night?" his father demanded.

"Yes, Dad."

Corey's father again looked worried. "You bloody drongo!" he snarled at Corey. Then back to Moira, "Where are your friends?"

"I told you, gone back to Corwa. They don't know I am here. They don't approve of my friendship with Corey," Moira explained.

Corey's father turned to Cass and said, "Do we get going now?"

Cass shook his head. "No, we go ahead with tonight, then we go."

"But what if they have gone to call the cops?" Corey's father asked.

Cass stepped close to Moira and hissed, "Have they?"

"N... no," Moira replied.

"Then we stay. We lose too much money if we don't hold tonight's meet. Lock her up," Cass said.

Corey's father nodded but looked unhappy. "What about her horse?"

Cass nodded and said, "Corey, you go and get the horse and put it down on the riverbank up past the far side of the west paddock, near that old shed. If anyone comes asking, we say we haven't seen her and we offer to help search. If they find the horse it isn't near here. And don't you let your feelings for this girl give you any weak ideas of helping her, or else. Now get going!"

Corey nodded and walked quickly off across the yard. His actions, or rather the lack of them, lowered Margaret's opinion of him even more.

What a coward! she thought.

Corey's father and Cass now hustled a terrified and protesting Moira through the doorway and into the shed. As they did, Kylie gripped Margaret tightly, warning her to stay still. Margaret found it hard to do as her every instinct was to run to her friend's assistance. But her mind told her it was futile.

We need to wait our chance, she reasoned.

As soon as the men with Moira were inside, there was a sudden outburst of noise as dogs began to bark and snarl. Margaret was appalled by the sounds. She turned to Kylie. "What do we do?" she whispered.

"One of us must go and get the police while the other one stays on watch," Kylie answered.

That was what Margaret had been thinking. "Who goes?" she asked.

"You... er... Shh!" Kylie started to say.

But she went silent and lay flat as the two men came back through the doorway near them. Margaret tensed, ready to run or fight. She found she was breathing fast and then she realised that her nose was tickling. A sneeze began building up. She gripped her nose and squeezed upwards to make her eyes water.

Cass climbed into the back of the van and passed a cage to Corey's father. In the cage was a dog, a Scotch terrier. Corey's father walked inside. As he did, there was another sudden outburst of savage barking from several dogs. Corey's father shouted at the dogs and then returned a few seconds later without the cage. Cass passed him another cage. This time Margaret gaped, and it was her turn to grip Kylie in warning. In the cage was a black and white terrier, Skip! She only got a glimpse of her but, she was sure.

Skip! She is alive! she thought, her heart leaping with hope.

More cages were carried into the shed. Some contained dogs but others had roosters and even guinea pigs. *What on earth are they taking all those creatures into that shed for?* Margaret wondered. Because of the continual outbursts of barking and growling from inside she had a sneaking suspicion, and it made her ill just to think it.

The men came back out and closed the door. For the next few minutes they stood talking near the back of the van. They were just too far away for Margaret to hear most of it, but she did get the sense that they were very worried and extremely angry. Then Cass closed the back of the van and both men walked off out of sight towards the other sheds.

As soon as they were gone, Kylie turned to Margaret. "This is our chance. They haven't locked that door. We will try to rescue Moira."

"What if she is locked in?" Margaret whispered back.

"We will at least know. Now, you go for help, and I will free Moira," Kylie replied. With that she crawled forward to the fence and began wriggling under the bottom strand.

Margaret knew it was good sense for her to go but was consumed by curiosity. "I will come too," she replied.

By then Kylie was halfway under the fence. "No! Go and get the police," she hissed back furiously.

"I will just have a peek inside," Margaret insisted. With that she began pushing through the grass under the bottom strand.

Kylie stopped arguing and wriggled through. She crouched for a second and stared in the direction the men had gone, then walked quickly over to the door. Margaret followed, ignoring the dirt and grass seeds she had collected in hurrying. By the time she reached the door Kylie had opened it and slipped through. As she did, there was another eruption of noise as dogs began to bark and growl. Margaret paused to glance anxiously over her shoulder and then followed her inside, pulling the door shut behind her.

It was dark in the shed, and it took a few seconds for her eyes to adjust. While they did, she stood in terror lest the snarling, barking and growling of several large dogs meant she was about to be savaged. But none attacked her, and as her vision adjusted to the gloom she now saw that they were in cages. It took her a few seconds to work out the layout of the place, but she now saw that there was a three level arrangement. On the ground level was a mass of interconnected cages full of dogs and other animals. Above that was a sort of half deck or working floor on top of the cages. Above that was another floor which Margaret mentally labelled a loft. There was a passageway right across the back of the shed and a walkway on both sides of the cages with sets of steps leading up to the working floor. A wall screened the cage area from the main part of the shed.

Along the wall on her left were more cages beside the passageway. These were filled with hens and roosters and guinea pigs. Under the steps leading up to the working deck was another cage and in it was a huge black boar which began squealing and grunting with rage. It lunged and banged at the bars and Margaret quailed in fear and hurried on past it.

Beyond the steps was the large set of interconnected cages, each containing one or more animals. In the semi-darkness Margaret strained her eyes, searching frantically for Skip and her heart hammering with fear.

Skip. Where is Skip? she thought, hurrying after Kylie across the rear of the cages.

The first cage on her left contained three large brown and white dogs which snarled and barked. Beyond them was a cage containing a large black dog that growled and banged at the steel mesh. Margaret moved on, every sense telling her to get out, but her thoughts focused on helping save Moira.

The next cage contained an ordinary looking dog that just barked and beyond that was another dog that just stood and stared. Two more large dogs, an Alsatian type and a Doberman, took up the next two cages. There was then a central passageway of mesh and then three more double sets of cages. The two cages beyond the passageway contained mixed breed 'pig dogs' which barked furiously but did not move to attack.

As Margaret reached the next, she saw Kylie recoil in horror at the large black dog that had sprung at her inside the cage. The dog struck the steel mesh so hard that the whole building seemed to shake.

Then Margaret recognised the fangs and evil yellow eyes and felt a thrill of pure terror.

"Brute!" she gasped, stepping away as the enraged animal sprang again in another furious but futile attempt to get at them.

Kylie began to cry and whimper and repeated over and over, "Skip! Where is Skip?"

Margaret gripped her arm and pushed her on. As she did, she stared at Brute's slavering jaws and was so scared she had trouble not wetting herself. Her mind kept telling her that what they were doing was stupid.

Those men must hear the racket, she thought. *And even if they don't, they could come back at any moment.*

Then she heard a distinctive yapping sound and Kylie grabbed her and pointed to the cage beyond Brute. Margaret saw a small black and white dog and then sobbed with emotion. It was Skip!

"Skip! We must save her," Kylie cried.

"But we must find Moira first," Margaret replied.

They found her a few seconds later. She was tied up and hidden away under the steps that led up to the other side of the working deck. There was another door there, leading through into the main part of the shed. As Kylie slid in under the steps to try to free Moira Margaret went to the door.

"I'll just check there is no-one in here," she whispered.

Carefully she turned the handle, her ear to the door. There was no sound she could hear above the yapping and growling of the dogs, so she eased the door open a fraction and peeked through. What she saw surprised her. Most of the shed was taken up by some sort of arena about 10 metres across. It was surrounded by a chest high wall made of concrete blocks. Outside this was a step and two rows of bench seats.

Surely, they don't get that many people in to watch such a horrible thing as a dog fight, Margaret thought in amazed disgust.

Seeing nobody she eased the door open further and looked through. She saw that the far end of the shed had a row of doors and a bar for serving drinks. As there was no-one in the hall she turned back and crouched to look in under the steps. Kylie was there struggling to untie the ropes binding Moira's wrists and ankles. Moira looked terrified but could not speak because she was gagged.

Kylie muttered and struggled with the knots but then looked at Margaret and shook her head. She scrambled back from under the steps. "The knots are too tight. We need a knife or something. See if there are any tools here."

With that Kylie hurried up the steps to where an assortment of ropes, bridles, whips and rods were hung along the wall separating the hall from the cage area. Margaret opened the dividing door and leaned through to see if there any sharp tools on the walls.

Seeing none she leaned back to tell Kylie she was going through to the doors at the far end. But at that moment a burst of brilliant light from her left caused her to freeze in terror.

Caught! she thought, glancing towards the light.

As she did, her mind worked out what she was looking at. The bright light was sunlight streaming in the open side door they had come through.

"Someone has just opened the door," she hissed at Kylie, who was halfway up the ladder leading to the loft. "Quick! Hide!"

Chapter 32

HORROR PILED ON HORROR

Kylie had begun climbing the ladder to the loft to look for a knife or sharp tool when the side door was flung open. She stared at the brightly lit opening in horror. Even as she heard Margaret gasp and say, "Hide!" she croaked the same thing herself.

A desperate glance around for a hiding place revealed none. For a few seconds she considered dropping down and crawling in under the stairs to hide with Moira but then she shook her head.

The men might check that Moira hasn't got free, she thought.

Moving shadows and voices just outside the door convinced her she had to move very fast or be caught. There seemed to be only one option, up, so she took it. She scrambled up the ladder and rolled onto the timber floor of the loft.

Even as she did, she was aware that a man had come through the doorway. All she could do was freeze and lie there terrified and hyperventilating, her eyes going blurry from fear. Then she could not hear because of the hammering of her own heart and her mind screamed in an agony of anticipation.

But there were no shouts of alarm or sounds of running boots, only the snarling and barking of the dogs so she lay on her side, silently gasping for breath and blinking to clear her vision. Then she heard voices. Two men were talking: Corey's father and Cass. They sounded angry but not as though they were searching. Cautiously Kylie peered through a crack in the rough floorboards and saw them. They were placing more small cages at the end of the row of boxes near the door.

Then another horrible thought came to Kylie: *Where is Margaret?*

A spurt of sheer panic grabbed Kylie so that she found herself frozen with fear yet panting for air and sweating. She rolled her head the other way and glanced around but could see no sign of her. Nor could she hear anything above the barking and snarling of the dogs and the frightened cackle of poultry.

Then she heard the men's voices closer and swung her head back to peek down through a gap in the floorboards. Just as she had feared they might the two men walked across the room to the stairs where Moira was held prisoner.

If Margaret has gone in under there with her she will be caught and they will suspect I am somewhere around as well and they will search. Then I will be caught as well. Then there will be no-one to save us, she thought.

For a few seconds fear for her own safety overrode her concern for the possible fates of her friends. Then Kylie felt ashamed and knew she must act to try to save herself, if only for her own sake.

If I get away, they won't do much to Moira or Margaret as they will know that the police will be told, she reasoned.

As the two men bent to look in at Moira Kylie rolled onto her front and very carefully raised herself onto her hands and knees. *If they come up here, I must have an escape plan,* she thought.

Fear of discovery made her look around. Now she saw that there was no obvious exit to the back or other side. The loft floor extended all the way to the walls. Nor was there much on the loft for her to hide behind; just a few small boxes, small coils of rope, some old rags and a lot of dust and spider webs. The only opening was at the front. Here the wall was only a few planks nailed to uprights. There was a clear gap between the top plank and the rafters.

To check what lay beyond, Kylie moved to peek through the planks. She saw that beyond the wall was a large room with offices and a bar at the other end. Directly below her was a U-shaped area about 10 metres long with a sandy floor. Around the arena was a chest high wall of concrete blocks. Outside this were bench seats and planks for spectators to stand on.

That is where the dog fight will be, she reasoned.

But where was Margaret? There was no sign of her, and the men were not calling out in alarm or searching. Instead one was walking around on the working floor below her and a change of light told Kylie that the other had gone into the big room. She was able to glimpse both through the cracks in the planks and that at least told her that Margaret had not tried to hide beside Moira.

Kylie watched Corey's father walk along the side of the big room and then go through a door into the offices at the far end.

If Margaret went to hide in there, he will catch her, she reasoned. She tensed ready for fight or flight.

But no angry shouts or cries of alarm sounded, and Corey's father did not reappear. Cass continued doing something to the metal catches of the cages and Kylie could only crouch and wait. Slowly her heart rate slowed and she was able to relax her muscles. But her nerves remained stretched, and she shivered from time to time.

As soon as that horrible man leaves, I am out of here, Kylie told herself, thinking to sneak back the way she had come to go and get help. *I won't try to find Margaret. It is more important that I get the police.*

But the minutes ticked by and the man did not leave. Worse still Corey's father re-joined him and both men worked on the working floor just below Kylie, so close she could have touched them if there had been no planks blocking her. She began to fume with impatience and also feared that they might hear her breathing or smell her.

She could certainly smell them. A nauseating stench of animals and sweaty, unwashed males rose to make her gag and several times she had to stifle a sneeze or cough.

Oh, why don't they leave! she thought.

Then her tense muscles began to cramp, and she had to force herself to relax. She lowered herself to lie on the dirty wooden floor and eased each limb in turn. Then she shivered and felt ill. Time continued to drag, and Kylie became more and more worried.

If I don't get away soon, I might not be in time to save Skip, she thought.

It was a ghastly thought and it made her thoroughly miserable. Apprehension grew into dread as the minutes ticked past.

Then the side door into the back of the shed opened and a person came in. Kylie moved to look and saw that it was Corey. She also noted that the light which had come in through the door was not nearly as bright as earlier.

The sun must be going down, she thought. That caused her some dismay as the idea of making her way back to Corwa in the dark did not appeal to her.

Corey's father looked down at him and called, "Well?"

"All done dad. Her horse is hidden down near Flannigan's pump," Corey answered.

"Any sign of those other girls?" Case asked.

"No. But I did see horse tracks heading back towards Corwa," Corey replied.

Cass grunted and then said, "Good. Now you get up here and help your dad fix this gate and I will take the van and go and start shuttling in the punters."

That dashed Kylie's immediate hopes. With a sinking heart she saw Cass leave and then watched Corey climb up to join his father just below her. It was becoming quite gloomy in the shed and Kylie began to consider climbing down the front of the wall into the arena area to see if she could get out through the door at the other end of the building.

Cautiously she got up and leaned out to look down, her eyes searching for hand and foot holds in the gloom. Suddenly the shed was flooded by bright lights and Kylie almost wet herself as a spasm of terror coursed through her. She jerked her head up and looked fearfully around, blinking in the bright light.

I have been spotted! she thought.

As this ran through her mind, she saw a door open at the far end of the hall and through it stepped a large and ugly woman. Instinctively Kylie ducked back below the flimsy planks and crouched in terror, her heart hammering fit to burst as she tensed ready to try to escape.

The woman joined Corey and his father and when Kylie heard Corey say 'Yes Mum' she understood that the woman was his mother.

Surely, she will step in to let Moira go? Kylie thought.

But she quickly had her hopes shattered. Corey's father took her to look at Moira. Kylie couldn't hear most of what was said but by straining her ears above the barking and growling of the dogs she did hear the words 'other girls' and 'looked for them'. Then she was absolutely chilled and dismayed to hear the woman say, "Well, we might have to take her with us and then make sure she disappears."

They are going to murder Moira and hide her body somewhere else! Kylie thought.

It was such a dreadful idea that Kylie felt ill and could only crouch and tremble. Slowly the fit of shivering passed, and she became aware that the horrible woman was now speaking to Moira, demanding to know where she and Margaret were. The sound of slaps and the disgusting threats the woman made caused Kylie to quiver with terror.

If Moira tells her then we will be caught, and these horrible people will do terrible things to Margaret and me. Then they will kill us, she thought.

In desperation, Kylie looked around for a way to escape. But there was none so she just pressed herself flat and waited, shivering with fear and sick with dread. To make it worse she had to desperately suppress the urge to sneeze. She did this in the way her brother had taught her, by pressing up on the base of her nostrils with her thumb until her eyes watered. It hurt but worked. Kylie was left trembling and in tears.

Then an opportunity seemed to present itself. Kylie distinctly heard Corey's mother say, "Time for tea. Corey, go and chain all those bloody guard dogs up. We don't want any of our punters bitten. Then come for tea."

All three people went out the side door. As it closed Kylie heaved a huge sigh of relief. *Now is my chance,* she thought. She slid down the ladder, then went down the steps to where Moira was held. As she did, some of the dogs began barking and snarling but Kylie kept moving, hoping that no-one outside would notice.

Moira was huddled in a whimpering ball in the corner under the steps. As soon as she saw Kylie, she began to call out hysterically, "Kylie, save me! Save me! They are going to kill me!"

Kylie was so shocked by the way Moira was yelling that it sparked her anger. "Be quiet!" she snapped back.

She was sure the people would hear and come back. When Moira kept calling out fear for her own safety moved Kylie to anger. Without thinking she swung her hand hard and gave Moira a vicious slap on the right cheek.

"Be quiet! If they hear you, they will come back and kill me too!" she snapped.

The blow had its effect and Moira subsided into whimpering sniffles. Kylie was terrified but determined. She now crawled right in close and set to work to untie Moira. She was not going to leave her there if she could help it. It took her several minutes to untie the rough knots and then another couple of minutes before Moira could get her cramped and swollen limbs to move. During this she continued to whimper, and several times cried out in pain.

Kylie became so anxious she twice scuttled up the steps to peek through the door into the main hall. Seeing no-one she came back and grabbed Moira's hand. "Come on! We've got to get out of here before they come back!" she hissed, fear putting and edge of anger into her voice.

Moira crawled out, still groaning and sniffling but Kylie was not in the mood to spare her any sympathy. Instead she hurried across the back of the room, ignoring the snarling, snapping dogs. When she reached the side door she pushed, and then stood in shock. It did not move. She tried again. Still it did not open. Frantically she began searching for a handle or lock but she could see none.

Moira hobbled over to join her. "What's wrong?" she asked.

"It must be locked on the outside," Kylie replied. She remembered seeing the men opening a bolt. *We must try the front door then,* she thought.

But that meant going through the main hall and she was afraid to do that. Still, there seemed no other option and she realised that she was nearly hyperventilating from anxiety by this time.

"This way!" she snapped at Moira and turned and hurried back across the building.

At the far side, Kylie cautiously eased the door slightly open. She peeked through and seeing no sign of anyone beckoned Moira to hurry up and join her. Then she began to open the door.

But as she did, the door on the left of the offices at the far end suddenly opened. Kylie pulled back, just leaving the door open far enough to be able to peek through. To her horror the man named Cass came into the hall. Luckily, he was looking back, talking to someone behind him so he did not notice the door move. With growing dismay Kylie saw four men and two women come into the hall behind Cass. They were shown to seats on the far side and Cass went to the offices and opened the bar roller door and brought out beer.

It was very obvious that there was no escape that way. *We will be seen at once,* she reasoned.

Moira hissed anxiously, "What's wrong? Why don't we go?'

"There are people in the next room. Let me try the other door again," Kylie replied. She pushed past Moira and ran across to the back door. But it was definitely locked and would not budge, no matter how hard she pushed. In her fear and frustration she banged at it but that immediately started the dogs barking. Fearing discovery Kylie stopped and went back to join Moira at the steps to the landing.

"We can't get out yet," she said. "You had better get back under there and pretend you are still tied up."

Moira looked horrified. "Oh I can't!" she cried.

"Shhh! You must. We will have to hope we get a chance to escape later," Kylie answered, angry that Moira might attract the notice of the men by her wails.

After more argument and a lot of persuading, Moira finally agreed and very reluctantly crawled back under the steps. Kylie crawled in after her and arranged the ropes to look like she was still tied up. That done she backed out and climbed back up to the loft. Here she lay down and tried to calm herself and to think rationally. Once again, she examined the roof, rafters and walls searching for a weak point or possible escape route. But there was none, and she lay back with her eyes closed, despair and anxiety flooding through her.

Then she heard more people arrive next door and she moved to crouch and peer through the planks. Seven people: six males and a hard-faced blonde female came into the hall and took seats. Several of the men went to the small bar where Case served them drinks. All Kylie could do was lie and hope.

Five minutes later seven more people came in. When she saw them, Kylie sucked in her breath in recognition. *Mr and Mrs Flawse!* she told herself. But seeing them was hardly a surprise. *That explains a lot,* she thought bitterly. Thinking dark thoughts she lay and watched them take seats. More time crept by and she became ever more anxious, dreading what she suspected was to come.

And she was not wrong. After another half hour, during which a dozen more people arrived, Corey and his father came into the back of the shed. They first checked that Moira was still there and then Kylie was sickened and disgusted to overhear Corey's father say to him that afterwards he could do what he liked to Moira as… "She won't be tellin' anyone."

Both men revolted Kylie further by proceeding to stir up the dogs and pigs by poking sharp sticks through into the cages. When the animals were really aroused and snarling, Corey's father made his way through into the hall and took up the role of MC. Corey stayed on the working floor.

Another glance into the hall showed Kylie that Cass was ushering more people in and that Corey's mother was behind the bar serving drinks. For a few minutes Kylie studied the people, wondering what type of person could pay to come and watch animals fight. To her surprise, very few of them matched her preconceived images. Most looked quite ordinary and only a few were the red-faced, burly brute type she had pictured.

Cass then stood on a stand and began taking bets and then the real horror began. Kylie had been desperately hoping that someone might have arrived with the police before the fights began but now two dogs were released into the pit. To her relief, neither was Skip but it was small comfort as she had a terrible dread of what was going to happen to Skip.

The two dogs then began to fight, and Kylie was so shocked and disgusted she felt ill. What appalled her as much as the savage snarling, biting, and lunging of the dogs were the reactions of the watchers. They cheered, shouted, yelled encouragement and advice to the dogs and in between drank and laughed. It was such a disgusting display of humanity near its lowest that Kylie was stunned.

Worse was to come. The first fight was between two evenly matched dogs. One ended up dead and its carcase was dragged away by Corey through the central passage in the cages. The sand was raked and more bets called and more beer drunk. Next a flock of hens was released into the pit, to the sound of much laughter and jeering. Bets were placed on how long it would take and then Corey goaded a large and savage Alsatian and guided it from its cage to the entrance by poking it with a steel tipped stick. Kylie now saw that all the cages were interconnected and that there were gates between them which Corey lifted vertically and then dropped again behind the animal.

When the dog was finally released into the pit, the hens all scattered in terror, cackling and trying to fly. The crowd burst into excited shouting and laughter and Kylie tried not to look. She covered her ears to try to block out the sounds. But the dog's growling, the terrified cackle of the hens and the sickening crackling and chomping sounds of the dog's jaws cracking bones still penetrated.

The pit was then cleaned out and the dog driven back into a cage by Corey. After more bets, drinking and laughter Corey released Brute into the pit. When Kylie saw this she went cold with fear lest Skip be sent in next. *She will have no chance!* she thought. In her heart she was sure that Skip would be matched against Brute at some stage.

But then a dozen guinea pigs were tossed into the pit by Corey. As he threw them in, he chuckled and yelled out. That sight totally disgusted Kylie.

What a revolting animal, she thought.

The crowd began cheering and shouting with delight. Brute at once went into a frenzy of attack. Terrified guinea pigs ran in all directions, but they had no chance. The sight reminded Kylie of their own dead guinea pigs and she began to cry, the tears streaming down her cheeks. She felt a strong desire to try to stop the killing, especially when Brute chomped onto the neck of a particularly cute looking guinea pig and then shook it and then held it down while it tore and savaged it until it was dead. Within minutes every single one had been hunted and caught. Kylie felt ill and gripped by such a strong sense of dread and stress that she wanted to scream.

By the end of that round Kylie was gasping and shivering. But worse quickly followed after another clean-up of the pit and more bets being placed there was another dog versus dog battle, between two pit bull terriers that snarled and snapped and tore at each other until both were bleeding and torn.

Kylie kept shaking her head and praying that something would happen to stop the horror. *Where is Margaret?* she wondered. *Did she get away? Has she managed to call the police or get help?* Not knowing was just another level of stress.

Then another ghastly event was staged. This was a fight between three big speckled white dogs of the bull terrier type and the wild pig. The pig was goaded through the now empty cages and then into the pit by Corey. As he did, this Kylie got glimpses of his face and was revolted by the glassy-eyed look of ecstasy on his face.

He is enjoying this. Oh, poor Moira! she thought.

Then the dogs were released and for Kylie horror just piled on horror. She found the spectacle so gripping that she could not stop looking. Within minutes blood had been drawn on both sides and the four animals whirled and lunged in a melee of snarling, grunting savagery. The pig used its tusks to rip open the side of one of the dogs and then to almost rip out the left eye of another. But the dogs had it by then and while one gripped its throat and shook it a second tore at its stomach. This burst open and the third dog, still fighting despite its terrible injuries, rushed in and sank its fangs in. It then pulled and to Kylie's horror the pig's intestines began pulling out like a string of pink and purple sausages.

It was too much for her and her stomach heaved. Desperately she tried to stop herself spewing. She held her mouth shut but that only caused squirts of foul-smelling and caustic liquid to pour from her nostrils. More vomit trickled between her fingers, and she was unable to stop it. Catching it in her hands was also a failure. To her dismay, some spew trickled onto the floorboards and began dripping down onto the working floor below. Fearful that Corey would notice, she used her hands and shirt to smear the vomit across the floorboards and then she lay on it to try to mop it up with her shirt. The smell was horrible, and she felt sure that Corey must notice.

But there were revolting smells coming from the now disembowelled and dying pig, so her mess was not noticed. These were so nauseating that Kylie wanted to vomit again and had trouble breathing. Several times she had to stifle sneezes and coughs and she found her eyes watering and her breath coming in short gasps. For several minutes she lay on her back feeling utterly wretched and wrung out.

Only slowly did it dawn on her that the obscene yelling and shouting had stopped and had been replaced by the disgustingly cheerful chatter and calling of bets that signalled a break between fights. Still stifling the urge to retch again she rolled on her front and peeked down through the cracks. She saw Corey and his father drag away the carcass of the pig, now torn and bloodied and trailing bleeding entrails.

Oh why doesn't help come? she thought, dreading the impending fight between Skip and who knew what.

Then her worst fears were realised. She saw Corey go into the cages and corner a dog. It was Thistle, the little Scotch terrier belonging to Emma. Thistle was tossed into the pit and then Corey turned and made his way back into the cages.

Oh no! Not Skip. Please God, not Skip! Kylie whimpered, biting at her knuckles in despair.

But it was Skip. As Corey cornered her and then grabbed her roughly, causing her to cry out in pain Kylie sobbed 'No', but how loudly she did not remember. To her horror, Skip was also thrown roughly into the pit. She rolled over then picked herself up and stood on unsteady legs looking around in a puzzled way.

Kylie just knew it would be Brute that was released into the pit, and it was more than she could bear. As she heard Corey annoying the big dog and opening the cage, she resolved to try to save Skip, come what may. Without really considering the consequences, she stood up and hurried to the ladder. Even as Brute charged out into the pit, she scrambled down it to the working deck.

As she swung onto the floor, Kylie glimpsed the small dogs dashing around in frantic attempts to avoid Brute's lunges. The crowd began jeering and calling out and the noise quite downed any sounds Kylie made. In front of her stood Corey. He was leaning over the railing and shouting crude encouragement to Brute. That so enraged Kylie that she dashed over and slammed into his back with both her fists. Corey cried out but was unable to regain his balance. He toppled over the railing and fell heavily into the pit, landing on top of Brute. The dog howled in pain and squirmed free.

In a flash, the enraged dog turned and clamped its fangs into Corey's left arm. Corey screamed and struck at Brute, enraging it more. Kylie looked down, both delighted and appalled at what she had done. She heard loud shouts and dimly noted that it was Mr Flawse who was screaming at Corey's father and pointing at her.

Then suddenly she had a plan. She ran on across the working deck to the landing on the far side and grabbed a cage of rats. Fumbling at the latch, she dashed to the front of the deck and hurled it into the pit. Rats began scurrying in all directions, causing the crowd to shriek in a mix of horror and delight. There were still some hens there too. Kylie decided that Skip's life was more important, so she tossed them in as well. Then she paused to consider what to do next.

She saw that Corey had freed himself and was standing with a bleeding arm at the side of the pit. His father had handed him a vicious looking goad and he used it to lash at Brute until the snarling dog turned away. Then the big dog lunged at Thistle, but she managed to avoid the charge. Then Brute turned and chased after Skip. Skip scampered across into the corner below Kylie and then turned to face the attack. By then Kylie was hanging on the outside of the railings and only dimly aware of the shouting, screaming humans who surrounded her. Seeing Brute bounding towards Skip she jumped, landing just in front of the charging animal.

Brute propped in alarm. Kylie saw the animal's yellow eyes fix on her and seem to glint. Growling savagely Brute bared his fangs and gathered himself to spring. Kylie stared in horror at the dribbles of saliva and blood dripping from the dog's jaws.

Oh God! I am in trouble now! she thought.

Chapter 33

MARGARET'S NIGHTMARE

When the side door opened Margaret was so scared that for a few seconds she froze. Then she saw that there was no way she could hide in the back room.

I will never get up that ladder in time, she calculated, seeing Kylie scrambling upwards.

She instantly rejected trying to hide under the stairs with Moira. There seemed to be only one option, into the big room, so she took it. Slipping through the dividing door she quickly turned and closed it.

She was just in time, catching a glimpse of Corey as she pushed the door shut. Fearing he might have seen her Margaret scurried down the steps into the hall and ran across to the far end. As she ran, she looked right and left for somewhere to hide but there were only the bench seating and that offered nowhere. Reaching the far end she took hold of the door handle on the first door, hesitated for a second, then turned it. She swung the door open and stepped through, half expecting to meet another of the gang.

But the room was unoccupied. She saw that it was some sort of storeroom and contained stacked crates of beer and boxes of bottled spirits. A large refrigerator took up half the space. A connecting door led into another room, so she cautiously opened it and looked. The second room was a bar and had two more fridges and rows of bottles under the counter. There was a closed roller window above the bar and another connecting door.

Hoping that this door led to the outside Margaret moved to it and leaned on it to listen. She found that hard to do as her beating was so hard. Hearing no sound she carefully opened the door and peeked through. The room was an office and contained a large desk against the front wall and there were several boxes and a filing cabinet. A laptop computer and a litter of papers lay on the desk. Two doors led out of the office, one into the hall and one in what looked like the front wall of the shed.

That is the door I want, Margaret told herself.

She tiptoed across and again listened. Unsure if she could hear anything or not she cautiously turned the handle and opened the door a tiny bit. Placing her eye to the crack she peeked out.

I was right, she thought. The door did lead into the open yard. But her hopes of escaping quickly plummeted as several large dogs were running loose in the yard. *Oh drat! I will never get past them,* she thought, remembering how the guard dogs had snarled and barked when they had first visited the yard.

So she went back through the rooms looking for a place to hide in case one of the gang came into that part of the building. But the only place, and that a very poor one, was under the table near the front door.

If I try to hide under there and someone sits at the table their feet will hit me, she decided.

But there was nowhere else, so she moved the chair out to make it easier to get under in a hurry. Then she cautiously peeked outside again. To her annoyance the dogs were still there. She also noted that the shadows cast by the afternoon sun extended right across the yard.

It will be dark soon. I must get going, she thought anxiously.

The sound of the dogs running and starting to growl warned her just in time to close the door. But the animals didn't start barking and she heard them run past. Then she heard Corey's voice outside and at once turned and crawled in under the table in case he came through the door.

Minutes went by and Margaret thought she could hear voices in the main part of the building. Very cautiously she snuck out and moved into the bar area and peeked through a tiny gap beside the roller. But it was very gloomy inside and she had trouble seeing anything. Twice she glimpsed movement and the murmur of voices, barely audible above the barking and growling of the caged dogs.

Once again, she returned to the front door and eased it open. She was just in time to see the white van reverse out and then drive away. A glimpse of the driver allowed her to identify the thin man.

Margaret waited until the sound of the van had died away and then eased the door wider. She saw that it was dusk but also that the dogs were still roaming the yard. One even lifted its head and looked straight in her direction. Fearing it had detected her Margaret closed the door and retreated to her hideout, her heart hammering with fear.

She was just in time. The door to the hall suddenly opened and

Corey's father came through it. Margaret could see his legs and boots and as he walked around to the front of the table terror almost paralysed her. She crouched in against the wall and tried to make herself as small as possible. She saw the boots stop only half a metre from her. A desk lamp was switched on. For a few moments she tensed as she was sure the man was going to sit down. But to her intense relief, he just checked some papers on the desk, then turned and went out the front door, slamming it behind him.

Margaret slumped down and sobbed. She found she was trembling with fear and for a few minutes could only take deep breaths and try to calm her shivering. She stayed there for another fifteen minutes or so and then resolved to get going.

It will be dark soon and it will be no fun trying to walk along that riverbank then, she thought.

Resolving to make a run for it regardless of the dogs she moved to the door again and carefully opened it. For several seconds she peeked through the narrow crack she had eased open, but it only gave her a view of a tiny part of the yard towards the back door. There was neither sign nor sound of any dogs, but by this time it was quite dark and she took a deep breath and summoned her courage ready to run.

Just as she was about to shove the door open, she heard the sound of footsteps on the sand of the yard. *Someone coming!* she told herself, a thrill of fear sending her heart rate shooting up and icy chills through her.

Quickly she eased the door closed and then turned and scuttled in under the table. Curling herself into a trembling, gasping ball she tried to make herself as small as possible in the corner nearest the door.

She was just in time. The door was flung open and a person came into the room. Suddenly the lights came on and Margaret almost cried out with fright. Biting her knuckles to stifle her breathing she peered out. A solid pair of female legs with slippers on the feet came into view only centimetres from her.

Corey's mother? she thought as the legs belonged to a middle-aged woman and looked particularly unattractive.

Margaret cringed in fear, her heart hammering alarmingly and her breathing coming in shallow gasps that she tried to keep as silent as possible. She made ready to spring out and fight.

But to her relief the woman did not sit at the desk or stay in the room.

Instead she opened the door leading into the main part of the building and went through, closing it behind her.

Margaret did not hesitate. *I must go now,* she decided.

As quickly and quietly as she could, she crawled out and made her way to the front door. Here she paused to nerve herself but the fearful knowledge that the woman might come back at any moment helped her to move. Summoning up her courage she took hold of the door handle and eased the door open.

The yard was silent and except for the bar of light streaming through the open doorway was in darkness. No sounds of dogs came to Margaret's ears, so she stepped through the door and pushed it carefully shut behind her.

For a second or two she stood with her back to the door, her mouth dry with fear as she listened for dogs. But none came rushing to attack or barked so she scampered around the corner of the shed to where she knew the back gate was. She reached it within seconds. It was shut but she just clambered up over it and dropped to the vehicle track on the other side.

Still no sound of dogs or of anyone raising the alarm. *Made it!* she thought, the relief coursing through her so that she trembled and had trouble breathing. *Now to get help!*

She set off down the dirt vehicle track towards the riverbank, anxious to quickly put as much distance between herself and the horrible people as she could.

But within fifty paces she had come to a halt. It was fear of snakes that was the cause as she remembered the large brown snake they had seen that afternoon. Perversely, it was not the darkness that caused her fears to increase but the moonlight. The moon was low, just above the hills across the river but it was strong enough to cast firm shadows. These patterned the ground with numerous interwoven dark lines as the moonbeams passed through the tree branches.

Is that a snake? Margaret wondered, straining her eyes and staring hard at a suspicious looking shape lying across the road.

For several long seconds she stood and studied the shape until she was unsure if it was a shadow, a stick lying on the ground, or a snake. She even wondered if it had moved or if her eyes were playing tricks on her.

All the while, images of that big brown reptile slithering into the long grass beside the narrow track kept forming in her mind. And the grass was a big part of the problem. On the bench cut sloping down to the river there were two-wheel ruts with long grass on both sides and in the centre, but she knew that all along the riverbank it was just a single narrow pad that wound through the trees and bushes.

Having decided that the shape was a stick, she changed to the other wheel rut and hurried on down to the bottom of the slope. But the effort cost her, and she found she was shivering and panting for breath. Fear gripped her and her throat went dry as she reached the end of the foot path. She took three steps along it before sheer terror brought her to a whimpering halt. The feel of that waist high grass brushing at her legs and the thought of what might be lurking in it was too much for her.

For several minutes she stood and tried to calm herself. Tears came and she sobbed in misery at her cowardice. But the frightening images remained. That snake had been real, and it lived somewhere along that track.

Thoroughly ashamed of herself she backed out and stood in the most open area she could find while she tried again to summon up the courage to walk. But she couldn't. *But I have to get help!* she silently wailed.

Then she wondered if she could sneak past the sheds and house along the road. *The road will be alright,* she thought.

But that meant going back up past the people and dogs. Still, that seemed to her less frightening, so she turned and walked back up the track. Even walking in the wheel rut was enough to scare her so that she was running by the time she reached the top of the slope. She came to a gasping stop near the gate.

What is that light? she wondered while standing in the middle of the track and sucking in great gulps of air.

Then it came to her. *Car headlights, and coming this way,* she realised. Feeling both foolish and scared she scuttled sideways behind the end of the big shed.

The vehicle came right into the yard and swung around before it stopped. Its lights remained on shining back along the road. Margaret risked a peek but saw no-one. She heard voices and noted the increase in light as the front door of the shed was opened but the people then went inside.

The door closed and then Margaret heard the vehicle door slam and she saw it drive away. As it went, its headlights lit up the access road. This allowed Margaret a good glimpse of the end of the next shed and of the front of the farmhouse.

Seeing nobody she decided to take a chance. *The dogs must be chained up or in cages if they are bringing people here,* she thought.

She knew that might not be the case but also realised that time was running out. *I must get help before Skip is killed,* she thought, then added Moira's name.

Summoning up her courage, she climbed over the gate and tiptoed across the back of the shed. At the corner she paused and peeked around. The yard was in darkness except for the moonlight but the only dogs she could hear sounded as though they were inside the shed.

"Come on coward!" she muttered.

After taking a huge gulp of air she walked quickly and quietly on across the yard, angling over to be next to the fence on her right. Beyond that was an open paddock. In twenty steps she had reached the end of the next shed and a few seconds later she was at an open gateway leading through to the front of the farmhouse. Here she again paused to look and listen in case there was someone in the house or a house dog on guard.

There were lights in the house but no sounds to indicate any people. Now her anxiety for Skip and her friends forced her to overcome her fears and she walked on, keeping to the grass beside the fence and as far away from the house as possible. She knew she would be visible to anyone outside the house as the moonlight was bright enough to light up the whole scene.

A minute later she was at another gate and past the house. This time she did not pause but walked quickly on. As she did, reaction set in and she began to shake and sob. But this time her fear of snakes receded. The road was clear gravel and in the moonlight she could see where she was walking quite clearly.

With every step she felt safer. Every few seconds she glanced back, and each time was relieved to see no sign of pursuit and to note that the lights of the farmhouse were getting obviously further away. In front of her she now discerned the dark line of trees she knew grew beside the road and railway and she could even make out the shape of the distant hills in the pale light of the moon.

Suddenly Margaret stopped. Off to her left front car headlights had appeared. They were traveling fast and she knew their course marked the main road. But were the people in the vehicle friendly? Biting her lip with anxiety she watched it. Then she saw it slowing down.

It is turning in here, she thought, stabbed by a sudden surge of fear. *I must hide!*

But where? There was only one obvious choice, in the long grass of the paddocks beside the vehicle track. Now worry about snakes was pushed aside by the more immediate fear of the man named Cass. Margaret scurried across to the fence on her right, pushing into waist high grass as she did. Then she went down on her hands and knees and began to crawl under the fence.

A sharp pain in her back told her it was a barbed wire fence, and she quickly learned the lesson of getting right down. Ignoring the grass, prickles, and fear of snakes, she went flat and wriggled in under the fence. As she did, she discovered that her shirt was still snagged on the bottom strand and after tugging in vain she realised she had to back up to pull it free.

By then the vehicle had turned onto the farm track and its headlights were lighting everything up. All Margaret could do was curl up in a ball and lie still, hoping desperately that she would not be noticed. The couple of seconds as the vehicle accelerated towards her seemed an agony of time.

Then the vehicle was past. Margaret gasped with relief and turned her head to watch. It was the same van. When it showed no sign of slowing or stopping, she tore at her shirt, ripping it free. Then she wriggled back and scrambled to her feet. A billowing cloud of dust engulfed her, and she found she could not see well enough to walk. Worse still she began to cough.

By the time the dust had cleared the vehicle had reached the farm and she saw its headlights swing around. Only as the beams swung towards her did Margaret remember how the vehicle had turned to face back the way it had come before unloading its passengers the previous time.

That sent her scrambling back into the long grass. As she wriggled through under the fence, she hoped that there had been enough dust in the air to hide her. For the next few minutes she lay, perspiring and shivering with anxiety. She also began to worry about what might be happening to Kylie and Moira.

"I must go fast if I am to help before Skip is put in to fight Brute," she muttered.

Having seen Brute in the cages she felt sure it would be him that was matched against Skip. So she lay still and fretted with anxiety and impatience. Her fear was such that the pain from the scratches on her back barely registered.

After what seemed like a long time, but was actually only a few minutes, the van came driving back towards her. This time Margaret was not as worried as she was further from the road and she kept her head very low and her face covered. She was right. The van drove past at speed, only slowing when it reached the main road.

But then Margaret was dismayed by the fact that the van turned left. She raised her head to watch and felt stabs or swirling worry. *That is the road I was going to walk along,* she thought. But did she now dare? *Will I be able to get under cover in time if it comes back?* she wondered. She felt sure it would come back and she also knew that she would have to hide from every vehicle on the road.

As she crawled back under the fence, her fears put her into a real state of nerves and she felt tears prickle. Dusting her hands and clothes she stood up and hurried on along the farm road. *Oh, what shall I do?* she worried.

Then the answer came to her. Margaret found herself at an open gate and just beyond it was the railway. She stopped in the middle of the tracks and stared along it. The two rails shone in the moonlight and seemed to light her path.

The railway goes right to Corwa's front gate, she thought. *And there will be no cars to bother me.*

So she turned left and began walking along the railway track. In the moonlight that wasn't too difficult. The only real problem was that the wooden sleepers were unevenly spaced, and many were rough and irregular on their upper surfaces. As a result she stumbled a few times until she adapted to them.

As she walked, Margaret kept looking back over her left shoulder to check how far she was from the farmhouse. She found it a relief to note how it was obviously further away each time and then its lights vanished from view, hidden by intervening trees.

She also kept glancing to her right, ready to hide in case the van returned. Her plan was to hide in the shallow ditch that ran along beside the railway tracks. But when she did see the flicker of vehicle headlights through the trees, they were so far away she did not do more than crouch. The vehicle was going fast and soon vanished behind her and she did not even hear if it turned off at the farm.

Margaret had known that the road and railway diverged but had not realised they were that far apart. But then she thought about it and remembered riding her horse along the vehicle track at Venture Creek. With that came the memory of the high rail bridge.

I will have to cross that to reach Corwa! she thought with dismay.

For a few seconds she pictured herself inching across those narrow planks and then the headlights of a train appearing when she was in the middle. Awful memories of the boys scrambling or jumping to save their lives came to her and she shivered. The rail bridge began to loom in her mind as a major challenge. However she nerved herself to face it.

I can't let Kylie and Moira down, she thought.

The thought of her friends suffering horrible fates and of Skip being torn into bleeding chunks caused a sickening chill of dread to grip her stomach. It also helped to keep her moving. Other unpleasant thoughts crossed her mind.

Mr and Mrs Lucas must be very worried. I hope they have called the police, she thought. Then she hoped they hadn't also contacted her parents. *I don't want mum and dad getting all worried,* she decided.

Then she thought of the horses. *Poor old Lucy. She will be getting sore with that saddle still on her,* she thought.

But then another, happier thought came to her. *If the boys are camped at Venture Creek, I don't need to cross it. I will go to their camp,* she decided.

Images of Graham and his friends sitting around a campfire helped motivate her and she sped up. For a few seconds she conjured up a fantasy of Graham standing up and hugging her before he rushed off into the night to get help. She knew he could be depended on to do that anyway.

Suddenly she stopped. It was the hissing noise that brought her to an anxious standstill. Instinctively she knew what it was, a snake. And this time it was not her imagination. She stepped back, every nerve quivering and the breath coming fast and hot into her throat. Straining her eyes she stared at the area the noise was coming from. She had heard of snakes hissing but had never thought to actually experience it. Now the sound sent chills of terror through her, and she had to use will power to stop herself from running back.

The snake was small, less than a metre long she calculated once she finally detected it. It was only the fact that its body was draped twice across the shining steel rail that she saw it at all. Only then could she focus and to her horror she saw that it had its head up, the upper body waving slightly and the terrifying sound coming from that. Later she was not sure if she had seen the snake's forked tongue flickering in and out in the moonlight, but she knew that the snake was warning her it would strike if she came near it.

By this time every muscle was tense, and Margaret was ready to try to spring back if the snake attacked. But it remained where it was, head raised and slowly swaying so she took the risk and edged back one foot at a time until she was sure it could not reach her with a single lunge. Satisfied she was temporarily safe she took another step back.

The snake stopped hissing and lowered its head. Margaret breathed out with relief, then stiffened up again. The snake slid off the rail and into the shadows under it and in the pool of darkness between two sleepers.

Oh help! Is it coming this way? she worried, her eyes flicking from side to side as she tried to spot the reptile.

But she could not see it, so she hurried back another couple of paces. Then she remembered that there might be more, and she hesitated while she glanced at the railway track behind her.

No threat was visible, so she stepped back again. Then she stared hard at where she had last seen the snake. *Where has it gone? Is it coming to get me?* she thought, her breath coming in rapid gasps.

She thought she heard the grass rustle on the left of the railway but then her mind began imagining more sounds and she knew her eyes were playing tricks on her. Every shadow seemed to move and she sobbed with anxiety.

But she could see no sign of it and her fear grew until she was on the edge of panic. A minute ticked by with her still rooted to the spot, then another. Then she stepped back another couple of paces and had to suppress the urge to run.

What shall I do? she thought. She glanced back along the railway lines and even considered going back to the road.

Then a wave of shame swept through her. *I am being a coward,* she told herself. *I am putting my friends in danger by not getting help.*

Horrible images of Skip being attacked by Brute helped her. So she forced herself to stand still and then she summoned up her courage again and ran forward. She kept to the right of the rails, her anxious gaze scanning the shadows in the hope she might just see the snake in time to avoid it.

At the place where she had seen the reptile, she almost tripped. As she stumbled, a stab of pure terror went through her. But she managed to keep running and not fall. A few seconds later she was past. Just to be sure she kept on running until a stumble on another uneven sleeper almost caused a twisted ankle. That sobered and steadied her and she slowed to a walk.

But now the whole trek became a sort of living nightmare. Now the snakes were not figments of the imagination but real. *If I have seen one there might be more,* she told herself.

But despite her fear she forced herself to keep walking. Except now it was like walking in a minefield. Every step took a toll on her sum of courage, and she was soon sobbing and trembling.

Despite that she forced herself on, her eyes aching from the strain as she stared at the shadows ahead of her. Tears began but then dried up and several times she stopped, unable to go on for a few minutes. Then her pride and shame motivated her to keep moving.

Kylie needs me, she told herself.

Suddenly she stopped and stared at the different pattern of shadows. For a moment she puzzled then realisation came to her and she sighed with relief.

Venture Creek Rail Bridge! she thought.

The huge structure stretched ahead of her in the moonlight. It seemed very long and the creek bed appeared lost in the pools of shadow under the trees. Then she noted moonlight glinting on water and the height of the bridge became even more apparent.

A flicker of light out to her left caught her eye and she looked that way, then sobbed with relief. It was a campfire. "The boys are there!" she gasped.

To reach them she had to walk and slide down the path in the long grass, crawl under the barbed wire fence and then run along the vehicle track. Having done it before made it easier but the fear of snakes drove her on. Once on the flat she ran as fast as she could, hoping to get past any snake before it could bite her.

Two minutes later she was at the bank of the creek and there were the four boys sitting around a small campfire on the open sand of the small island. Margaret saw a face turn as she began splashing into the water.

"Graham!" she cried.

Chapter 34

BRUTE'S FANGS!

Brute snarled and Kylie saw dribbles of saliva drop from his jaws. His mouth opened to emit a snarl and she saw those horrible fangs. Fear coursed through her and her heart leapt into her mouth. Frantically she cast around for a weapon, knowing in her heart that she had made a bad mistake. Her eyes focused on a scurrying, yapping bundle of fur. It was a Scotch terrier.

"Thistle!" she cried.

Without considering the consequences she turned her back on Brute and snatched at the little dog. She managed to grab him by his left hind leg. Thistle let out a shrill yap and began howling as Kylie swung him off the ground. As she did, she was struck in the back of her left calf and almost knocked off her feet. Sharp stabs of pain told her that she was being bitten. A glance confirmed it. Brute had her by the leg and was now tearing at her jeans and worrying her.

Kylie lost her balance and fell but as she did she had the presence of mind to toss Thistle high up over the wall surrounding the pit. She feared he would be injured but still thought it was the best option. Then she was down in the blood-soaked sand and the fear and pain had her screaming.

Her senses swam as terror and panic surged in her. Her vision blurred but she noted scampering, scurrying, and fluttering rats, dogs and hens going in all directions. Her focus narrowed down to Brute's head and the fangs that were embedded in her flesh. Blood was trickling and spreading on her clothes and the cloth was being torn. The sight of the crazed yellow eyes of the dog sent new stabs of terror through her and she screamed even louder. Then she began hitting at Brute, punching at his head.

A black and white dog raced past her face, barking in a high-pitched, penetrating yapping tone that was audible above the uproar of yelling people and barking dogs. *Skip!* Kylie thought. She saw Skip pounce on Brute, sinking his teeth into the bigger dog's left haunches.

Brute at once let go of Kylie's leg and let out a shrill yowl of pain.

Then the big dog snarled and swung to bite at Skip. Kylie sat up and saw that Skip had latched on really hard and was worrying him.

"Good girl Skip!" Kylie shouted.

But then she saw that Brute had managed to curl himself around to get his jaws around Skip's body. *Oh no! He will kill Skip!* she thought.

She sprang to help, straddling Brute's back and grabbing at his head. As she did, she noted that Skip had been torn from her grip but in the process had left a bleeding and torn mess of sinew and muscle. The sight sent a spasm of nausea through Kylie. But this was replaced by dismay as Brute squirmed and wriggled around under her, his legs scrabbling for purchase in the sand. The sheer strength of the animal appalled her, and she felt the urge to let go and flee.

But Brute had Skip's small body in his jaws and Kylie determined to save her. So she clung on grimly, tightening her knees and lower legs around Brute's furry body. Then she reached down and tried to prise the big dog's jaws open. Her fingers encountered slime, blood, saliva, and wet fur. She could feel the fangs and hot breath and it was all revolting. But she clung on and kept trying.

Skip whimpered and Kylie saw one eye roll and look at her. She thought she saw recognition and a silent plea for help, so she redoubled her efforts. Unable to lever the slimy jaws apart she moved her left hand to place it over Brute's nostrils. Ignoring the pain from Brute's claws as they tore her trousers and leg, she tightened her grip on the dog's muzzle.

But it did not seem to be working and she saw Skip's eyes roll up and then her head seemed to go limp. In desperation Kylie used her right hand to claw at Brute's eyes. "Let go you mongrel!" she screamed.

Then even louder screams caused Kylie to flinch and glance around in fear. Her first impression was of people all running and scrambling away towards the front door. But then she heard the screams again and saw that it was Mr Flawse. He was climbing over the wall of the pit!

"Let my dog go, you little bitch!" Mr Flawse screamed as he dropped to his feet in the pit.

His big hands were clenching and unclenching, and Kylie experienced a spasm of sheer terror. Mr Flawse began lumbering towards her, his right fist clawing.

Kylie felt paralysed as waves of fear swamped her. But she did not let go. *He is going to hit me!* her mind told her.

But it seemed so unreal it did not really influence her actions. She continued her desperate efforts to release Skip even as she noted Mr Flawse's grasping hand reaching for her throat.

There was a sudden loud shout and a blur of movement. A person appeared from her left side, travelling downwards from the top of the wall and striking Mr Flawse with his boots. Mr Flawse and his assailant both fell to the ground at her feet. Through eyes gone blurry from stress Kylie saw that it was Graham who had come to her rescue.

Graham! How…? Her mind raced to try to comprehend.

But then she realised that the drama was not over. A loudly swearing Mr Flawse was rolling away and scrambling to his feet while Graham lay on his back on the blood-soaked sand!

But at least Brute had let go. Kylie saw Skip flung aside and watched in horror as Brute turned with a snarl, only to let out a shriek of delight when Brute suddenly rushed in and latched onto Mr Flawse's left leg!

Mr Flawse screamed and hit at Brute with his fists until he obeyed and let go. He then grabbed the dog's collar and heaved him around to face Graham. Now Kylie screamed again and moved to help Graham, who lay there writhing. Into her very focused vision came an image of Brute's fangs, now dripping blood as well as saliva.

Oh no! she thought as she saw the ferocious animal crouch ready to attack. Savage snarls and bared teeth added to the horror.

There was a thud beside her and she was shoved aside. Margaret appeared, standing over Graham, her feet braced and in her hands the steel rake Corey had been using to restore the pit after each bout. As Brute sprang Margaret lunged, swinging the rake up to block his attack. Kylie simultaneously yelled in fierce delight and winced in horror as the sharp steel tines struck at the big dog, sending it tumbling sideways.

"Oh well done!" Kylie cried, the word 'tigress' flitting across her mind at the sight of Margaret shoving hard against the scrabbling dog. She glanced down and saw that Graham was now rolling over to get to his feet.

"You okay?" Kylie queried, anxious lest he had been really hurt by the fall.

Graham gasped and stepped back to lean on the wall behind Margaret. "Just winded. Look out!"

For Brute had recovered and started snarling again while showing his fangs. Next to the dog, Mr Flawse was screaming encouragement to 'sool' him to attack. To emphasise this he slapped at the dog's head.

Which was a mistake.

Brute suddenly whirled and with a savage snap of his jaws he grabbed Mr Flawse's wrist. The chomp was so loud it registered in Kylie's brain as a snap that made her wince. But so did Mr Flawse's scream. He tried to shake Brute off and kicked at him with his boots. But the animal did not let go. Instead it began to worry and drag, and Mr Flawse tumbled to the sand, kicking and shouting obscenities.

"Oh save him, Margaret, that dog will kill him!" Kylie cried.

"Serve the mongrel right!" Graham yelled angrily.

Kylie wasn't sure if he meant Brute or Mr Flawse but she was so appalled by the viciousness of the dog's attack as it mauled Mr Flawse that she was impelled to intervene. But Margaret just shoved at Brute with the rake and Graham didn't help by pushing in and trying to take the rake off her. The three of them stumbled and tripped against each other.

There was more yelling, and as Kylie stepped forward to try to grab at Brute she was puzzled by the sudden appearance of a red object in the middle of Brute's back. Then her eyes focused and she saw it was the feathering at the back of a dart. Then Graham hauled her back.

"Keep back, Kylie!" he shouted.

Then other voices penetrated and Kylie glanced up to see two policemen leaning over the edge of the pit. One held a gun with a large barrel and the other had a pistol aimed at Brute. This one waved his arms.

"Get out of there, you kids! I can't shoot with you there. Go back!"

Kylie did, Graham beside her and Margaret beside him, rake still held up ready to fend off any attack. Graham then pulled at Kylie.

"Ricochet," he said

"What?"

"The copper won't shoot in case the bullet ricochets off the block wall," he explained.

As he did, the policeman sprang down into the pit between them and Brute. He aimed his pistol at the back of Brute's head and Kylie was horrified.

But the policeman did not need to shoot. Brute suddenly staggered and his back legs crumpled. He let go of Mr Flawse and then flopped down. The tranquilizer in the dart had obviously taken effect.

Kylie nodded but her focus had now moved from Brute to Skip. "Skip! Where is Skip?" she cried, looking anxiously around.

Then her eyes lit on Skip. The puppy was lying on the sand, all crumpled, soiled and bloodied and she forgot about Brute and Graham. With a cry of anguish she hurried across to where Skip lay.

"Oh Skip!" she wailed, not wanting to touch the battered little body.

But then she saw movement in Skip's chest. "She's alive!" she cried.

Very gently she touched Skip and began to feel her for broken bones. As she did, Skip opened her eyes and lifted her head. Skip's eyes met hers and she opened her mouth slightly and gave her tail a tiny wag.

Kylie scooped Skip up and cradled her in her arms. Graham knelt beside her and gently stroked Skip's head. Skip poked out a tiny pink tongue and licked at his fingers. Kylie burst into tears. These fell unheeded on Skip's fur.

Then more police were there and so were Mr and Mrs Lucas. Peter, Stephen and Alistair also appeared. Kylie handed Skip to Margaret and was helped from the pit. The adults at once hurried her out of the room past all the angry and unhappy people who had been arrested. Once outside she took Skip again and then clung to Margaret and sobbed herself dry. The boys joined them and she saw that the yard was full of police cars, four or five of them. There seemed to be police everywhere.

Then Graham wrapped his arms around her. "You are safe, Sis," he murmured.

Kylie pressed her head against his chest and sobbed with relief. Margaret joined them and Graham put out his arm to draw her into the embrace. For a few seconds the only emotion Kylie could feel was relief. Then she shuddered and began to cry, but with happiness.

An ambulance arrived with flashing lights and siren. Kylie was helped over to the back of it and the paramedics placed her on a stretcher and quickly set to work on her scratches and bites. As she lay there, Kylie still cradled Skip while Margaret held her hand. Fits of trembling shook her and from time to time she burst into tears.

Then into the light came Moira, being helped as she could only hobble. Moira looked at Kylie and then at Skip and also burst into tears. She was seated at the back of the ambulance while the paramedics checked her over.

While they did this Corey, his father and mother and the thin man named Cass were led past. They were followed by a scowling Mr Flawse and angry Mrs Flawse. All were handcuffed. Kylie saw Corey glance at Moira and then look away. Seeing him in handcuffs caused Kylie a fierce sense of satisfaction.

Good! What disgusting animals he and his family are, she thought. But there was also sympathy for Moira. *How does a girl know what a boy is really like?* she worried.

Before the stretcher was pushed right into the ambulance, she saw Margaret casting loving and hopeful looks at Graham. *Now, if bonehead brother will realise she is the girl for him at least Margaret will get a good man,* she thought.

Then the ambulance door was closed and the trip to the Cairns Base Hospital began.

* * *

Skip survived. She always walked with a limp but she remained a brave, loyal and happy dog. And for Kylie, Margaret, Graham and his friends there were other adventures ahead. And did Margaret become Graham's girl?

You will have to read on and find out.

Enjoy more C.R. Cummings stories

The Air Cadets

The Navy Cadets

The Army Cadets

 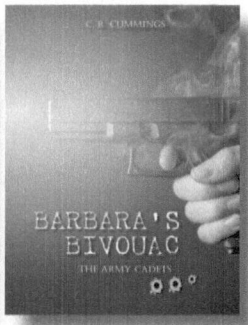 

www.ingramcontent.com/pod-product-compliance
Lightning Source LLC
Chambersburg PA
CBHW031554240626
47153CB00002B/509